THE METANAUT

ALSO BY MEGAN BLEDSOE

Glitching the Matrix: *a novel . . .*
The Metanaut: *a supernatural thriller*
Girl, Incorrupted: *a love-horror story*

THE *CORBIN KOHL IN HELL* SERIES
fun low-fantasy mysteries
Corbin Kohl Adrift in Hell
Corbin Kohl Baited in Hell
Corbin Kohl Cornered in Hell

MEGAN
BLEDSOE

THE METANAUT

Arched Brow Books
VANCOUVER

THE METANAUT

Published by Arched Brow Publishing
Arched Brow Books is a trademark of Arched Brow Publishing

Cover design by Megan Bledsoe

Cover design elements by Bragi Kort (Northern Lights), Jeannette Katzir (redwood trees), and Adi Arianto (silhouette) via canva.com
Ending text image by GDJ via pixabay.com
Cover and interior typefaces by Georg Duffner (EB Garamond), Pria Ravichandran (Palanquin), Steve Matteson (Open Sans, Tinos), Christian Robertson (Roboto), Carolina Short (Mansalva), and Yvonne Schüttler (Voltaire) via fonts.google.com, and by Emily Conners (Bergamot Ornaments) via myfonts.com

Bledsoe, Megan, 1980–
The Metanaut / by Megan Bledsoe.
First Edition. | Vancouver : Arched Brow Books, 2025.
FICTION / Fantasy / Contemporary
FICTION / Mystery & Detective / Women Sleuths
FICTION / Thrillers / Supernatural

Summary: A scientist must work with a psychic to defeat a deadly paranormal anomaly in the California Redwoods.

ISBN 978-1-969265-06-8 (hardcover)
ISBN 978-1-969265-00-6 (ebook)

For Mom

Because she said this one was excellent.

THE METANAUT

HALLOWEEN

On October 31, at 4:58 pm, the sun cast a reddish hue on the old ornate buildings that surround the University of Washington's Red Square plaza.

The square was hosting a night market. Halloween themed.

Yuri Palming had gotten there early to set up his scarf-on-a-milk-crate psychic's table at the base of a steel sculpture, an upside-down obelisk balanced on the tip of a pyramid. It was a great spot, centrally located between two aisles of brightly lit stalls, and primed to catch the attention of anyone wanting a reading.

He'd already had half a dozen clients. Mostly costumed college kids. They roamed the stalls, trick-or-treating and bartering for trinkets. Their laughter rang in the air, mingling with the smell of oncoming rain and imminent thunder.

Usually after one client left, Yuri would catch the eye of another curious co-ed and wave her over. But something else had caught his attention.

To his right, the sun was setting in the gap between Meany Hall and the three brick towers that Yuri had once thought were viewing elevators, but later learned were ventilation stacks for an underground parking garage. The lower the sun sank into the gap, the redder it became—until it was the same color as the carnation in the black raincoat lapel of a man across the square who had his eyes locked on Yuri.

He was beelining his way over.

The man had grayish-white hair and a stiff gait. He was at least four, maybe five decades older than the rest of the market's young crowd. He sidestepped a costumed ghost and paused his stride to let a group of Care Bears pass in front of him. But little by little, the man was getting closer.

It was weird.

But the thing that really had Yuri's spine stiffening inside his purple wizard costume was a woman flanking the man's left shoulder.

She was both there . . . and yet not there.

To Yuri, the woman was clear as day.

She was taller than the man she flanked, but her clothes were more drab: a long wool gray skirt and a cream shapeless top. She had a hawkish nose and graying blonde hair styled in tight curls, like a helmet. Yuri could see the details of her clearly.

But he could also see the bright red sun shining through her body, like she was nothing more than a diaphanous swath of gauze.

Yuri doubted a single other person on the plaza could see the woman at all.

Did the older gentleman know he was being followed? The woman walked just behind him, practically breathing in his ear. Like she was his second. Or a bodyguard. Or his wet-work gal. She reminded Yuri of Baba Yaga, a character from fairy tales with iron teeth.

Yuri was still young, just fifteen, but not stupid, not even close. He always set up shop in the busiest part of an event, and this was the busiest part of Red Square on one of the busiest nights of the year. He should be safe.

But the chill rising up his spine was telling him to worry.

He kept his eyes focused on the man, if only to keep from looking at the woman still flanking his left shoulder, still there and yet not there. He just had a feeling he shouldn't look at her, shouldn't let her know he could see her.

The strange pair came within kicking distance of Yuri's scarfed milk crate, and the corner of the man's mouth rose with amusement, like he was scoffing at the idea of fortunes told and crystal balls.

"You do readings?" the man asked, pointing at Yuri's crayon-on-cardboard sign that advertised as much.

Yuri nodded, feeling cornered. If he were standing, he'd probably be taller than the man—taller than the woman, too—but he was sitting on the sculpture's cold concrete base. The milk crate was pressed against his knees, blocking him in.

"Twenty bucks," Yuri said.

The man opened his black raincoat and pulled a long billfold from the inside pocket, opened it like a book, and pulled out a crisp hundred-dollar bill.

"I don't have change for that," Yuri said, sensing that a fistful of the man's cash would come with a stomach full of worries.

That same chill that told him not to let on that he could see the diaphanous woman was also telling him to pretend that he was a charlatan and not the real deal, that his readings were phony, too.

The man dropped the money, letting it flitter down to Yuri's table like it was just another dead autumn leaf. "You can keep the difference."

Yuri picked up the bill and tucked it beneath his right hip. People sometimes asked for their money back. He'd learned the hard way that it was easier to give it to them than to argue—and easier still if it wasn't in his pocket.

The woman stepped around the milk crate and up onto the sculpture's platform, invading Yuri's space. She bent down low and peered at him, her face inches from his own, like she was testing him. Like she was testing whether he could see her, whether her presence made him squirm.

That was a big fat yes. But hopefully only on the inside. Yuri couldn't help stiffening, but he otherwise tried not to react to her. He tried to look oblivious.

But he could see her out the corner of his eye. Her hawkish nose. A witch's nose. Not unlike Baba Yaga's. Her hair was more blonde than gray, but it was curled in the way some elderly women do to make their thinning strands seem thicker. Yuri had a hard time guessing her age. But he placed her at fifty, give or take a decade or two. Which made her a decade or so younger than the man.

"How long have you been doing this?" the man asked.

Yuri had been reading people whether he wanted to or not for as long as he could remember. But truth wasn't the correct answer. Not for this man.

"Not long. A couple years, maybe. What's your question?"

Baba Yaga stood up straight again and stepped behind Yuri.

He pretended to rub his chest, feeling for the protective crystal he wore under his hoodie. *You're safe*, he told himself, repeatedly, trying to convince himself that whatever the woman planned to do while she was behind him, she wouldn't—shouldn't—be able to hurt him. She was just a ghost.

"I have this brother," the man said. But instead of getting a feel for the man's brother, an image of Yuri's own brother flashed into his mind. "Do you have any brothers?" the man asked.

Yuri had last seen his brother almost a year ago, when Josh had left for his latest assignment. Yuri missed him every day, and didn't want to talk about him with this man.

But Yuri was more than just good at reading people. And he could feel that now was not the time to lie.

"One," he said.

"He older or younger?"

"Older."

"Mmm," the man said, his tone disappointed, as if this difference between them meant the milk-crate psychic wouldn't understand his issue. And yet Yuri knew the man was secretly pleased with his answer. "Mine's younger," the man said.

The man's ghostly bodyguard snort-laughed—and Yuri heard it. He tried not to frown, not to react, at the strangeness of hearing the sound. But she was unlike any ghost he had ever seen before. She had clarity of figure. He could see her whole body, every detail, from the grays streaking her curly helmet hair to her round-toed boots that looked to be made of something soft, like gray felt. And she had clarity of consciousness. She was aware and focused. And she moved like she had a mission—and solid form. Yuri could have sworn she'd just tugged at the hundred-dollar bill beneath his hip, with her foot. It took all his focus to resist the instinct to check.

"My brother and I don't get along too well," the man was saying. "Do you and your brother get along?"

Yuri shrugged, using the motion to release some of the tension in his back. He felt the woman behind him, an energy without heat. He took a deep breath to keep from shrinking away from the feel of her.

She stepped around him and down off the platform, reclaiming her position at the older man's flank. Yuri was pretty sure she could have walked all the way around him, platform be damned—a normal ghost would have—but she hadn't. She'd stepped up, and then she'd stepped down.

She acted physical.

Still human.

"Yeah, I think that's the way of brothers, to not get along," the man was saying, "to love each other, but to compete. To put each other down and deny their better differences."

The woman shifted her weight and then stepped behind the man, watching Yuri as she did so. Yuri once again felt like he was being tested, like she was trying to see whether his gaze would jump from the man's face to her own and reveal his gift for what it truly was. It took all of Yuri's concentration to keep his eyes on the man, to keep them from jumping to the woman.

He missed what the man was saying.

"You okay, son?"

"I was picking up on a feeling." Yuri rotated his wrist as if reeling in a thought, which wasn't untrue. "What was your question?"

"How do I heal the rift with my brother?"

The man didn't have a brother. Yuri had received that clarifying thought the moment the man had uttered the lie, but the image of Yuri's own brother had clouded it. He still wondered why, and wondered why the man was here, but thinking on those answers would have to wait until later.

Yuri tilted up the milk-crate table, where his backpack was hidden, and pulled out a tarot deck. He didn't need props, but most people felt they weren't getting their money's worth unless he used them.

He halved the cards and shuffled them nine times.

"One shuffle for each word in the question," he explained. It was habit, one he'd settled on for his own amusement. Most people got this look on their face like *Oh, no, did my question use the right amount of words?* But the man just nodded, like the rule made total sense.

His invisible bodyguard, however, frowned.

Yuri flipped over three cards.

As the sun dropped below the horizon, so did the temperature. Yuri shivered against a sudden bite of wind that carried with it the smell of fried bread, cloyingly sweet. He pulled the hood of his wizard's robes up higher around his neck, then adjusted the three cards he'd placed atop his makeshift table so that they were equidistant apart. Despite the fact that he didn't need props, he found that divination tools produced surprisingly accurate results.

And he didn't like what he saw: The Tower and the Three of Swords, both upright. And The Moon, upside down.

Disruptive change.

Secrets and deception.

Sorrow, suffering, and pain.

Yuri shivered, then reached inside his robes and zipped his hoodie, hoping to play it off as a response to fall night air cooling quickly now that the sun had fully set.

"He needs encouragement, your brother does," Yuri said. It was one of those classically vague, applicable-to-everyone answers.

But the man looked pleased.

For a millisecond.

Then he frowned. "He's in his fifties."

"Yes, but you're only older. Not wiser."

The words had come unbidden. The man didn't have a brother.

But he'd been thinking about someone.

The man's brows rose, deepening the lines in his forehead, and he released a big, boisterous laugh that caught the attention of people passing by with their market bags and candy baskets.

The man's ghostly bodyguard, standing to the side, startled at the man's laugh. But then she turned an intense gaze on Yuri. He was still only looking at her with his periphery, which blurred a lot of details. But he could feel it. He could feel her.

She wasn't as convinced about Yuri's act as the man was.

She suspected Yuri wasn't a fraud.

Don't look at her. Don't look at her. Don't look.

The man pulled his wallet from his inside pocket again, opened it like a book, and dropped another hundred-dollar bill on the milk-crate table.

"Thanks, kid," he said, and he walked away, back across the square, shaking his head as if still laughing.

The ghost woman hung back. She was still in Yuri's periphery, which was harder to maintain now that the man was gone. When people stare at your back, you turn around, you make eye contact. The urge is even stronger when they stare at you from the front.

And she was *staring* at him, daring him to stare back.

Yuri picked up the hundred—thank goodness for that hundred, for a place to rest his eyes—and took his time gathering the first bill from under his hip, folding the two together. He kept his eyes down.

But just beyond the milk-crate table, he could see Baba Yaga's gray felt boots.

He shifted to one hip and stuffed the hundreds into his pocket.

The gray boots quarter-turned and followed after the man, picking up enough speed that she probably wasn't looking back over her shoulder.

Yuri chanced a look.

Across the square, the diaphanous woman caught up to the man, slowing as she reached his side. He put on a pair of glasses and turned toward her, as if looking at her. As if speaking to her. She nodded, and then she was gone.

The man pulled a phone from his pocket.

But Yuri lost sight of him when a pink bear paw waved through his view.

"Excuse me," said the pink bear paw's owner. She was a college-aged girl, one of a dozen wearing colorful Care Bears costumes. The pink bear pointed at Yuri's cardboard sign, still advertising, in colorful crayon, *Fortunes Told $20.* She had two hearts on her white stomach. Love-A-Lot Bear.

"Can you tell me if I'm gonna get my promotion?"

The answer came unbidden: *Eventually, but not this round. And that's not the question you most want answered.*

Yuri nodded and gathered up his previous client's cards, glancing up to see if he could still see the old man. He could. At the top of the stairs between Meany Hall and the three red-brick towers. The old man was pocketing his phone.

The pink Care Bear leaned into Yuri's view. "Are you trancing right now?"

Yuri smiled. *Trancing* implied he could turn off the broadcast.

If only.

"One shuffle for each word in the question," he said, receiving the customary horrified expression as she undoubtedly repeated her question and second-guessed its phrasing. He shuffled the deck, trying to inhale calm and exhale composure with each flex of the cards.

But then a man appeared.

A man wearing a dirty black T-shirt under dirty fatigues.

From out of nowhere, he just suddenly appeared in front of the Care Bears.

Yuri flinched backward, startled, and lost his grip on the cards. They shot out of his hands and all around the table.

Yuri scrambled to his feet. "Josh?"

His brother. He was just standing among the Care Bears. Thirteen years older and buffer—but no longer taller, and with new lines around the dark almond eyes they'd shared with their mom. It was the first time Yuri had seen his last living relative in almost a year.

The Care Bears had all shrieked and bent down to collect the scattered cards, leaving Josh standing alone. His dirty camos were green and reddish-brown in a pixelated pattern. Perfect for winning the award for Most Authentic Costume.

But Yuri knew better.

Josh's eyes darted around the square like he wasn't sure where he was. Or how he'd gotten here.

"Josh?" Yuri said again.

Josh locked eyes with Yuri—then winced as the pink Care Bear, reaching for a wayward card, crept through his body.

Yuri sucked in a breath. It wasn't the first time he'd seen a disembodied being. It wasn't even the first time he'd seen a disembodied being today. He'd known the truth the moment his brother had appeared. But still. This was Josh. So new. Only just recently—

Deceased.

A hollow feeling grew inside Yuri's chest, creating pressure in his throat, even as it left him completely empty below the sternum.

Josh's lips moved. Yuri didn't hear the words so much as receive them. Almost like he was thinking them himself.

You were right, Yuri. A rift. 41.82555, -123.98445. Big Beauty. Hurry, kid . . .

Yuri didn't scramble for a pen. He knew he'd remember the coordinates. He wasn't so sure he'd remember his big brother. He tried to memorize Josh's face, his love, as he flickered, already fading . . .

Yuri closed his eyes and tried to imprint this moment, this man, on his memory. He sat with his feelings, breathing into them, beginning the long process of getting used to them, to what it really felt like being the only Palming left in the world.

"Here's your cards," said the pink Care Bear.

Yuri opened his eyes and took the cards from her, then gathered up his tablecloth and sign, packing everything into his backpack.

"The most reliable way to connect with dead loved ones," he said, softly, just for her, just for the pink Care Bear who'd wanted to ask this question but had asked another instead, "is to remember them when you're enjoying yourself."

She blanched, her face becoming as white as her furry heart-centered stomach. "What?"

Yuri hiked his backpack onto his shoulder and picked up the milk crate. "So go have fun," he said.

Ignoring the Care Bears' rude dismissives, Yuri hurried across the square toward the steps between Meany Hall and the three brick towers. He pulled out his phone and typed an email to himself with the GPS coordinates his brother had given him, along with the words *rift* and *Big Beauty*, whatever they meant. Then he scrolled through his contacts for the only phone number he'd never called before.

Yuri dialed the number and held the phone to his ear, listening as it rang and rang.

Darius Jackson heard a siren. He put a protective arm around his wife and looked over his shoulder as an ambulance zoomed past, its exhaust stinking up the air. He waved his hand around, trying to keep the smoke away from Marisol. He held his wife by the elbow, letting her lean into him as she clutched at her belly, like maybe she could pull it in enough to see around it to the red curb below. No go, though. She kicked outward, her black ballet flat making contact, then inched forward and stepped up.

"Got it," she said, picking up speed toward the sliding glass doors under the big red sign that read *EMERGENCY ROOM*. They'd gotten lucky and found a parking spot in one of the closer feeder lanes, but the emergency room's sliding glass doors had been opened when they'd pulled in and Jackson had yet to see them close, what with how many people were filing into the hospital.

"Most of them are pregnant," Marisol said, her voice strained. "You seeing that?"

"Yeah," he said, not liking it one bit.

Up ahead, to the left side of the walkway, only two wheelchairs remained available for patients who needed extra assistance. One of them was already being detangled from the other by a man a lot younger than Jackson, who got it free and rolled it into position for his own pregnant wife.

Darius looked behind him at the parking lot and down the sidewalk both ways. He and Marisol were close enough to get the last wheelchair, but they weren't the only couple arriving who could use it.

"Leave it," Marisol said, thinking the same thing. "I'm okay. That woman's way further along than I am." She jerked her head backwards, over her right shoulder, where a woman who was almost certainly in her fortieth week was waddling up behind them. Marisol still had two months to go.

They'd been enjoying a nice dinner when all of a sudden Marisol had pitched forward at the table, her mouth dropping open in a silent gasp of pain, one hand bracing herself against the table, the other clutching the bottom of her belly.

Really, that last symptom was the only one Jackson would have needed to jump out of his chair, haul Marisol out of hers, and rush her out to the car. In his limited experience, hands on top of the stomach meant ease, contentment.

Hands clutching the underbelly meant trouble.

He'd been thankful that the best hospital in Sacramento, California, was only a few blocks away. But pregnant or not, it looked like Marisol would be in for a long wait.

The brightly lit waiting room smelled like industrial hand sanitizer and lingering sickness. Rows of light-blue vinyl chairs filled the room, and nearly every one of them was occupied.

Many by people in costumes who looked like they'd had a rough night.

Too many by expectant women grimacing and clutching their stomachs.

"There's one," Marisol said, pointing out an empty chair in the middle of the room. "I can make it. Go check me in."

She let go of him and reached for the seatback of the nearest chair, apologizing to the occupant when she brushed his shoulder.

Flat screens in the high corners of the room and at the tops of support posts were showing a subtitled rerun of Friends.

Better than the news.

Reports of a rise in complications and pregnancy loss had been all over the airwaves in recent weeks, but local reports had started in the Midwest about ten or eleven months ago, right before Jackson had received his current assignment. He'd been so excited to get one close to home. He and Marisol had just gotten married and they were both running out of time to become parents. They'd heard about the reports in the Midwest, but by then they'd already heard all kinds of horror stories. They figured, at best, the report was fake news, and at worst, it wasn't anything new.

But the ratio of pregnant women to other patients sitting in this Sacramento hospital's waiting room said the problem *was* new, it was different, and it was making its way to the coasts.

Jackson's phone buzzed and vibrated against his hip. He

unhooked it from his belt and checked the screen. The number was post, his latest assignment.

Jackson ground his jaw. Not even loss of limb was a big enough emergency to warrant his team bothering him right now.

He answered after the second ring, keeping his head down, his voice low, and his hand over his mouth. "Jackson."

"Finally. Where's Josh?"

The caller was male, but his voice was young.

Too young.

"Who is this?" Jackson asked.

"Yuri Palming. Is my brother still there? I want to come get him."

"Palming?" Jackson had a Palming on his team. Under civilian circumstances, he might acknowledge the connection, but the job and everyone involved was top secret. "How'd you get this number?"

"Josh gave it to me. For emergencies."

"Not this numb—"

Jackson stopped himself. If what the kid was saying was true, it meant no one had answered the phone at command post. He'd expected his team to eventually get comfortable with their cushy mission—they were used to more adrenaline; to days in the field, rather than months—but they wouldn't test him while he was with his wife. Jackson felt a sensation in his stomach that he was trained to work around but never quite got used to.

"How long was the phone ringing?"

"I don't know. It clicked over about a billion times, and then you finally answered. What happened to him?" said the caller. "What's the rift?"

The word sent a chill across Jackson's shoulders. He'd only heard the term himself last week. From his team. There were so many questions he wanted to ask the caller, but there was nothing he was allowed to say.

"You know what, dude? Never mind," said the caller. "I already have your coordinates. I'm coming either way."

Jackson hung up on the kid and dialed command post. The

phone rang and rang, clicking over several times, and then, as someone finally answered—

"Jackson?"

—he heard a baby cry. His heart leapt. He looked up and glanced around the hospital's waiting room, looking for Marisol, not finding her in the seat she'd been aiming for. He started to lower the phone but then he heard his name again.

"Jackson?" A female voice on the phone. And a baby crying in the background.

"Doc?"

Jackson had earned his team's reputation for discretion in part by stipulating in every mission contract that his team always have a doctor on retainer, one that he could call at a moment's notice. The arrangement was best for team safety, for keeping client secrets, and for maintaining team and family morale. Jackson had a few doctors he trusted all over the globe.

Gabriela Ceja was his "Doc" in the American Southwest.

She was also his favorite.

But he did not like that she was answering his phone.

"Jackson!" Doc said, the relief in her voice tainted by strain.

"Where is everyone?" he asked, his irritation slowly giving way to dread. "How come no one's answering the phone?"

"They were out at the clearing. They . . . they . . ." Jackson did not like the tone in Doc's voice, a woman who had seen it all and then some. The hesitation, the terror, punctuated by the baby's wail. Jackson feared he'd been wrong:

There was a big enough emergency.

"Who's left?"

"Danny's bringing the last of them back now."

Jackson waited for Doc to add more names, but on the other end of the line, Doc was cooing, trying to soothe the baby.

"Wait. That's it?" Jackson asked her. "Just Danny? No one else?"

"I wanted to go out there too, help Danny bring them back, but with Gaia here . . ." Doc's voice broke. Doc was Gaia's primary caretaker for the next little while because Gaia's mother, Doc's young granddaughter, couldn't be with her right now. Doc sniffled congestion as she cooed the crying baby. But Gaia's cries sounded distant on the phone. Like the baby was in her carrier. Which meant Doc was probably already tending someone on Jackson's team. Doc sniffed, and her tone sounded a little more normal. "You know how it gets out there."

He didn't, actually. Back in January, his team had been tasked with guarding a clearing in the woods. "Consider it a break," his handler had said, "easy money." Jackson was happy to do so. The post was even close to home, close to Marisol. He got to see her a lot more often. But once they found out she was pregnant, Jackson had mostly left his team to handle the mission on their own. He'd mostly just listened to their reports.

"When'd it start this time?" he asked.

"I don't know. I could check the logbooks."

Jackson didn't say anything. Moments later, he heard a few sounds through the phone: footsteps, a door creaking open, rain, lots of rain. Then a door closing, the flipping of pages. Jackson figured Doc was consulting the logbooks.

Still two people from the head of the line at the check-in desk, Jackson turned to look for Marisol and found her in the chair she'd aimed for, in the center of the room. They met eyes immediately, like she'd been watching him this whole time. Her forehead was creased. He knew those worry lines were for him, rather than for herself. So he flashed her a smile and shook his head that his phone call was nothing, hoping she wouldn't continue to worry about him. She needed to focus on herself.

In his ear, Doc said, "Jackson? You still there?"

"Here."

"It looks like they started reporting activity about forty-five minutes ago."

Jackson checked his watch. That was about how long ago he and Marisol had left the restaurant.

It may have been a while since Jackson had been to the clearing, and the clearing may have been quiet every time he did go, at least to his eyes and ears, but Jackson still had his suspicions.

His team had been watching the clearing since January.

The rise in pregnancy complications had started about the same time.

Logically, it was just a coincidence. It didn't make sense that his assignment could relate to, let alone cause, the rise in pregnancy complications. But both the clearing and this, this pregnancy loss pandemic, had occasional upticks in activity. And those upticks, at least to Jackson's eye, sure seemed to happen at about the same time.

He looked around the emergency waiting room, feeling the eeriness of seeing so many expectant women in this sterile, sick-smelling place, all of them here at one time, at the same time.

And his eyes landed on Marisol. Still watching him. She gave him a small smile. He tried to smile back. But he didn't know how to help his wife and child.

At least not here.

Above him, a PA system announced a Code Purple followed by a Code Pink. Neither code was as well known as Code Blue, but the patient demographics in the waiting room tonight made them easy to figure out. Jackson swallowed hard. And made his decision.

"Everything okay?" Doc asked him over the phone.

Jackson ignored the question. "There's a file in—"

His voice broke. In his thirty-three years of having top secret clearance, he'd never once broken mission parameters, let alone trust.

"A file?" Doc said. "What file?"

Jackson cleared his throat. The sanitized air didn't have enough oxygen.

"In my desk. It's called *Supplies*."

A fake name for a dangerous suspicion and an even more dangerous solution.

But he couldn't take it back now. He was grasping at hope.

Hopeless hope. It was crazy for him to think that a clearing in the woods could be connected to his wife's pain, to his child's survival. But if checking it out had even the slimmest chance of saving their lives, it was worth the sacrifice of his own.

"Give the file to Danny," he said to Doc, "and tell him to go get her."

CHAPTER 1

Anja Copenhagen had chosen to walk back to work from the Oregon Convention Center, in Portland, Oregon, hoping that the ten minutes of beautiful, sunny morning and fresh air and autumn leaves would clear her head of the disaster that had been the last hour.

She was still muttering to herself as she opened the main door to her brightly lit science lab. But as soon as the door shut behind her, she let out a big sigh and felt herself finally relax.

She loved the lab. Just being in the white room lightened her mood. She loved all the expensive shared equipment set up in the center. Loved the brass nameplates above the green doors that were spaced every eight feet along the walls, one of which was her very own office. She loved the glassed-in meeting room that sat at the back and provided a nice place to have lunch or catch up on a show while the back brain worked.

The air filter was rumbling, but the room smelled strangely of banana runts, sweet and full of chemicals. One of the fume hoods must've been acting up again.

But she didn't mind. Not today.

It was ten past eleven on a Saturday. She'd gotten back from her first science convention as a presenter in less time than it had taken the security guard to escort her off the dais. But at least she hadn't had to travel far to get home.

Still, she couldn't believe she'd given a whole hour of her weekend to that waste of time.

She made it into the lab as far as the first white equipment table before dropping her bag on the floor and plopping down on the nearest stool. She had less than an hour left before Farhad would come in and kick her out—rightfully, even though they never used the same equipment.

Her mentor, a man she hadn't heard from in years, had called late this morning, asking her, last minute, to fill in on a panel.

She'd been so thankful for the opportunity.

She'd arrived at the conference center a few minutes before her panel was scheduled to start. The conference center smelled like fresh carpet cleaner, and it was filled with people—but not the kind she'd been expecting. She'd thought there would be suits, a few at least, and definitely business casual. Instead, some of the attendees were wearing costumes, many of them dressed as ghosts and ghostbusters, like they hadn't gotten enough of Halloween the day before. Too many others were wearing T-shirts and hoodies, their phones out and their heads down.

An escort met her in the lobby and rushed her to her panel. A dais had been erected beneath a giant white projector screen. It held a long table and a dozen chairs, but only two of them were occupied.

Her escort pulled out a chair for her near the center of the table before heading back to the lobby. The table was covered in a burgundy tablecloth, and Anja had to fight with it to scooch in her chair. That was the first red flag. She should have left then and there.

She didn't know the other two people on the panel, but she recognized the gentleman sitting furthest away. He was not a scientist. Well, maybe he used to be, was trained as such, but he'd long ago abandoned the science credo. He was into spiritualism or some such now. That was the second red flag.

Sitting closest to her, the moderator was a young guy who seemed in no great hurry to start. And one of the members of the audience looked ready to take advantage of that. Unlike everyone else, he *was* wearing a suit, and Anja recognized him right away, having spoken with him before. He was pleasant enough, even though his mission was reprehensible.

She smiled and spoke before he reached her. "Still not interested in a job, John."

"You sure?" John Stanton said. He was a headhunter. Worked freelance. But he reminded Anja of your stereotypical smarmy stockbroker. "Compensation has gone way up, given the state of things. Did you see the news this morning?"

She hadn't, but she figured her assistant, Ming, would fill her in.

At precisely ten o'clock, the moderator called everyone to attention and announced the name of the panel.

"Thank you, everyone, for coming and for sticking around despite our change in guests. This hour's panel is entitled Sci vs. Psy."

The moderator had gone on to introduce his two panelists, starting with the other guy, but Anja wasn't listening.

Sci vs. Psy? She wasn't sure she'd heard right, so she glanced around the table, looking for an agenda, a program, anything. She looked up at the projector screen and there it was: Sci vs. Psy.

She knew what *Sci* referred to, but *Psy?* She could only guess, and she didn't like what she was coming up with.

The third red flag.

And yet, there she sat.

"Also with me today is Anja Aura Copenhagen." Anja cringed at the moderator's use of her middle name. Where did he even get it? "She has a PhD in biology and is currently studying luminescence, which, as I'm sure many of you are aware, is the new theory of proving a nonphysical side of things. We're glad she could fill in today, and we're very excited to have her here."

The crowd had applauded.

But Anja had been livid.

She exhaled now, trying to relax, trying to get back into work mode. When that wasn't enough, she screamed and shook her arms and legs, trying to release her annoyance.

"How was it?"

Anja startled. She frequently booked the lab on Saturdays for the guaranteed access to community equipment, but mostly for the solitude. She looked around the lab's perimeter. All the green office doors were closed.

"In the conference room," the voice said on a laugh. Anja recognized it now. She picked up her bag and ventured further into the lab.

At the far end of the community space was the glassed-in meeting room with a large conference table, snacks, and a projector. Her lab assistant, Ming Lee, had pulled down the screen and was both watching the news and reading the paper, with her feet on the table. She was wearing orange, old-school Converse. She waved, then pointed at the screen. "Your mentor's on TV."

"Oh, yeah?" Anja felt her stomach tense, but she entered the conference room anyway. Jim Lugner hadn't been her mentor since he'd left her PhD program at the beginning of her second year, eight years ago. But she'd mentioned their connection once before, when he was on the news, and now Ming pointed out his every appearance. "What's he doing?"

"Adopting a kid."

"What?"

The conference room smelled like fresh coffee. Anja sat at the table and peered at the screen.

Jim Lugner, tall and fit with a full head of neatly trimmed grayish-white hair and wearing his signature knee-length black raincoat with a red carnation on the lapel, descended the steps of a charter plane with his hand on the upper back of an eight- or nine-year-old Asian child.

The boy was dressed in simple, maybe even handmade, blue cotton pants and a white shift shirt. He had a presence, a way of carrying himself, unlike any Anja was used to seeing from an American kid.

"From China?" she asked.

"Doubt it," Ming said. "We don't give our sons away." She gave

Anja a cheeky grin from behind her sweep of bangs. Ming hailed from LA and had a picture of her toddler on her desk, but her son lived with his father. "I think the kid's from the Midwest or something, been in foster care a few years. 'Older kids need love too' and all that."

Anja nodded. Even she had heard certain circles chanting adoption as the solution to the rise in pregnancy loss.

"Good for him," she said. "So, you're here to watch the news?" she asked Ming.

"Big screen. Free paper. Free coffee." Ming held up her twenty-ounce cup, still watching the screen. Someone in a blue suit was opening the door to a limo, and Jim and the kid climbed inside. The news pundits closed the segment with their usual reminder that Jim Lugner was running for Senate after having started a foundation following the murder of his twenty-year-old son eight years ago this week.

Ming turned off the TV and got up to make herself another latte. The lab boasted a fantastic one-touch espresso machine. The milk frothed.

"You should be thanking me, by the way," Ming said. "Farhad tried to steal your time."

Anja snorted and rested her head on the table glass. She closed her eyes. Not even noon yet, and it had already been a long day.

"So," Ming prompted. "How was it? How's it feel to be officially invited to speak on panels?"

Anja smelled old ketchup. One guess said Aman had left her half-eaten eggs on the counter again, instead of pushing them a foot to the right, into the trash. Yup, there they were. Anja debated throwing them away, but they'd continue to stink regardless, and she wasn't the maid.

Nope, she was just a scientist whose work and time no one respected.

"It was a sci versus psy panel."

"A what?"

"Half the people there weren't even scientists. They were ghost hunters. The crowd turned it into a superstitious free-for-all."

"Whaaat?"

"I kid you not. Dressed the part and everything. One of 'em asked if human bioluminescence is, in fact, the soul."

Ming laughed.

"It's not funny," she said, but Ming had a high-pitched and contagious chortle, and Anja was soon laughing along with her.

Anja had tried to get the panel's conversation back on the science track, but the audience was having none of it. They quickly moved on to asking about the scent of souls and the fluorescence of ghosts: sensory experiences that, they argued, were real but were reserved, most inconveniently, for a select—nay, *chosen*—few.

Ridiculous.

"After life, we die," Anja said now, for herself, for good measure, to keep laughing and to avoid remembering the last question she'd been asked, about her family. "We die, that's it, and thank goodness."

"I'm sorry," said Ming, still laughing.

Anja shrugged. "Live and learn to say no." She'd wanted the publicity, to convince the more prestigious journals like *Science* or *Nature* to publish her research—which, in turn, would help her renew her grant, due at year's end—but now she could only hope her attendance wouldn't tank her credibility entirely. "Oh, and John Stanton was there."

"The headhunter?"

"*USBS, Anja.*" She sleazed her voice to imitate the talent scout's schmooze, and the acronym the pharmaceutical industry had given their new cash cow. USBS. Unexplained Stillbirth Syndrome. "*People* need *pharmaceuticals.*"

"Wha'd you tell him?"

"That unborn children need drugs like my fluorescent worms need salt."

Anja wanted to resolve problems, not make a buck off the people suffering them. She wanted to work on something that mattered.

She checked her watch. Farhad would be here in twenty minutes. Probably less. She thanked Ming for the pick-me-up and headed to her office, to get to work.

Ming followed her out, complaining about her stomach growling and offering to pick up lunch for the both of them.

"Oh, and I got your mail," Ming said. "You got another letter from your mom."

CHAPTER 2

Anja's private office looked like someone's sterile white kitchen. It had a small desk and chair, but its main features included a sink and counter space over lower cabinets, and upper cabinets with glass-fronted doors that made it easy to find her glassware.

Her fluorescent worms lived in a tank of dirt on the counter, to the right of the lab door. Whenever her colleagues brought their kids in to show them what mommy or daddy did for a living, they'd always stop by Anja's office, third green door on the right, and ask her to turn on the blacklight. The worms would glow.

"Cool" was the most frequent response, followed by "How do they do that?"

"They've got something in their bodies that absorbs the ultraviolet light from the blacklight and then immediately releases that light, as visible light. In this case, blues and greens."

Occasionally, the kid's eyes would go wide with understanding, but usually they just frowned in confusion.

Was it Einstein who said if you can't explain it to a six-year-old, then you don't understand it yourself?

Soon after she'd started as Anja's assistant a couple years ago, Ming had designated the worm tank's lid as Anja's inbox, and sitting on top of the mail pile now was a white envelope, hand-addressed and thin, like it held a lone half-sheet of paper.

Odd. For one thing, the letter was at least five days early. Her mom contacted her once a week, rotating through phone, letter, and email, and Anja had just ignored a call from her two days ago.

For another thing, the envelopes were usually colored—the last one was pink—and they were usually stuffed as full as could be and affixed with extra stamps.

Still, Anja opened the bottom drawer beneath the worm tank and tossed the slender, white, unopened envelope in with the rest.

Next in the pile was a printed email from *Quantum*. The publication wasn't as prestigious or as well known as *Nature*, but according to their email, they were just as unwilling to publish Anja's research. Anja sighed. Her paper was good. Important even. And not just to the superstitious of the world, the ones who wanted to use her findings to prove the existence of souls and the afterlife and the nonphysical and whatever other nonsense interested them. It was important in the *real* world, to real people, to progress . . .

She dropped the printed email into the trash.

The main lab was quiet—seemed Farhad was running late—but Anja still shut the door and put on her headphones. She counted to five, intending to get to work, but the seven-year habit wasn't strong enough to balance her focus. She sulked on her lab stool, letting the meditation music soothe the rejection, letting the pillowed cushions covering her ears offer her comfort.

She couldn't think of anywhere else to submit. *Quantum* had already been a stretch. And what was with all the rejection, anyway? It wasn't like she was in a creative field where worthiness was a matter of opinion. This was science. She'd thought that all she had to do was follow the scientific method and her results would be added to the broader conversation.

But along with the insult of being ignored, rejection also came with an injury. If she couldn't publish her work, then she had no way to show progress in her research. And her funding was up for renewal at the end of the year.

She opened the drawer of unopened letters from her mom, the thin, white anomalous one on top. She told herself it was just curiosity—why was it so thin, so early?—but there was something about giving your dreams your all and still not quite making it, still failing, that made her yearn for contact with someone who clearly loved her no matter what.

Anja had just gotten her thumb under the loose edge of the envelope's flap when there was a knock at her door.

She sighed—Farhad was always complaining about the way she left the machines—and opened the door.

"What did I forget to do this time . . ."

The man at the door was not Farhad. He wore pixelated reddish-brown and forest-green camo pants and a black, fitted T-shirt, and he had excellent posture. But his dark hair was too shaggy and his beard a day too old to be active military. A Halloween costume, maybe? Except he looked too old for Halloween, let alone to carry it over to November 1st. Early thirties, maybe?

"Anja Aura Copenhagen?" He sounded exhausted. And irritated.

Great. He was probably one of the crazy people who had attended the Sci vs. Psy panel, someone who thought she owed him something and so had followed her back to the lab. Anja glanced across the room, at her office phone. Too far. He'd get to her before she could reach it, let alone dial security.

"Look," she said, slowly closing her office door. "I told you guys at the conference, I can't help you prove the existence of ghosts."

His brows puzzled together, never taking his eyes off her, but he shifted his weight to one hip, sliding his boot against the jamb so she couldn't shut the door.

"Not why I've come," he said.

"Good to hear." She shifted closer to the counter and reached beyond the worm tank to where she kept her scissors. But they were just out of reach. "You should also know that I'm not interested in creating pharmaceuticals and definitely not interested in creating weapons."

His brows puzzled tighter, and he looked down at his military fatigues. Anja reached for the scissors and came up with them.

When the man looked up at her again, his eyes widened. He showed her his palms and backed away a step. Anja thought that might be all the room he'd give her, but he backed all the way up to the main lab's nearest equipment table.

The room's overhead light shined harshly on his face and glinted off reddish-brown stains on his camos. Could have been mud, but not any kind of mud found in the Pacific Northwest. She thought it might be blood. Maybe he'd helped a fallen comrade a while back and couldn't get out the stain. Except it looked textured. Which made it fresher than the last wash.

Holding his empty hands out at his sides, he said, "Ms. Copenhagen, I don't know the specifics of your assignment, but *my* assignment is to collect you. People died today. It's imperative that you come with me now."

People? Anja lowered the scissors a little. "I didn't hear anything on the news." And Ming would have told her if there had been any new catastrophes. "What happened?"

The man opened his mouth to speak, but no words came out. He shrugged and shook his head. Then straightened, seeming to shake it off. He still had his hands out. She put down the scissors, and he lowered them. "Can you please just come with me? Please?"

"What's your name?"

"Danny."

"Danny what?"

"Danny Diega."

"Do you have identification?"

"Not anything that's going to convince you I'm legit."

She stared at him. "And *that's* supposed to convince me?" She shook her head. "I'm sorry about whatever happened, but I have work to do. My grant's up for renewal, and—"

"The Chesterton-X grant?"

Anja nodded slowly, trying to decide if the award was common enough knowledge or whether she should brandish her scissors again.

The man stood taller, suddenly more confident and relaxed, if still exhausted-looking. "Facilitated by the Veritas Progress Foundation?" he said. "Funded largely by an anonymous donor?"

Almost entirely by an anonymous donor. Anja nodded again.

"Helping him in the field could go a long way in making up for your lack of progress in the lab."

Anja felt the slight, but only its implications held her attention. "*You* know my donor?"

"Not personally. He funds my work same as yours. If he says pick up Anja Aura Copenhagen, well . . ." He held his hands out, palms up. *Here I am.*

Anja had never experienced the beck-and-call of a donor's request before, but her lab mates had. She knew how it worked.

Still, she didn't feel comfortable leaving with a stranger. She pulled out her phone to call Ming.

"Leave your phone."

"I need to let my family know."

He shook his head. "Your mom won't know the difference, and the sooner we get going, the better chance I have of getting you back here by Monday. So work doesn't need to know either. Leave the phone."

Anja never really called anyone except Ming, her therapist, and her favorite takeout spots—the Chinese place down the street and the best gyro place in the city, near her apartment—but putting down the phone felt like surrendering a lifeline.

"I can hold onto it if you insist, but choose fast. I need to get you to post by sunset."

Anja hesitated.

"Either leave your phone or give it to me. We're not leaving until you choose, and we need to go now."

Anja handed it over.

"Got any tape?" the man asked.

Despite the fact that he was kindly kidnapping her, Anja had the sense that he was trustworthy, that he, too, was acting against his will. "You gonna write my name on it?"

"Something like that."

"You have a lot of phones you need to keep track of? Am I gonna find myself shackled in a van with a bunch of other idiots who gave you their phones?"

"Tape."

"Masking? Scotch?" She got a piece of masking tape from the supply cabinet and wrote her name on it with a Sharpie. When she turned around, Danny had her phone dismantled and was putting it back together with a tiny screwdriver kit. He looked up for the tape, saw her name written on it in thick black Sharpie, and snorted a smile. He used the tape to secure the SIM card and battery to the outside of the phone, then slid the phone into the cargo pocket on his right pantleg. "You'll get it back when you're done. Do you have any other shoes?"

Anja looked down her white blouse and designer jeans to her cream ballet flats. "Not here."

Danny shook his head. "Fine. Let's go."

Anja grabbed her raincoat and her bag, then looked around her lab, wondering if she'd ever see it again. Then she wondered if she'd ever hear her mom's voice again.

But anger still trumped regret on that topic, so she opened the bottom drawer beneath the worm tank and tossed her mom's last letter back inside.

"What are you doing?" the man asked.

"Packing." She grabbed the box of granola bars she kept in her desk and a couple bottles of water. "Hard to do when I don't know where I'm going and the guy taking me there is wearing fatigues."

Out in the main lab, the entrance door *kachinked* open. "Hey, Anja, everything okay in here?"

Ming.

Anja stepped out of her office, expecting the man to hide behind a pillar, but he turned to face the opening door and resumed his perfect posture.

Ming entered the lab juggling takeout bags, her lab key, and a handwritten sign.

"Looks like Farhad wants the place to himself," she said, flashing the sign: *Noxious gas spill—Lab closed today.* "I figured you'd call me if it were true."

She set the takeout bags on the lab table nearest the door. "Is Farhad even here yet?" She looked around—and spotted their visitor.

Ming glanced at Anja with wide eyes, then hubba'd her eyebrows. "I didn't get enough food for three, but if your hot friend likes phad thai, I can leave, and he can have mine."

"Ming Lee?" the man asked.

"Yeah . . ."

CHAPTER 3

Outside, a newish but very dirty Ford Explorer was parked in the loading zone, right at the end of the building's walkway, where the curb is painted yellow. Danny peered at his windshield and half-smiled. Anja looked too and didn't see a ticket.

But he'd been parked long enough to get tagged.

A layer of freeway dust covered the SUV's forest-green paint, and someone had written *Wash me* on the rear passenger door's window. Beneath the dust, the lower side panels and wheel wells were splattered with reddish-brown mud. It was dry and flaking off where it was thickest.

Danny pointed his key fob at the SUV and it beeped unlocked. He opened the rear passenger-side door. "You can both sit in back, if you want."

"Sounds good to me," Ming said, climbing in and sliding across the middle seat to take the one behind the driver.

"Aren't you worried about us being behind you?" Anja asked.

"No. I figure if you're both in back, you'll talk quieter, and I can concentrate on the road. Get in."

Anja did. The interior smelled like vanilla. A little yellow air-freshener tree hung from a knob on the front console. The tree still had its clear plastic packaging wrapped around its bottom half.

Danny gently shut Anja's door, then walked around the back of the vehicle.

"Moody," Ming said. "What's his deal?"

Ming put one elbow on the back of the seat and turned to watch Danny as he made his way around to the driver's side front. The third row of seats had been flattened to increase the cargo area. A dark blanket lay spread out in back. It was covered with the same stuff that covered Danny's pants—and the bottom of the SUV, come to think of it. That strange red mud, and something that might be blood.

Anja shrugged. "Something happened."

"He looks tired. Think he can drive?"

Before Anja could answer, Danny opened his door and climbed in the front, reached over his left shoulder and pulled down his belt, snapping it in place with a click.

"Seatbelts," he said without looking at them first to see if they'd already put them on. They hadn't.

Anja buckled her seatbelt. The Explorer had strange upholstery. It was dark gray. Like leather, but not. It seemed nicer than leather. Sturdier.

Ming did the same, then shrugged at Anja as if answering her own question about Danny's fitness to drive with a hesitant affirmative.

Danny started up the engine and pulled into traffic. It was heavy, being lunch time and all, but as soon as they were on the freeway it lightened up considerably.

"So where are we going?" Anja asked.

"South."

"I see that. How far south? How directly south?"

"Feel free to take a nap. It might be a good idea anyway."

Anja felt Ming's fingers grope across the bench seat and grab her hand, giving it a squeeze. It scared Anja just how much she appreciated the comfort, and she wondered not for the first time whether she and Ming were idiots for having gotten into Danny's Ford.

Anja was nowhere near trusting him enough to take a nap, but his driving was smooth. Easy and calming. Even with brake lights flashing every so often up ahead of them. She soon found her eyes closing, her head falling against the door frame.

When she woke up, they were still driving south on I-5, seeing signs for Grants Pass, Oregon. She'd been asleep for something like four hours.

"You guys hungry?" Danny asked. He took an off-ramp and pulled into a fast-food parking lot.

Anja didn't open her door to get out. She awaited instructions, figuring Danny would stay in the car with either her or Ming while the other one went inside to place their order. Like they were kidnap victims. Or at the very least like they were in a hurry.

But such instructions didn't come.

Danny got out of the car and started trudging, head down and tired, toward the restaurant's entrance.

Then he stopped and looked around himself, looked back over his shoulder. Frowning, he came back to the Explorer. He leaned down and peered into Anja's window.

"You guys coming?" he said through the glass.

Anja and Ming climbed out of the vehicle, and they walked into the restaurant—Danny holding the door open for them—like they were three old friends on a road trip making a pit stop.

Anja and Ming took their time in the restroom. Peeing, sure, but also debating whether this was the most laid-back kidnapping ever or whether Danny was legit and, if so, what could have possibly happened. Ming said she hadn't heard about a thing. Anja was hoping to borrow someone's phone so they could at least call someone and let them know where they were. But no one walked in with a phone.

They exited the bathroom and found Danny seated in the nearest booth, facing the restroom. He had one bag of food. It smelled of grease, but Danny pulled out three salads.

"No burgers?" Anja asked, sliding across the bench seat and opening her salad. A green salad. Not even a good chef salad with meat and cheese. And the dressing was a vinaigrette.

Danny opened his own salad and forked off the croutons. "I don't eat that stuff," he said. "And you shouldn't either. We need you sharp."

He didn't rush them as they ate, but he did check his watch a lot. "It would be best to get you there by sundown," he said.

"What time is it now?" Ming asked, looking around the restaurant for a clock. "Three? Four?"

Anja checked her watch. It was five after four. The restaurant's dinner crowd was just starting to trickle in.

"Sunset's at, what, six-ish?" Ming asked.

Anja didn't know. She didn't pay much attention to that kind of thing. If she needed a light, she just flipped one on. Hooray for science.

Ming asked, "Where can we get in two hours?"

Anja shrugged. "Mount Shasta?"

"For work?" Ming asked.

Anja shrugged again.

"What say you?" Ming asked Danny. "Any guesses where we're going?"

Danny had obvious smile and laugh lines. They suggested that, under friendlier circumstances, he might withhold the information with a playful grin.

But not today.

Tired eyes lifted from his salad for a second but then drifted somberly back down as his mouth quietly chewed. He looked almost shell-shocked. Like he was lost in his own thoughts, and like those thoughts were heartbreaking.

"You look beat," Ming said. "Do you want me to drive?"

Danny looked up like he wanted to take her up on the offer or at least say *more than you know*, but all he said was "Can't."

They finished their salads in crunchy silence, but Anja began looking at Danny anew.

His camo fatigues hid it well, but they were filthy, covered in that reddish-brown muck. Whatever the reason Danny had come to collect them, he looked like he'd left to do so while still in the thick of it—and not by his own choice. He looked like the last place he wanted to be was here, chauffeuring Anja and Ming.

And yet the way he let them take their time in the restaurant . . . he wasn't in a hurry to get back either.

When they got back into the car, Ming started in on Danny again. "Why can't you tell us where we're going?"

Danny sighed as he buckled himself in. "I was supposed to have you two wear blindfolds." He reached down into his footwell and came up with two thin black towels. "But we've gotta pass a border checkpoint, and blindfolds would look bad." He tossed the towels back into the footwell and started the engine, started backing out of the parking spot, then stopped. "Actually, can one of you sit up front?"

Anja looked at Ming, who frowned back at her.

"Please?" Danny asked, checking his watch. "We're cutting it close, and I'd rather they see the California plates, note nothing suspicious about our seating arrangements, and wave us on through."

Anja climbed out of the back and into the front as Danny picked up a tri-tab manila folder about an inch thick off the front passenger floor and slotted it into the narrow space between his seat and the door.

Anja didn't figure he'd tell her, so she didn't bother asking him what it was.

"So I take it you're just the brawn of this operation?" she said as she buckled herself in beside him.

"As opposed to the brains?" He said. "Funny. And, no. I wouldn't say I'm the brawn."

Danny pulled the SUV up to the parking lot's curb ramp and waited for an opening in the traffic. But instead of heading back to the I-5 freeway, he turned onto US 199 south, toward somewhere in western California.

And he said, almost absently, "You might say I'm what's left of the heart."

CHAPTER 4

Jim Lugner sat behind his mahogany desk and fretted his knuckles while the ten-year-old boy he'd finally managed to adopt from China played on the rug, in front of the crackling fire, with the old yellow lab that once belonged to his dead son.

The kid was gentle with the dog, slowly and repeatedly running a tiny palm over the mutt's huge head as it panted happily in the boy's face.

Every now and then, though, the boy would sneak a glance at Jim.

Jim tried to remember to smile.

He was impatient to ask the kid to give a demonstration of his skill—and was even more eager to get started with the kid's training—but the Russian had been right. The boy should acclimate first. Delaying for one day wouldn't make that much difference. And anyway, the boy's previous handlers had told Jim that the kid performed better when first put at ease.

But what was Jim to do with himself in the meantime? Worry that the lost day *would* matter?

Or worry that it wouldn't, but only because it was almost dinner time and he still hadn't received word?

He'd expected to receive the message by noon.

And once it came, there would be no turning back.

At the sound of footsteps, Jim looked up and was surprised to find that the pocket doors at the far end of his office were open. *But, that's right.* Normally he kept the doors closed. But the kid had shuddered, wrapped his arms around his knees, tucked his head, and shook when he'd started to close them.

Jim leaned to the side to get a better view of the corridor through the pocket doors. The whole west side of this particular home had wall-to-wall windows overlooking the Pacific Ocean. Just now the setting sun was casting a long shadow across the hardwood floor. An *approaching* shadow.

Without knocking first, the Russian stepped inside Jim's office.

She stood before him, framed tightly by the doorway, the long hallway stretching behind her into oblivion—where he hoped she would soon take them. She was taller than him. More mobile, too. But she also had more weathering on her face and an older woman's sense of style. Long wool skirts and shapeless tops in drab colors. Shawls covered her short and grayish-blonde hair and draped over her shoulders. The muted colors with occasional pops of red stayed the same over the years, but the fabric choices, and later the brands, had quickly grown more and more expensive. This one—an Hermès, wrapped to show the trademark on her left shoulder—cost more than some people's rent.

The scarves, her hooked nose, her stern eyes reminded Jim of Baba Yaga, the witch of Russian fairy tales. The woman could be thirty or seventy for all he knew, but he guessed it was somewhere in between.

She had with her an opened plastic mailer bag. It rustled as she pulled out what was inside.

She said, "Do you want to tell me what is this?"

She peered down her bumped nose at him, reminding him of the nuns who'd taught him at St Francis, how they'd appeared when trying to be patient but were actually about to whack his knuckles with a ruler.

She held the uniforms he had ordered. A loose-fitting technical fabric in a shade of cream.

Unfortunately, the insignia he had asked to be embroidered into the material was so big that he could see it from behind his desk, nearly fifteen yards from where the Russian was standing. It was supposed to be a tiny, insignificant mark that he'd hoped everyone would assume was the branding mark of the clothier.

He'd asked for the embroiderer to make the size in millimeters, but she must've assumed he'd meant centimeters.

Jim sighed.

"You, you will deny this?" the Russian said.

He would have, yes, if the insignia had been the proper size, but as it was, the insignia looked like a uniform patch. Embroidered in, rather than sewn on top, so that it couldn't be so easily torn off.

Even now the Russian was rubbing her thumb against the stitching. He'd been hoping she wouldn't know the true, occult reason behind all the symbols on all the patches of all the uniforms in all the world.

But of course she would. She knew more about that kind of thing than he did.

"He not wearing this," she said.

Off to the side, the kid was kneeling next to the dog, hugging it around the neck. His face was pale, and his dark eyes darted back and forth between Jim and the Russian.

"You're scaring the boy," he said.

The Russian glared at him, her eyes narrowing, her lips pressing into a line. He gave her a moment, but still, she didn't say a word. Lest she scare the boy.

An unexpected benefit.

Jim smirked. "Should I tell you it was an error at the clothier?"

"Is one thing for tragic accident happen on mission," she said. "Is another thing for you to"—she glanced at the boy, opting for euphemistic words—"to plan your benefit from it."

The kid stiffened, squeezing the dog's neck. Too tightly, apparently, because it barked and wriggled away. The kid got up and chased after it, but instead of following the dog out the pocket doors, he ran to the Russian's side and clung to her thigh like an oversized toddler, his cheek pressed to her hip, his wide eyes staring back at Jim.

The Russian startled at the boy's touch, but recovered quickly enough.

She had known that he had been looking for someone with a particular skill to add to their team—it was she who had made the suggestion in the first place, after failing at the skill herself—but she hadn't known that Jim had selected a child until yesterday.

Jim had expected her to be a severe schoolmarm type, but it seemed she reserved that demeanor for adults.

She now put a protective hand against the boy's back, shifting the bundle of uniforms to the crook of her other arm. "He not wearing this," she said again.

"I got one for you, too," Jim said. "Hope for the best, plan for the worst. Waste not, want not."

She shook her head. "I find this work interesting, what we do together. But I don't like where I think you are taking it. I will let bad things happen to bad people, if those are orders. But this"—her index finger tapped against the boy's shoulder, still clutching him as he held fast to her thigh—"this is not bad person. I will not wear your mark into battle. And neither will he."

"If you want us to track you," Jim said, "protect you from radiation, then you will wear it."

"Technical fabric?" The Russian raised an eyebrow and looked at the garment anew, rubbing the fabric between her thumb and forefinger.

It wasn't as special as all that—that was a lie—but the fabric was supposed to be soft, with a nice feel over the skin. He hadn't spent much money or time getting it, just enough that she wouldn't mind wearing it, and his insignia with it.

"Very nice," the Russian said. But she wadded up the cream uniforms and the mailing package in both hands and brought the bundle to her chest like she was about to pass a basketball. "Still, I think no. Could prove too tempting for you, yes? A sudden *oops*?"

The Russian tossed the uniforms toward the fireplace.

Jim jumped to his feet. "No!"

The boy reached his tiny hand into the air like he was trying to block the shot, but the cream fabric sailed on by . . .

But it didn't land in the fire. The wad of plastic and fabric suddenly stopped, halfway between the talented duo and the flames burning in the hearth, then it dropped to the floor.

It happened so quickly, a casual observer might have thought the boy had gotten a hand on the pass after all, or that the Russian had flubbed the toss.

But Jim knew better.

This wasn't the skill he most wanted to see from the boy—wasn't the reason why he'd requested this kid in particular—but that almost made witnessing the feat all the more satisfying.

Of course a kid like this would have additional talents. Of course he would.

All kinds of talents.

Because he was the real deal.

The United States wouldn't know the real deal if they saw it sitting behind a milk crate on the White House steps. They'd long ago turned their nose up at the idea of paranormal abilities.

Don't ponder more than the physical, the material, or we will mock you, shun you, ostracize you.

Fortunately for Jim, the rest of the world wasn't as close-minded.

Or as high-minded.

When the Chinese government had learned of this kid, they'd rewarded his family and taken him for observation and development. He'd been prized.

But he'd also been merely one of so many gifted children that Jim had been able to acquire him in exchange for using his budding political clout to get thirty thousand of China's one-child-policy boys into the States, ostensibly to find wives. Jim didn't believe that for a second. But if he accomplished his mission, which he needed the boy to do, then China's true intention wouldn't matter.

It had been worth the risk.

And now Jim was sure that risk was going to pay off.

The boy hurried to the fallen pile and separated the fabric from the plastic mailer bag. He shook out the fabric, letting the bigger uniform fall to the floor. He threw the top of the smaller uniform on over his white shirt, then, still dressed in his own pants, shoved his feet into the uniform's flowy pantlegs, dressing in a flash.

He snatched the Russian's uniform off the floor—the plastic mailing packaging, too—and hurried to her side. He clung to her leg again, like he was five years old instead of ten, and looked up at her. With pleading eyes, he held up her uniform.

The Russian glanced at Jim, glaring daggers that could only be Russian Kizlyar Supremes, tempered with resignation. Then she smiled wanly down at the boy. She patted his head, ruffling his black bowl cut.

She took the uniform.

Jim's phone buzzed, but he only smiled. He didn't need to look at the message to know what it said. The moment he'd been waiting for had finally arrived. And with perfect synchronicity. A good sign.

The Russian would wear his insignia.

And Anja Copenhagen would soon be in California.

CHAPTER 5

It was getting dark out. Danny had the headlights on, but Anja could still barely make out the road they were following.

They had left the world of smooth pavement and were now driving uphill, on a heavily rutted and potholed street with no name and no painted line down the center separating the two lanes.

And yet Danny seemed to be driving faster. He had said he wanted to get them to wherever they were going by sunset. Anja figured they'd make it.

Outside her front passenger-side window, the bumpy road wound through a dense forest. She spotted a few Douglas firs and cedar trees—trees she was used to seeing in the Pacific Northwest. But the early darkness was thanks to the dense canopy of another species. The trees towered over them, on either side of the Explorer. They had spindly lower limbs and reddish-barked trunks, some of which stretched more than ten feet in diameter. Massive.

"These are redwoods," Anja said.

"This particular grove is about twenty-five acres," Danny said. "And there are more groves besides. We can't have you knowing which one you're in, though. It's for everyone's protection."

Anja stared at him. That was a surprising amount of information freely given.

But it fit with her assessment of Danny. He was telling them as much as he possibly could, which wasn't much, because he didn't know much himself.

"There's no bioluminescent phenomena in the redwoods," she said. "Unless . . . Did you discover something?"

She tempered her hope, but the thought was exciting. Most bioluminescent organisms lived in the ocean or, on this continent, east of the Mississippi. Finding bioluminescence in California at this late stage of civilization would be . . . well, it seemed impossible. "Did you?"

As he drove, Danny glanced at Anja. His expression said she wasn't wrong.

"You did."

But the worry in his eyes said it wasn't anything like she was thinking it would be.

"What did you find?"

Danny pulled off to the left side of the road. He put the SUV in park and got out of the car, leaving the engine running.

Up ahead, the road looked to be blocked by brush.

Ming leaned forward between the seats. "Do you think they really found something?"

"I don't know. But I don't know why else we'd be out here."

In the beam of the right headlight, Danny leaned against the brush and it swung forward, out of the way.

A camouflaged gate.

"Whatever it is," Ming said, "they don't want anyone else to know."

Danny hopped back into the SUV, put it in drive, and rolled forward, just enough to clear the gate, then hopped out and shut it.

Back in the car, he rolled forward again.

"So is there?" Anja asked. "Is there bioluminescence here? What did you find?"

Danny pulled the SUV up to a log building with a sharply pitched roof.

"I'm just the brawn, ma'am," Danny said, turning off the engine. "Let me take you to the brains."

Anja looked out her window. The log-style building was old and maybe forty feet wide, with windows on either side of a centered door, and a portico roof. It reminded Anja of the place she'd stayed in the last time she'd gone into the field. It had been a school trip to study the southern lights, led by her mentor, Jim Lugner. It had been fun. A hopscotch trip down through South America.

But not fun enough to ever do it again. Anja was a lab rat. She liked the clean, sterile, buzzing comfort of the lab.

And yet she'd been summoned to study something not just in the field, but in the redwoods. The coasts of southern Oregon and northern California were the only place on earth where these trees existed. They were wondrous in their own right. So it was too cool to think that she might discover something new here. But these trees were also a tourist attraction. She couldn't imagine anything relevant to her field of expertise going on in these woods, left undiscovered until now.

Danny and Ming both opened their doors to get out, and a smell wafted into the Explorer.

Anja covered her nose. "Is that skunk?"

"Sorry about that," Danny said. "We use skunk bombs to keep people away from the area. You get used to it."

Anja got out and met Ming in front of the SUV, and they shared a look of disgust. Anja felt better having Ming with her. With Ming around, she was not alone. And Ming was feisty. Even as she grabbed Anja's hand and squeezed.

Danny had already started toward the log building. He turned back to them, motioning with bare, empty hands for them to follow him faster.

Ming looked at Anja, unsure. But Anja was not afraid of Danny. He was a strange man in a very dirty set of camos who had more or less abducted them and taken them into the redwoods, but Anja was not afraid.

At least not of him.

The woods were another matter. They gave her a strange feeling, like a buzzing sensation. She'd felt something like it before, felt it many times in fact. Different, definitely different, but similar. Every time she witnessed bioluminescence, she felt this warm sense of wonder fluttering in her stomach, her heart, stretching out through her limbs. She felt that feeling now, except it wasn't generating from inside her. It was in the air.

"I've never been to the redwoods before," Anja said. "Does it always feel like this?"

"I've never been here before this mission either," Danny said. "But no, it doesn't always feel like this. Sometimes it feels even greater than this."

"What is it?" Anja asked. "Some nuclear reactor? Some radiation signal?"

It wasn't lost on her that she'd only named negative things that might make the air feel this way and give her this tingling feeling. She expected Danny to grin and shake his head, no, of course it wasn't something so bad. But he gave her a look that said he wished he could tell her no and put her mind at ease, say everything was all right, but it wasn't. It probably wasn't some nuclear reactor or radiation signal. But it probably wasn't something benign either. His eyes said he thought it was something even worse.

Anja followed him to the log building, pulling Ming along with her. He wasn't going to hurt them. Far from it, in fact. He seemed reluctant to have brought them here. He didn't want them anywhere near whatever was causing this feeling. He didn't want to put them at risk. No, indeed, he was the protective type. He would protect them if he had to.

Danny used a set of keys to unlock the door beneath the log building's portico roof.

"Welcome to base," he said, opening the door.

The interior was a twenty-by-forty-foot room, toasty warm, and smelled like infrequent showers, day-old spaghetti, fried eggs—although it was a definite improvement over the skunk.

A rectangular, laminate conference table with ten metal folding chairs placed around it took up most of the space.

To the left of the door was a bar-style desk and a wall of monitors.

To the right was a kitchenette, with a small half-bath in the back right corner.

Dishes in the sink, sweatshirts on the backs of chairs. People had definitely been stationed here for a while. Weeks at least, if not months.

But the building was silent and empty. Not one of those people were here.

"Where is everyone?" Anja asked.

Danny looked down, like he didn't want to talk about it. "Be here in a minute," he said.

Anja looked around the room, but there wasn't much else to see. She walked the room's perimeter and looked at all the monitors, but they just made her eyes glaze over.

Danny told her and Ming to have a seat at the table and offered to get them sodas from the fridge.

Ming asked to use the loo, and he pointed to the door in the back right corner.

"So," Anja said, taking a seat. "Everyone else, are they driving in like we did, or—?"

At that minute, Anja heard a crunching noise outside. Danny's head jerked toward the front of the building, like he'd heard it too. And a moment later the doorknob turned.

CHAPTER 6

The door opened and a man entered. He was average height and in his fifties, wearing a black T-shirt and camo pants, like Danny's, only clean. And Anja recognized him immediately.

"Darius?"

"Hey, kid."

Anja ran around the end of the table and Darius opened his arms wide for a hug. She laughed and returned the embrace, wrapping her arms around his middle and pressing her temple to his chest. He squeezed her back like he was more than just saying *hi*, like he'd needed a hug, and he let out a big sigh that, if she wasn't mistaken, hitched just this side of tears.

She pulled away to take a better look at his face, at his coal-black eyes, to gauge how he was doing.

Darius Jackson. She hadn't seen him since her brother's funeral. He'd been single then, and he'd sat by Anja's parents in the row reserved for family, even though he was just her dad's friend from college. He'd gotten grayer since that day. Anja had heard he'd gotten married, too.

He smiled down at her with sad, darkened eyes—but they held a story for another time. Darius Jackson was sticking to business. "Have a seat."

Jackson gestured for Anja to take the metal folding chair at the head of the table, the end closest to the monitors.

Danny remained standing, leaning against the wall opposite the door with his arms crossed, facing the two of them but mostly watching the monitors.

"How you doing, Danny?" Jackson asked him.

Danny nodded, his face more stoic than it had been on the drive down. "You?"

"I got the new guys settled in at the lodge in town. Half of them are on duty now."

"Okay," Danny said.

Jackson squeezed Danny's shoulder, and Danny gave Jackson a frowning smile, adding another chapter to the story for another time.

Then Jackson took the chair to Anja's right, tipping it on the corner so that his back wasn't totally facing the door, and Danny returned his attention to the monitors.

"I heard you got married," Anja said. It was probably the least important of her many questions, but she was nervous. "Did you?"

Jackson nodded, looking more sad than happy about the whole affair. Anja felt too young and childlike to press him on the issue.

"How's Mom?" she asked.

"She's good," Jackson said, perking up. "Haven't seen her since I've been stationed here, about a year now, but last I saw her she was good."

He glanced at Danny and the monitors. One of the monitors seemed to have some static, some feedback racing across the screen. Jackson closed his eyes and sighed. He looked tired.

"Why am I here?" Anja asked.

"Danny, have you got the file?"

Danny stepped forward and held out the inch-thick, tri-tab manila folder.

In the back corner of the room, next to the kitchenette that lined the wall opposite the monitors, the toilet in the tiny half-bath flushed.

Jackson put his hands on the table and rose halfway out of his seat, suddenly alert. "Who's that?"

"Ming Lee, sir," said Danny. "She was in the file."

The bathroom sink turned on and water flowed.

"Ming Lee?" Jackson said.

"She's my lab assistant?" Anja said.

Jackson reached for the file and opened it up on the table.

Anja's face, laser-printed in black and white, lay on top. Jackson flipped the pages, revealing a thick dossier.

"What is all that?" Anja asked.

Jackson kept flipping until he found another printout of Ming's face.

The bathroom door slid open and Ming stepped out, rubbing her hands on her pants and leaving wet marks.

"What?" she asked. "Why are you all looking at me like that?"

Anja didn't know. She glanced at Danny who seemed just as puzzled as she was about Jackson's reaction.

But upon seeing her in person, Jackson seemed to remember: "Oh, yes. Ming Lee. Yes. I put this file together back when Marisol first . . ." He waved away the rest of the thought.

"Marisol," Anja said. "That's your wife, isn't it? Is she okay?"

"She fine. She's . . . under the weather."

"Oh," Anja said, unsure what else to say. She glanced at Danny for a clue. He met her gaze, but if he knew anything, and Anja was pretty sure he did, he wasn't letting on. "I hope she feels better." She grabbed Jackson's hand and squeezed.

He squeezed back, tighter than she would have expected if Marisol had just had the flu.

"Let's just stick to task," Jackson said. "Thank you for coming, Ming."

"No problem." Ming walked down the length of the table and sat next to Anja. Anja almost thought she might put her orange Converse up on the table, but she didn't. Just leaned back in her chair and interlaced her hands behind her head. "Not like Commando, here, gave us much choice."

"Thanks, Danny," Jackson said.

"Sir," Danny said, and he resumed his position against the wall, where he could both join the conversation and watch the beeping, flashing monitors and, judging from his stance, react quicker than the rest of them should the need arise.

"So?" Anja said. "Why are we here? I asked Danny if we should bring some equipment, a microscope, things like that, and he said no. He said those weren't his orders."

"His orders were to bring you." He glanced at Ming. "But I don't think microscopes will be necessary. You're at Stumptown University now, aren't you?"

"Offsite, but yeah. I share a lab. I'm working with bioluminescence."

"You're working on emission versus absorption, right? And how it relates to the electromagnetic field?"

Anja narrowed her eyes at him. She'd completed her study and had written an article on her findings. It was a paper and accomplishment she was quite proud of. But no one had accepted it for publication yet. No publication had even asked her any follow-up questions. "How do you know that?"

"Have you identified the substance that causes emission?"

Anja licked her lips and ultimately nodded.

"It's not what everyone thought, is it?"

Anja chewed the corner of her mouth and ultimately shook her head.

Jackson nodded. "There's something we need you to look at."

"In the redwoods? Have you found a new bioluminescent species? Is it a mushroom?"

"It is in the redwoods," Jackson said. "It's not a mushroom."

"Animal?" Tingles ran over Anja's arms. A new discovery could jumpstart her career. Most bioluminescent species were sea animals or mushrooms or sometimes bugs. Bugs or mushrooms would be most likely, here in a forest. But Anja could tell from Jackson's hesitancy that what he'd found was bigger than that. More important.

She was suddenly thrilled to be here.

"Where is it? Can I see it?" She twisted in her chair and looked around the room for a cage or a jar. "Do you have a sample here?"

Still looking at the monitors, Danny scoffed and shook his head. Anja looked at Jackson, who looked perplexed.

"I need you to resolve an anomaly," Jackson said.

"Resolve an anomaly? I don't know what that means."

"Ideally, it means it's gone, undone, whatever you have to do to make it go away. But I don't know what that is. It attacked my team. I need you to figure out what it is, how it attacks, and keep it from doing so again."

"Your team?" Anja said. But then she looked around the room. She considered the many empty chairs and the smell of many foods and many bodies. Definitely more than just the two men who stood before her now. "Where's the rest of your team?"

Jackson looked down at his file. Danny hung his head lower.

Jackson sighed and said, "Before we can get into any specifics, I need to secure your cooperation and your confidentiality."

He pulled a document from the manila folder and slid it over to her. Danny plucked a wayward pen from the nearby desk and handed it to her.

"It's a standard NDA," Jackson said. "You can't tell anyone about anything you see or hear while you're with us."

"So you're telling a scientist that if she sees something phenomenal, she's not allowed to study it and report what she finds?"

"Not in any way that can lead anyone back to the here and now."

"What about funding?" Anja said. Any chance to raise money that didn't require her to schmooze was a chance worth taking. She gestured toward Danny. "He made it sound like if I came I'd get more funding."

Jackson smiled. "I'm pretty sure what he did was imply that if you didn't come, you wouldn't get any more funding."

"And now you're saying that if I don't stay . . ."

"If you don't help us fix this, there won't be any funding left to give you. There might not be anyone left to give you anything. There might not be anyone left, period."

"Wait, what?" Anja shook her head. "Bioluminescence hasn't been known to hurt humans. Are you sure it's me you need here? How dangerous is this thing?"

Jackson glanced at Danny, then back at Anja. "We think it's an electromagnetic anomaly," he said.

"I don't do electromagnetism," Anja said. "I mean, I understand it some, from school, and it's tangentially related to my research, but it's not my area of expertise."

It had been her mentor's area of expertise.

"Well, this thing we're dealing with is probably no one's area of expertise," Jackson said. "We've just been assuming it's an electromagnetic anomaly, because that's what people assume weird things are."

"Okay," Anja said. She was suddenly getting the whiff of a distasteful subject. But she held her tongue for now.

"Sign the NDA and I'll explain," Jackson said.

Anja felt put on the spot, but she trusted Jackson. He wouldn't do that to her if it wasn't necessary. She started to sign, then looked at Ming.

"Do you have another form?" she asked Jackson.

"You can both sign that one."

"But it's only got my name on it."

"It's fine."

"Okay." Anja scribbled her signature on the document and then handed the pen to Ming, who did the same.

Jackson slotted it into the folder.

"About a year ago my team was hired to guard something in the redwoods. A piece of land," he said. "There were concerns about vandalism, or so we were told. We don't usually defend things. We usually do more active missions, offense, but the requester—who so far remains anonymous, despite my efforts to uncover their identity—they specifically asked for us."

"Your team?" Anja asked.

"Yes."

"Why?"

"That's a good question. A few weeks after we got here, some tourists came out here looking for ghost redwoods or Big Beauty or solitude, who knows. This campground and the surrounding trails and sites have been decommissioned and quietly removed from local maps, but people still show up. These two tourists had their dog with them. They said they saw light in the woods, like the aurora borealis or alien spaceships. I don't know. Anyway, the dog gave chase. Apparently their instincts told them not to follow, and they were wise to listen. They left and went to the ranger station, who later questioned us. We said we'd keep a lookout, but by then we'd already found the dog."

"What happened to it?"

Jackson shook his head. Danny was staring at the floor.

"Another good question," Jackson said. "I don't know. But whatever we're guarding, whatever attacked that dog, last night it attacked my team."

"Attacked," Anja said, still feeling way outside her wheelhouse. "What do you mean 'attacked'?"

Jackson shrugged. "Just as I said. Last night, the site we're supposed to be guarding took out my entire team, save Danny, here, and—"

"What?" Anja said, flinching. "Are they okay?"

Jackson didn't answer. Anja looked over her shoulder at Danny.

Danny shook his head.

"I'm asking you to help me," Jackson said. "Help me figure out what the hell is going on so we can neutralize this thing."

"Wait—neutralize? I'm doing my best to listen for how Ming and I fit in here, but I work with glowing worms in a lab. If you've found some bioluminescent bugs deep in the redwoods, I'm your girl, but if not, then I have no idea what I'm doing here. I wouldn't know the first thing about solving a set of mysterious deaths."

Jackson nodded. "I understand. But unfortunately, spot-on qualifications weren't as important to me as picking someone I can trust. I have been on many missions. But this is the first time we've been asked to guard something from people when really it's people—*my* people—who are threatened by the thing we're guarding. By the time we get involved, intelligence is vetted, accurate. I'm usually given reliable information. I feel like I was lied to this time around. It could be an accident, but it's all so strange I just don't think so."

Anja frowned and looked at Danny, who looked like he was hearing all this information for the first time, too.

"Didn't you say the people funding my research are funding your operation?" she asked him.

"Don't blame Danny," Jackson said. "I needed you here. I gave him some talking points."

A quick frown flashed across Danny's face, for which Anja gave him credit. She turned her glare on Jackson. He rubbed his face with both hands, massaging his brow and his eye sockets. Anja found herself doing the same, rubbing her mouth with one hand. She wasn't the right person for this. Jackson had to see that.

In the silence, a noise came from behind her, from the other side of the long wall opposite the door. Anja turned her ear toward the noise.

But Danny shifted as if to distract her.

"It's six o'clock," he said. "Sun sets in ten minutes."

Jackson nodded. He pushed back in his chair and stood. "I think it would be best to just show you."

Anja stared at him, mouth agape. "I'm sorry about your team, Darius, I really am. But I can't change the past and I don't know how to help you go forward. And if you were lying about this being the path to funding, then I need to get back to my lab, or else I'm going to be out of a job." She looked at Ming. "We're both going to be out of a job. I have to finish my proposal."

Anja pushed away from the table, Ming following suit, but Jackson grabbed Anja's hand.

"I have broken protocol by inviting you here."

Jackson's voice was laced with fear, but Anja could tell it wasn't his own violations that had him scared. And that scared her.

"And if the government hired us, I'm also breaking the law," he continued. "I don't care. I'm not turning this investigation over to the client, not when they're the reason we weren't better prepared. You're the only person I trust who's also any kind of scientist. I'm sorry, Anja, but I can't let you leave. Through is your only way out."

CHAPTER 7

They climbed into Danny's Explorer—Jackson in the front seat, Ming and Anja in the back—and Danny took them back out past the camouflaged gate, to the no-name road, and back down the hill to town. The woods were dark now. No more sun filtered through the canopy, nor did any light from the night sky.

Almost immediately, Danny took another right down another dirt road.

If you could call it a road.

In the headlights, Anja could see big gouges in the grading, some at least a foot deep, the removed clumps left where they'd fallen. Danny said the road had been purposefully chopped up after being decommissioned decades ago. He turned the wheel this way and that, maneuvering around the bigger obstacles. The Explorer thumped and knocked and complained the whole way. It was the bumpiest, jerkiest, and—although Danny insisted it was less than half a mile—the longest car ride Anja had ever had in her life. Her stomach churned.

But the car ride wasn't the reason why.

Nor was it the smell of skunk, even though the further they traveled down the decommissioned road, the worse the smell got.

No, her stomach was nervous because she had no idea what to expect. She didn't like the whiff of superstition she'd gotten from the conversation with Jackson back at base.

But of course she had no reason to worry. Wherever they were going, the place wasn't going to *do* anything out of the ordinary. That was just ridiculous.

And yet she was here. And Jackson and Danny had gone far, far out of their way to get her here.

But that wasn't everything. There was also the upside. Even though it was a one-in-a-million chance, how cool would it be if this adventure actually led to some new light discovery that she could not only study but introduce to the world. She could make a name for herself. Could bring her area of science forward, into the mainstream.

But chances were more likely that whatever all this hubbub was about, the thing in question likely had a rational, easily understood, and already discovered explanation. Chances were it was something some other physical scientist was better equipped to deal with. And chances were she was wasting her time.

And yet a part of her couldn't help both wondering and worrying that it might be something unfathomable.

The road dead-ended at a rustic, waist-high split-rail fence that stood in front of a giant redwood tree. Its red bark trunk stretched twenty feet, at least, in diameter, dwarfing the width of the SUV.

Danny put the Explorer in park, and Ming was the first to open her door.

"Wow," she said as she hopped out. "Look at this tree."

Danny got out and went around back, popping open the SUV's back hatch.

Anja joined Jackson and Ming in front of the Explorer. Its headlights were still on, and the circumference of the massive trunk in front of them stretched beyond the width of both beams.

"This is Big Beauty," Jackson said. "She would be on the tourist map of trees to visit, but she's near a spot of white ghost trees and the road's getting bad and there isn't money to keep everything safe or in good repair, so the park rangers have just let her slip quietly off the map. People still know she's here, of course, but not many. Fewer and fewer every year."

Big Beauty was just that. She was huge and she was spectacular. Her trunk was wide enough to drive a full-size truck through, maybe even a semi, but no one had disparaged her like that yet.

It was too dark to see all the way up to her top, but Anja imagined she rose high and straight into the sky and was crowned with a symmetrical spread of needles. Standing before her, Anja couldn't help but feel a sense of wonder at all that the world offered, and all that it still held secret but would share willingly if we would only appreciate what was and listen quietly.

The Explorer's hatch clunked closed.

Danny came around front and handed out flashlights.

"Here, clip these on," he said to Anja and Ming, and he handed each of them something that looked like an old-school pager from the '90s.

Except this one you didn't want to hear beeping.

"What is it?" Ming asked.

"A dosimeter," Anja said, hefting it in her hand and resigning herself to the idea of having to wear one. If it beeped, it would mean that her surroundings held unsafe levels of radiation. It probably wasn't a problem though or they would all be wearing protective suits.

Still.

She clipped the dosimeter to the collar of her coat, not at all loving the fact that she'd been conned into working on a project that required her to carry one.

"This way," Jackson said. He and Danny quickly hurdled the fence. Anja put her palms on the top slat and put a ballet flat on the bottom slat and hoisted herself over without snagging her slacks too much. Danny nodded, seemingly impressed with her agility, which pleased her. She didn't do so much CrossFit for nothing.

Ming looked longingly up at Big Beauty, then scrambled over the fence and followed after them.

The woods were eerily quiet. There were no birds chirping in the branches, no animals scurrying beneath the ferns that covered the forest floor. Not even insects buzzing or wind rustling through the trees. The only sounds were their footsteps and the distant roar of the Pacific Ocean.

Redwood fluff covered the narrow path, but the ground felt hard beneath Anja's feet. Very easy to walk on. Like it hadn't rained in a while, even though it was the first of November. There were roots and small shrubs growing here and there, but the canopy prevented anything too thick or too big from growing. Aside from a huge fallen tree they had to duck under, Anja was finding the grove easier to walk through than she'd anticipated.

Up ahead, Danny shined his flashlight onto the lower limbs of a small redwood tree. Its flat needles were white.

"Ghost tree," Jackson said. "Albino redwood. They lack chlorophyll, so they siphon nutrients off the root system of their neighbors. They're rare, and some people think they have mystical significance."

"This is starting to feel like the beginnings of a haunted experience," Anja said. "You remember I'm not interested in that, right?"

Jackson neither confirmed nor denied. But his tight-lipped, guilty expression said he did indeed remember.

He gestured for Danny to keep leading the way.

They were traveling in a line—Danny leading Anja, and then Ming, with Jackson bringing up the rear—walking among the giants in the dark, when Ming suddenly hurried to Anja's side.

"Do you feel weird?" Ming asked.

Sure she did. Anja felt weird being here at all. They'd been *summoned* (if she was feeling generous; *kidnapped*, if she was not) to work on a project that was sounding more and more outside her wheelhouse. And now she was traipsing through a redwood grove, in the dark, in her favorite ballet flats, which were holding their own for now, but were unlikely to survive the trip.

But Anja knew what Ming meant.

Ming wanted to know if this place, itself, was giving Anja a weird feeling.

As a scientist, Anja had to admit that she was feeling something.

But feelings in the body are just chemicals released in the brain, caused by sensory experience of things perceived.

In other words, she was cold and damp and struggling to see, let alone walk, the root-marbled path with her too-dim flashlight—and the skunk-laced woodsy smell in the air wasn't helping things. Of course her body was feeling like something was off.

In this case, the off feeling could just be her body responding to a low-pressure system in the atmosphere—rain was coming, maybe even a storm.

Or it could be an allergic reaction to the artificial smell of Danny's skunk bombs.

Or it could be based on nothing more than Jackson's superstitious suggestions triggering her overactive imagination. She usually put it to good scientific use, but everything has its flip side.

"No," she lied. "Why? Do you feel weird?"

Ming looked around, then over her shoulder. She shivered. Then shivered again. Then didn't stop shivering. She was trembling. "Nah," she said. "I'm good."

Anja put an arm around her friend and rubbed her arms, in case she was cold. In the Pacific Northwest, the first day of November can still be pretty warm. Rainy, maybe, but warm. And it seemed Northern California's weather was about the same. Now that the sun was gone, the temperature was dropping quickly, but for now it was still in the low fifties.

But as much as she wanted a chill in the air to be the cause of Ming's angst, Anja knew that wasn't the problem.

The problem was in this grove.

And when they reached their destination, Anja needed no one to tell her that they had arrived.

CHAPTER 8

The redwood grove opened onto a clearing about the size of half a football field. Maybe a little bigger. It was tough to see, what with the dark and all the fog. There wasn't a single tree in the clearing nor any grass really, just a few scattered rocks.

"Was there a fire here?" Anja asked. She'd seen similar clearings before, one in particular, when someone threw a cigarette out their car window and into the woods near her grandparents' house. For the next year, nothing grew there but weeds.

Although, now that she thought about it, there were no weeds in this clearing, either. There was nothing green at all. Not even pine needles or other shed foliage. The clearing was just dirt, as far as Anja could tell.

But that wasn't the strangest thing about it.

The clearing had a subtle glow. Not a spotlight glow, as if from a full moon breaking through the clouds. This was an inherent glow coming from the center of the clearing. The center-center. From within the fog, not on the ground. As if fireflies, emitting their light, were hovering stationary in the air.

Except the glow wasn't dots of light, either.

It was more diffused. Like the effervescent off-light that shines around the moon in a total eclipse of the sun. It took Anja's breath away. It was spectacular.

If this light was indeed bioluminescence, then it reminded her of the kind she might find in the deep, dark parts of the sea. Like the deep-sea shrimp, which spits a luminous substance that looks like glowing smoke once it's dispersed in the water.

Except nothing was spewing the smokey light in the clearing, at least nothing Anja could see or otherwise sense.

But there were ways to make invisible things visible. She'd likely get her chance to do so tomorrow.

Still, unexpected light wasn't the only issue with this clearing, with whatever was in this clearing.

Danny stopped about ten yards from the clearing and pulled out a walkie-talkie with a big red button on the side. Anja tried to walk past him, to get closer to the glow, but Danny grabbed her arm and pulled her back.

He pushed the walkie's red button. "Perimeter Two? Anything I should be concerned about? Over."

The walkie crackled, then came a voice. "Nothing that I've seen. Over."

"What about the fog? Over."

Silence.

Danny looked over Anja's and Ming's heads at Jackson. They exchanged raised eyebrows, and then Jackson looked down at Anja and said, "Maybe we should—"

"I don't see any fog. Over."

"*Move.*" Jackson grabbed Anja by the arm and yanked her back toward the Explorer. Danny did the same to Ming. "Let's get out of here. Go, go!"

Then, on the walkie. "Rover, this is Perimeter One. The fog came in from the south, south-west. I think it's just normal fog."

Danny released Ming and turned back to the clearing, narrowing his eyes as he studied the fog. Aside from the weird glow, which was fading even now, the fog looked normal enough to Anja.

Danny pushed the walkie's red button. "Copy that."

Jackson let Anja go.

"The dog?" Anja said, rubbing her arm. "Is this what hurt the dog? And . . . and your team?"

Jackson didn't answer, just looked to Danny.

Bioluminescence wasn't dangerous in itself, but it could signal that danger lurked along with it. Some dinoflagellate and firefly species produce toxins, and there are millipedes that glow with cyanide. In fact, the Motyxia millipedes were found in California, but they were in the Sierra Nevada Mountains, on the central eastern side of the state.

It was possible that this glowing mist in the clearing was indeed dangerous. But somehow Anja doubted it.

Then again, it was easy to doubt the danger of something so beautiful.

"Something here is lethal," Danny said. "And whatever it is, it strikes with little warning."

Anja shivered, then looked a question at Ming, who shrugged.

The four of them now stood at least twelve yards away from the clearing, and neither Danny nor Jackson seemed in any hurry to regain their ground. They were exchanging those raised eyebrows again. They were inching further away from the clearing, if anything.

Anja sighed. "Guys. It's what you kidnapped and brought us here for." She marched forward, taking the lead. "The sooner I take a look, the sooner I can tell you it's nothing, and the sooner Ming and I can get out of here. So let's go."

Danny ran ahead of her, reclaiming the lead. But he led them down the overgrown path toward the clearing for only a few more paces before they heard someone scream.

CHAPTER 9

The night fell silent again. No snapping branches, no wind rustling through the canopy. The scream had been short-lived, like someone surprised rather than terrified.

But Anja figured her own terror made up for it. The air smelled damp with a hint of spice and earthy undertones.

"What was that?" she asked, clinging to Ming, who clutched her back.

Even Jackson looked ruffled, steadying himself against the nearest tree trunk.

Danny put a finger to his lips and shook his head. He unhooked his walkie-talkie from his utility belt and clicked the big red button. "Anyone got a visual?"

Danny released the button, and they waited. Anja's heart pounded. Ming's fingers dug into her arm. Jackson looked around, head cocked, listening.

Anja had never heard such silence. The forest seemed absent of birds, bugs, even wind, despite whatever was slowly pushing the fog along.

No one answered the page.

"Shit," Danny said.

Just then, far in the woods, on the opposite side of the clearing, Anja heard a man yell, "Stop right there!"

It was followed by the pounding of footsteps and a thrashing of branches. Another scream. This one lower pitched. The scream of struggle, of someone being captured and contained.

"Let me go!" yelled a terrified voice, closer now. Still on the other side of the clearing, but nearer. "Who are you?! Where's Josh?! What did you do to him?! Let me go! Let! Me! Go!"

Then silence. Not even a whisper of wind through the towering trees. Anja stood stock still, not daring to move, wondering, not for the first time, what the hell she was doing here. This was not her element. No, not at all.

The walkie-talkie crackled to life.

"Rover?" said a tinny, electronified voice.

Pressing the red button, Danny said, "Go ahead."

"This is Perimeter One. We found a kid on the northeast corner of the site."

Danny listened with a frown growing on his face.

"A kid?" Jackson muttered. "Great. One more thing to deal with. Some teenager, out smoking pot or writing poetry. Well, I can tell the skunk bombs are fresh." He put the back of his hand to his nose. "Is the caterwaul deterrence not turned on?"

"The mountain lion sound?" Danny said. "It should be. I turned it off at base and just around here, so as not to scare them"—he nodded toward Anja and Ming—"but it should still be working further out. They're motion-activated though. I'll check them when we get back."

Jackson nodded and made a give-it-here gesture. Danny handed him the walkie.

Before Jackson could speak, the walkie crackled in his hand.

"He's got airline tickets," the tinny voice said. "Looks like he flew down from Seattle early this morning. Landed in Oakland, then up to Crescent City. Looks like he got in about, maybe five hours ago. He has a GPS app open on his phone. And he has the coordinates."

Danny and Jackson shared a look. Jackson brought the walkie up to his mouth and pushed the red button.

"Boss here. How far from the site?"

"I can't see it, so I'm guessing, but maybe seventy-five yards?" the tinny voice said. "But the kid says he can see it."

Jackson blew out a breath and frowned up at the sky visible above the clearing. Clouds covered the stars, and night was growing darker by the minute.

"The kid can *see* it?" Danny said. "I can barely see you, and I've got a flashlight. What do you want to do?"

"I want to talk to him."

"Want them to take him to base?" Danny said. "Probably shouldn't bring anyone new to the clearing."

"Kid's already seeing it apparently, and I'm not sure I want him knowing where base is," Jackson said. Then, as if to himself, "He says he can see the clearing now? How does he even know there's anything to see?"

Jackson clicked the walkie's button. "Can you bring him to the tree?"

Jackson released the button, and they waited for a response.

Danny slowly panned his flashlight back and forth, casting a beam of light into the fog in the clearing. Anja had no idea if it penetrated the fog enough to reach into the trees beyond.

The walkie crackled. "I can, but be advised, he wants to come."

Jackson shared another look with Danny, then clicked the red button.

"Understood."

CHAPTER 10

Anja climbed over the low, split-rail fence that separated Big Beauty from where Danny had parked the Explorer and joined Ming, Danny, and Jackson near the back bumper to await the arrival of their mystery guest.

It was full dark now, the waxing moon just high enough in the sky to shine through a sparse section of treetops. Anja heard footsteps coming toward her, and three men appeared in the beams of Danny's flashlight.

Two were average height, just under six foot, and dressed like Danny, in reddish-brown-and-green fatigues that matched the forest. But their outfits didn't fit them as well as Danny's. On one man, the jacket was too tight in the shoulders; on the other, too tight at the waist.

The man on Anja's left, with the wide shoulders, held something in his hand that Anja thought, at first, was a walkie-talkie. But as he came closer, she saw his walkie on his utility belt.

The second patrolman, with the paunch, held a blue backpack.

Between them, they held a young male by his biceps.

The kid stood taller than the two patrolmen, and he was gangly. Late teens, if that. He had mud on his blue jeans. His blue-and-purple tie-dyed sweatshirt was zipped up to his chin with the hood pulled over his head and cinched down tight. His face was scrunched into the shape of an almond. The pulled-tight hoodie strings hung loose down his scrawny chest, toward the hoodie's pockets, where he'd stuffed his hands.

"Guess I found the right spot," the kid said, his voice cracking. Anja wasn't sure if that was fear cutting through his bravado or hormones changing his vocal cords.

Danny shined his flashlight into the kid's eyes.

The kid squinted into the light and held up one hand to block the glare. The straps of a headlamp dangled from his wrist. He looked capable but harmless.

And Anja had a thought. If the kid could get in, then maybe he could help Anja and Ming get out.

But she'd have to get him alone in order to ask him, not to mention get started on the journey, and that didn't seem likely to happen anytime soon.

"What's with all the skunk?" the kid said, cupping his nose and mouth with his other hand. "It's been smelling like skunk for hours."

No one answered him.

Danny kept the glare from his flashlight locked firmly on the kid's eyes, keeping him blind and blinking. An intimidation tactic no doubt. But Anja wasn't sure it was working.

Shoulders said, "He tripped the monitors on the east side."

"The east?" Jackson said, as if the east side was the least likely direction to approach the clearing. And Anja supposed it was, since it appeared to be the opposite direction of the way they'd come in, the furthest from any roads.

Danny continued to not say anything, just kept staring at the kid and shining his flashlight into the kid's eyes.

Shoulders nodded. "And he didn't wander in here willy-nilly."

He held up a phone.

Anja peered closer. The phone's big screen was almost entirely green, a map of an area with dense vegetation—the forest they were standing in, presumably.

A red destination marker had been plotted in the center of all that green. But Anja wasn't seeing the typical blue dot that would indicate where on the map the phone was located, so she had no idea how near or far the phone was from the red marker's location.

Danny took the phone and peered at it, then held it closer to Jackson.

Jackson glanced at it but showed no reaction.

"Why these coordinates?" Danny asked the kid.

"I need to find Commander Darius Jackson," the kid said.

Anja frowned and looked at Jackson, but she noticed that the three men dressed in fatigues remained plain-faced and Jackson himself made no indication that he was the man the boy sought.

"So," said Shoulders, "what do you want us to do with him?"

Jackson made a give-it-here gesture.

Danny took the kid's backpack, and the two perimeter guards released the kid, who shrugged them off. The two patrolmen turned heel, in separate directions, and vanished into the forest, returning to their posts.

Danny and Jackson waited until they'd disappeared entirely into the fog before talking again.

"We can't let him go," Danny said.

"No," said Jackson. "We'll take him back with us."

Jackson dipped his head in attempt to look at the kid's face. "What are you doing out here?"

"I told you," said the kid. He was still squinting against Danny's flashlight beam and trying to block the glare with his forearm.

"Wait a minute," Danny said. "Put your arm down."

"Put the flashlight down," said the kid, still shielding his face.

Danny lowered the flashlight beam to the kid's chest, leaving some light illuminating his face but sparing his eyes.

The kid dropped his arm to his side. He could have stood taller than Jackson, but his posture slouched with defeat, robbing him of several inches. He stared at the ground and heaved a big sigh. The bravado was gone. Now he just looked lost.

Danny tugged on the top of the kid's hood, loosening the cinch.

The kid swatted at his hands, but Danny was still able to pull down the hood.

"Oh, shit," Danny said.

"What?" Jackson said, jumping a little, like he'd been startled.

"Well, look at him," Danny said.

The kid had shaggy dark hair and spectacular amber-brown eyes that right now had a worry line creasing between them. His nose was on the larger side, and he was biting his full bottom lip, which right now had a slight tremble.

Danny said, "It's Josh's little brother."

CHAPTER 11

"What's your name, kid?" Danny asked.

"Yuri. Yuri Palming," the kid said, standing a little taller. "Josh Palming is my brother."

Jackson narrowed his eyes and studied the kid. "How'd you get the coordinates?" he asked, sounding like he didn't really want to know, like he knew he wouldn't like the answer.

"Josh gave them to me," said the kid. He pulled a piece of paper from his pocket and held it out to Jackson.

Jackson took the paper. Anja peeked over his shoulder, Ming peeking over hers. It was a handwritten note that listed two decimal-pointed numbers—the coordinates, Anja presumed—and the name *Big Beauty*.

"That's the tree," she said.

"What tree?" the kid asked, and Jackson gave Anja a silencing look. "What tree?" the kid asked again.

Jackson held up the paper with the coordinates. "You say Josh gave you these?"

The kid nodded, but Anja noticed he was suddenly no longer willing to make eye contact.

Jackson shot Danny a look.

Danny shrugged. "I can check the call log, but he would've had to get to town to make a private call, and I can't remember the last time he went. That was Nick's gig."

The kid peered at Jackson.

Anja's flashlight dangled in her hand, by her side. She shifted it, angling it so that its beam offered a little more light to illuminate Jackson's face.

The kid's eyes widened, and he took one small step closer to Jackson.

"Are you Darius Jackson?" he said.

Jackson said nothing.

"Where's Josh?" the kid asked. "I . . . I know he's dead, but he's all the family I've got, and I want to take him home. He wants me to take him home."

Jackson massaged his brow with his fingertips, then rubbed his hand down the side of his face. He looked askance at Anja, seeming to wilt when they made eye contact. She frowned at him, not knowing what to make of that. Jackson sighed and said, "*When* did Josh give you these coordinates?"

The kid opened his mouth, but then he frowned and stepped back again, like he'd been about to say one thing but had reconsidered his response.

"You already know when he gave them to me," the kid said to Jackson, his tone accusing, angry. "And you"—the kid turned his attention toward Danny, and his voice broke—"you were there. What happened? What happened to Josh?"

The corner of Danny's mouth rose in a smile. Anja didn't know him all that well, but she thought it meant he was impressed.

But impressed or not, Danny didn't give the kid an answer.

Neither did Jackson.

"Let's get back to base," Jackson said. "You two okay if he sits in the middle?"

Anja looked at the kid, expecting him to make a face of anarchy, but he just stared back at her, his face and body slack with fatigue.

Still. "You checked him for weapons, right?" Anja asked.

The kid snorted, shaking his head and looking away, offended.

Danny said, "The guys would have, but I can check him now, if you want."

Anja looked at the kid—who definitely seemed more sad-angry than violent-angry—then conferred silently with Ming, who shrugged, opened the door to the rear passenger-side seat, and climbed in. Ming looked tired, too.

"We'll be fine," Anja said.

Danny opened the rear driver's side door for the kid, but as he climbed in, Danny said, "You're not gonna do anything stupid, are you?"

"You mean like kill my brother?" The kid slid across the bench seat into the middle and then searched around for his seatbelt. Poor guy's knees were kissing his chin. "No, I'm not the murderer. You guys are. Where's Josh?"

Anja climbed in after Yuri, shoulder to shoulder.

Danny shut the door behind her, then went around back to put the kid's phone and backpack into the back cargo compartment before climbing into the driver's seat, next to Jackson.

Danny waited a minute, then turned in his seat to look into the back.

"I'm Danny," he said to the kid.

Anja felt the muscles in the kid's shoulder, arm, and thigh relax.

"Diega?" the kid said.

"Yeah," Danny said.

"I've heard of you," said the kid. "From Josh. You're the funny one."

Funny? Anja pulled a face. She had yet to see or hear anything she would've described as *funny* coming from Danny. Then again, it sounded like the past twenty-four hours were providing a good reason for that.

"I'm Yuri," the kid continued.

"Yuri Palming, yeah. You look like him. Like Josh," Danny said. "Smaller, maybe. Josh is pretty massive. But you look like him."

"Look*ed*," said Yuri, emphasizing the past tense.

"Yeah," Danny said, his face falling. He mustered a small smile for the kid, then turned front again and started the engine.

CHAPTER 12

Anja figured on a quiet, if bumpy, ride back to base, followed by a night of questioning their unexpected guest. Standard procedure. No one likes to converse in the car. But Danny had barely put the Explorer into drive when Jackson pulled down his visor mirror and started in on the kid.

"How'd you get here?"

"Took the bus."

"Not to here," Jackson said.

The Explorer entered the choppy, decommissioned stretch of road. The kid braced himself against the back of Danny's seat. "Got as close as I could, then I hiked in."

Jackson and Danny shared a glance, like they were deciding whether that was plausible and whether it mattered either way.

Anja couldn't tell what they'd decided. The Explorer dipped into a rut, knocking her into the window, then knocking her into Yuri.

"Sorry," Danny said.

"So are you Darius Jackson, then?" Yuri asked. "I told you something was wrong. What happened to my brother?"

Jackson braced a hand on the dashboard and turned in his seat to face into the back. He peered at Yuri, his bottom lip quirking. Anja didn't know what conversation Yuri was talking about, but none of Jackson's fleeting expressions suggested that *he* didn't know what the kid was talking about.

The kid stared back unfazed, knees up to his chin, his long arms folded on top of them, waiting Jackson out.

Jackson's face eventually settled back into impassive interrogator mode.

"How'd you know to come *here*?" he asked.

"I told you," the kid said with a whine.

"Josh," Jackson said.

The kid sighed. "If you aren't going to believe me, then quit asking me questions."

In the rearview mirror, Anja saw Danny's eyes lift off the road and look back at the kid's reflection. The kid looked from Jackson to the rearview mirror, and Anja thought she knew why. In this scenario, Jackson was the bad cop. Danny was more on the kid's side. And Danny seemed to know, somehow, what the kid was thinking.

Jackson noticed their connection, too. He sighed and turned in his seat, facing front again. "Go ahead," he said.

Danny looked to Jackson, and Jackson nodded.

Permission.

"When did Josh give you the coordinates?" Danny asked.

"Last night."

"Impossible," Jackson said.

Danny took his right hand off the steering wheel and gestured to the kid sitting in the back seat. *And yet . . .*

Anja could attest that he was definitely wedged between her and Ming.

Jackson covered his mouth with one hand and rubbed his jawline with his middle finger. He had stubble, and the gesture made a scratching sound.

"Why's that impossible?" Anja asked.

But she didn't get an answer. Jackson looked out his side window, and Danny kept quiet. It started to rain. Light droplets tapped against the roof.

Anja nudged the kid with her elbow and whispered, "What's impossible?"

"My brother gave me the coordinates."

"Yeah, why's that impossible?"

The kid gave her a look and a small shrug, as if to say it wasn't. It wasn't impossible.

But up front, Danny said, "Because he died last night."

Anja flinched as if Danny's words had been flung in her face.

Because that *was* impossible.

There was no way this kid could know what he knew in the way he was claiming. He couldn't have gotten information from a dead brother. He must have gotten it some other way.

"Are you a hacker?" Anja asked. "Did you hack the computer system? Steal a logbook? Is there some other way he could have gotten the coordinates?" Anja asked the men up front.

Jackson nodded, though Anja wasn't sure it was in agreement. And she noticed that Danny wasn't making any agreement motions at all.

"Where is he? Is he here?" the kid said. "I want to see him. He wants me to take him home."

Danny looked at Jackson, who looked back at Danny. They seemed to have a silent conversation deciding whether or not to speak aloud.

Danny said, "I left them with Doc—"

"Who's Doc?" asked the kid.

"She said you wanted me to go north," Danny said, ignoring Yuri. "As soon as I got Tyrese—he was the last one—I left."

Jackson nodded but didn't say anything.

Danny hedged. "Did you . . ."

Jackson shook his head.

The kid's eyes shifted right and left, watching each man. "Does that mean he's still here, or not?" he asked.

Anja wondered the same thing. All she knew was that Josh and the rest of the team shouldn't be here. Not under normal circumstances. There'd been plenty of time between last night and now for someone to get them to the hospital or the morgue.

She looked around Yuri, to Ming. Ming looked to be following the conversation as well. She looked back at Anja and shrugged.

But the kid's question as to whether Josh was here or not got no reply.

They rode the rest of the way back to the log building in silence, but Anja kept an eye on the kid through the reflection in the darkened window.

He mostly faced front, leaning forward over his knees, looking out the front window. But when Danny got out to open the camouflaged gate, Anja felt Yuri stiffen. He looked side to side, back and forth, out Ming's and Anja's windows. He started scooting around in his seat, like this trip couldn't end fast enough.

"What?" Ming said.

The kid shook his head. "Nothing."

He leaned back in his seat and closed his eyes. But he tilted his head at an odd angle, and then another, like a dog hearing and honing in on a distant sound.

Danny finished closing the gate and continued down the driveway.

The kid's eyes flashed open. He leaned across Anja's lap, looking out the window with more purpose, shifting in his seat and ducking his head to get a better look into the dark woods, as if something ought to be out there.

"What are you looking for?" Anja asked.

Yuri met her eyes, studied her face, like he was gauging whether or not he could tell her the truth.

Jackson grunted. "What aren't you saying, Yuri?"

"What aren't *you* saying?" Yuri said.

Danny's gaze darted from the road to the rearview mirror, and his eyes narrowed. Not in anger, Anja noted. In sympathy. In curiosity.

"Can we roll down the windows?" Yuri asked.

"No," Anja said. The rain was picking up, the taps becoming a steady drum.

Yuri leaned across Ming and reached for the window knob, but Ming elbowed him back into his center seat.

Through the gap between Danny's seatback and the door, Anja saw Danny move his left hand off the steering wheel and onto the door panel. The windows' master control.

But Jackson said, "We're almost there," and Danny put his hand back on the steering wheel.

Next to her, the kid heaved himself back against the seat with a huff and closed his eyes, like he was turning off his vision to heighten his other senses.

Anja closed her eyes, too. She listened for things. Inhaled deeply to see if she could pick up some strange scent.

She didn't hear or smell anything, other than rain and skunk.

For a second, the thought flashed in her mind that Yuri was closing his eyes to heighten what some call the sixth sense. Intuition was the softest name for it, but Anja always rolled her eyes whenever she heard anyone referring to their intuition as their source for any kind of knowledge or information.

Instinct sat better. Instinct was all gut and immediate action, no time for thought.

But intuition? That was slower. More deliberate. More knowing you're acting on nothing concrete. Some called it faith.

She called it foolish.

CHAPTER 13

The log building with its centered door and portico roof came into view, and Danny parked the SUV about thirty-five yards from the building, about the same spot he'd parked in when they'd first arrived earlier that night. Anja couldn't believe that was only a couple hours ago.

She unbuckled her seatbelt and opened her door—and heard Yuri suck in a breath.

She felt him behind her, subtly pushing her to exit the car faster.

Never liking to be hurried, she slowed her movements, taking even more time to slide off the back seat. And Yuri's pushing suddenly stopped.

Anja looked over her shoulder and saw him climbing out after Ming. He pushed past her and started running.

"Wait, where are you . . ." Danny started to say, but then he gave up the words and just chased after him.

Danny was at least fifteen years older, and the kid was fast. But he wasn't running away. He was running like he was on a mission.

And like he knew exactly where to go.

"Where's he headed?" Jackson said, lumbering to keep up but falling behind. Anja and Ming jogged along with him.

Yuri started yelling.

"Josh! Josh!"

He ran to the log building's front door and turned the knob, but the door wouldn't open. He pounded on it, saying, "He's not dead! He's not dead."

Danny caught up to him quickly, but he didn't grab the kid or try to restrain him. He put a hand on his back and looked him in the eye.

"Josh is dead," Danny said kindly. "I pulled his body out of the circle myself."

"He's not dead. Open the door! He's not dead. He's not dead!"

Danny stepped back and let the kid pound away at the door, without interfering.

Anja stopped a few feet away, not knowing what to do, what to think.

Jackson used his keys to unlock the door, and the kid pushed inside. Jackson went next, followed by Danny. Ming shrugged at Anja, and they followed inside, too.

Anja had a sinking suspicion about what was going on, what *kind* of thing at any rate. She didn't want the next few moments to validate her concerns, but she didn't want to miss out on anything either.

Yuri ran around the table, to the wall opposite the door. He placed his hands on the wall, a few feet left of center.

"He's here," Yuri said. He looked back at everybody and then looked around the room. Anja looked around, too. There weren't any other doors besides the one they'd entered and the one standing open to the half bath.

"Where is he?" Yuri said, and he pounded the wall. "He's here. He's . . . He's right here."

Anja watched the reactions of the other two men. Jackson looked dumbstruck, his mouth slack, his arms hanging at his sides. But Danny had that look again, that knowing, impressed, believing half-smile.

Danny looked to Jackson as if for instructions—or permission.

And Jackson gave it.

"Take him."

Yuri whipped around to face them, his face alight with hope. “He’s here?”

Danny stepped outside, and the kid raced around the table after him. Anja glanced at Jackson, who gestured toward the exit. *After you*. Anja grabbed Ming by the arm and they hurried out the door.

Danny led the kid, and the rest of them, around the left side of the log building.

What Anja had thought was open ground around the building was actually a wide dirt path or maybe even a road. Maybe two cars wide.

On the side of the road opposite the log building, trees and thick brush separated small lots that were covered in low-growing plants. Like an old, out-of-use campground. The kind her dad used to take her and her brother to when her mom came along, with a welcoming center and running water and other amenities her mom claimed she needed. Anja had to admit camping had always been more comfortable when her mom came along.

Ten or twelve such campsites formed a half circle around the back side of this campground’s log-style welcoming center. And most of the campsites, eight or nine or so, starting on the right side of the half circle, had twenty-foot shipping containers parked on the grass.

But that wasn’t the weirdest thing.

The weirdest thing was that the back side of the log building had its own door.

A light shining above it illuminated not only Yuri—who’d reached the door first and was standing under the light, bouncing on his toes, eager to get inside—but also the front end of a black, late-model Honda Accord.

Maybe the Honda was Jackson’s?

Anja didn’t know. But neither Jackson nor Danny seemed surprised to see it parked beneath the light.

Anja thought they’d wait for Jackson to use his keys to open the door, but they didn’t.

Danny knocked.

CHAPTER 14

The door opened, and on the other side was a woman in her sixties with a long, gray-streaked braid, and a baby strapped to her chest. The baby was held in place by a big, colorful swath of fabric, wrapped in some complicated fashion around the woman's back and over her shoulders. The baby was sleeping. Seemed it had either slept through Yuri's pounding or the log building had some serious kind of soundproofing. Anja figured the woman was the infant's grandmother.

"You're a doctor," Yuri said, posturing like he would have pushed past her to get inside, but for the baby. "My brother . . . ?"

The woman looked at Danny, who shrugged. The women then swept curious but not surprised eyes over Anja, which turned to questions as her gaze swept over Ming on its way to Jackson. Anja looked too slowly at Jackson to see his reaction. But it must have been acquiescence, because the woman stepped aside and gestured for them all to come in.

Yuri entered first, but barely. Danny went in next, almost just as eager. Anja was going to let Jackson go next—it was his team after all—but he gestured for her and Ming to go before him.

Like everything else Anja had seen so far, this side of the log building smelled like skunk. But it also smelled of disinfectant and natural, herbal remedies.

The room was about twenty feet by forty feet, the same size as the monitoring room next door, with the same half-bath and kitchenette. Except in this room, the bathroom and kitchenette were on the left-hand side. And the kitchenette was stocked with medical supplies.

Seven men, wearing reddish-brown-and-green fatigues like Danny's, and just as dirty, lay on cots set up against the walls or on dark wool blankets spread out on the wood floor.

None of the men moved. None of them made a sound.

Yuri tiptoed between two men lying on the floor and fell to his knees beside one of the men lying on the cots.

"Is that Josh?" Anja whispered.

"Yeah," Jackson said softly.

Josh's cot stood a few feet to the right of the wall's center, Anja noted, exactly opposite the part of the wall Yuri had been pounding on in the other room.

But that had to be a coincidence. Yuri must have received a map of the place in addition to the coordinates, because he'd seemed to know exactly where to go.

Except he apparently hadn't known about this side of the log building. Somehow Yuri had gone straight through the welcoming center's front entrance to where Josh was, to as close as Yuri could get to him anyway, without knowing the layout of the building.

Jackson introduced Anja and Ming to the doctor, whose name was Gabriela Ceja.

"Do we know yet what happened to them?" Jackson asked her.

Ming grabbed Anja's hand. Ming looked pale and sad, and no wonder. The man nearest them looked so still, so vacant. He and some of the others had low-grade burns and abrasions. Anja wondered why he and the others hadn't been covered yet, from head to toe, with a finalizing white sheet. But maybe Doc didn't have any. She didn't seem to have much by way of supplies.

"Not yet," Doc said.

Across the room, Yuri looked up from his brother. "He's not dead."

"No," said Doc.

"What? I checked them. They weren't breathing." Danny knelt beside the man on the floor nearest him and put a hand a few inches above his mouth, then placed his ear against the man's chest. He grabbed the man's wrist and started shaking his head. "No pulse, no breathing."

"They're breathing," Doc said, "but just barely. They seem to be in a coma, all of them. But it's not like any coma I've ever seen before."

"Like those trained monks," Ming said, and Anja jolted, startled, and stared at her. Ming hadn't said much of anything since they'd arrived, and Anja hadn't been expecting her to say anything now. "Where they slow down their body functions so much—heart rate, breathing, metabolism—that they appear to not be doing any of those things. But they are."

"Is that it?" Jackson asked Doc.

Doc shrugged. "It's not unlike that, I guess, but while your men are highly trained"—she smiled softly, fondness fighting with the sadness—"I'm willing to bet they've never even considered monk training."

"Yeah," Jackson said, smiling softly, too. "Kumar, maybe, but not the rest of them."

"If they're not dead, shouldn't we be getting them to the hospital?" Anja asked. "I mean, no offense. I'm sure you're capable. But you don't have any equipment. These guys don't even have beds."

Doc shook her head, and Jackson said, "You know that NDA I asked you to sign?"

Anja's mouth dropped open and she stared at him. She didn't need him to finish.

They—he and Doc—had already decided they weren't going to do anything to help the team.

And Anja and Ming had agreed not to tell.

"You can't be serious," Anja said. "You're just going to leave them here?"

"I'm not doing nothing," Doc said softly. "I've been practicing medicine for forty years. And I've seen more than my share of odd cases, both inside and outside the emergency room. Hospital protocols will require them to put the boys through test after test after test, even though the vast majority of doctors on the floor will know their tests aren't going to show anything useful. But for legal reasons, they have to be seen as doing everything they can. And for insurance reasons, they'll have to do it in a certain order. In such cases—and we've discussed this in the past"—she gestured between herself and Jackson—"less medical interference, especially when the patient is stable, is better in the long run."

"And better for the mission," Jackson said. "We don't want any questions. We don't want people or law enforcement poking around up here. For everyone's safety. I know that probably doesn't satisfy."

It didn't. Not even a little. Not even if there *was* something more going on here.

"What happened to them?" Yuri asked.

"I've run through all the things that could cause this: electromagnetic disturbance—"

"No," Yuri said, "I don't mean what's your diagnosis. I want to know what happened to them."

"We're not sure," Doc said, with a glance at Danny.

"I was watching the feeds," Danny said, pointing to the room's back right wall, where, on the other side of the wall, all the monitors were. "They were patrolling the area. All of them, because it was Halloween and we'd heard that people like to come hunting for ghost trees in greater numbers on Halloween. The—"

Danny stopped himself and looked to Jackson, asking permission.

"We're getting more out of him than he'll ever get from us," Jackson said, giving it.

But Anja frowned at Jackson's comment. Was he saying that Yuri's lucky guesses were actually meaningful?

Danny said, "The clearing you saw tonight? Something showed

up there about ten, twelve months ago. We were hired to watch it, to protect it from people."

"What showed up in the clearing?" Anja asked.

Danny shrugged. "It's just a clearing as far as any of us could tell, but people were getting hurt. Tourists, dogs, trees. I noticed Josh had started taking notes in his journal. I asked him about it, but he said he didn't have anything yet. He's particular." Danny shrugged. "He was always saying that he didn't want to make that fallacy where you see something only because it's what you're looking for."

"Confirmation bias," Anja said with a nod. She decided she liked this Josh fellow. Strange that the brother, Yuri, was so different.

"What happened on Halloween?" Yuri asked, and Anja had to remind herself that that was just yesterday.

"I don't know," Danny said. "All I can say is the video feed on the monitors got brighter."

Anja narrowed her eyes, suddenly more interested, wanting to ask if by *brighter* Danny meant the site was glowing. Glowing was her area of expertise.

But glowing things didn't usually hurt you. Unless you ate them. And even then, only in rare cases.

Then again, what Danny was describing didn't sound like the glow they'd seen tonight. Which had been faint. So much so that she doubted it would have shown up on the monitors at all.

"It just looked like a bright blob to me," Danny continued. "But the way the guys were reacting on the comms, they had to be seeing something more than what the monitors were showing. To me, though, everything just got bright. The monitors went pure white . . . and then the comms went silent. Total silence. I got in the Explorer, and . . ." He gestured around the room, at the men, his fallen comrades, still lying perfectly dead-seeming on the cots and the blanket-covered floor.

"He brought the first ones back here," Doc said, "and then he called me."

CHAPTER 15

"So let me get this straight," Anja said. "There is something in the clearing, but you can't see it, but sometimes it glows, and it's huge, but it's really just a blob, and somehow it exploded or something, giving some of these guys burns and abrasions and putting them in a coma, and to top it all off, you brought me here to . . . figure out what it is?"

Jackson looked a bit sheepish.

The baby awoke and made gurgling sounds. Jackson let it wrap its tiny hand around his finger. "We can't let this happen to anyone else," he said.

"No," Danny agreed, standing up.

"Can't you just put up signs?" Anja asked. "Tell everyone to keep out of the clearing?"

"Can't risk it," Jackson said. "And I doubt it would be enough anyway. We'd have to do more, fence it in."

"Too much *no* just adds to people's curiosity," Danny said. "Gets them wanting to come in, hopping the fence, telling the media."

Jackson shook his head. "Could you imagine? We can't have everyone down here with their cameras, poking around, and then all of a sudden something happens and we've got more people like this to deal with." Jackson gestured at his seven fallen men. "The world's already dealing with the whole stillbirth—"

"*Cht,*" Doc said. She passed it off like she was cooing at the baby, but Jackson stopped mid-sentence and didn't pick it up again.

Anja stood in silence for a while, and so did everyone else.

Doc bounced the baby and made quiet soothing sounds.

Jackson looked down at his hands and twisted his wedding ring.

Danny stood at attention with his body but not with his eyes.

Yuri, across the room, continued kneeling beside his brother's cot.

And Ming stood beside Anja and took deep breaths, her shoulder touching Anja's shoulder.

Yuri said, "Now that you mention it, the stillbirth thing, that's kind of what it felt like out in the clearing, what it feels like with Josh, with these guys now. They feel like empty vessels. They have no auras. The clearing . . . it doesn't feel like life. It feels like suffering. It feels like something that's begging for help."

Anja stared at him open-mouthed. When nobody immediately said anything to shut him up, she slowly shifted her gaze to look at everyone else's reactions. Doc still cooed the baby. Jackson still looked at his hands, but seemed to be nodding. And Danny looked pensive. They looked like they were actually considering what Yuri was saying, like it was actually valid.

"Are you guys seriously taking him seriously?" she said. "Auras? Yeah, we've all got an electromagnetic field, and that clearing in the woods might have one too, I'll give you that. But *auras*? The clearing is begging for help with its aura?"

"*He* called *me*," Jackson said, jabbing a finger in Yuri's direction. "Last night. Before I knew about any of this. Before Danny or Doc had a chance to call me themselves. While they were still dealing with the problem, he called me. *He* already knew."

Anja stepped back and hit the log wall. She didn't know what to say. She stared at Jackson, speechless. Then stared at the kid.

"I didn't ask you to come," Jackson said to Yuri, "but I guess I'm not surprised you're here."

"Me neither," Danny said.

"Josh never really talked about his personal life, but he started talking about you a lot in the last couple weeks," Jackson said. "Saying he should have listened. Saying he was sorry."

"Saying you could help," Danny said.

"I don't like that you found us so easily," Jackson said. "I'm still not comfortable with how you got the coordinates for our location—"

Anja snorted.

"—but now that you're here, I think I'd be a fool to send you away."

Danny sighed, seemingly with relief, his shoulders and face relaxing, his attention, his focus, coming back into his eyes. And he focused on Yuri. Like the kid was a long-wished-for gift that, until now, he'd thought might be taken away.

Anja couldn't believe it. Couldn't believe what she was hearing.

And she dreaded what she knew was about to happen.

"I assume you can stay," Jackson continued. "I assume you intended to stay, and I guess I'm saying I'd like you to stay. I'd like your help."

Yuri nodded and gave Jackson a small smile, like he'd never expected anything else, then turned to face his brother once more, bowing his head and closing his eyes.

"I knew it," Anja said, and she pointed at Jackson, hackles rising. "You expected that this thing, the clearing, had a-a"—she waved her hands, unwilling to use the first word that had come to mind, or the second—"an *unworldly* quality all along. You know how I feel about . . . about that kind of thing. And you brought me down here, tricked me into coming down here anyway."

Jackson had the good grace to look a bit guilty. He'd been a good friend of her dad's when she was growing up. He was fully aware of what had happened to Anja's brother. Of what had happened between Anja and her parents as a result. He'd been a comfort to her parents then, when Anja had refused to be. So for that, a part of her felt that she owed him.

But Jackson knew full well that she didn't jive with any kind of supernatural, paranormal crap.

"Why me?" she demanded.

Jackson sighed. "Many reasons. And I'm sorry to say that your history is one of them. There's a rational cause for all of this, and I know that you will stay true to that course. But there also seems to be a luminescent aspect to all of this as well as an electromagnetic aspect. I know you're doing bioluminescence now, but if memory serves me, your mother said you did some graduate work with a mentor who was studying electromagnetism. That makes you more qualified than others who specialize in just one field or the other. Plus, and most important, I know you. I trust you. But . . ." He put out his hands in a helpless gesture. "But you are going to need an open mind."

"An *open mind*?"

Minds *that* open got people killed. Ask her how she knew.

But she was becoming overwrought. She took a deep breath and tried to calm her tone. "I'm assuming whoever hired you can afford some real subject-matter experts, so why not get some out here and have them take a look at your clearing?"

Jackson looked around the room, at Doc, cooing the baby, and at all of his fallen men. "Maybe we should take this to the other side of the building."

Yuri said, "I'm not leaving Josh without a good reason, and the only reason I can think of is because we know what did this to him and, a better reason, how to undo it."

"I'm good here, too," Anja said. She didn't want any distractions deterring the juice of this conversation. Change the location and all of a sudden people are looking for dinner or other forms of entertainment. No, she wanted to be here, with the injured men. No one could look at them, not moving, barely breathing, and say that this secrecy and reliance on her wasn't crazy.

Jackson said, "We weren't hired to investigate the clearing or to even protect people from it. We were hired to protect *it*." Jackson didn't say so, but Anja heard it in his disgusted tone, an implied order to protect the clearing at all cost, at the expense of everything else, even their own lives. "We were asked to keep it hidden and to keep it secret. If we violate the contract, we won't get paid, and worse, these men . . . if we can't figure out what did this to them and how to undo it, their families will get nothing. No compensation."

Anja sighed. She knew all about secrecy for money's sake.

"I won't tell," she said, and she elbowed Ming, who shook her head vigorously in agreement.

Jackson nodded. "I've got to be getting back to the hospital," he said, and then he spoke to each of them in turn: "Doc? Thank you. For everything. Danny? You're in charge. Use your best judgment with the new perimeter guys. Keep them away and need-to-know for now. Anja? I expect this whole thing to have a rational explanation. A *scientific* fix. And I expect you to find it."

Anja looked around the room, at the seven fallen men, and nodded. She expected it to have a rational explanation, too, and she would do everything she could to find it, to figure it out. For these seven men.

Jackson's gaze drifted over Anja's left shoulder, to Ming standing beside her. "Ming," he said, but then he just stared at her, looking puzzled, not finishing his thought.

"I'll help Anja," she said quietly.

Jackson nodded and looked away, looked around at his fallen team again, and alighted on Yuri.

"And kid," he said, "Yuri. Yuri Palming. I expect you to . . . I don't know. Do what you do. Do what Josh knew you could do, what he knew you would do. Help Anja."

On the other side of the room, still kneeling beside his brother, Yuri nodded, looking relieved that he wasn't being sent away from his brother but not so excited about being asked to help.

Anja was about to protest on both their behalfs when she honed in on something else Jackson had said.

He was headed back to the hospital.

"Everything okay with Marisol?" She asked.

"She's . . ."

"Going to be fine," Doc insisted.

Jackson considered this, doubt creating worry lines all over his face, but he ultimately nodded agreement.

Then he turned toward Anja, squeezed her shoulder, and gave her a small smile. "Give the kid a chance," he said quietly. "With you two working together, I know we can solve this. I know we can set this right."

Anja tried to reassure him with a smile of her own, but it was tight. Mention of the paranormal had that effect on her. "When will you be back?"

Jackson didn't immediately answer, just looked around the room at his men again, his face crestfallen. Like he needed to be in two places at once and could have used a second body.

"Take as long as you need," Danny said, patting him on the back. "We'll be fine. I'll keep you posted."

Jackson nodded and then headed for the door.

Good. Anja put on a worried face, trying to look distressed that Jackson was leaving right this minute, that she had no idea when he'd be back, but she secretly felt relieved.

He may have assigned her to work with a so-called psychic, but if he wasn't going to stick around to make sure that happened, then she could pretend it was never mentioned.

Yuri Palming could stay in sick bay, keep watch on his brother, help Doc, whatever, so long as he stayed out of Anja's way.

She would find out what happened to the team and how to help them.

She would tend to this so-called rift.

After most everyone else had gone to bed, one person found a quiet place, uncovered a forbidden satellite phone, and sent a text:

> *Today's arrivals at the site:*
> *8 new team members*
> *a scientist*
> *the scientist's assistant*
> *and a psychic.*

CHAPTER 16

It was still dark outside the small window opposite Anja's cot. Danny had set them up in the metal shipping containers—conexes, he'd called them—that stood in most of the old campsites that surrounded the back half of the old log building. Anja tried to get out of bed quietly, but her feet thudded onto a floor that was closer than she was used to.

At the other end of the twenty-foot conex, Ming said, "You think Danny's got an extra conex to spare? You snore. Bad."

"Just get up," Anja said on a laugh, because, sadly, that wasn't the first time she'd heard that she snored. "The quicker we resolve this thing, the quicker we can go home to our own beds. Mind if I turn on the light?"

"Go for it."

Anja padded two steps toward the other side of the conex, where the door was, and flipped the switch, illuminating the small space. Two beds and a dresser with two columns of drawers sat against the wall opposite the door and the light switch, and desks sat at either end. Ming's side also had a small bookshelf next to the door.

The bathroom was in another conex, one campsite over.

Anja had left her pants and jacket on the desk, but sitting on the floor, just inside the door, she found two sets of rain gear. Coats and pants in camo colors that blended in with the forest, and rubber boots, low-profile with elastic goring on the side and a pull tag on the heel. They looked expensive. "Where'd these come from?"

Ming got out of bed, pulled her dark hair into a high ponytail. "Danny?"

"Nice of him."

She handed Ming a set and took hers to the desk by her bed.

The pile included black shirts and socks. No undies, unfortunately. But Anja understood how that might have been weird.

Anja layered the new shirt over the one she was already wearing, then tried on the boots. They were a little big, but good enough with the extra socks, and they were better than the muddy ballet flats she'd now have to throw out when she got home.

Also included with the rain gear were two sets of travel toiletries.

"Toothbrush," Ming said with delight. "And toothpaste! I'll be making use of you after breakfast. Thank you, Danny." Then, "You ready, boss?"

Ming had dressed fast and was standing with one hand on the doorknob.

Anja finished zipping up her coat. "Ready."

They headed out into the cold, damp, early morning dark and crossed the packed dirt road to the welcoming center, their flashlight beams guiding the way.

Last night, before they'd all gone to bed, one of the perimeter guys had ducked into the monitoring room's kitchenette to change the batteries in his flashlight, so Anja figured she'd find whatever handheld equipment they had available in the kitchen.

But if they expected her to figure out what, if anything, was in the circle in the woods and harming people, she would need some heavy-duty equipment as well.

She and Ming hadn't taken more than a few steps when Anja heard ferns rustling and branches breaking nearby, less than twenty feet away.

"What the hell is that?" Ming said, grabbing Anja's arm. "A bear? A cougar?"

Anja shined her flashlight in the direction of the sound. She still heard the commotion, heard rustling ferns, but she wasn't seeing any rustling ferns.

She looped her arm through Ming's and hustled her toward the welcoming center. "Come on, let's hurry."

But Ming was still peering into the dark, panning her flashlight from side to side. Her beam brushed over a figure.

Anja screamed.

"Oh, it's you guys," Danny said, stepping into the beam of Ming's flashlight. He wore camo rain gear, like her own. He looked at something in his hand, some kind of remote, and pressed a button.

The noise in the woods suddenly stopped.

"What are you guys doing out here?" Danny said, clipping the remote to his belt. "Come inside. I'm making oatmeal."

"Oh, good. I'm so hungry," Ming said as they followed him into the building.

"Are you monitoring us?" Anja asked.

"The grounds," Danny said, opening the door for them. The room was bright and warm and smelled of nutty, earthy carbs. "There's motion sensors all over the place."

Danny took Anja's flashlight and pointed the beam at a couple devices set up at the base of the trees.

"Aren't the monitors constantly triggered by animals?" Ming asked.

"You know we thought they would be, but no, not once, in fact. There's nothing living but trees and ferns for about a mile in all directions around the site."

He gave Anja back her flashlight, then made his way to the stove. One of the burners was warming a pot. He picked up a wooden spoon and gave the oatmeal a quick stir.

Ming elbowed Anja. "I know what keeps the animals away," she said with a grin. "It's the ghosts, like Yuri said."

Danny looked over his shoulder and made a face like, *You laugh . . .*

Anja rolled her eyes and whispered to Ming, "Let's just eat and get out of here before he wakes up."

Along the wall, beside the door, Anja found the box the perimeter guy had sorted through when he'd changed out his batteries. Black plastic with a yellow lid, maybe twenty-eight gallons in size. Inside was a bunch of batteries. Anja dug through them, hoping to find something more, but it was just a big box of batteries.

"Where do you keep your equipment?"

"What do you need?"

"The only things I can think of that *might* cause a few people in a specified area to develop coma-like symptoms are rogue electromagnetic fields. Very, very strong ones. So I could use an EMF detector. A frequency counter would be good too, if you've got it. I'd also take a barometer, a thermometer, and a full-spectrum camera—video camera, if you've got it."

She watched Danny for a reaction, wondering if he knew that the equipment she was asking for was the kind of equipment ghost hunters took with them into allegedly haunted houses. But if he did, he didn't let on. Just nodded slowly, face solemn, taking her requests very seriously.

"I'm assuming you've already set up a Geiger counter," she asked.

Danny suddenly perked up—which caused her to deflate. Jobs are tough without tools.

"We've got a Geiger counter." He pulled one from a smaller box near the battery box and handed it to her.

Anja looked it over. It was army green, fancier and more durable than any kind she'd ever seen before. Probably military grade. The dosimeters clipped to their clothes hadn't gone off when they'd visited the clearing the night before or at any other time, so there probably weren't dangerous levels of radiation in the area. But that didn't mean there wasn't any radiation.

"Have you tried it?" she asked, holding up the counter. Ionizing radiation was an obvious thing to check for, but given the state of

Danny's team—and Jackson's eagerness to add Yuri-the-psychic to hers—Anja wasn't confident they had done so.

"Yeah," he said slowly, not elaborating.

"And?"

"There's some radiation in the area."

She waited for more, but Danny returned to the stove to stir his oatmeal.

"And?" she asked.

"It's clean."

"But there's something," Ming said, "some kind of unexplained radiation?"

"Occasionally," Danny said. "Yeah."

"Probably just wind and rain," Anja said. Not that they created radiation, just that they moved it around, carried it down from the atmosphere faster.

"Except it's windy and rainy outside here, too," Danny countered, gesturing around the building.

"Okay, well, we'll take this with us," Anja said, and she pocketed the Geiger counter. "What about the other devices?"

"We've got cameras up, full-spectrum—you mean infrared, right?"

Anja nodded. "And ultraviolet."

"Okay, so full-spectrum-ish. We've got cameras with infrared monitoring the rift for human heat signatures, but they're not set up for ultraviolet. As for an EMF detector, barometer . . ." Danny shook his head, then perked up again and looked around. "I've seen a thermometer somewhere. Yeah, here it is."

He pushed past her, around the table, and found a mercury-based thermometer hanging by the door. He removed it from the wall and handed it to her.

"Right," she said, handing it back. "I was looking for more of a digital thermometer, something that'll react to change in temperature instantaneously."

"You know, I think Darryl might have one of those. I'll check his room before we head out."

She nodded, hoping the thermometer would not only be there but would have a fast enough refresh rate to be useful.

But it still wasn't much to work with.

"So, what equipment *do* you have?"

"Surveillance and deterrence," Danny said. "Cameras, motion detectors, skunk bombs, caterwauls, but the skunk bombs work better. Mountain lions are rare and more likely to flee than fight, so people try to catch a glimpse. We learned that the hard way. But unless they see a problem, even forest rangers veer wide of skunk."

Anja nodded, waiting for him to list off more equipment items.

Outside, a gust of wind roared along the building's old logs and whistled through its tiny cracks.

"That's it?" Anja asked.

"We don't even have firearms," Danny said, taking three bowls from an upper cabinet. "Our mission is strictly to keep everyone away from the site without anyone knowing and wondering why we're here. We're invisible babysitters."

"Of the clearing in the woods?" Ming said. "That's one strange baby."

"Yeah, and we're protecting *it*, not people from it. So believe me when I say I feel your frustration. But right now I don't have anything for you that's high tech."

"How do you expect me to resolve whatever's going on here if I don't have any equipment?"

"Just to be clear, *I* don't expect anything. And Jackson, as far as I can tell, only *hopes* you can fix whatever this is. My only job is to make sure you do it safely and as he ordered. And I've been up, without sleep, for more than forty-eight hours now." He scooped oatmeal into three bowls and set two of them on the table. He pushed them toward Anja and Ming. "Make that fifty hours and counting. So why don't you just tell me exactly what you want and I'll see if I can get it for you."

"How long is that going to take?"

"Depends on what you need. Twenty-four hours probably."

Anja sighed. That was actually way faster than she'd expected—way faster than she could have gotten something sent to her lab back in Portland—but Ming was giving her a look that mirrored everything Anja, herself, was feeling: *I don't want to stay here any more nights than I have to just so we can play high-tech ghost hunters.*

"What about a compass?" Anja asked. "You look like a former Boy Scout. Do you at least have a compass?"

"That I can do." Danny reached into his pants pocket and pulled out a set of keys. He maneuvered a keychain off the ring and handed it to her. It was your basic circular compass with a red-tipped magnetic needle.

Anja stepped outside. It was still pitch black out, so she reached back inside the door and flipped on the exterior light. The space beneath the portico roof lit up.

At her feet, just outside the door, was a welcome mat decorated with a compass rose. But the mat was sideways and slightly skewed, putting North off to Anja's right.

Anja pointed down at the mat. "Is this accurate?"

Danny smiled sadly. "Darryl put that there. I'm sure it's accurate."

The red tip on the keychain compass pointed in the same direction as the mat's compass.

While she was at it, Anja thought she might as well get a base reading for the Geiger counter. She turned it on and got a few random clicks. Nothing out of the ordinary.

"What about a light?" Anja said. "I'm looking for a lamp, something big, better than these flashlights."

"Yeah," Danny said with hesitation, "I can get you a light, but it's got to be turned off by seven, seven-thirty."

"Like, in the morning?" Anja said.

"It's a Sunday, and it's supposed to be dry today. People will start driving up that hill"—he pointed at the welcoming center's camouflaged front entrance gate, toward the main road—"around sunrise. Maybe sooner. Dawn, probably. And we're supposed to be invisible, remember?"

"So no equipment and no light. Awesome." Anja flopped down into a seat at the table and pulled her bowl of oatmeal in front of her. Sure, the sun would eventually rise and fill the clearing with light—at high noon. But until then, the forest canopy would keep the area dim and filled with shifting shadows cast by all the trees.

"Wait," Ming said. "Isn't it daylight savings today?"

Danny frowned and went to his monitoring station.

Anja glanced hopefully at her watch—6:16—then looked for the time on the wall of monitors, which she assumed would update automatically. The two times were different. The monitor said it was an hour earlier, 5:17 a.m.

"So we have an extra hour? Kind of? Okay. Awesome," she said with less sarcasm.

"It's fall back," Ming said.

"Yeah," Danny said, consulting a website with an astrological calendar. "Dawn is at 6:20 a.m. today."

"So I've lost an hour?" Anja said. "Are you kidding me?"

"I'll pack up lights and a little power station for you," Danny said, returning to the table, "but don't get too attached to using it."

"Sure," Anja said.

He'd agreed to get the light. That was good enough for her. For now.

In addition to oatmeal, he'd put out a spread of maple syrup, dried fruit, and apples.

"Not that I'm complaining," Ming said between tiny bites, "but I was kind of expecting eggs and bacon."

"Oatmeal's easy, healthy, and it's shelf stable," Danny said, eating his oatmeal plain. Anja couldn't help the disgusted face she made. She doused her oatmeal with maple syrup and tucked in.

"Do you happen to have any bananas?" Ming asked.

"They don't last long. They get eaten or they go bad. We only shop once every few weeks or so."

"Who's 'we'?" Ming asked.

Danny looked up at her, then looked around the table, at the seven empty chairs. Everything very quiet.

"Guess that would be me now," he said.

CHAPTER 17

Danny finished his oatmeal first. "I'll get the light," he said. "You go get Yuri."

Anja laughed. Ming chuckled, too.

"You're supposed to work together," Danny said. "He might have some insight."

Anja laughed harder. "*Insight*? Into what? Spirits? Ghosts? Whatever this is, it isn't . . . whatever Yuri thinks it is. It has a scientific explanation."

"Okay, sure," Danny said. "But the kid knows things. You saw him. He was right about . . ." He jutted his chin toward the wall that separated the monitoring room from Doc's sick bay, where, as Yuri had said, the teammates Danny had thought were dead were actually alive, albeit barely. "Just let him tag along."

Anja felt bad for being hard on Danny and thought maybe she should give him less trouble. He had lost his friends, hadn't slept in two days, and was still managing to be kind and accommodating.

But this was literally a matter of life and death.

She tried to keep her tone kind but firm. "You took me away from my work and drove me all the way down here for my opinion, my scientific opinion. At least let me form one without the superstitious distractions."

"But he knows things," Danny said. "First off, I don't know how else he could have gotten the coordinates other than the way he said. From Josh, after this all went down. The whole team has the coordinates, but you aren't the only ones who had to give up your cell phones. The only phone available on base is for emergencies only, and the call log gets sent directly to the client and to Jackson, and there were no calls that night, not until I called Doc, and then again later, when Doc called Jackson. That's it. But more than that—the kid wasn't *using* the coordinates when we found him last night. GPS signals are notoriously unreliable around here, and his wasn't working. But he got here anyway. In the dark. On foot."

Danny shook his head, his jaw slack, in a classic expression of astoundment and awe. The kid impressed him.

"And that's still not all of it. I debriefed the guys watching the perimeter last night. They told me Yuri never tripped the sensors."

"What does that mean?" Ming asked.

Anja was hearing all this—she couldn't help it—but she was resolute in her decision not to participate, not to entertain any of these superstitious notions that Yuri was somehow higher-powered.

"I don't know," Danny said. "The wires trip physically, if you walk past them. But the perimeter guys said Yuri got past them. They didn't want to mention that in front of him and let him know that we didn't have this thing under control. But they said the only reason they knew he was there was because they'd heard him scream."

"He wasn't screaming because they'd caught him?" Ming asked.

"Not at first, no."

Anja remembered those two screams. The first sounded scared, the second frustrated.

"What happened?" Ming asked.

"They don't know. They said he kept whispering, 'Did you see that? Did you see that?' But he couldn't, or wouldn't, tell them what he saw, just that . . . just that it was magnificent. And terrifying."

"Well, jeez," Ming said, "part of me wants to take him with us just to hear what he might say next, but if he's special—"

"Not you too," Anja said.

Ming laughed, revealing that she wasn't taking all this Yuri talk seriously.

But she continued: "But if he *is special*, and this scary thing came out to play because of him—he's the brother of one of the guys who was attacked, right?"

Danny nodded. "Josh."

"So maybe it's something about them, the brothers?"

Danny shrugged. "Josh noticed some things, but I don't think he's got Yuri's . . . ability. It sounded to me like he'd always doubted Yuri's ability. But in the last couple days he was realizing that maybe . . ."

"Maybe it was real and useful after all?" Ming said.

Danny shrugged.

"Okay," Anja said, because someone had to be reasonable. "He says there's ghosts. Fine. Whatever. It can't be proved. But it can be faked."

Danny and Ming stared at her, neither looking mentally calibrated to reality.

Anja huffed, chastising them both for entertaining such ridiculous ideas. The sooner she performed her tests and formed her opinion, the sooner they could resolve this thing. She just needed to keep everyone on track. They'd thank her in the end.

"Okay, try it this way, then," she said. "For the sake of argument, let's say you're right. If this kid is really as magical as he claims, as you all seem to think he is, then he'll probably know, from right where he is, whether there's anything to be seen or *felt* out there at the clearing, and he'll figure out where we are. He's already proven he can get there on his own. Therefore, he doesn't need us to take him."

Danny started to protest again, but Anja cut him off.

"Yuri and his theories have no place here, Danny. He'd prove a distraction at best and at worst an uncontrolled element. He's not going to get you any kind of diagnosis you can actually work with and resolve. And your friends in sick bay"—she jabbed a finger toward the building's other room—"need me to not waste my time indulging some illogical charlatan that will only interrupt me with asinine suggestions that are categorically incorrect. So let's just let him stay here, with his brother, while we figure this thing out. Now get the light and let's go, so I can have some time to use it."

CHAPTER 18

Anja's breathing blew white air into the glow of her flashlight, so she knew it was no warmer out than forty-five degrees. The dark and early morning was damp. Very damp. The moisture from last night's rain hung on the ferns. The wet ground sucked at her new boots as she walked the path through the trees, toward the clearing and away from Big Beauty, where Danny had parked the Explorer.

She checked her dosimeter, clipped to her new rain jacket, and wondered how the humidity would affect the readings and the internal machinery of her equipment, what little she had.

Danny carried a portable power station in a surplus backpack, with two folded up lamps clipped to the sides. The load had to be heavy, but Anja still had a hard time keeping up with him. And she had a feeling he was taking it easy to accommodate her and Ming.

Ming, for her part, was doing a better job keeping up. She'd started the trek out behind Anja, but upon reaching the first downed tree, she'd scrambled over it, given Anja a hand, and then scrambled ahead. Now Anja brought up the rear.

"You gotta see this," Danny called back to her. He stood atop a low hill, pointing ahead and allowing them to catch up.

Ming reached his side first and sucked in an audible breath. If Anja wasn't mistaken, it had been a gasp of awe.

Anja hurried up the small rise to the crest, where the other two stood, and scanned the huge trees, though what Danny pointed at was unmistakable.

Straight ahead, in the space between two redwood trunks and about thirty yards beyond them, just barely visible, perhaps a single lumen, maybe less, dimmer than candlelight, the clearing glowed with a violet light.

Anja shivered.

But she stayed focused.

"It's a natural, explainable glow," she said, shaking off the shivers and trying to get a jump on dispelling any awe or reverence or mystical inclinations being entertained at the moment by her companions. And herself. She forced one foot in front of the other and continued trekking toward the clearing.

"There's no tree canopy here, so moonlight is making its way into the clearing. The moon's, like, two days shy of full today, so it's bright right now. And it's blue because blue light is scattered through the atmosphere easier than other colors. It's why the sky looks blue during the day."

"Still pretty," Ming said. "Dare I say *awe-inspiring*."

Anja couldn't disagree.

Because Anja wasn't telling them the whole truth about the light, and she knew it.

First, the moon was low enough in the sky that the light should have been coming into the clearing at an angle, not straight down like a column.

The light seemed to be shining down from the heavens—or from an alien spaceship, take your pick, as both were equally implausible. Nothing scientific shined beams down like that, except Search and Rescue, and their light beams moved around. This beam was stationary and, as far as Anja could tell, almost the exact size of the clearing. The light enabled her to see all the trees that bordered its perimeter.

Second, the moon was high enough in the sky that the atmospheric scattering shouldn't be noticeable: the light should be white, not the distinct violet-colored light she was forcing herself to march towards.

Which meant other factors were at play here.

Air pollutants were an obvious consideration. But they would only account for the blue color, not the light itself.

There was only one thing she could think of that could account for both the light and its color, and the possibility dared her to hope that this trip wouldn't be such a waste of time after all.

It was possible that bioluminescent organisms were causing the light and its violet color. Maybe even a new, undiscovered microorganism. Like an airborne dinoflagellate, maybe. Something indistinct to the naked eye. Something that thrived in open-air spaces hidden in redwood groves. The possibility raised goosebumps on Anja's arms.

She ventured closer to the edge of the clearing and its faint, violet glow.

Up close, the column of light was just slightly brighter at its base than higher up, making it seem like the light rose from the earth to the sky rather than the other way around, like she'd previously thought. From where she stood, right next to it, Anja couldn't see how high the column went before fading out, thanks to the redwood canopy, but it reached at least as high as that, as high as the treetops.

When neither Ming nor Danny joined her at the edge of the clearing, she looked over her shoulder.

Danny had stopped next to a giant redwood, a couple dozen paces behind her. His face looked pinched around the mouth and the eyes. His nostrils flared. Anja knew that look. She'd seen it on the faces of field scientists.

Awe, but also wariness.

Nature was often at its most dangerous when being its most beautiful.

"What is it?" Anja asked.

Danny lifted his chin and breathed in.

Anja looked at Ming to see if she, at least, would answer.

"Just the uninteresting-now-that-you've-totally-explained-it light through the trees," Ming said with a smile.

Anja smiled too. But now she was even more concerned about Danny. She walked back to him and touched his arm.

"You okay?" she asked. "What do you sen—see," she finished. She'd been about to say *what do you sense,* and was relieved that she'd caught herself. Someone had to remain rational in this whole affair.

But Ming would probably stay on her side to the very end of this thing. She'd probably make a joke of everything, too, which Anja welcomed. Humor would help them get through the next, well, however many days this took.

And then Anja sensed it. A shift in the air. A new scent was rising above the smell of humidity and damp earth.

It smelled like fresh baked cookies. Soft molasses, like her grandma used to make when she and her brother would visit their grandparents' house. It always smelled like something sweet and made with love was baking in Grandma's oven.

But Anja didn't recall seeing even a toaster oven back at base, let alone out here at the clearing.

"Do you guys smell that?" she asked.

"Like the top of a baby's head," Ming said. "I love that smell."

Anja rounded on her friend. "What?"

Ming took a step back. "You know, that powdery soft newborn smell. I love that smell. Why? What does it smell like to you?"

"Not babies," Danny said. "I've got four nephews. That's not what they smelled like. This smells more like . . . my dad's aftershave."

"No, it doesn't," Ming said.

"Well, it doesn't smell like a baby's head," Danny said.

And just like that, the scent was gone.

"Anja, what do you smell?" Ming asked.

Anja shook her head and inhaled, trying to recapture the scent of her grandmother's cookies. But it was gone.

"Nothing," she said. "Just wet dirt and trees. Let's get to work."

CHAPTER 19

"So what's the plan?" Danny asked, after setting up the lamps.

If the circular clearing were the face of a clock and the path leading from the SUV and Big Beauty opened onto the clearing at six o'clock, then the first lamp and the power station were placed at four o'clock, and the second lamp was placed at eight o'clock. An extension cord stretched across the clearing, between the two lamps. It was taut enough that it hovered a few inches above the ground.

They hadn't turned the lamps on yet. Jackson wanted Anja to eradicate anything that wasn't supposed to be in the clearing, but to do that they first had to figure out what they were dealing with.

Anja wanted to start with the clearing's subtle glow, which was already beginning to fade with the oncoming of twilight.

The glow could be caused by a concentration of millions of bioluminescent airborne microorganisms. Or it could be caused by fluorescing airborne particles, although that explanation would also require discovering the UV light source that was causing them to fluoresce.

Thing was, she'd been watching the glow for about twenty minutes now, and the light breeze coming off the Pacific Ocean, through the trees, wasn't causing any deviation of light away from the main column.

Which made airborne causes increasingly unlikely.

Which meant the glow had a cause that Anja, at this moment, couldn't fathom.

With all the superstitious talk she'd heard from Jackson and Danny and the kid the night before, she didn't know how to feel about that.

Still, she took air samples, which Danny said he could probably send to a lab. She didn't have proper collection containers, so she'd made do with a few empty water bottles.

She'd come up with an idea for how to test the cause of the glow. And assuming she could find some rudimentary supplies back at base, she could MacGyver the test today. But it would have to wait until nightfall.

Until then . . .

"Our equipment's limited," she said, "but we're going to walk the clearing in a grid pattern and take baseline readings with what equipment we do have."

Danny, who'd set up the lamps and then retreated to his protective tree near six o'clock on the clearing's metaphorical clock face, was grimacing.

"Okay," he said. "How about this. You two stick to the perimeter of the clearing—don't go in it, just walk around it—and I'll keep watch."

"Keep watch?" Ming said.

"Don't go in?" Anja said. "We have to go in. I get why you wouldn't want tourists walking into an area that may be radioactive, but we're the people you kidnapped in order to test whether it is. Someone's gotta go in. We'll wear protective suits if you've got them, but this little gadget you gave me"—she patted the dosimeter clipped to her jacket—"says we should be safe from radiation, and this guy"—she held up the barely beeping Geiger counter—"confirms it. What else should we worry about?"

"Airborne pathogens?" Ming said.

"Right. But we've got masks and goggles." She'd found a black storage container full of them in one of the lower kitchenette cabinets. She pulled hers out of her pocket and put them on. They were medical style rather than industrial, but they were better than nothing.

Ming put hers on, too.

"Anything else?" Anja asked.

"Just your garden-variety superstitious bunk," Ming said.

Anja smiled, relieved but also feeling affirmed that Ming was definitely on her side despite any jokes she might make suggesting the contrary. "And we don't believe in superstitious bunk, so . . ."

"Say what you want about Yuri, but he's not wrong," Danny said, completely serious. "That"—he pointed at the clearing—"is not normal. It's beyond normal. And I'm pretty sure that's the definition of *paranormal*. And whatever's in there acts up occasionally. Gets bigger. Attacks people. But before it does, it gives off signs, and I—"

"Like warning signs?" Ming asked.

It occurred to Anja to disapprove of Ming indulging any ideas that bumped against Yuri and his superstitions. But then an image of Danny's team, all lying broken on their cots in Doc's sick bay flashed in her mind.

But even more than that, Danny's tone commanded compliance, and he still wasn't venturing any closer to the edge of the clearing than he had to. He was dead serious about what he was saying. He was scared.

And that scared Anja.

Danny scanned the clearing, left to right, his eyes squinting. Anja looked at the clearing too, wondering what he saw. But there was nothing to see.

The sun was beginning to rise, and in the growing daylight, still dim under the tree canopy, the clearing looked like nothing more than a circle of dirt, like the site of an old fire, where the char had washed away but nothing green had grown back yet.

He didn't answer Ming. He was cautioning them about the

clearing's warning signs, warning signs he, apparently, would watch for, but he wasn't telling them what those signs were.

Anja snorted and rolled her eyes. "You don't know what the signs look like, do you?"

"I've never seen them in person," Danny said. "I've always been on the monitors. On the monitors, it just looks like the screen going bright white. I imagine that means the clearing lights up, but . . ." He shrugged and gestured toward the circle of dirt, as if that explained it.

Anja supposed it did. The clearing was just a circle in the woods, empty of trees and brush, and silent of birds. It was empty. And, sure, yeah, it was eerie. But that was all. How could it possibly light up?

But it had. She had seen a lumen or two of its light herself.

And she couldn't deny the men in sick bay.

"Fine," Anja said, trying not to sound antagonistic, and failing. "You keep watch and we'll walk the clearing. Just the perimeter, I promise. Ming, do you want the compass or the thermometer?"

Ming took the thermometer and grinned. "Less work, Boss. Can we start on the other side?"

Anja frowned at her. It was a circle in the woods. Yes, supposedly it had hurt the team. Yes, a psychic had found the place. Yes, the only remaining member of the team seemed scared to death and wasn't coming any closer than twenty yards. But still. "Why?"

Ming glanced at Danny. Not only was he not coming any closer, he seemed to be backing further away. "What if he's right?"

What if indeed? Anja's heart pounded faster, and warmer. What it would mean for her career, for her curiosity about what took her brother from her, if the superstitious of the world were right.

"He's not right," she said.

Ming looped arms with Anja. "Does it seem quiet to you?" she whispered.

Anja stilled. Far in the distance, the Pacific Ocean rolled rhythmically along the rocky shores.

"How so?" she whispered back.

Ming shrugged. "Not seeing land animals is one thing, but birds? Where are the birds?"

"Kinda late in the fall for birdsong," Anja said, knowing that wasn't exactly true.

"Sure," Ming said. "But they still gotta eat. Early bird and the worm and all that."

The Eastern night was brightening with every passing minute. If there were birds in the area, now would be a good time to see them.

But Anja said, "I remember hearing somewhere that redwood bark is inhospitable to bugs, so birds aren't attracted to the area."

"Well, I saw a documentary that a third of the country's species live in the redwoods. Hundreds of species," Ming said, her tone growing insistent.

Anja looked at Ming, at all her seriousness, and laughed.

"What?" Ming demanded, her voice growing louder. "Where are the birds, Anja? They may not be singing this time of year, but they should still be flying around."

"The birds don't like the clearing," Danny said from his safe distance away.

Anja snorted. "They *don't like* the clearing?"

But his strange phrasing set Anja back on her heels. If Yuri had said it, she would have brushed it off as Yuri's paranormal mumbo-jumbo. But this was Danny. True, she'd known him for less than twenty-four hours, but he . . . well, he just didn't speak unless he had something that needed to be said.

"I've seen a few birds back at the base, on the far side, but once you start heading toward the clearing, there's no sign of them."

"Maybe they're smarter than we are," Ming said. Elbows still linked, she squeezed Anja's arm.

It was another notion Anja would have normally rolled her eyes at—not to be a cocky ass, but nothing and hardly anyone was smarter than she—but instead, Anja just looked at her friend, at Ming's genuine unease. Humans may have trained themselves to override their better judgments, but animals' instincts have served them well enough for millions of years.

And something was keeping them away.

"We're fine," Anja said. "Hit the lights, Danny."

Danny held out a fob and clicked a couple buttons. First the power station came on, and then the two lamps flooded the circle.

Anja was impressed. She could see the whole circle, and the power station was so quiet that she didn't have to raise her voice to be heard. About ten feet in front of her, the reddish dirt beneath her boots met dark dirt, marking the edge of the clearing, a circle of blackened earth and a few rocks, maybe fifty yards across.

"I'm sure you're right. We're fine," Ming said. But then she pointed at the trees on the opposite side of the clearing. "And I still want to start over there. Do one side of the circle and then the other. So that we're almost always moving closer and closer to home—"

"Base," Anja said.

"—rather than further and further away."

"Fine. Whatever. After you."

"Thank you," Ming said, and she started walking toward seven o'clock, eight o'clock, leading the way around the left side of the clearing, rounding giant tree trunks when they stood too close to its edge. "And just so you know, if we have to make a run for it, I'm not waiting for you to catch up."

"Back at ya," Anja said.

CHAPTER 20

Anja and Ming reached the twelve-o'clock point of the clearing, opposite where Danny remained standing near his protective redwood and the path back to Big Beauty and the Explorer. Ming was humming softly. A light wind blew through the trees and smelled like earth and bark.

Anja asked Ming which side of the clearing she wanted to map first.

"The other one," Ming said, pointing at the circle side opposite the one they'd just speedwalked around.

They took a reading where they stood, made a few notes, then took a few steps closer to one o'clock and did it again, tracking the measurements of magnetism and radiation on their rudimentary equipment. Which was easier said than done. Anja's compass pulsed like a heartbeat, the little needle quivering as it pointed toward the center of the circle.

"See anything?" Ming asked when Anja failed to keep up.

"I don't know yet."

Anja tried to parse out what the needle's unsteady pulsing meant. She'd read somewhere that a less rhythmic cardiovascular pulse was actually healthier than one that was steady-state. A variable heartbeat meant that you had an easier time adapting to whatever was going on around you without getting too stressed out about it.

But she wasn't sure what a variable pulse meant in the context of a bouncing compass needle responding to the center of a clearing. It had a scientific explanation, of course. Had to have. No such thing as the paranormal. She wasn't going to get excited just because her instruments were acting up. It didn't mean there was anything paranormal here. It just meant . . .

Well, maybe a big piece of magnetic metal was buried in the ground.

She lowered to a crouch. The needle stopped bouncing, and it migrated around its face to point in a different direction. She was standing at about the two-o'clock point on the clearing's perimeter.

She yelled across the circle. "Hey, Danny, which way's north?"

He pointed back down the path to Big Beauty and the Explorer. Same direction the needle pointed to when it was closer to the ground.

And, if she wasn't mistaken, the tip of the little red needle seemed to be rising off the compass's face.

She stood back up again.

The needle settled back into position, pointing toward the center of the circle. And it resumed bouncing.

Anja checked her dosimeter and the Geiger counter. No radiation. At least not enough to give cause for concern.

Okay, then. Only one thing left she could think of to do.

Should she?

Well, it was probably pointless. But if she did it anyway, no one had to know.

So she shifted perspective to that of a ghost hunter—just for a second, grinding her teeth as she did—and considered whether a ghost hunter might find something interesting about her measurements. But the readings still didn't seem very significant.

Ugh. Had she just hedged and qualified her thought with the word *significant*?

She had. But you know what? She would stand by that decision. And she was going to round down as well. Nothing to see here, folks. Everybody move on.

"I think I've got a broken compass," she said.

"Broken how?" Ming said, taking it from her. Anja hovered at Ming's shoulder.

Ming tapped the compass's face, then held it up to eye level and looked at its edge. Then she held it at chest level. She walked it closer to the clearing's three o'clock, and Anja followed after her, sticking right next to her shoulder.

The compass did not point north, towards Danny. It pointed straight ahead, into the circle.

Ming stretched her arm out, putting the compass closer to the center of the clearing. Anja rose on her toes and held onto Ming as she leaned forward to peer at the compass's face.

"It's quivering faster," she said.

Ming took the compass in her other hand and stretched it out toward the trees.

Anja peered at the face. "The needle's stopped bouncing. And it's less decided about where to point. It's not pointing north, but it's not pointing as hard at the clearing, either. Any other ideas?"

Ming made duck lips as she thought about it. "Let's keep walking."

So they did, slowly, but Anja didn't like it. There was clearly something here, some kind of magnetic or electromagnetic reading. But knowing that didn't tell her what was giving off the signal. And she didn't like the options her mind was considering.

Stupid paranormal suggestions invading her thoughts.

"Wait, what's that?" Ming said, pointing into the clearing. The sun was rising higher and higher, filtering light into the circle. Until now, Anja had noticed nothing but dirt and roots and rocks, but from this spot, this angle—and thanks to the sun getting higher in the sky—she could see that one of the rocks near the center of the clearing, about the size of a basketball, had at one time been painted fluorescent orange.

The paint was mostly faded and worn away now, but from this angle some of the color was still visible.

"Hey, Danny," she yelled. "Is that a painted rock?"

"That?" Danny said, shining his flashlight on the rock. "Yeah. Josh put that there."

Anja pulled a face.

"I know what you're thinking," Danny said, "but Josh is nothing like Yuri. He was skeptical. Like you. But he noticed that the site was changing. Getting bigger. The site's pretty quiet, and we . . . well, we weren't taking the babysitting job very seriously back then, so no one believed him at first. But it used to be about a third of the size it is now." Danny dragged the beam of his flashlight away from the center rock and a few feet closer to the center, at another rock that showed signs of having also been painted. "Anyway, once Josh realized the circle was growing, he started marking its growth with painted rocks."

Danny used his flashlight to point out other rocks, each spaced a few or more feet away from the rock before it, and closer and closer to the edge of the clearing. Collectively, they marked the boundaries of a set of concentric circles, each circle a further development in the clearing's growing size.

"When we got here, there were big redwoods and ferns in there, in these outer rings, but over time the trees just . . . disintegrated. We don't know how or why. The camera feed goes white or fails when it happens."

"So, not like this?" She gestured at the lingering subtle glow in the clearing, which was fading in the sun. And she backed away as she did so.

"No," Danny said, but it sounded more like a question. "I've only seen it on the monitors. But it's blinding white, explosion white. I'll check the feeds when we get back, but I doubt this glow even shows up on the screen."

"Do other things ever show up on the screen?" Ming asked.

"Like what?" Anja whispered before Danny could answer.

"I don't know," Ming said, turtle-shelling her shoulders. "But cameras can pick up colors just beyond the visible light spectrum.

Ultraviolet. Infrared. Even cameras not designed for that. We're scientists, Anja. We gotta ask."

"Fine. You're right." Then, louder, to Danny. "So? Do other things ever show up?"

"I'll show you the feeds," Danny said.

"That's not a no."

Danny neither confirmed nor denied.

"Huh," Anja said. It was a lot to unpack. "Wait, so the rocks don't disintegrate when the trees do?"

"Don't seem to."

"Hmm," Anja said. She had no idea why this would all be, but she'd leave the ancillary questions for some other researcher. She needed to stay focused on the more pressing issue of helping Danny's team.

"Does he have the dates?" she asked. "Josh? Does he have the dates that the circle grew?"

"Probably. They'd be in his notebook. I'll see if I can find it for you. But I can tell you that it seems to be happening at a faster and faster rate, and each new ring is bigger than the last."

Of course it is.

"Well," Anja said. "I think the compass might be responding to that rock."

Danny hesitated, his eyes narrowing, his stance subtly shifting, preparing for action. But all he said was, "Okay."

Anja stared back at him. It would be easy to confirm whether she was right about the rock. All she had to do was walk into the circle and get it.

She took one step closer to the center, still several feet from where the reddish dirt met black and marked the edge of the clearing. Something within her felt that she shouldn't step any closer.

But without any indication of danger from her dosimeter or Geiger counter to corroborate the feeling, she felt she had no choice but to do her scientific duty.

She took another step, crunching dirt beneath her boot.

"Anja," Danny warned.

But then something beeped.

Danny checked something on his utility belt. Then he pulled his walkie-talkie from his belt and turned tail, heading back down the path toward the Explorer. Anja couldn't hear what was being said on the walkie. It sounded like mostly static. But Danny stopped suddenly, turned back, and raced past the power station and the first lamp, into the woods.

Anja stepped up to the clearing's demarcation line. This was her chance to get answers. She took a deep breath and blew it out, trying to calm her nerves. But she couldn't deny that her body was abuzz.

It was telling her something. But what? That she was nervous?

That had to be it. Nothing more.

But the hairs on her arms rose like there was something in her surroundings, shifting past her.

She looked at Ming, wondering if she, too, was feeling something strange. But Anja couldn't bring herself to ask. Instead, she took a close assessment of her assistant. Ming's silky black hair seemed fuller, almost staticky. Was it full of humidity or standing on end? Was that a raindrop on her forehead, or was she sweating from sudden fear?

Anja focused inward, checking in with herself, not knowing what she was looking for but feeling like she was treading way too closely to Yuri's silly territory.

But she needn't have worried. She didn't find anything troublesome inside herself. No strange feelings, no urge to leave. She felt a jittering in her stomach. She could interpret it as fear if she wanted to, but it felt better just to call it what it was.

Excitement.

CHAPTER 21

Anja stood on the clearing's demarcation line, where reddish dirt met black, halfway between the three o'clock mark and where Danny had set up the power station and the first lamp at the four o'clock mark. Everyone was afraid of it. Jackson, Danny, Yuri. Sure, yes, something had happened to Danny's team. But whatever it was, it wasn't happening now. It couldn't be happening now. She was fine. Ming was fine. The clearing was just a clearing.

She lifted her foot.

"Don't go in there!"

Behind her, through the woods, Yuri and Danny were racing back to the clearing. Yuri had probably received the same camouflaged rain gear she had, but he wasn't wearing it. He had on his jeans and his blue-and-purple tie-dyed hoodie.

Anja had thought Danny was fast, but Yuri was young. He easily raced ahead of the seasoned soldier, waving his arms.

"Anja, don't go in there," Yuri said as he stumbled over ferns and roots.

Anja stared at him, waiting for him to say why she shouldn't. But she wasn't about to ask him. She wasn't about to encourage his superstitious ideas.

And she didn't trust her voice, her words.

Her heart was pounding.

She could see it in Yuri's eyes. Whatever the reason he didn't want her going into the clearing, he believed it.

He wasn't looking at her. He was looking beyond her. He might even be seeing it now. No way was she going to peer into the clearing for what he saw, though, no way. There was nothing to see. Not for her, anyway.

She stared at Yuri, eyes to eyes, and stomped her raised boot onto the black dirt.

And nothing happened.

See? Nothing unscientific here.

But then she felt something brush across her skin. Like a chill wind rushing past her. And she shivered. Because there was no wind. There wasn't even a light breeze. The foliage beyond the clearing wasn't moving. She had no idea what had caused her to shiver.

Or why she was still doing so.

Oh no. What had she done?

She checked her handheld devices. Still no radiation that was cause for concern. But the numbers were increasing slightly. And the compass was bouncing. Becoming less and less certain about which way was north.

As a scientist, no immediate explanation for these readings came to mind.

She once again thought about shifting perspective to that of a ghost hunter—but no. Not even. Just because she felt weird did not mean anything paranormal was going on here. It just meant that she'd been momentarily reckless with science and the scientific method. Like Marie Curie and the guy who discovered X-rays. And the guy who ruined wheat. And the people who thought that adding fish DNA to tomatoes was a good idea. And let's not forget her own personal favorite: the guy whose family decimated the dinoflagellate population in the Puget Sound over the course of a few summers, which prevented her from ever seeing her hometown's living light for herself.

But the advancement in science was worth it.

And a lot of those people had received Nobels.

Good company to be in, all around, let's be honest.

"Get out of there," Yuri yelled. He reached the edge of the woods and rounded the clearing, coming toward her.

But he was too far away and she was already inside.

"I just want to check the rock," she said.

She forced herself to keep walking toward the center. She had about twenty-five yards to go, about a quarter of a football field.

On her left, an extension cord stretched from the power station to the second lamp, parallel to her path. If it could manage, so could she.

But the closer she got to the center, the more her body buzzed with energy.

"No, get out of there. He's right behind—"

Anja stiffened.

But she couldn't say it was in response to Yuri's words.

She felt it on her shoulders. A weight. Then a pressure on her left temple, like a headache. Except that instead of pulsing from the inside out, it pressed into her skull. Her head tilted to the right. It was too much effort to hold it up straight, too much pressure, too much resistance pushing on the left side.

"Come out of there," Danny yelled.

Anja blinked, clearing her vision, bringing her out of her aching head and shoulders and back into the clearing.

Danny was sending Ming and Yuri back to the SUV at a run. Yuri was looking back at her as he moved, but he no longer looked scared for her. Now he just looked sorry.

"Anja, get out of there," Danny begged, his arms waving frantically. He was beckoning for her to come with them—and backing away as he did so.

He was not going to come inside the clearing to get her.

And something about that realization frightened Anja to her core.

She did what he said.

She ran for her life.

She ran as fast as she could. But her head still felt tilted, her balance was off.

She tripped over the extension cord.

She stumbled but managed to stay upright, stay on her feet. She kept running.

But the jerk of her foot getting caught on the cord pulled the power station into the circle.

The air crackled with electricity, sparking against her skin, and then—

BOOM.

"Ahh!" she cried as she ran.

She'd felt it more than she'd heard it, like an ultrasonic boom. She ran to the edge of the clearing, eyes on the edge of the woods and the start of the path back to the SUV, twenty feet, fifteen feet away. Danny was bouncing on the balls of his feet and waving her home, like her old softball coach.

She reached him and kept going, racing to catch up with Yuri and Ming. Danny fell in step at her side, one hand at her back, pushing her to go faster.

CHAPTER 22

Danny parked the Explorer off to the side of the log welcoming center, about twenty yards away. No one had said a thing as he'd sped along the potholed ground, away from Big Beauty, to the main road, and then tore into the old campground.

As Anja climbed out of the vehicle, on still shaky legs that threatened to collapse beneath her, Danny asked her if she'd gotten everything she needed.

"Hardly," she said, shutting her door and leaning against the SUV's back fender. The sun was rising, but the light beneath the canopy stayed dim. Ming and Yuri joined her and Danny in front of the vehicle's back hatch.

"There's something magnetic there," Anja continued. "The painted rock, probably." Although, given that the compass needle wasn't as active near the ground, parallel to the rock, as it had been at chest level, that theory wasn't as solid in her mind as she was making it out to be. "But I wasn't able to confirm, because . . ." She sighed heavily and her eyes rolled from Danny to Yuri. "I told you he'd just be a distraction."

"What scared you, Yuri?" Danny asked.

Yuri looked like he was about to answer with something specific and indeed scary. Anja glared at him, daring him to. And he must've felt it, because he made eye contact with her. She stared back pointedly. She couldn't help it. She knew her expression made clear that there was only one acceptable answer.

Yuri looked away and hung his head and gave it. "Nothing," he said.

But his gaze almost immediately popped back up and found Anja. Not a glare. Nothing so negative. Anja was pretty sure the kid was incapable of judging harshly. She stood there, leaning her weight against the car, staring back at him, her arms crossed. And yet the look in his eyes as he watched her was one of fascination. Like she was doing something impossible and he didn't want to miss a beat.

Danny narrowed his eyes, pursed his lips, like he didn't believe the kid, didn't believe that nothing had scared him. But he didn't press the issue. He clicked his key fob, locking the SUV with a honk, making Anja jump, and headed toward the welcoming center.

Anja, Ming, and Yuri followed, and Anja noticed that Yuri was hovering just beyond arm's reach, watching her closely.

But not just her. It was as if he was also watching the air, the space, just around her.

She stopped walking, halfway between the SUV and the log building, and crossed her arms. "What?" she asked him.

"You okay—you *feel* okay?"

The way he asked her. Such empathy. It was disarming. She uncrossed her arms and let them rest at her sides, taking the question seriously.

She felt heaviness throughout her shoulders, pressure on the left side of her head, blurry eyes, and sort of a queasiness in her stomach. Though that was probably just nerves because this was all new to her and she wasn't sure what was going on.

Whatever had or hadn't happened back at the clearing, she couldn't say she didn't feel it, feel something. She'd felt it upon entering the clearing, and now that feeling had followed her home.

Still.

"I feel fine, Yuri. Why wouldn't I?"

Danny and Ming turned back to join them. Danny looked at her with a studied eye.

"The boom?" Ming asked, and Anja shot her a betrayed glance.

"You guys felt that?" Yuri asked.

Anja frowned, noting that he said *felt*, not *heard*.

Danny and Ming nodded.

"What was it?" Yuri asked, and Anja snorted a laugh. Because wasn't he the one who was supposed to have all the answers?

But maybe that was unfair. He and Ming had been running back to the SUV, and were probably at least halfway there, when the boom happened.

For a while everyone just looked at each other. But Anja felt the other three were mostly looking at her. And she didn't want to say anything. She knew what events had taken place in the clearing, but she didn't know how those events could have caused the result.

Danny said, "I don't know what caused the boom, but I can tell you it happened when she tripped on the extension cord and pulled the power station into the circle."

Yuri flushed and took a step back. "She what?"

"Oh, quit being so melodramatic," Anja said. "A power station isn't going to cause any . . . problems just because it shifts a few feet."

"Halloween was two days ago," Yuri said. "People think the veils between worlds—"

"The *what*?" Anja said. She blinked and shook her head. "What are you even talking about?"

"I'm talking about the ability of the physical to connect with the nonphysical," Yuri said. "Some traditions—or sure, myths, fairytales—"

Anja snorted.

"—they call it the veil. People think it's thinnest on Halloween. But Halloween isn't as old as astrology."

"Omigod," Anja said, rubbing her forehead and turning away from their little circle of stupidity.

"No, keep going, Yuri," Danny said behind her. "Keep talking."

"Scorpio is the sign that governs the realm of the dead and the underworld and that kind of thing," Yuri said, his tone earnest. "And Scorpio is considered a span of time when the veil is thinnest.

Scorpio runs from about October twenty-second through November twenty-second. Halloween fits in there nicely, and the veil *is* thin at Halloween. But the thinness of the veil isn't consistent. It starts to thin at the beginning of Scorpio and gets thinner until the middle, when it starts to close again, or at least become more thick, more opaque, toward the end of November."

"So you're saying the veil is thinnest sometime on November sixth?" Ming asked.

Anja couldn't help the look of disbelief she shot at her assistant.

Ming shrugged back at her. "What? You're not talking, and someone's gotta listen." Then, to Yuri, "Is that what you're saying? That the veil's getting thinner over the next four days?"

"That is what I'm saying."

"Okay, but what does that mean for us?" Danny asked. "What can we do?"

"Well, even if not at its thinnest, the veil is still thin, and we've just agitated it with an electrical source."

"So what?" Anja said, turning back around to face them. "Are you saying we let ghosts through?"

"Ghosts were already through," Yuri snapped at her. "What's the language of the brain?"

"What do you mean?" Danny asked.

"She knows," Yuri said, nodding at Anja. "What's the language of the brain?"

Anja felt tingles rise up her arms—and not the good kind, like when she'd made a breakthrough. This was the disturbing kind. Same rise of skin, but different electrical impulses running up and down her arms.

Similar to the language of the brain.

"Voltage," she said.

The force that pushes electricity from one point to another.

"Right," Yuri said. "I know scientists think we're all a bunch of robotic meatbags, that thought is just a process in the brain, and that when the brain dies so do all the thoughts and feelings and whatever else. But just for the sake of argument, what if that's not true? What's the language of the soul?"

Anja kept her eyes on Yuri, refusing to answer. But she felt the eyes of Ming and Danny on her, studying her, waiting for her.

But she didn't have to answer for them to know the truth. If there were souls, then their language, too, was—

"Voltage," Ming said.

"Right," Yuri said. "And what might pushing an electrical source into a disembodied soul's electromagnetic field do?"

Anja chewed the fleshy knob at the inside corner of her mouth.

"Well," Danny said, "we know it creates a spark and an ultrasonic boom."

"Then it could act as a catalyst to brain waves," Ming said. "Not unlike a defibrillator to the heart . . . which has neurons."

"Bingo," Yuri said.

The four of them sat with that for a while, and Anja could sense Danny and Ming siding with Yuri.

But then Danny shifted his weight and made a face that Anja found encouraging.

"So these ghosts," he said, "you said they'd already come through . . ."

Yuri nodded. "But they were lost then. Wanderers. Like drunks meandering the street. Unfocused, unaware. They're not so unaware anymore."

"Why didn't you say anything about them before?" Danny asked.

"Because I knew that's not what you were looking for, and that you didn't want to talk about them. And because I don't know of any ghosts who can do what was done to Josh and his team. Take advantage of the situation, sure, but not create the situation themselves. And there are lots of ghosts. To not see ghosts would be weird. They're everywhere."

"Here?" Danny asked, waving at the welcoming center and their sleeping conexes set up around it in the old campground.

Yuri glanced at Anja, then focused more neutrally on Danny.

"Not really. Not with the clearing so close. They're drawn to borders, liminal places. Places where land meets water, or mountaintop meets sky. Where woods meet a clearing. Those are hotspots for ghosts. So they wouldn't hang around here when the clearing's just over there. Seeing them roaming around anywhere doesn't raise any alarms. But . . ."

Yuri's gaze slowly shifted back to Anja. Make that *around* Anja. His gaze studied the air just outside the lines of her body.

She shifted her weight. "What? Just say it."

"But there is a ghost clinging to you," he told her. "And it wasn't there when I met you last night."

Anja shivered. She didn't want to know and wasn't going to ask what he claimed to see in her, or on her, or around her, or whatever the hell—it was all nonsense.

But that knowing didn't keep Yuri's earnestly shared belief from unsettling her to her very core.

Ming seemed to sense Anja's fear, and share it, too, because she gave Anja a hug—a quick one, Anja noted—and let the subject drop.

But Danny didn't.

"Well, for the sake of argument," he said with a laugh that didn't quite hide that he was completely serious, "is there anything we can do to protect ourselves from ghosts?"

"Omigod," Anja said, turning on her heel and heading for the welcoming center and away from this conversation. She had to think about what to do next.

Danny called after her. "Well, just to be on the safe side, why don't we all go see if Doc is here."

"Why? So she can check me for ghosts?" Anja said.

Danny didn't say anything, but he, Yuri, and Ming were all staring at her.

"I'm fine," Anja said.

But she let them take her to the back side of the building.

CHAPTER 23

Anja and the other three were walking around the back corner, on the left side of the log building, when Anja heard a speeding car.

Doc, in her black Honda, sped around the building's right side and slammed to a stop in front of the door to sick bay.

Danny ran to meet her as she got out of her car. Anja, Ming, and Yuri were right on his heels.

"What happened?" Doc said. She opened up the back seat, pulled out the gurgling baby, and quickly wrapped it up against her chest. "Are they okay now? Why aren't you with them?"

"What are you talking about?" Danny said.

"The team." She pushed past him toward the back door. "I have a pager that beeps me if there's any noise in sick bay. The boys are moving. They are *moving*."

"They're awake?" Yuri said.

Doc wrenched open the door. The sounds of groans and cot squeaks carried outside. Yuri and Danny filed into sick bay after Doc, but Anja grabbed Ming's arm and held her back.

"Why didn't Yuri know they were moving and awake?" Anja asked Ming. "We've been standing over there the whole time. Yesterday"—had it only been last night?—"he was jumping out of the Explorer and pounding on the wall as soon as he got here. So, why no sixth sense about his brother now?"

Ming considered for a moment, glancing inside sick bay and then back at Anja. "He only said he was alive yesterday. He didn't say anything about any of them being in a coma. Maybe he only has a sense of aliveness."

Anja shook her head. "I think he's a fake. I think he came up the road—who hikes through the woods when there's a road?—found the building, found the team, and so he knew they were awake."

"But wouldn't he then have also known they were in a coma?"

When Anja didn't respond, Ming shrugged and headed into sick bay. Anja trudged after her.

Inside, the team was moaning and shifting on their cots. All of them.

In addition to the four cots set up against the right and back walls, three more cots were now set up in the middle of the room, holding the men who had been laid out on the floor. Danny must've spent part of the night making sure they were comfortable instead of sleeping himself.

The metal creaked under their shifting weight. Anja would have thought they were having seizures, but the man lying nearest her, on her right, was gasping and moaning, his closed eyes squinting, his head jerking, like he was having some kind of nightmare.

Across the room, near the kitchenette, Doc stood hunched over one of the men laid out against the back wall, the one making the biggest movements with his limbs. She wrestled with one of his legs as his other leg kicked at the wall.

"Come on Tyrese," Doc pleaded. "Just let me . . ."

Danny grabbed Tyrese's kicking leg and held it still for her. She secured a strap around his ankle with a click and let go. The strap had some slack in it. She ratcheted it down until Tyrese's knee could still bend and flex wildly, but his foot stayed more or less in place. Danny helped her with Tyrese's other leg, and they left his less active arms free.

Doc stood up and put her hands on her lumbar like she was stretching her back.

"What happened?" she asked.

"Tough to say," Danny said.

"No, it isn't," Yuri said, sounding defeated as he struggled with Josh's limbs.

Josh wasn't kicking as wildly as most everyone else, but as Yuri tried to hold his legs down, Josh got one free and kicked Yuri in the back. Yuri yelped, then grabbed Josh's kicking leg, pulled both straight, and sat on the inside of Josh's cot, so that his back was against the wall and his own legs draped over his brother's shins. Effective enough.

He blew out a sigh of accomplishment and then pointed at Anja. "She did this."

He sounded more sad than angry.

"Not possible," Anja said. "I just got here. I've never even touched them."

"Science hurts people all the time without touching them."

Anja scoffed. "Whatever."

"And what about quantum entanglement?" the kid continued. "Spooky action at a distance?"

Anja rolled her eyes—if she wasn't careful, they might unscrew entirely and fall out. But everyone always brought up quantum entanglement as if it were the magic bridge between science and new age crap, and she was tired of it.

"You're *right*," she said. "Maybe I *did* do this."

"You might have," he said. "We don't know what we're dealing with, so how can we know how it works?"

"Because we know the general principles. And let me tell you the first one with my apologies to Newton: There is no nonphysical; there is no nonphysical that affects the physical; and there is definitely no nonphysical that jumps over a bunch of giant redwood trees to affect some distant physical."

They stared at her, and she took a breath, calming herself down. Doc and Ming might realize she was talking out her ass, but the two who really mattered, Danny and Yuri, wouldn't know any better. She just had to keep it together. The important thing was that only the physical mattered, physical proof, and they didn't have any.

But she did have an idea about how to get some. And if they would just let her work in peace, she might have it for them soon.

She asked Doc, "How long have they been like this?"

"It takes me about an hour to get here," Doc said.

Anja checked her watch, then caught Ming's eye and shared a grimace.

An hour was about how long ago she'd dragged the power station into the clearing.

"See," Yuri said, pointing at Anja. "That face you just made. You know you did this. You stepped into the circle—"

"After Jackson and I both told you not to," Danny said.

"—and they . . ."

Yuri trailed off, leaving his thought hanging. But he raised his arm and pointed at the wall, to somewhere out past the building, toward the clearing, which made Anja think he wasn't referring to anyone in this room.

Fortunately, Danny and Doc were too busy with the team to ask the kid to finish his thought.

Doc opened one of the kitchenette's drawers and pulled out handfuls of leather and metal.

Straps.

"We need to restrain them," Doc said. She tossed the straps to Danny, who passed them out.

Anja took the guy to her right, grabbing and wrestling with his arms and restraining them with the straps. It turned out to be easier than it looked. Maybe the men were getting tired. An hour was a long time to thrash around in bed.

Once the men were all restrained, Doc went to another cabinet. She pulled out a box of something that rattled softly and a large multi-dose glass jar of some kind of liquid. She set both on a small rolling cart and rolled the cart over to Tyrese. She opened the box and pulled out a syringe.

"This should give them some peace," she said, plunging the needle tip into the top of the jar and siphoning up a dose.

Anja nodded. Tranquilizers made perfect sense to her.

"Don't," Yuri said. But he seemed to see the futility of arguing. "At least not to Josh. I can't speak for the others, but please, don't do it to Josh."

Doc started to protest, but Danny placed a hand on her arm.

"Why not, Yuri?" he asked. "What aren't you saying?"

"They're . . . they're fighting something," Yuri said. "We don't know what caused this. And just like we didn't know what caused the rift and yet took action against it anyway, to unintended consequences"—he gestured at the team still moving, but less so, in their restraints—"we don't know what consequences might arise from any . . . additives. It could hurt their ability to fight."

Danny considered this and turned to Doc, who answered his silent question.

"Look," Doc said. "Until they tire themselves out, restraints won't keep them from hurting themselves."

She gestured to Tyrese. His legs jerked in their restraints and his left hand sometimes banged the wall. Two cots to the right, Josh swung his arm and hit Yuri, underscoring Doc's point.

She lifted Tyrese's pantleg and swabbed his ankle. "Whatever they're up against, this will shut down unnecessary activity so that they have more resources to fight it, and can do so in more comfort."

"You're assuming the ailment is physical," Yuri said. "What if it's not?"

"What else could it be?" Doc and Anja both said.

Yuri looked like he had something more to say but couldn't see the point in saying it.

When he kept quiet, Doc said, kindly, "Even if it's mental, it's still physical."

Ming stood next to the guy that lay along the log wall, opposite the kitchenette. She held his hand, keeping him from hitting the log wall. Every time his arm swung, she bent her knees and tensed so that he wouldn't knock her off balance. "And if they aren't tranqued," she said, "we'll probably spend more time in here helping Doc instead of figuring out what's going on in the woods."

"But we don't know why they're acting this way," Yuri said. "So we don't know if the tranquilizers will play well or make things worse."

Anja flashed on her brother, on finding him that day, that final day.

But the memory lasted barely a second. She was practiced at shaking it away.

Doc held up a syringe and squirted out some liquid, then pricked Tyrese's ankle.

"Don't," Yuri said. "We don't want to mask symptoms when we don't yet know the root cause."

Doc said, "Once we get them settled, I'll still need to work on them, take care of them, which will be a lot easier—"

"On you," Yuri said.

"Yes," she said, still holding the syringe, unpressed, in Tyrese's ankle. "There's seven of them. It would be a lot easier on me if they were cooperative."

"I don't know about you," Anja said, "but I side with the expert on the subject. The expert the team brought in to deal with just such issues."

Yuri looked at each of the other people standing in sick bay, quickly passing over Doc, Anja, and Ming, and landing his pleading gaze on Danny.

"If I asked Jackson about this, he'd tell me to do what Doc says," Danny said, and he nodded to Doc. "Do it."

Doc pressed the plunger.

"Please, not Josh," Yuri said. "If you want to use the other guys as guinea pigs, there are obviously more of you than me, and you're gonna do what you want. But please, don't do it to Josh. I'll sit with him. I'll keep him calm. Just, please, don't do Josh."

Doc gave him a sympathetic but unyielding smile as she set the used syringe on her cart and prepared another.

Anja smiled too.

But Danny said to Doc, "Don't do it to Josh. But why not, Yuri? What aren't you saying?"

Yuri sighed with relief, but then he looked forlornly at the other six men lying on cots, and said nothing.

Danny sighed and headed for the door. "I'll be in the other room, on the monitors."

As he passed by Anja, he leaned in and whispered, "You've got some smug on your face."

Anja smiled wider. Psy had been put in its place, and, for a while at least, she wouldn't have to deal with Yuri.

Excellent.

Ming followed Danny out.

"Where are you going?" Anja asked.

"Lie down for a sec."

Anja nodded. That sounded good. But she had something else she needed to do. She smiled a goodbye to Doc. Doc sort of returned it, but then it morphed into a frown.

"Are you okay?" Doc said, approaching Anja. "You look—"

"I'm fine," Anja said, turning to leave. She darted a look at Yuri—*keep your mouth shut*—and followed the others out the door.

She needed a quiet place to think, and then she needed to talk to Danny. If she could find the right equipment by sundown, she might just be able to get a look at what was in the clearing.

CHAPTER 24

Anja, Ming, and Danny left Doc alone while she tended to the team, but Yuri insisted on staying with his brother. He sat on the inside of his brother's cot, between his brother and the interior wall, with his knees resting over his brother's shins. He held his brother's rough hands so that Josh wouldn't jerk them around and hurt himself.

The other members of his brother's team seemed to be responding to the tranquilizers Doc had given them. They were all lying still. And breathing again.

It had been less than two days since the team had been . . . well, it depended on who you asked.

Incapacitated was Doc's word of choice.

Commander Jackson liked *attacked*, and Yuri most definitely agreed with that.

Anja agreed Doc's word was most descriptive while being least presumptuous, and Ming just considered them all *out of it*.

Clearly they were out of it.

Even so, Josh seemed better off. Sure, he was still thrashing, maybe even thrashing more than before.

But the thing Yuri saw around all seven men wasn't thickening over Josh like it was over his teammates.

Not that Yuri could convey that information to anyone around here.

Doc took Tyrese's blood pressure. And frowned.

Yuri wasn't surprised. Science often thinks it knows everything, only to charge ahead and be found out wrong.

He didn't ask Doc what she saw. It would only be symptoms, either of the real cause or of her attempt to dampen other symptoms so that the team would look and behave more like they were quote-unquote supposed to.

Yuri doubted he was seeing the real cause either. But he was pretty sure it was giving more information about the real cause than anything Doc was seeing.

Josh jerked his hand away and Yuri scrambled to get ahold of it again.

"If you change your mind, let me know," Doc said.

But Yuri would never change his mind. He did not want Josh tranqued. He didn't want the others tranqued either. But what was a lowly psychic kid to do among a bunch of arrogant scientists?

Yuri just hoped that tranquing Josh's teammates wouldn't prevent them from fighting, that it wouldn't force them to succumb and die.

While he didn't like Doc's quick usage of chemicals when she didn't know what she was dealing with, Yuri did like Doc.

Maybe it was the baby, the way she kept the baby strapped to her—and in front, no less—despite the obvious inconvenience.

And he liked the way she worked. Methodical, without playing favorites, even though he was here and she could placate him by tending to Josh first and last.

At first he thought Doc just tended to the men in order by location in the room, circular from the door. But now he realized she was triaging. She'd probably triaged them in the first place, when they'd been brought here and placed around the room.

Tyrese, in the worst shape, to Doc's eyes and to Yuri's, was closest to the kitchenette, where Doc's supplies were.

The team's leader, who had the fewest marks on him and had probably been furthest from the attack, was along the log wall, opposite the kitchenette. Juan, his name was. Yuri learned that because Doc talked to them while she was working on them. Juan, Tyrese, Josh, Kumar, Darryl, Steve, and Nick.

They all had what Anja had.

A presence about them that wasn't their own.

Anja's foreign presence was just . . . there. There, but not interfering. Like a shadow.

But the foreign presences around the team were behaving differently.

Yuri could feel their suffocating energies and smell their musky, fear-based focus more than he saw them. Though sometimes he could see them, too.

Dark.

They weren't quite so much shadows as blankets. Damp woolen blankets that had been left to dry out. Like dirty cats.

Yuri hadn't told Danny or Anja yet because it was clear they weren't ready, because they wouldn't believe him, because he couldn't prove it.

But more, he didn't know how to fix it, and they wouldn't know either.

And he wasn't sure he wanted to fix it.

Scary and unsettling as the blanket-things were, they were serving a purpose at the moment.

They were keeping Josh and his teammates alive. Alive, but distant, at bay.

They were keeping their bodies alive, but had shooed away their souls.

But Yuri wasn't so sure about Doc. The room smelled of sick and medicine and antiseptic, but it also smelled of herbs. Despite being a doctor, a scientist, probably not interested in the so-called supernatural, Yuri thought Doc might be able to hear him if he told her what he knew. Hear him and listen, maybe even try to understand, if only because she couldn't deny that clearly something had happened, and they had no other explanation and no other leads.

"Anja's test did this," he said.

Doc was checking all the straps put on by the others, loosening or tightening them as needed. "What?"

"Not the original coma, obviously, but the . . . the seizures."

"How so?"

"When they were out at the rift, they took some equipment. I think Danny thought they were just going to do investigative testing, trying to figure out what was present, what was anomalous. And they did. But that wasn't enough for Anja. I think she provoked the rift."

"You think she attacked the rift, and the rift attacked back?"

Yuri nodded, but otherwise remained silent, letting Doc process the information and gather her thoughts uninterrupted.

"If the rift attacked back, then why aren't you hurt?"

Yuri had been expecting that question. He'd been thinking about it since last night when, with trepidation, with expectation of suffering the same fate as his brother, he'd wandered into the precise coordinates Josh had given him—and nothing happened.

He'd seen the ghosts. He'd sensed something was there, in the circle, something that wasn't normally there, not that it *shouldn't* be there, just that it wasn't normally there, not normally perceivable.

He couldn't see it, but he could feel it, its energy.

But nothing happened. He was fine. And then when he was caught and the perimeter watchers apprehended him, as they called it, when there was noise and a rise of anxious and threatening energy, when there was a commotion and a struggle . . . still, nothing happened.

And then today, Anja attacked the rift, pushed the power station into the circle, he knew she did, and still, nothing happened.

And Yuri thought he knew why.

"There's a cycle," he said. "Not the predictable kind, the development kind. It's more susceptible at times and it's more aggressive at times, and it's probably getting both weaker and stronger, respectively, until . . ."

"Until what?" Doc asked.

Yuri groped for an answer but could only shrug.

Until what? That was the question.

Yuri thought that would be the end of the conversation, that Doc would dismiss him, like everyone else, and continue her work. But she was a keen multitasker, Doc was, and also open-minded.

"What might cause it to cycle?" she asked. "Or what might cause it to jump from one . . . rotation, to continue the cycling metaphor, to another rotation?"

"Why 'jump'?" Yuri asked.

Doc was quiet for so long, he wasn't sure she was going to answer him. She continued to work on Nick, talking to him, but glancing, occasionally, at Yuri, as if deciding.

Finally, she stood and went to the kitchenette, bouncing a little, for the baby.

"Come here," she said. "I want to show you something."

Yuri carefully climbed off of Josh's cot and followed.

"The team wasn't the only attack," Doc said.

"Was it a dog?" Yuri asked. "I did some research, on the bus out here. The news said a couple lost their dog in this location a while back."

Doc nodded. "About nine months ago now. We said the dog was lost."

"Not lost?"

"Not lost," Doc said. "Too damaged to give back. Too anomalous to put down."

She opened a large bottom drawer in the kitchenette. It had been outfitted with a cushion and some monitoring equipment.

Lying inside was a bully mix. Probably a bully-lab. It was white with big, light-brown patches. Thick and somehow still muscular, with that certain kind of lab's cow-like head. Its paws were swimming and its tail wagging. Usually when dogs did that they gave off little whimpers, but this dog was silent.

In the same state as the team.

Except there was no foreign presence surrounding the animal. At least not one that Yuri could sense.

"And the next attack?" Yuri asked.

"Why do you think there's another?"

"Twice is a coincidence. Three times is a pattern. And you can't have a sense for something jumping as opposed to cycling, happening randomly or happening on a schedule, until there's a pattern."

"I heard you're a student," Doc said. "What are you studying in school?"

"Nothing applicable here," Yuri said with a smile. "Just the usual high school stuff. But I like statistics."

Doc nodded. "There was another incident. Two, actually."

"Not animals?"

"Not animals."

"Not team members?"

"Not team members."

"I didn't read about any missing persons reports."

"Not people," Doc said.

"What then?"

Doc smiled, sort of. "The trees," she said. "I'm from around here. That clearing wasn't always a clearing. And it wasn't always that big."

Yuri sat with that a moment. "So the dog was attacked, and then later suddenly trees, what, disappeared?"

"Disintegrated," she said. "And the trees happened first. And they're still happening."

"And it didn't happen at a certain interval apart?"

"I don't know about the trees. And the team found the dog. Must've been February, maybe? It was still pretty rainy."

"Found it in the clearing?"

"Thereabouts. Ask Danny. I'm sure one of the boys logged it."

She shut the drawer and moved on to Kumar.

"It may be cycling through something, but it's not doing it on a predictable schedule. At least not yet," she said.

"So maybe something's triggering it? What might trigger it?"

Doc shrugged. "That is the question," she said. "One you're supposed to help Anja figure out."

CHAPTER 25

Anja spent the afternoon at the conference table in the welcoming center, with Danny and eventually Ming.

Ming sat with Danny at the monitors, watching the feeds, asking him questions about his tech and anything anomalous she saw on the screen.

Which, so far, always turned out to be nothing.

Despite it being the end of a weekend, people seemed to be staying away from the clearing. Danny's aversion methods—his skunk bombs and caterwauls—seemed to do the trick.

After a while, Danny asked Ming to take over the monitoring, and he opened a laptop on the conference table.

Anja was sitting on the other side, so she had no idea what he was looking up. But every now and then his eyebrows would pop up. Whatever he was researching, he seemed fascinated by it.

Danny had set Anja up with her own laptop, but she didn't have much access to anything useful. The team's computer guy, Steve, one of the guys who'd been on the floor that first night in sick bay, had set up firewalls to keep anyone from using certain internet sites. All of them, as far as Anja could tell.

At least at first. She eventually learned that she could read research papers on Google Scholar, but she couldn't check her email or any forums or any site that offered a means of communication.

So far, her online research wasn't getting her anywhere.

Then again, how could it?

Research papers were scholarly science, and what she'd been doing today was decidedly not.

What she was absolutely *not* doing, absolutely not, was wondering if her skin felt a little cooler than usual, but warmer at her neck as if someone with heated breath were whispering in her ear, giving her thoughts that were not her own. Like how she might check for ghosts and make them visible. The thoughts were out there, far-fetched, scientifically speaking.

Should she listen to them?

Should she trust them?

Or should she carry on with her plan to neutralize the charge she'd accidentally emitted at the clearing?

She had a feeling that cat wasn't going back in the bag.

At lunch time, after Danny had returned to the monitors and Ming had taken his laptop, he looked over his shoulder and announced that if he were alone, he'd do it himself, but since Anja and Ming were here, he'd like to keep an eye on the monitors and would one of them go over to the little kitchenette, fill the big pot with water, and set it to boil.

Ming hopped up and said she'd do it. She then rifled through the cupboards and pulled out a bulk-sized bag of elbow noodles.

"Were you thinking pasta?" she asked.

"Little comfort food might do this party some good," Danny said. "Unless you're gluten intolerant, in which case sorry about that. People who do this kind of work tend not to complain about food intolerances."

"I'm good with it," Ming said. "Anja eats cake every chance she gets, so I know she's good with it. And we don't care what Yuri thinks. Right, Anja?"

Anja snorted but didn't deny it. She was too busy coming up with her next plan of action.

She wanted to test whether she could affect conditions enough at the clearing to see what might be going on. What might be present in what, so far, she could only see as air and empty space?

This morning she'd taken air samples to see if she could identify some kind of bioluminescent, airborne, microscopic organism.

But bioluminescence wasn't the only way things could glow.

While Ming was pouring tomato sauce over the noodles, the door opened.

Doc held it wide as Yuri entered.

Interesting.

Had she and Yuri bonded over there, these past few hours?

Well, even if they had, it didn't mean they had bonded over shared opinions about how to deal with the clearing. If anything, they'd probably bonded over stories about Josh and the team.

Either way, Anja wasn't going to worry about it. She'd supported Doc's professional medical opinion to use the tranquilizer. If and when the time came, Anja expected Doc to support Anja's professional scientific opinion about the problem she'd been summoned here to resolve.

The five of them sat down to lunch. Danny turned around in his monitoring chair to sit at the head of the table. Anja stayed where she was, on the interior side of the table, to the left of Danny, and Ming sat next to her. Yuri and Doc sat across from them, with their backs to the front door.

There wasn't anything green, unless you counted the canned green beans dumped into a bowl and nuked in the microwave, now sitting untouched by all but Danny in the center of the table. Nor were there any rolls or French bread. Ming had toasted some regular bread she'd found in the freezer and had put out pats of butter on the table. If she was being honest, Anja might admit the spread was no worse than what she'd make for herself at home. She was more of a takeout girl.

Anja was just biting into her sauce-soaked bread when Doc nudged Yuri. "Tell them," she said.

Yuri sighed like he'd been hoping he wouldn't be put on the spot like this.

"I've got something to share, too," Danny said, and he looked at Yuri. "Do you want me to go first?"

Yuri shrugged and put his head down as he forked a noodle.

"So, here's the thing," Danny said, "I know it's all taboo, and getting more so every day, to give any credence to the supernatural in this country, but other countries are taking it seriously."

"Like who?" Ming asked.

"Brazil, Russia, Portugal, France, China. And by the way, China's been taking it seriously since at least 1980."

That got Anja's attention. "Really?"

Danny nodded. "I'll let you do the math."

And it was exactly the math that had Anja so concerned.

Two years was the general probationary period for a new avenue of consideration in government-funded research.

That two-year period could be extended, but only if you saw results.

To carry on the study of something for over forty years . . .

A large, wealthy country could learn, reverse engineer, and exploit a lot about a subject in that amount of time.

Capturing the Roswell spaceship in 1947 and landing on the moon in 1969 were the most obvious examples that came to most laymen minds. But there were truly scientific examples as well.

Not that she was going to validate what Danny was telling them by saying any of that out loud.

"I see I've got your attention." Danny twisted in his chair toward the wall of monitors and pushed a button on a keyboard.

The screen on the biggest monitor changed to a news article on some website, but only one word of its headline jumped out at Anja:

SUPER PSYCHICS.

"China's super psychics are healing cancer in under three minutes, maturing plants in seconds, pulling dice out of glass jars without taking off the lids. And that's just what they've deigned to make public. Who knows what they're keeping secret."

Danny looked around the table.

Anja did as well.

Doc was smiling like a proud mama bear at Danny.

Yuri's jaw was hanging open as he stared up at the article.

Ming met Anja's eye and shrugged.

"I think they're ready for you," Doc said to Yuri.

Yuri looked at each of them in turn, lingering on Anja and landing on Danny, at the head of the table, who nodded encouragement.

"It's two things, really," Yuri said, like he'd had time to distill it down to its two bare essentials. "One is that there are ghosts over there, at the rift, and, like I said, they were more or less harmless or at least uninterested before." His gaze cut to Anja and then down to his plate. "But the boom got their attention."

"Meaning what?" Anja asked.

"Could mean nothing. Could mean a lot of things."

"Are you sure you're not a scientist?" Ming said with a smile.

"I wouldn't be surprised if there were more ghosts milling about the next time you visit the clearing. You're visiting again, right? Tonight?"

Anja had been hoping that everyone but Ming would stay home. But Danny had already said he'd be going, and now it looked like Yuri would be coming along as well.

"So, the second thing," Yuri said, "is that . . . is that the rift, the thing in the clearing . . ." He looked to Doc as if asking her to finish for him.

Anja couldn't blame him. He probably should've had Doc deliver his entire speech. She would have given it more oomph, more credence, more acceptability.

"Tell 'em," Doc said.

"We think there's a cycle," Yuri said, "to the attacks."

"How so?" Ming asked.

And Danny said, "Josh noticed that. The expansion. The rocks. I didn't know what he was doing at the time. We weren't taking the job as seriously back then, and he was keeping his notes secret, but I saw him sitting on his heels at the edge of the clearing, poking his pen at the plants or the dirt or something, and then writing notes in his journal."

"Where's his journal?" Anja asked. Data. That was something she could work with.

"I don't know," Danny said. "I looked through the office conex, but couldn't find it. Maybe you've seen it? You're sleeping in his bed."

Anja wasn't sure how to feel about that. She looked down at her half-eaten pasta.

Danny said, "Anyway, Josh was doing that same crouched-inspection-of-the-ground thing one morning, and later the clearing blew up and expanded so much no one could argue otherwise, and then he started doing the crouching stuff even more. Or, as much as a person could do in the twelve hours before, well . . ."

"The next attack," Doc said, nodding. "Appearance, dog, expansion—maybe a couple expansions?—and then the team. So far. Did it expand two nights ago?"

Danny shook his head. "I don't know. I was never really out there. I saw Josh doing his crouching thing on the monitors."

"Well," Doc said, "for lack of a better term right now, Yuri and I are calling it a cycle. But if it is a cycle, it's not yet predictable. There's anywhere from hours to months between attacks." She sighed, picked up her fork. "Anyway . . ."

"So we're looking for the trigger," Ming said, and despite her reservations about the conversation's subject matter and conclusions, Anja smiled.

There was a reason Ming was her assistant, and she rarely failed to demonstrate that reason. Ming was sharp, a good listener, and pretty much contributed only when she had something solid . . . or something she thought was funny.

"Any ideas?" Yuri said, and he gave Anja a look she could only describe as faith in the presence of fear.

She felt it disarm her.

But she put her shields back up before she answered.

"I might have a few."

Anja couldn't do anything with a ghost hypothesis, so she would pretend it hadn't been said. But she could do something with a hypothesis about a cycle and its trigger.

But she'd work on that tomorrow. Their cozy conversation had done nothing to change her mind about her plans for tonight's trip to the clearing.

But first she had to get Danny to let her go to the store.

CHAPTER 26

Somewhere in the world a ten-year-old boy sat in the corner of a large room being watched over by a large Russian woman.

They'd just met.

The boy didn't have to stay in the corner, but he liked it there. The warm, crackling fire was there, and so were the plush chairs and couch. He'd never been in a room as big or as extravagant as this one. One wall looked out onto a roaring ocean. Everything was burgundy and gold.

Real gold?

Maybe.

Nor had he ever been in a room so scary.

"You're fine," said the woman, in English.

The boy's English wasn't great, but neither was hers, even though she looked like hers should be. Still, they understood each other.

At first he'd thought that *she* was meant to be the scariest thing in the room.

And how could he not have? She was taller than the man who'd brought him here, and very skinny, almost skeletal. She had a large, hawkish nose and feet to match. They were bare now. From the couch where he lay, he listened to her bare feet stick to the wood as she paced across the wood floor.

"You're fine," she said again.

He nodded, hoping that his agreement might keep her from saying it anymore.

And so it did.

"You can do this," she said.

The boy closed his eyes.

The first time he'd realized that he could do what he was about to do next, he'd been sleeping, had woken in a dream, still dreaming—but not for long. The shock had woken him for real.

But he didn't wake screaming. He woke in awe.

Do it again, he'd thought.

The second time he'd done it was a long time coming, or at least it had felt that way. Even back then, at age four, he could feel the passage of time speeding up. It had probably only been a week or two before he did it again.

He stayed with it longer that time, more real than a dream.

It was dark, but a full moon. He recognized the rice paddies his dad worked in, and his grandparents. They seemed to be going dry. When he woke in the morning, he rushed to tell his dad. His dad had dismissed him.

But not for long. Not after he got home from those same paddies.

His dad soon read in the papers that the government was looking for children, kids like the boy. Special kids. To be sent to a special school.

The boy went. He said he was happy to go, even though he'd miss his mom. She didn't want him to go. But it was an honor to go. For him, for his family. His dad said so.

While there, he learned that he didn't need to be sleeping to be special.

Lying on the plush couch now, in the burgundy and gold room, the fire crackling, the ocean roaring, the woman's bare feet sticking to the floorboards, the boy closed his eyes and exhaled, letting every muscle relax, letting every muscle release . . .

Until it felt like he'd been dropped—

From someplace high.

From a skyscraper or an airplane.

And without a parachute.

He sat with the feeling of falling for as long as he could comfortably remain without air.

And, as his lungs began to draw in air again, he lifted his self.

Lifted it up and out like he was a snake shedding his skin, a snake that weighed no more than a feather, a feather that had been picked up by air . . .

And like the wind would take him anywhere he wanted to go.

"Da, good," said the woman.

The boy heard her, and yet did not hear her. His body heard her. His body translated her words and made them part of his dream.

That meant he wasn't as clear yet as he could be.

Clarity, he thought.

And he was suddenly in the same luxurious burgundy and gold room—but viewing it from the height of standing position, and facing the woman.

His body still lay on the couch.

"Da, very good," she said, her voice less sound now and more a second speaker in his mind. "Now we make see what you can do."

The boy showed her that he could do a lot.

And soon another presence joined them in the room. The man who'd brought the boy here in the first place.

"The rift has been tampered with," he said.

He leaned over the couch and looked down at the boy's body lying on the cushions.

"Anja's found the rift and done something to it. They're messing with it. We need to stop them. Is he ready?" the man asked.

The woman stopped pacing across the floor.

"Mmm," the woman said to the man. But she looked at the boy and then frowned sadly at the boy's body, like she didn't want to risk him.

They had only gotten to know each other over the last couple days. But she had told him that she'd missed out on the opportunity to have children of her own, and that she was taking a liking to him.

They were the same, she'd said, she and him. In the ways that mattered.

In ways that others wouldn't understand but would try to exploit.

He didn't ask what that meant. He could tell from her voice it was bad.

But she couldn't do what he could do. She'd told him so.

And so she couldn't take his place.

"Is like trial run?" she said to the man.

"Call it whatever makes you feel good," he said. "Can he do it?"

"He is born to do it."

"Good," said the man. "Go with him."

CHAPTER 27

At dusk, Danny parked the Explorer in front of Big Beauty, and Anja climbed out. The skunk smelled strong, like it had recently been renewed, and the caterwauls were on. It was already dark under the trees. She turned on her flashlight. This was it. She'd either see something or she wouldn't.

She didn't know which to hope for.

Convincing Danny to go to the store hadn't taken much work at all, because food was running low and he'd gotten a call that part of his equipment order had come in. He'd set one of the new guards up on the monitors, then drove Anja and Ming into Crescent City, about 30 minutes away.

Anja was expecting to find nothing and to have to do some serious MacGyvering to make her test work, but she lucked out thanks to a post-Halloween sale and the delivery item they picked up, an electromagnetometer. What a boon. The rest of her supplies were rudimentary, but she had everything she needed.

Danny lifted the Explorer's back hatch and once again took most of the equipment load. Ming and Yuri carried nothing. Anja carried a pocketful of makeshift excitation filters and the electromagnetometer.

She hadn't let it out of her hands since she'd gotten it.

She climbed over the split-rail fence and headed for the clearing, holding the clicking electromagnetometer out in front of her. Danny had gotten her a nice one. The clicking was part of its standard operating function. It had a visible display that changed from green to red as it picked up anything. But if it found something truly anomalous, it would sound an alarm.

Anja didn't know whether she wanted that to happen or not.

If it didn't sound, she could feel good about being right.

If it did, she'd at least have new data to work with.

She decided she hoped it did sound, because if this experiment didn't work, then Anja didn't know what else to try.

But the image of them traipsing through the woods carrying ghost hunter equipment—at least half of their team looking for such ghosts and one of them claiming to see such ghosts—was a lot for Anja to accept.

But everything can become something else with a shift in interpretation.

To those with a superstitious eye, they were ghost hunters.

To those steadfast with science, they were field expeditioners.

I am a field expeditioner.

Even if she was about to hold her electromagnetometer up to an empty space in the woods that she had been warned held ghosts.

She wouldn't allow Ming to use the electromagnetometer on her earlier, since, you know, supposedly Anja was hosting her own ghost.

But she did get a moment to test herself in private.

The tool had shown her that there was some sort of activity present.

But that could have just been the electronics in the building, or atmospheric electricity due to weather and cloud formation, or telluric current in the ground. Or maybe something about the metal conex.

Ghosts should always be the last acceptable interpretation.

Needless to say, she'd shut the tool down right away.

Anja now crested the rise in the narrow path, and the clearing came into view. The moon was low in the sky, well beneath the redwood treeline, but it was almost full, and its ambient light allowed her to see the clearing. It wasn't glowing violet as it had been that morning. Not even a lumen's worth of glow, as far as Anja could tell.

A part of her hoped that wasn't because of the incident with the power station.

Before she could get to feeling too guilty about that, she held her tool up, toward the edge of the clearing. The electromagnetometer's display showed three bars out of twenty.

Same as it had shown back at Big Beauty.

She walked a little closer, maybe forty yards from the edge, and the display pulsed a fourth bar.

Curious, but she didn't tell the others.

A little closer, maybe thirty yards away from the clearing, and the display settled on four bars and started to pulse a fifth.

"You see any ghosts?" Danny asked.

Anja glanced back at him and was about to say no and explain the display's reading, when she saw that Yuri had stopped several paces behind everyone else. He was nodding. And he had everyone's attention. Including Danny's.

"How many?" Danny asked him.

"Dozens."

"Dozens," Ming repeated, deadpan.

"And more arriving."

"What?" Danny said. "Where are they coming from? How are they getting here?"

Yuri bit his lip and shook his head. "There's too many to see."

"Maybe we should reconsider this," Danny said.

"It's just a little fog and spotlight," Anja said. "I think it'll be okay."

"I think we should leave," Yuri said. "Some of them are . . ."

Yuri took another step back.

"What?" Danny asked.

"Interested."

And that was about enough for Anja. "Look, guys, we're not

going in. In fact, we're taking a step back. I'm hoping this will help us—all of us—get a look at what we're dealing with."

She motioned for Danny's pack. He set it down. Anja unzipped the top and pulled out her fluorescence tools, then walked closer to the clearing.

"Come on, Ming."

When she and Ming were still ten yards away, Danny said, "That's close enough."

Anja wondered if Danny's statement was made at Yuri's behest. But she agreed that she was close enough to conduct the test, and nervous herself, so she didn't press the issue.

Anja and Ming set up their equipment: a fog machine and another big lamp, even though the first two lamps from that morning were still set up around the clearing. She then went to the lamp at the four-o'clock point on the clearing's edge, took a deep breath, and pulled on the extension cord, removing the power station from the clearing. It came without incident, and Anja released the breath. She hooked the power station up to her new equipment.

When she was done setting up, Anja exaggerated putting her finger on the equipment's ON switch. "Five. Four."

Ming hustled backward to stand with Yuri and Danny, at Danny's favorite protective redwood tree, and the three of them started whispering.

Whatever.

Anja counted louder.

"Three. Two." She flipped the switch.

Ultraviolet light and fog flooded the clearing. The smoke from the fog machine got caught up in a current, revealing movement in the air. A counterclockwise rotation in the shape of a giant triangle, rising high into the sky. It was bigger than anything Anja could have expected.

Much bigger.

The triangle's corners breached the edges of the clearing,

stretching far into the woods on either side and descending deep within the earth beneath it as it rotated.

She could see it. She didn't even need to use her makeshift filter. She could finally see the rift.

She'd heard Yuri use that term, the *rift*. And now she could see why.

The center of the rotating triangle was like a hole in the atmosphere, tattered and torn at the edge.

Behind her, Danny muttered, "Holy shit. Do you always see things like this?"

If Yuri answered, Anja didn't hear it.

Ming said, "You okay up there, boss?"

The triangle was . . . well . . . not stationary, but it wasn't trying to get her.

She nodded.

With a shaky hand, Anja reached into her coat pocket and pulled out a makeshift excitation filter, a piece of glass she'd colored herself with black and blue markers and colored plastic wrap. She's created a few different filters with different combinations of marker and plastic wrap, not knowing which combination might work best.

They probably wouldn't work at all. But they were meant to block the ultraviolet light of her lamps from entering her eyes so that she could see the fluorescent light being excited by the ultraviolet light, in the clearing. If any. Heavy on the if any.

She brought the filter up to her line of sight.

CHAPTER 28

"Wow," Anja said.

But that was an understatement. Her makeshift filter worked. As Anja peered through the filter, she could see in the clearing something not unlike a subdued rave.

Florescence.

Everywhere.

Greens and oranges and pinks and blues and more. Every color of the rainbow and maybe even colors on either side of the spectrum, infrared and ultraviolet. They all shined back at her through the filter.

But they didn't just shine.

They had shape.

Human shape.

And they moved.

Anja still wasn't willing to say ghosts, but she was definitely seeing something people-shaped milling about the clearing, as if coasting on some drug's chill high, grooving under a blacklight.

Maybe someone had put something in her macaroni.

Still, Anja put the electromagnetometer under her arm and, from another pocket, pulled a notebook she'd found and started her first night here.

She wrote down every detail she was seeing. And she looked for anything, anything at all, that could tell her, in physical terms and principles, what was causing this rift. These shapes. What she was seeing.

She wanted to conclude that the rift was just an eddy—two wind currents at variance, causing a swirl, like a giant cyclone tipped on its side—and she could have, if the swirl's shape were circular.

But the rift was triangular. How? How was this possible?

And how could she explain all that fluorescence, those vaguely human shapes, like a crowd of people, standing in front of the triangle? And moving—swaying—like an unfocused mirage.

A mirage.

Anja smiled. Finally, something she could explain. Temperature-gradient air creates mirages. It was cold out, but the floodlight was warming the air closest to it, making the light curve toward the cooler air, causing a shimmer.

She noted this in her notebook.

She also noted that it looked like Yuri had been wrong: turning on the equipment hadn't bothered the rift.

But *could* it be bothered?

Hoping it could be—it would give her more data—she put her notebook and the electromagnetometer into her jacket pockets and looked around on the ground for something to test her theory.

The scientist in her was nothing if not thorough.

"What do you see?" Danny said, coming up behind her.

Still looking at the ground around her, Anja absently handed him her filter.

He brought it up to his—

"Holy shit," he said. "Holy shit, you guys. You have got to see this. Is *this* what ghosts look like to you all the time?"

Ming got to him first and took the filter. Just peering through it, however, apparently wasn't enough. She moved the filter left to right, up and down, as if looking at each . . .

Anja considered the word *specimen*. Yeah, she could work with specimen.

Ming moved it around as if looking at each specimen before calling it incredible.

Yuri held out a hand for a filter, but Ming wasn't giving it up. "You made extras of these, right?" she said.

Anja reached into her pocket and handed Yuri a filter.

"Wow," he said. "No, this is not how ghosts usually look to me."

"No?" Danny said.

"No. They usually just look normal, only more or less diaphanous. Some are more solid than others. Some are barely visible. This," he said. "This is incredible. What's making them do this?"

"Some invisible material in the clearing is absorbing the ultraviolet light and immediately emitting a lower-energy color," Anja said. "The filter helps block the ultraviolet light."

"Isn't ultraviolet light invisible?"

"Yeah, as a color, but it's still light, and even though we can't see it directly, it overwhelms the fainter fluorescent glow without the filter."

Yuri handed the filter back to Danny.

Danny elbowed Anja in the ribs and grinned, then held the filter out half an arm's length away so they could both peer through it together.

The fluorescent human shapes were still there.

"Ghosts," Danny said. "What do you think of that? Proof."

"Proof?" Anja said, finally spotting a softball-sized rock. She stooped to the ground and picked it up.

Anja's throwing arm was non-existent. So, with her rock in one hand and her notebook in the other, she stepped closer to the rift and the shimmering mirage.

"What are you doing?" Yuri asked.

"Just stay there."

Anja pulled her last filter from her pocket. She held it up to view, took a few more steps toward the clearing, and brought her throwing arm over her shoulder.

"No!" Yuri cried.

Too late.

The rock sailed through the specimens and smashed into the rift.

Anja wasn't sure if it went *through* the rift or *into* the rift. But either way.

The rift reacted.

Fluorescence poured from the tear. What hadn't been visible in the triangle's tattered center was suddenly as bright as a Hunter's supermoon in October. And she didn't need the filter to see it.

It was breathtaking.

Anja patted her pocket for her notebook. She had to get this all down.

In her other pocket, her electromagnetometer started to beep. But Anja barely noticed. The sight before her, all that light, all that luminescence, that fluorescence. It held her captive. She scribbled down what she saw.

"Anja!"

She heard pounding footsteps retreating into the distance, but it was Danny who'd hissed at her. And Anja realized that he'd called her from somewhere behind her.

Way behind her.

She turned around, still momentarily confused by the beeping and dazed by the awe and splendor and wonder of what she was witnessing for the very first time, for probably anyone's very first time.

A rift.

A tear in the veil.

Danny, near his protective redwood tree, bouncing and ready to flee, had fear written all over his face as he pointed behind her, back toward the rift.

"Look out! LOOK OUT!"

She whipped back around to face the clearing, bringing up her filter to see. And what happened, it happened so quickly, and yet she saw it all so clearly.

The human shapes had been haphazard before, as if looking at nothing in particular, as if bored as they mingled in front of the rift.

But they were focused now. The whole shimmering mirage. They were all focusing their attention on one thing, the same thing, and Anja could feel it. They were focused on her.

The started ambling toward her.

And one darted for her.

The electromagnetometer's beeping doubled in speed.

"Get to the car!" Danny yelled.

For once, Anja didn't argue. She stepped backward, one foot, then the other foot.

"Anja, come on! Get the hell outa there!"

But she had to see.

The hazy, humanoid shapes were gaining on her. But one of them was brighter and closer—and faster—than the rest.

The shape was distinctively female, if far taller than average, with short, curly hair. Slender but with what some might call birthing hips. And when Anja looked at where the specimen-woman's eyes should be—

Eyes, indeed, she saw.

"Anja, what are you doing?! She's right there! Run, run!"

And the mandate finally sunk in.

Anja turned and bolted for the narrow path through the redwoods back to the Explorer, following the blinks of light that were the team's flashlights and headlamps.

The moon filtered through the trees, and the dim light helped her leap over occasional roots and shrubs. She ran. And she didn't dare look behind her.

All she could see of Ming and Yuri were their flashlights, and sometimes not even that. But she could see the back of Danny.

"How close?!" she yelled. "Danny! How close?!"

Ahead of her by maybe thirty feet, Danny slowed enough to turn around yet keep moving. He held up his filter.

"Don't slow down." But he slowed his own pace a little more, allowing her to catch up while he watched her back. "Keep coming, keep coming."

She didn't know if that meant he did still see something behind her or he didn't but didn't want to take any chances.

She kept running, tried to run faster. But her heavy rain gear, her heavy boots . . .

She wasn't fast enough.

The beeping became one solid buzz as a cold, burning sensation scraped down Anja's arm, from her shoulder to her fingers.

She dropped her notebook.

Instinct made her stop for it.

She turned and was challenged by brightness, by light and silver.

By a human face.

Anja gasped. She put her head down to block the bright. She found her notebook at her feet, grabbed it, and kept running.

Danny let her run on past him before continuing his own run, right on her heels.

The SUV's left-side doors were open, and the vehicle was running. As soon as her butt touched the back seat, Danny had them moving, bumping along on the decommissioned road back through the woods.

Anja pulled her legs in and slammed the door.

She turned in her seat to look out the back.

Through the trees, and using her filter, she could just make out the haze of human-like shapes loitering at the edge of the clearing, like they couldn't come any closer.

And the one bright one was gone from the path.

CHAPTER 29

She'd made it back to the Explorer. Thank goodness. Anja sighed and faced front.

Ming was sitting beside her, staring silently out the window.

"Did they get you?" Danny asked, eyeing her in the rearview mirror as he guided the SUV over the bumpy road.

Anja's shoulder hurt.

She decided she must've twinged it when she started to run away and shifted too quickly over loose dirt.

"I'm fine," she said.

"Did you see that?" Yuri asked from the front seat. "Did you? Tell me you saw it."

Anja noted that Yuri wasn't looking at her or Ming. He sat in profile, looking at Danny. Out the front window, the Explorer's headlight beams illuminated the chopped-up dirt road.

"I saw," Danny said, "I saw a big hazy triangle, circling. And . . ."

"Say it," Yuri said.

"And people," Danny whispered.

"Louder," Yuri said. "Say it louder."

"People," Danny projected. "I saw people."

"Yeah," said Yuri, leaning his head against the headrest.

Then he pulled down the visor and looked in the mirror, into the back seat. "Ming, what about you?"

Anja glanced at her assistant, afraid of what she might say. Ming was leaning against the door, her forehead pressed against the window, her breath fogging up the glass. She didn't answer.

"Exactly," said Yuri.

Anja snorted. "What an astute scientific conclusion."

Yuri twisted in his seat and met Anja's eyes. "You still think this is a purely physical phenomenon?"

His tone wasn't hostile. But Anja wasn't sure she could offer him the same.

She held his gaze, but her whole body trembled. She hoped it was too dark for him to notice.

It had been a long day. And there could have been moisture in the air from earlier rains. Humidity could cause a sighting of the sort she'd just seen. She decided that was all it had been: a trick of the light, humidity and water.

She considered telling Yuri her theory about the temperature gradient air. But it would just encourage conversation. And she didn't want to hear any more.

What they were saying . . . it resonated with her own experience just now in the clearing, but none of it fit her worldview.

She wanted silence.

She needed to think.

"Let's talk about it tomorrow," she said.

Yuri pointed at Anja's shoulder. "Did they get you?"

Anja scowled. "No." Her shoulder hurt, but how did he know that? There wasn't any blood. No tears in her clothes. She rubbed it. "Just twinged it a little, getting my notebook."

Yuri peered at her shoulder, like he saw through her lie.

The Explorer finally reached the end of the choppy road. Danny stopped the SUV perpendicular to the main road, turned on his blinker, and pulled smoothly into the non-existent traffic. The road became much smoother.

But it didn't make the ride any easier.

"So were they?" Danny asked.

"Were they what?" Yuri said.

"Were they people?"

"In part," Yuri said. "Maybe, an aspect of people."

"Like ghosts?" Danny said.

Anja snorted and shook her head.

"Maybe," Yuri said. "But one of them—"

"Curly helmet hair," Danny said. "Brighter than the others."

"You saw her too?" Yuri said.

"Yeah, I saw her," Danny said, sounding like he wished he hadn't. He caught Anja's eyes in the rearview mirror. "She disappeared when you picked up your book."

Anja shifted in her seat, feeling like Danny was taking the long way back to base. She couldn't stand the way her body was humming, vibrating more and more with every word that was said. It was too childish to cover her ears with her hands, but her shoulders hunched, attempting to do the job themselves. She no longer wanted to know anything about the rift. She didn't want to be on the team. Jackson didn't need her, not with Yuri and his asinine theories. If she had to listen to any more . . .

"She seemed familiar," Yuri said. "But did you see the rope she was holding?"

"Rope?" said Danny.

Yuri didn't answer. Rain began pattering on the windshield.

"What do you mean rope?" Danny asked.

"He doesn't," Ming said, and everyone in the vehicle glanced at her. Danny, over his shoulder. Yuri, in the visor's mirror. "He means a silver cord. And she wasn't holding it."

"You saw it?" Yuri asked.

Ming said, "It was coming out of her chest."

Anja stared at her assistant. She, herself, had seen no such thing. And she'd thought Ming hadn't stuck around long enough to see much of anything.

But a flash of silver was dancing across her mind.

Yuri said, "I've heard of other people seeing silver cords, but I'd never seen one before. Your lights made them visible."

A smile spread on Yuri's face, and his gaze cut to Anja.

She looked away, closing her eyes against the image, hoping that the picture in her mind of a bright flash of silver, of a human face, was just that—an image forming from their suggestions, and not a memory.

"What does it mean?" Danny asked.

Yuri faced front. "I don't know yet. I want to experiment with something first."

Experiment? How dare the charlatan use such words to describe what he does. If Anja had to listen to any more . . .

"What experiment?" Danny asked.

Yuri glanced at Anja, then said, "I'll tell you later."

"What was she?" Danny asked. "The brighter one. Any idea?"

"I'll tell you later," Yuri said, and he jerked his head toward Anja, as if reminding Danny of the scientist's skeptic presence.

"You think it's ghosts?"

"I'll *tell* you later."

"Worse than ghosts?"

"What's worse than ghosts?"

"Disembodied humans?"

Anja grabbed the backs of both their seats and shook them, screaming, "There's no such thing!"

She closed her eyes and sat back and laced her fingers behind her head and squeezed her forearms against her ears and rocked softly. *There's no such thing, there's no such thing, there's no such thing . . .*

CHAPTER 30

Back at the log building, after shifting the SUV into park but before anyone had taken off their seat belts, Danny turned to Yuri, in the front seat, and said, "You were saying something this morning about ghost protections."

"Omigod." Anja flung off her seatbelt and hopped out of the vehicle before anyone could utter another ridiculous word.

Those things at the clearing? They were a mirage. They were a trick of the light. They were rationally explainable. She just needed time to come up with the explanation.

She was suddenly happy that Ming had complained to Danny earlier about her snoring and had gotten her own conex—and that she wasn't trying to catch up to Anja now. Anja needed a moment to herself.

She marched straight to her eight-foot by twenty-foot metal conex without looking or speaking to anyone.

Anja checked her watch. She couldn't believe it was still only November 2. It was 6:32 p.m. A little too early for bed. Ming and Danny would probably start cutting up the stir-fry ingredients they'd bought for dinner when they were in Crescent City. Anja lay down on her cot anyway, grabbing her journal out of her raincoat pocket, even though she knew she was too exhausted to start writing any more notes for the day.

She flipped onto her side, shoving her journal under her pillow to give it more height, and let herself relax. If she dozed off, great. If not, at least she was getting some alone time.

A two-shelf bookshelf stood on the opposite wall, next to the door. It was mostly used in place of a dresser, filled with one of Danny's team members' folded clothes, but there were a couple of books. She was gazing at them through her heavily drooping eyelids, wondering if she should fight the exhaustion and get up and check to see if any of the books were Josh's journal, when she thought she saw something.

Someone was in the room. Someone tiny with shiny, straight black hair styled in a bowl cut. They were crouched in a flat-footed squat to the left side of the bookcase, their back to Anja. The person's tiny right hand reached out further and further to the side as it ran a small finger over the spine of each book, like they were reading the titles.

Anja blinked and reared back, pulling her pillow in front of her. "What are you doing here?"

The person looked back at her and stood—and surprised Anja again. He was just a kid. A kid in a cream-colored tunic and flowy pajama pants, with little black slippers on his feet.

In the woods? He was just a little kid. Ten years old, tops. But probably younger.

His eyes went wide and he sucked in a breath. He turned back to the bookshelf, yanked out a spiral notebook, and—

"I don't think so." Suddenly wide awake, Anja sat up on the edge of the cot. She wasn't worried about capturing the kid. He'd have to stop and pull open the door to get out of here, and the door was less than five feet away from her. She stood and grabbed for the kid's shirt.

And felt nothing.

Saw nothing.

The door was still closed.

And there was no one else in the room.

CHAPTER 31

Anja ran out of the conex, around the side of the log welcoming center, and burst through the front door.

"I just saw something," she said.

Ming, watching the monitors, jolted upright in her rolling chair and clutched at her chest.

Danny, standing at the kitchenette counter and cutting up veggies for stir-fry, turned to look at her with more measured movements.

He was wearing the same thing he'd been wearing since the morning Anja had met him. Dirty camo pants and a black T-shirt. But now there was a silver medal around his neck. It hung from what looked like a couple heavy-duty shoelaces tied together and was about the size of a Kennedy fifty-cent piece.

He set down his knife and calmly walked toward the monitors.

"You went out to the clearing?" he asked Anja.

"No. In my room. Snooping around the bookshelf. And when I caught him, he . . . he . . ."

She knew what she'd seen.

But she also knew she would never believe someone else telling her this same tale.

"Did you see anything?" Danny asked Ming, putting a hand on the back of her chair and leaning in for a view of one of the smaller screens.

Ming shook her head. "What did he look like?" she asked, rolling her chair back into place. "How'd he get here?"

Those were very good questions. But Anja still hadn't delivered the most troublesome part of her freak-out.

"I don't know," she said, "but probably the same way he left."

"He's gone?" Danny said, and then his lips worked like he was silently testing out ways to chastise a clearly upset woman for failing to capture and detain a trespasser.

But there was no way she could have.

"Poof," she said.

She had no other way to explain it. That was what the kid had done after all. Maybe even with the sound effects. It had all happened so fast, and she'd been dozing. She'd been groggy.

But no, there was clarity in the memory as well. She knew what she'd seen.

"Poof," she said again with more certainty. "The kid was there, pulling out books by the spine, and then . . ."

"He was gone?"

"Hugged a notebook to his chest and was gone."

"That's not possible," Ming said.

"I would love to agree with you," Anja said.

Danny looked up at the screen that still showed the headline they'd discussed at lunch:

SUPER PSYCHICS.

"He was Asian, I think," Anja said before she could stop herself. "It was fast, and I was more concerned about a stranger being in my room than studying his face for his specific ethnicity, but . . ."

Was she really considering the truth of psychics? Super psychics no less? Super psychic little boys?

"You said a kid, right?" Danny asked. "As in not a man?"

Anja nodded.

"How old?"

"Beats me. Fully functional but nowhere near puberty? How old is that?"

"That's interesting you mention it in terms of puberty," Danny said. "Because from what I read, the Chinese search for kids in particular, because their abilities tend to peak and then fade away at puberty. Not everyone. If what I'm reading is true, then there are definitely kids who grow into adults with all their pre-pubescent powers and then some. But just before puberty seems to be when they're pretty powerful."

In her mind, Anja tried to make the intruder taller, broader; hell, she tried to give him facial hair.

But he'd been so small.

Young.

There was no mistaking it.

And she was having a hard time chalking it all up to coincidence.

"Did you see anyone on the monitor?" Anja asked.

"No," Ming said. "And no one triggered the alarms either."

Anja had forgotten about the alarms. To reach her sleeping conex, the kid would have had to traipse through the woods, past the perimeter patrols and their trip alarms. Come to think of it, the kid would have had to pass through all of Danny's skunk bombs and caterwauls, too. Poor kid must've been terrified.

But he didn't look scared. Not until after she'd said something to him.

And he didn't look like he'd traipsed through the woods, either. His slippers and cream-colored pantlegs were clean. It just didn't make any sense.

The door opened. Doc and Yuri came in and headed for the kitchenette.

"You guys see anyone outside?" Danny asked.

"No," Doc said, opening a cupboard and pulling out a box of crackers. She opened it and took a few and handed the box to Yuri. "Is someone here?"

Anja told them about seeing someone in her conex.

"He was just a kid though," she said. "I'd say maybe he was homeless and just looking for food, but he looked well taken care of, if dressed wrong, and he was looking at the bookshelf. Plus, what kid these days would come out into the woods for food?"

"Maybe he got lost," Yuri said.

"Yeah, but whatever his reason for being here, why didn't he trigger the perimeter alarms?" Danny said. "I know they're working. One of the new guys triggered them a couple hours ago. We saw him do it."

Danny pointed at Ming, who looked back at Anja, Doc, and Yuri and nodded emphatically. "Heard him, too," she said, "cursing on the mics."

"So why isn't the kid on the screens now?" Danny finished.

Anja shifted her weight, knowing the impossible answer but not knowing how to tell them the rest.

CHAPTER 32

For a moment, nobody moved or said anything, just watched the feeds on the monitors. Ming and Danny watched them up close. Yuri and Doc watched them from the kitchenette, frowning as they munched on crackers. Anja stood alone, next to the door, working up the courage to speak.

But then Danny grabbed his raincoat. He asked Ming to keep an eye on things and for someone to finish the stir-fry. Then he pushed past Anja and headed out the front door.

As soon as he left the building, he showed up on one of the monitors. Anja watched him jump from screen to screen, wondering what he was doing. Because, really, what could he do about a long-vanished little boy?

"I'm going with him," she said.

"Me, too," Yuri said.

Doc said she would finish the stir-fry.

Outside, light rain pattered against Anja's hair and raincoat, dampening the smell of skunk. The sounds of caterwauls and things in the brush triggered as she walked past the sensors. She followed Danny's flashlight beam around the right side of the log building. He was headed toward the conexes set up in the half-ring of campground sites.

Yuri caught up to Anja. She didn't rush to stay ahead of him, though. Yuri seemed to want to say something, and for some reason—maybe it was the strangeness of the moment, of the day—she was willing to listen.

"This person you saw, did you see him clearly?"

"What's that supposed to mean?"

"Oh, I don't—I'm not, I'm not, like, questioning your ability to see." He stuffed his hands into the pockets of his blue-and-purple hoodie. "I was wondering if he looked clear. If his body was clear—transparent! That's the word."

"Still not making any sense."

"Like, could you see through him?"

Anja thought back to when she'd grabbed for the boy. He'd seemed just as solid as she was. But as she'd reached out her hand, her flesh and bone hand, the boy's body had suddenly seemed decidedly less solid.

And he'd only gotten less solid from there. Quickly. Instantly. Her hand had gone right through him. And then there was nothing.

But how could she say that? It was impossible.

"He was solid," she said. *Until he wasn't.*

Yuri gave her a questioning look.

"He was solid," she said with more finality.

He nodded, and she picked up speed, moving into a jog to catch up to Danny.

Yuri probably could have kept pace, but he let her pull ahead of him.

When she caught up to Danny, he was crouched in front of her conex, shining his flashlight on the ground.

"I don't see any prints here," Danny said, "not anything that might belong to a kid anyway. How tall was he?"

"Little. Four, maybe four and a half feet. And he wasn't wearing shoes."

"What?"

"He had on some kind of sock-like slippers."

"Well, that would leave something closer to bare feet than shoe tread, I'd think. Unless they had those little nubby things on the bottom that keep you from slipping. Either way, I'm not seeing anything like that. I'd say he maybe climbed a tree and is hiding out until the coast is clear. Or maybe he came in by tree and that's why he didn't trigger any alarms. They're all pointing at the ground, not the canopy. But there's no tree limbs to grab on to here, not from the door."

"Think he climbed onto the roof?" Yuri said, eyeing the side of the building.

Anja thought someone with very strong fingers might be able to climb up the spaced vertical ridges on the conex's exterior side panel, but she sure wouldn't be able to do it.

Danny steadied a foot on the side panel, gripped the ridges with the tips of his fingers, and tried to haul himself up. He got his other foot steadied on the panel before his hands slipped.

"Maybe," he said. "I've got nephews that can scale the inside of a doorway. But those are narrow enough to kind of wedge your way up. Not so here. Climbing this is straight-up strength." He curled and flexed and then rubbed his fingers. "And spidey hands. And the condensation doesn't look like it's been disturbed either." He wiped at the moisture collecting on the side of the building, where his feet had left marks. "Except by me."

Danny pulled out his walkie, turned it to a new station, and pressed the red button. "Hey, Ming, can you check the tops of the buildings, sleeping quarters in particular, for signs of anyone."

"Which monitor looks at the roofs?"

"Six through eight, but you gotta use the joystick."

"Oh, right." Then, "I don't see anything."

"Okay. Thanks." Danny changed the station again and used his walkie to ask the perimeter guys to keep watch for a boy crossing out of the perimeter. Then he put his hands on his hips and sighed.

"What's with the necklace?" Anja asked him.

Danny fingered the silver-dollar-sized charm and looked at Yuri.

Yuri looked back at him without saying anything.

Danny said, “My mom gave it to me.”

Anja raised an eyebrow.

“It’s a St. Christopher medallion.” He lifted it off his chest for her to see. The half-dollar-sized silver circle read *SAINT CHRISTOPHER PROTECT US* around the edge, and the center showed a guy with a walking stick carrying a child on his back.

“St. Christopher protects travelers,” Danny said, “and I travel a lot.”

“How come you’re wearing it on a shoestring?”

“Well, I usually just keep it in my bag, but Yuri said that anything you believe can protect you will protect you. And he mentioned St. Benedict, so I figured St. Christopher would work.”

“Work to what?”

Danny looked at Yuri, who was now staring at the ground and still not saying anything. He settled the medallion back on his chest. “Protect me from ghosts.”

Anja chuckled. It started small and then grew bigger.

“Yeah, yeah, get your laughs in,” Danny said. “Are you sure you saw something?”

Anja stopped laughing and didn’t answer. She couldn’t, not after laughing.

And she couldn’t blame Danny for misunderstanding her earlier. She would have done the same in his position.

She supposed now was her best opportunity to muster her courage and better explain what she’d meant by *poof*.

That the kid had disappeared.

As in *vanished*, not as in *ran*.

But Danny couldn’t do anything with *poof*. There were no actions to take to resolve the problem of someone going *poof*.

And that was assuming he even believed her. Which he probably wouldn’t. She knew *she* wouldn’t. And she didn’t like being questioned like she was a liar.

She was a scientist. She told it like she saw it.

At least, she did the best she could.

"I'm going to bed," she said. "Tomorrow we'll see if we can put together a hypothesis for Jackson."

"You got one?" Danny asked.

"Not yet, but I've got some ideas. I'm gonna go gather my thoughts tonight, and then tomorrow we'll do any final tests."

Yuri sighed and shook his head.

Anja ignored him. He didn't have to come. And come to think of it, if her tests could aggravate his brother and the rest of the team, didn't they need to know that? Didn't they need data in order to figure out what this thing was, what was causing it, what in turn it was causing, and how to stop it all?

Yes, yes they did.

Yuri's brother was already in a coma or something like it when Anja got here, and that was not her fault. Sometimes things got worse before they got better. Yuri was young. He probably hadn't learned that yet. Not her problem. She wasn't going to cater her approach to someone who, while invited to stay, had not been sought out to answer the question of the rift. That was her job. And she was going to do it. She was ready to get out of here.

"You want us to come get you for dinner?" Danny asked.

Anja shook her head no and headed around the side of her conex to the front door.

Yuri followed her.

"What are you doing?" Anja said.

"Going to bed?"

"What about Josh? Not staying with Josh tonight?"

Yuri shrugged. "Doc's here."

"Yeah, but she has medicine. She might give him some." Her teasing tone was harsher, bitchier, than she liked it to be, but she couldn't help it. She didn't understand Yuri. And if today's events were any indication of what understanding him entailed, then she was becoming less and less interested in understanding Yuri.

But he hadn't given up on her, it seemed.

He wasn't going to let her get a rise out of him, either.

"I don't think she will," he said. "You're in Josh's room, right?"

Anja sighed. "Yes, why? Do you want to trade or something?"

He looked like he did, but he shook his head. "No. Danny gave me Tyrese's, next door."

"Fine," Anja said, stepping into her conex.

Yuri said, "If I see any more snooping kids, I'll let you know."

CHAPTER 33

Before she could go to sleep, Anja had to get the day's events out of her mind and into her notebook.

She wasn't using her usual notebook, of course. She'd come to the redwoods with nothing but the proverbial clothes on her back. She'd found this notebook in a box in the welcoming center, in the kitchenette cupboards. Found a decent pen, too.

She now pulled the notebook out from under her pillow and opened it up to the fifth page, dated it, and sighed.

What a day. Had she really only gotten here last night?

In order to get to the logical stuff, she first had to expel the emotional stuff.

She started her journaling with her complaints about Yuri. About having to work with Yuri. About how his so-called abilities were inconsistent and must therefore be fraudulent.

Her pen flowed for page after page, and when it petered out, she turned her focus to today's two visits to the rift.

She couldn't believe she'd tripped on the extension cord and pulled the power station into the clearing.

And the repercussions. The unintended consequences.

The team's reaction. She'd denied the blame. But what if it was her fault after all?

And Yuri had said he could see something around her. She'd denied that, too. But she couldn't lie to herself now and say that she wasn't feeling any differently after this morning, when she'd stepped into the clearing.

It wasn't anything . . . how to describe it in a scientific way? It wasn't anything tangible or physical or exterior to her person, but inside. She felt something inside. Like a calm she didn't deserve under the circumstances.

And then this last visit to the clearing. What she'd seen. Anja closed her eyes, reliving the swirling fog, the fluorescence, the awe, the wonder.

Had what she'd done with the power station affected what she'd been able to see in tonight's visit to the rift?

Had she caused those . . . those specimens to gather around the clearing? They'd milled about like they were waiting for something, for instructions, for purpose.

For someone to throw a rock.

For something to attack.

So that they could retaliate?

An image of the woman with the eyes, the bright specimen woman, flashed in Anja's mind. And shivers struck along her shoulders.

She shook them off and readjusted on the bed, then put pen to paper again. She had to observe and record. She had to describe what she'd seen. The colors. The movement. The specimens. The woman.

She didn't want to admit it, but she felt like she'd touched something untouchable, injured something that shouldn't be vulnerable. Partaken in something she hadn't realized was going on and still didn't understand.

Good thing this notebook was new and had so many blank pages. She wrote and wrote, hoping that some kind of understanding, some kind of peace of mind would come over her. There shouldn't be any reason for her to doubt herself or question her methods or their results. The power station had been an accident, and the rock . . .

But she did doubt herself. She wrote and wrote until she was not only repeating herself but writing the repeats verbatim, her pen pressing hard into the paper.

She shifted to lie more fully on her side and rest her head on the pillow of her arm, the notebook still open before her.

She still had to write about the woman, how aware she'd seemed, how focused. How fast. The woman could have caught up to them if she'd tried. Probably wouldn't have even had to dodge the trees.

So since she'd bothered to give chase at all, why would she have stopped?

Anja's eyes began to droop. She let them close as she pondered the question.

She heard a soft thud, and her eyes popped back open.

But the noise was just her pen falling out of her grip and onto the pages.

She shifted, and the pen slid off the notebook and got lost somewhere between her and the top of the bed.

She lay on her back and hoisted up her hips, digging her hand around beneath herself, for the pen.

At the foot of her bed, someone with shiny, straight black hair parted down the middle was crouched and peering over the mattress at her.

"What the—?"

Anja startled backward and her vision cleared enough to see that there was nothing to see.

No one was there.

She laughed at herself and settled back on the bed again. She decided to give in to sleep.

Only, as usual, now that she'd decided she wanted to, it wasn't so easy to come by. She flipped onto her left side, her back to the wall, and dozed . . .

The notebook shifted, waking her up.

Probably from one of those pre-sleep full-body twitches.

Anja exhaled and opened her eyes a little.

The notebook slid off the bed.

But it didn't fall.

It hovered in midair as it moved toward the door.

Anja snorted. She didn't need a dream to tell her she was losing control of the rift project.

Wait. If she knew she was dreaming, was this one of those lucid dreams?

Funny. She hadn't had one of those since her brother died.

But if this were a lucid dream, then she should be able to reach out and touch the book, right?

As she thought this, she began to feel more awake.

But her notebook continued to float away, toward the door.

She reached out for it, but the book was too far away. She leaned forward to paw at the book. Her fingers touched its solid edge. She gripped it and pulled.

The book came easily.

Then fell to the floor with a crash.

She was suddenly wide awake.

Awake enough to see the book lift again. Only this time it wasn't all by itself. It was connected to a hand, an arm.

A boy.

A boy with shiny black hair. He wore cream pajamas, black slippers, and a determined frown. He was trying to pick her notebook up off the ground.

Anja blinked, but the boy was still there.

"What are you doing?"

The kid glanced up fast, as if shocked—no, *frustrated* that he'd been seen. Even though he was out in the open with nowhere to hide and making no moves like he'd been trying to hide.

He snatched the notebook and turned for the door.

"Hey!" Anja grabbed him, but her arms went through him—and yet they got caught on something. The notebook. She got hold of it again.

But so did the kid. He seemed to be fading in and out. This was the craziest dream Anja had ever had.

"Give it," she cried as she and the kid yanked at the book, the solid book.

Then Anja was shoved in the chest. Hard. She lost hold of the book and fell backward onto the bed.

The kid pulled the book close to his fading chest and was gone.

Anja tried to get up but she couldn't.

There was nothing in the room with her—nothing!—but she felt the weight of someone climbing on top of her, straddling her, digging their boney knee into her stomach. Nothing there, but the knee dug deeper, and a boney forearm pressed against her neck, crushing her windpipe.

Anja couldn't breathe.

"Stop," she tried to say.

But it came out like a breathy croak. She waved her arms, she kicked her legs, trying to dislodge whatever was on top of her. But her legs kicked the conex's metal walls; her arms hit empty air.

And yet she continued to choke.

"Help," she said with strangled breath. "Help me. Danny. Yuri. Someone. Help me."

Her chest burned with the need to suck in a lungful of air. She stared upward, eyes blurring over, into the empty air of her attacker, at the conex ceiling overhead.

What the hell was going on?

Was she going to die like this?

The grip on her throat tightened.

Her efforts, like her heart, began to fail.

She was going to die here.

She was going to die in this strange place by strangulation, and yet alone.

It was impossible, and yet . . .

CHAPTER 34

The door to her conex burst open and banged against the wall.

Danny rushed in. "Anya? We heard—Anja?"

For an instant, he pulled a face, something between confusion and disgust.

She could only imagine what he was seeing, what he was thinking, watching her writhe on the bed, trying to claw something that wasn't there away from her throat.

"Help," she tried to say.

He calmly knelt by her side and pulled her hands away from her neck.

The force around her throat tightened.

Anja gasped for air and tried to yank her hands free from Danny.

He let them go, saying, "What do I do? What do you need me to do?"

She re-wedged her fingers back between her neck and the nothing strangling her, gaining just enough leverage to suck in half a breath.

For a split second, Danny just watched.

Then he leaned over her. His St. Christopher medallion dangled between them. He slid his fingers up Anja's wrists and over the tops of her knuckles. Then he burrowed his fingertips down between Anja's clenched fists and the skin of her neck.

His face went pale—and then fierce.

His hands clenched around hers, and he pulled with her. Pulled against the invisible counterforce tightening around her neck.

Anja gasped, sucking in a larger breath. She stared up at him, her eyelids spread so wide he was blurry. She moved her lips, trying to mouth the words *pull harder, pull harder*.

His lips pursed with determination.

She could feel his added strength on her hands.

But no extra air in her lungs.

Whatever had her by the neck was tightening the noose.

Anja's eyelids started to droop.

"No-no-no," she heard Danny say. Then, "Help!"

He pulled tighter on her hands, jerking her body and jostling her awake. He looked over his shoulder toward the open door. "Doc! Ming! Anybody! Help!

It was strange. Anja started to feel both more awake and less awake.

She saw a flash of silver.

Then another.

Two flashes.

Two distinctly silver cords.

Something snapped, and the grip on her neck slipped.

She saw the flare of something cream. Wide-legged cream pajama pants—like the kid's, only bigger, longer—and a black sock-like slipper.

And just for an instant, the flash of a blue-and-purple tie-dyed hoodie.

The weight on her body lifted.

Her lungs filled with air.

"Anja!" Danny said. "Are you okay? What happened? What happened?"

She rubbed her neck. It was sore to the touch beneath her probing fingers.

Who knew what kind of soreness she'd find in her abdomen.

Her throat didn't feel ready to speak yet, and she didn't know what to say anyway. She was neither physically okay nor mentally sound, was she? So she just nodded. It was true enough.

Whatever had attacked her, whatever had saved her, they were gone.

Behind Danny, Ming appeared in the open doorway.

"What's wrong? Everything okay?" She looked around the room, which was empty but for the three of them. "I heard you yelling on the speakers. Do you need me to get Doc?"

"No," Anja said, struggling to get up. She expected Danny to tell her to sit, but he helped her to stand. "We need to check on Yuri."

"Yuri?" Danny said. Then, to Ming. "Go check him."

Ming ran out the door and Anja and Danny followed as fast as Anja could go, getting faster with every step.

When they reached the conex next door, they found Yuri lying on the cot to the right, propped up on his elbows.

He sighed with relief when he saw Anja. He beckoned her closer.

She stepped toward the bed. Yuri looked exhausted. She reached for his hands, and he let her take them. But he kept one hand clenched in a fist.

"Are they gone?" he asked.

"Is *who* gone?" Danny asked.

But Anja just nodded.

She stared into Yuri's eyes, bracing herself for a round of I told you so. But Yuri shifted his gaze away from her and onto Danny.

"Your Chinese super psychics," he said.

"Seriously?" Danny said. "That stuff I read about is for real?"

"But there's still something else," Yuri said. "I know how the kid got here."

"How?" Danny said.

"He was out of body." And before they could ask, he just started to explain. "He removed his soul from his body and that's how he got here."

"That's not possible," Danny said.

"It is," Anja said. "Yuri can do it too."

"What?" Ming and Danny both said.

"He's the one who saved me from the attacker," Anja said. "Aren't you?" She looked to Yuri, waiting for him to take credit.

But he did her one better.

He opened his clenched fist and showed them all what he held in his hand.

A black slipper.

Too big for a little boy.

Anja gaped at it for a moment, then grabbed for it. She expected Yuri to pull it back, to play keep-away, but he let her take it.

It was soft in her hands, though she couldn't name the fabric. A silk blend, maybe. She sniffed it. It smelled clean, more or less. Maybe a little earthy, but not like sweaty feet. She stuck her hand inside. Definitely not child size. It was a big slipper. Women's size ten at least, maybe larger.

Not the size of the specimen that grabbed her notebook.

This was the size of the one that had tried to strangle her.

"So was it you?" she said.

Yuri studied her as if he was debating whether or not it was worth saying anything to her, let alone the truth.

She couldn't blame him. He had to be wondering if she would believe him. If she would roll her eyes and ridicule him again. If it would be better to lie, say he didn't know what she was talking about, and just roll over and sleep it off.

"Was it?" Anja said, trying to convey in her tone that while she may not have been as open-minded before, she had witnessed a lot in the last twenty-four hours and had experienced a lot in the last few minutes. She rubbed her throat just to be sure.

Yup. Still sore.

Whatever had happened to her—even though she couldn't see it, had only caught a glimpse of it—it had been real. The evidence was in the pain and, likely tomorrow, the bruises.

And it was in the slipper. Tangible. Solid.

Real.

Yuri sat up slowly and nodded. Twice. Two small nods. Barely perceptible.

And still the gloating didn't come.

Anja sat on the edge of his cot and squeezed his hand. "Thank you."

She leaned back far enough to rest her back against the metal wall, and rubbed at her neck. Fidgeted with the black slipper.

Wait—

"Oh no," she said, bolting upright.

She ran out the door and back to her own conex. Lifted her pillow, looked under the cot.

Danny, Ming, and Yuri filed in after her.

"What?" Danny said.

"They got my notebook."

CHAPTER 35

The things an old guy has to do to make a difference in the world.

A world that was increasingly becoming a negative and disappointing place.

A place that would harm you where and when possible, making it imperative to protect yourself.

Politics and laws didn't actually make anything better. And things were getting worse, if the news was accurate.

But that was all just a partial list of the things Jim Lugner hoped to fix by what he and the Russian were doing.

It was morning, earlier and darker than he preferred, but needs must. Daylight savings had ended yesterday, and Jim was still adjusting. At his age, adjusting usually took him the whole period, right up until they switched it back again. It was enough to make him consider moving to Arizona: no daylight savings. But he was in Kansas now, his plane having landed less than an hour ago, and he would remain here until he finished his mission.

Lebanon, Kansas, to be exact. One of the first things Jim did after securing the old, hand-bound book he was flipping through at his desk in his subterranean office was buy this precise piece of land in the center of the United States and build this compound—an iceberg of a building surrounded by laurels and other quick-growing privacy shrubs. Many of the rooms were strategically wrapped in aluminum wire mesh. He'd told the contractors via his lawyer that he was electromagnetically hypersensitive and anthropophobic. All things considered, he supposed it was more of an exaggeration than a lie.

He sipped his green tea with pomegranate and flipped the page in this, his most prized book. It was an old book, judging by the cover, having somehow survived who-knew-how-long despite not being made of leather. He didn't know what the cover was made of—old wool perhaps—but it had been varnished stiff with some kind of oil. The pages, too. They rustled when he turned them, and his fingers always felt parched after flipping a few. He should have probably been wearing gloves as he read it—for the sake of his fingers and the book—but he was still bitter, and the squirts of lotion he was constantly rubbing into his dry hands left smudges on the pages. A small but satisfying rebellion.

He flipped the page, leaving another smudge. The book was in a language he couldn't identify, let alone read. But there were drawings. And it was clear they told the story of a secret process. He'd spent years finding someone who knew what the drawings meant, who could piece them together. The Russian had gotten them pretty far with the process and proven herself worth the cost of putting up with her. But she didn't have all the skills the process required. They needed help to take Jim's plan the rest of the way.

All the way.

Further than anyone had ever been.

If they made it, they would be the first to do so. Jim was sure of it.

And help had finally arrived. And it had proven its skill to Jim just last night. Finally.

Jim had been working on this plan for eight years. Ever since the senseless murder of his son.

Ever since Jim's subsequent sabbatical to Brazil and his meeting with the wise man.

And ever since Jim had done what he'd had to do to come home with the sage's book.

This book. This old and oiled book.

He felt that familiar pang in his chest threaten to push up into a lump in his throat, into wells in his eyes. He sniffed and shifted in his chair, hoping to soothe it. *One life for billions is worth it*, he reminded himself.

One life and eight years for a final task that would likely take less than an hour.

They'd missed the window last year. Didn't have the right people yet. But this year, now, in less than a few days if everything went according to plan, he might just earn himself a Nobel Prize.

Not for science. (Though that might come years from now. Posthumously, of course.) But for peace.

A Nobel Peace Prize. Him. My, how life can change a person.

But he had to be careful. His people had to be careful. This was unexplored territory they'd be entering. People had long said that space was the final frontier.

But people were wrong.

He heard footsteps outside his iceberg's office and then a knock, just two taps before the heavy wooden door pushed open.

"How's he doing?" Jim said, flipping another page in his prize book.

The Russian stood silent, her fingers interlaced but flexed like the spiked, crossed logs of a Frisian horse barrier in a medieval battle. He could almost hear the stern vibrations he most definitely felt emanating from her. He looked up, pretending to do so merely for another sip of his tea. He was the boss after all. The one with the plan, the one with the resources.

But she was the one with the skill.

"He is scared," she said.

The man couldn't blame the kid; he was scared, too. Though that was mostly because he had to rely on others to do what he couldn't do himself. But if he'd been the kid—in Anja's room, seen by her, grabbed by her—Jim had to admit he would be scared, too.

But scary encounter with Anja or not, the boy had come through.

Jim flipped through a second book. Anja's journal. It had only two days' worth of entries, but they proved interesting in their own right. He couldn't imagine what his former protégé must be thinking. She'd been his most science-staunch student back at the University, eschewing anything with even a whiff of idealism or superstition. He might have been able to steer her better if he'd known then what he knew now. But by the looks of her journal, she was coming to know things on her own. And even to experience them.

"I was under the impression he did this sort of thing all the time," Jim said.

"And so he does. But he was attacked."

"Attacked?"

"Something like. Is best word I think of."

And there would be no challenging it.

"What happened?" he asked.

"She saw him. Tried to grab him. Tried to take book."

Jim nodded. If he'd seen a kid trying to take his book, he would've done the same thing.

"He is scared he will fail," the Russian continued. "Scared of you. Scared of me. He fears he will disappoint us."

The man was scared of her, too, but he'd seen the two of them together. Her and the kid. She was an entirely different person with their newest teammate. Almost motherly.

"We have a few days," he said, "and that's assuming Caleb Weatherbee, here, is accurate." He patted his current copy of the *Farmers' Almanac*, which most famously predicts the weather, but which he consulted for its more esoteric predictions. "You can warm him up in time."

He tried to make the statement sound like a commanding suggestion, but the tone of his voice rose just slightly at the end, making it sound more like a question. Like deference. He'd heard it, and the twitch at the corner of the Russian's mouth told him that she had heard it too.

"I can," she said. "That is not real problem. I come because we have real problem."

He sighed and closed his eyes. Julian would've been twenty-eight tomorrow. His mother was already preparing for the party. Jim would attend with a forced smile, but he knew he couldn't stomach another.

And Anja. If Jim could accomplish this now, then Anja would remain just part of the plan. But if he delayed his mission and gave his best student a whole nother year to study the rift, she would find him out. She would become a threat.

So Jim could either finish this now or move to damage control.

One life for billions was worth it, it had to be. But he preferred the mission not require any more.

"What problem?" he asked.

"Your dead wise man?" said the Russian. "He assists your scientist. And that student we visit, psychic brother you call charlatan? He protects her, too."

CHAPTER 36

"So, Yuri," Jackson said, his face peering out of the biggest monitor in the welcoming center as Anja and the others ate their morning oatmeal at the conference table. "Danny tells me, and I can't believe I'm about to say this out loud, but Danny tells me that a disembodied being—a person—from the rift—came and took Anja's notebook and that you fought him off."

Yuri shrugged an admission.

"While also disembodied."

"Out of body, sir. Yes, sir."

Jackson nodded, his expression speaking volumes, and Anja could imagine what he was thinking. Hearing something strange had happened was one thing, one ignorable thing. But talking to the person who'd done the strange thing and being corrected on your terminology required another layer of acceptance.

But apparently it was a level Jackson was ready for. "Can that be taught?"

Yuri looked at Danny, as if he needed an interpreter.

"Is it something only psychics do?" Jackson clarified. "Or can you teach these guys?" His hand appeared on the monitor, gesturing to the remains of his motley team: Danny, Anja, and Ming, who, since last night, was now carrying around a spaghetti sauce jar of self-blessed holy water. Apparently Yuri had told her that if she didn't have a talisman with her, like his blue-and-purple fluorite crystal or

Danny's St. Christopher medallion, the self-blessed holy water would work.

"It can be taught, sir," Yuri said.

"Good, then—"

"But, sir? The chances of them learning in the timeframe I assume you're looking at—"

"Yesterday?"

"Right. Outlook not so good."

"How about tomorrow?"

Yuri laughed a little, but it was clearly out of stress rather than humor because everyone was taking the conversation entirely seriously. Jackson wanted the four of them to go out of body.

"Are you thinking of getting the notebook back?" Anja asked. "Yuri said that's an unbelievable skill, that he's barely heard of it being done by accident, let alone on purpose."

"No point in getting the book back," Jackson said. "If it was just a day's worth of notes, it's already been read by now—although I do want a briefing from you on what was in it. No, I want to go on the offensive. Danny said that there are ghosts around the rift, that some lady seemed to come out of it. If that's the case, then we're going in."

"Into where?" Anja asked.

"Into the rift," Jackson said. "Danny says it's a tear in the veil, like a vortex or a portal. Is that accurate, Yuri?"

Yuri nodded.

"So it sounds to me like a doorway," Jackson said. "Sounds to me like people—something anyway—is guarding that doorway, coming out of it when they want to, wreaking havoc on my team when it suits them, doing God knows what to the people of this country, to the babies . . ."

Jackson leaned back and sucked in a breath, seeming to catch himself before he went off on a tear.

Anja caught Danny's eye. She didn't know him well enough to communicate with looks. But she thought he was giving her a look that said there were things they could discuss later, after Jackson ended the call.

Anja could wait until then.

Jackson was saying, "Can you go in, Yuri?"

Yuri seemed to sense that this wasn't a time for the usual *well, it depends* . . . kind of answer used in academia or the law or pretty much everywhere that's not life or death in the field. He let out a breath and said, "If they're coming out, then, yes, sir, I think we can go in. Or we can at least try. I can try to go in myself, now, if you want."

Danny shifted his weight, a movement that looked like moving the muscles before they got stagnant and fell asleep, but Anja was getting better at reading him by the second. Danny didn't want Yuri to go. He didn't have a problem going in, but he didn't want Yuri to go, not alone.

But he didn't say so. It wasn't his call. He would take the orders as given, no debate. He made this assessment and decision and conveyed it all in his body language instantaneously.

But Jackson took his time considering Yuri's offer.

"Not yet," he finally said, and Anja noticed that Danny's shoulders relaxed just a skosh. "If push comes to shove and you're the only one capable, I might ask you to do that. But right now all we know is that these people are clearly smarter about and more skilled at this . . . this going-out-of-body stuff than we are. You should at least have backup."

Yuri nodded, and Anja was getting better at reading him, too. He'd been sitting up straight, like he was trying to remain stoic, but now he slouched some and took a bite of his previously untouched oatmeal, like he was secretly relieved.

Anja smirked and glanced at Ming to see if she—who was so good at reading Anja like a book—was finding these new opportunities to get to know people's idiosyncrasies and tells just as amusing as she did, but Ming didn't seem to be paying attention. She was staring off somewhere in the middle distance between Danny and Yuri. Anja decided she'd check in with Ming later when she had the chance.

Jackson said, "So what do you need from me in order to get them trained?"

Yuri shrugged. "I guess that's the beauty of going out of body. You leave all the worldly trappings behind. But if you guys have anything that helps you concentrate or reminds you that you can do anything. Something that gives you both confidence and encouragement—"

"You mean something we brought despite being told to leave everything behind and even being stripped of our phones?" Anja asked.

"Oh. Right," Yuri said, looking and sounding like the battle was already lost considering Jackson wanted this done yesterday, but now it was also a non-starter. "Well, I guess we're all set then."

"Start in a minute," Jackson said. "I want to talk to Anja first."

"Okay," Yuri said. "I'm gonna go check in with Doc and Josh and the team."

"I gotta check in with perimeter patrol," Danny said, following him out. "Don't get started without me."

CHAPTER 37

After the room cleared out (Ming requiring a bit of a nudge and Anja agreeing to watch the monitors even though she didn't know any of the buttons), Jackson got right to the point. "What's in your journal?"

"That's the part that strikes your curiosity?" Anja said. "The kid *took* my journal. He may have been out of body, but my journal most certainly was not."

She was still letting her brain's synapses puzzle that one out. And never mind that Yuri had somehow stolen a nonphysical black slipper. That feat was even more disturbing than the disappearance of her journal.

"Well," Jackson said, far more calmly than Anja. "While the method of travel and transport is unexpected, he came here for a reason, and that reason seems to be your journal. So yes, above all else, at this moment, I want to know what was in your journal."

"Nothing, really. Just the last twenty-four . . . hours . . ." Just all of her notes on the redwoods and the clearing and the rift. And the glow. And the smell. And her tests. And the boom.

She grimaced.

"Just everything?" Jackson asked.

Anja felt her face go hot. She felt like she was the one being blamed here, and so she shrugged, if only to herself, like it was no big deal. "Yeah."

"So you wrote about visiting the rift and the power station and the team and the fluorescence and the ghosts, the one that chased you and the one that attached to you—"

"No, I didn't write about that," Anja said, feeling alarmed.

She'd thought it complete nonsense when Yuri had first mentioned the ghost he supposedly saw hovering around her, despite the new sensations she'd felt and the way those sensations had changed. And she'd forgotten he had said it.

But now that she was reminded, now that she knew what Yuri was capable of . . .

She looked across the table at Yuri's empty seat, wondering if, as he'd sat there just moments ago, he'd been seeing her—or the ghost attached to her.

"Oh, good," Jackson said, not with blame but with defeat, "just every other secret we're supposed to be protecting." He leaned back, looking to the side and out of his element.

"When are you coming back?" Anja asked. She'd been hoping to have a hypothesis ready for Jackson this morning, a best guess about what the rift was and what had caused it, and a plan of action for how to shut it down. But new data just kept flowing in, and she didn't know what to do with the information she'd received—experienced—last night.

She looked at Yuri's empty chair again. She needed to talk to him. Alone.

"I don't know," Jackson said. "Marisol's not doing well."

"What's wrong with her?"

"She's pregnant."

"What?"

Jackson nodded solemnly. "Her due date's late next month."

"And the baby's still okay?"

Jackson shrugged. "As far as I know. As good as can be expected."

Anja nodded, not knowing what else to say. No wonder Jackson wasn't around. And he probably wouldn't be making it a priority to come around, not with his family in trouble. That was understandable. But it also meant he wouldn't be much help in the coming days.

"Can you grant me a favor?" she asked.

"What?" he said, and Anja was encouraged by his tone. He seemed open to whatever she might ask. But given what he had asked of her, what he had tricked her into doing, that was only fair.

"I need help here. Real help. I'd like to contact another scientist."

Jackson's face ashened. His head slowly tilted up as he tilted back in his chair.

"Who?"

"I trust him," Anja said.

"*Who*?"

"My mentor," Anja said. "You might've heard of him, actually. Jim Lugner?"

Jackson's ashen expression softened into a frown. "The guy in the news telling everyone to adopt older kids?"

"That's him."

"He sounds more like a politician than a scientist."

"He's a scientist. Or was. He's who I studied with back when I was focused on electromagnetism. Since then, he's just, you know, developed other interests."

Jackson didn't look so sure.

"His son died, and he left the field to start a foundation."

Jackson nodded like that tidbit rang a bell. "Shot trying to protect someone else?"

Anja nodded. Julian's friends said he'd been shot standing up for a stranger who was being bullied outside a bar. It had happened in the middle of fall quarter. Her mentor had taken a leave of absence for the rest of the term. And then a sabbatical in Brazil. And then made a permanent move to the Oregon coast. It was part of why she'd changed disciplines. Continuing his work without him just reminded her of why he was gone and distracted her from making progress. Which then made her feel bad for complaining about her own life when he was so much worse off.

"You trust him?" Jackson asked.

"I trust him more than I trust anyone else," she said. And not just about the facts. She trusted him to understand the implications if word of any of this crazy stuff leaked into the science world, and she trusted him to keep quiet about her involvement.

"Okay," Jackson said. "But blind copy me, and keep it need-to-know."

CHAPTER 38

"Okay, then," Anja said once she, Ming, Yuri, and Danny were back in the monitoring room. They'd pushed the conference table against the back wall, stacked the chairs to one side, and laid the blankets from their beds on the floor in preparation to learn how to get out of body. And now they were all standing around like lost children. And Anja was stalling on getting them found.

"Before we go all out learning how to . . . whatever. I want to get clear on why we're doing this in the first place. Clear about the mission. So, let's recap. We're charged with figuring out what's going on in the clearing and how to vanquish it. There are ghosts in the clearing." The fact that she said the word *ghosts* as if it were a normal part of her vocabulary was not lost on her, but apparently it had become so familiar so fast that she just kept talking. "There's something . . ."

"Like a portal," Ming offered.

Anja nodded. Sure. Why not? "Like a portal in the clearing. It's swirling. It's spewing something with fluorescent properties. And, most interesting, someone is sending a child—"

"A skilled child," said Yuri. "Taking a journal? I'll say it again, that's an incredible skill. I've heard of it happening, in legend, but even then it happened on accident. I don't know of anyone who's done it on purpose."

"Okay, then," Anja said, "someone is sending a skilled child into our camp—"

"With backup," Yuri added.

"Yes, with backup, to steal what we know about the rift."

"That's the key," Danny said. "Who's sending this kid in? Because I doubt it's the backup that came with him. Someone's gathering themselves a little army of skilled OBErs to deal with the rift."

"Or create it in the first place," Yuri said.

"Yeah," Danny. "He's an Asian kid, you said?"

Ming scoffed. "That doesn't mean anything."

"Maybe it *shouldn't* mean anything, but in my line of work it often does. Especially when the kid is wearing slippers and flowy pajama pants instead of tennis shoes and jeans. And when we know that China's got themselves a growing group of super psychics that they start grooming from toddlerhood. Was he Chinese?"

Anja looked at Ming. When she smiled, her eyes all but disappeared in order to make room for a fan of smile lines, but right now they were pinching toward the bridge of her nose, not a laugh line in sight.

"I don't know," Anja said. "Could be. Probably? I don't know."

"Even if he is, the woman with him isn't," Yuri said. "Ethnically, anyway. I suppose she could be based there."

"For the sake of argument," Ming said. "Let's say he is Chinese, they're both Chinese. What does it matter? How does that change what we do?"

"Honestly, it would be easier if the kid's local, if his handlers are local. We can do something about that. If he and his handlers are based in China or some other country and he's just appearing and disappearing . . ." Danny shrugged. "There may be nothing we can do. Us, anyway. There's always something a different team could do."

Anja recalled some of the movies and books she'd read, where secret contract killers snuck in and . . . well . . . killed. She wondered if that would extend to the kid.

"Well, anyway," Danny said, seeming to pick up on the disconcerting train of thought the idea of involving a different team had led to. "Let's stay focused on what we're here to do. We're here to figure out how to shut down the rift. Is it man-made or man-exploited? I think we all agree we have to start collecting all the information we have about the rift. And"—he met Anja's eye—"I think we're all finally in a state of mind, now, to listen to everything everyone here at the table might have to say on the subject."

Anja exhaled heavily, then lifted a hand in acquiescence. She didn't like this, not any of it, but she couldn't argue against their next step.

She offered Yuri a small, encouraging smile.

"Okay, kid," Danny said to him, "tell us what you know."

CHAPTER 39

"But start from the beginning," Danny said, sitting cross-legged on the blanket he'd laid out on the floor.

Ming sat too. She'd looked dazed and confused all morning, but apparently she'd been listening, because she looked interested now.

Anja followed suit, figuring she might as well get comfortable. She couldn't deny that she still felt uneasy about all of this, but she was ready to listen. She now had some context to help her understand.

"Start with your brother," she said. "How'd you get the GPS coordinates?"

"Yes," Danny said. "The coordinates. How the hell did you get out here? Maybe that's how the other kid got out here."

"Except Yuri got caught by perimeter control," Anja said. "The other kid appeared and then disappeared."

"Here's an idea," Ming said. "Why don't we just let Yuri tell it."

Anja caught her excitement and reeled it in, but it stirred and pulsed like dancing fireflies in her stomach.

Yuri stared at the floor, and his cheeks puffed as he blew out a breath. He hadn't laid down a blanket, but he sat on the floor with them, facing them.

"Where were you when you got the coordinates?" Danny asked.

Yuri nodded. "Outside, at a night market. I do fortune telling and palm reading."

"Seriously?" Anja asked, and immediately hoped it hadn't come out reeking of sarcasm.

Yuri shrugged, taking her for sincere, and she sighed with relief.

Yuri said, "It's not my forte, but it doesn't really matter. Most people don't want to know the truth, they just want some vague happy prediction delivered with a little pomp and circumstance, so that's what I give them."

He winced.

Danny wagged his finger at Yuri's face. "You just thought something. Tell us everything. Whatever it is."

Yuri said, "Before Josh appeared, there was this old guy who came up to me, tailed by this disembodied—*that's* who the woman is! I *knew* she looked familiar."

"Wait, what?" Danny said. "You lost me."

"The bright ghost at the rift, the backup. She's not a ghost. She's out of body, and I've seen her before. I saw her with this old guy who paid me two hundred dollars for a reading. She was scoping me out, I knew it. I had this feeling like I should pretend I couldn't see her. I bet that's what she was doing, trying to get me to break. And the old guy was asking me about his brother, but he didn't have a brother, and the question made me think of Josh, and . . ."

Yuri trailed off and all his excitement turned to pale dread.

"And then Josh appeared and gave you the coordinates?" Ming asked.

Yuri's head pivoted on his neck, acknowledging her, and he nodded, looking like his brother had died all over again.

"Did they hurt him on purpose?" he asked.

Ming rose on her knees and scooted to Yuri's side and gave him a single-armed hug.

"I saw that guy use his phone after he talked to me. What if he . . ."

Yuri shook his head, and Anja guessed what he was probably thinking. That was a lot of coincidences—too many, and so probably not any at all. But how had a guy in Seattle caused the clearing to attack the team?

Eventually, Danny broke the silence and got them back on track. "I gave the coordinates back to you, didn't I? Do you have 'em? Can I see them again?"

Yuri pulled a piece of paper from his pocket and handed it to Danny. Anja leaned to her left to peer at it over Danny's shoulder.

A rift. 40.26504, -123.88445. Big Beauty.

"He called it 'a rift,'" Danny said, as if to himself, chuckling a little and shaking his head. "We'd just been calling it the clearing, but then that day, Josh started using that word, rift. And I noticed Jackson just called it that as well, and he wasn't around to hear Josh use it as far as I know. Josh and Jackson never talked except in person with the rest of us. If Jackson was gone but needed, Juan's the one who'd always call him. You know, before."

Danny handed the paper back to Yuri. "The word doesn't mean anything to me, except, you know, as according to the dictionary. 'A fissure or cleft; a break in friendly relations; a fault; and to burst open or split.' I looked it up earlier," he said, answering the confounded expression Anja felt spreading across her face. Then, to Yuri. "Does the word 'rift' mean something different to you? To any of you?"

Anja shook her head. Ming did, too, and moved back to her own blanket, beside Anja, giving Yuri back his space.

"Yuri?" Danny said.

Yuri's hands were fidgeting, one thumb and index finger rubbing the other thumb. Anja could tell he had something to say.

"Everything," Anja reminded him, hoping it offered him encouragement, too.

"Well, um, a rift is something of a different name for . . . Have you ever heard of piercing the veil?"

"Like in the legal sense?" Anja asked. She remembered hearing the term once, when one of her lab mates was sued a while back.

"No," Yuri said, grimacing. "Remember yesterday, when I mentioned the veil between worlds?"

Anja's eyes widened at the same time her hackles rose. She did remember. She remembered how she'd acted. And she remembered what had happened since then. "Remind me."

Poor kid looked like that was the last thing he wanted to do.

But he said, "Okay, so, it depends on what mythology or belief system you're working with, but the veil is what separates our realm from the, well, the term *veil* is from a system I know you're not gonna like, so let's just call it the nonphysical realm, including the realm of the dead. So piercing the veil is like opening a portal between the two, between our realm—the physical realm—and the other realm, or another realm—the nonphysical realm."

Yuri shook his head like he knew he wasn't making any sense.

"So a rift is like a portal," Ming said.

"Yes," Yuri said, sounding surprised and encouraged. "And after what Anja showed us in the clearing, I think that's exactly what that is. A tear in the veil. A portal. A rift. Call it what you want. Usually the veil is thin in certain places, like at the boundaries of places, where the land meets water or mountain meets sky."

"Or woods meet clearing, like you said yesterday," Danny said.

"Yeah. When I saw the ghosts in the clearing, I figured they were just meeting where clearing meets forest. But then after you and your lights and filters and whatnot showed us what's *really* in the clearing—an actual hole, a swirling vortex, with far more ghosts there now than before . . . That's why they're here. Those ghosts are in the clearing because there's a rift. Josh was right. There's a rift, and like moths to a flame, our world and all it promises is drawing any of the ghosts within sensing distance to come here."

"So you couldn't see the rift before we looked at it through the lights?" Danny asked.

Yuri shook his head. "I saw the ghosts. But the big swirling vortex thing?" He shook his head again, this time with his bottom lip pushed out. "No. I've never seen anything like it."

"Then how do you know it's a pierced veil?" Anja asked.

"I don't. Not for sure. But I don't know what else it could be. And if what Doc says is true, that it's attacked four times, I say it's probably shifting. It's gearing up for something. What, I can't say. If it had stopped at three shifts, I would have said that's probably all it's going to do. But it's shifted at least four times. I'd say it shifts at least three more times to make it seven, if not more. Nine, ten, twelve times."

"Why not stop at four?"

"Three, seven, and twelve are the most likely. They're sacred numbers. Numbers that appear everywhere. It's just a guess, but it wouldn't surprise me."

"Then we'll proceed like it's going to shift again," Danny said.

Anja was still trying to understand. "So the rift is a hole in the . . ."

Veil was not a word Anja could work with. She tried *fabric of reality* and didn't like that one either.

"The field," she said aloud.

Yuri nodded side to side as if weighing her world choice. He didn't look like he loved it, but he didn't argue with her, so she took his silence as acceptance.

The rift was a hole in the field.

She had a hypothesis.

Now all she had to do was figure out a way to test it.

"What about the ghosts?" Danny said,

Ah, yes. The ghosts. Did the *field* allow for the coming and going and awareness of *ghosts*?

Anja chuckled to herself. One problem—and eye-popping revelation—at a time, please.

No, really. One a day.

Tops.

Please.

"The ghosts?" Yuri said, then shrugged. "They just seemed like ghosts at first. Gave me the same heavy feeling when I got close to them. Didn't seem particularly interested in anything or anyone."

But Yuri glanced at Anja. She shifted her hips on the hardwood floor and pulled her blanket up over her knees.

"They were just here, near a boundary," Yuri continued. "Seemed normal, if kinda weird because of the lack of people out here. But I don't get out in the woods much, so . . . I don't know, that's what I figured. Until I found all of you out there again, and one of them . . ."

He glanced at Anja again, and this time he didn't look away, though his eyes seemed to shift and focus on something that was her but not her.

Anja shivered. "What do you see?"

"I don't think he means you harm," Yuri said. "I think he's trying to help you, but I can't communicate with him. He's not interested in me at all. The rest of you, either. He's not even watching us right now. He's got his eyes closed, his hands folded in front of him. I'm not even sure he's listening. It's almost like he's tuning us out, like he's meditating. How do you feel?"

Anja found herself taking stock for a minute, but only because it seemed like the thing to do, like it was expected, not because she needed to.

She knew exactly how she felt.

"Good. I felt fine on the way here, on the drive down, and then I felt something, like heaviness, now that you mention it, when we first went to the rift, and that kind of stuck with me all night and most of the next morning, but that's more or less gone away, and I feel pretty good actually. Despite the weirdness going on, dare I say I feel fantastic."

"What about you guys?" Yuri asked.

"I've been better," Danny said, rubbing at the St. Christopher medallion hanging around his neck. "But my team's a garden of vegetables in the room next door and I'm ipso facto in charge of you guys and you haven't exactly been making it easy, and I still haven't gotten any sleep, so I figure par for the course." Danny shrugged. "You?" he said to Ming.

Ming was sitting cross-legged, holding her jar of holy water in the space her legs made. "I'm about dead," she said. "And I'm usually full of energy."

"Yeah," Yuri said. "That's what I would expect. Even though we've got our protective stuff, we're still surrounded by these ghosts, and the more that are here, the stronger and farther-reaching their influence. I feel it, and I'm usually protected pretty well." He pulled on his crystal under his sweatshirt. "But you're not feeling the effects," he said to Anja. "You're almost getting a boost—*are* getting a boost. And I think it's him." He pointed right at her, through her, as if the man were standing right behind her.

Anja shivered, realizing that he probably was.

"He should be siphoning your energy, and it's like he knows that. It's like he's trying not to, and that's why he's meditating."

"Does he ever do anything else? Besides meditate?" Anja asked.

"Maybe, probably, but he mostly just looks like he's meditating. He could be concentrating on telling you something, or showing you something. Any weird dreams?"

"No. I've slept pretty well, actually. Why?"

Yuri shrugged. "It's one of the symptoms of an attachment and possession."

"Possession?" Anja said.

"He's not possessing you," Yuri said quickly. "If he were, I wouldn't be able to see him like I do, and you wouldn't feel good. But attachments and possessions have similar symptoms, and that's one of them. Nightmares though, usually, not dreams. Nightmares."

"What do you mean attached?"

"Just what you're probably imagining," Yuri said, "Siamese-twin style."

Anja got another chill. "How are we attached?"

"Right now? He's bowing his head to yours. Like this."

Yuri rose onto his knees and moved closer to Danny. He pressed his right temple to the side of Danny's head, like an adult might do when cuddling a child. Yuri closed his eyes, and this calmness, this contentment, came over his face. And when he opened his eyes, they shimmered. Not just with tears, but with insight.

"He loves you."

Anja shivered like she'd never shivered before and jerked away from her invisible cuddler.

"Brian?" she said. "What's he look like? Is he my height? Skinny? My coloring? D-does he look like me?"

Anja was up off the floor, scrambling away and trying to somehow see what apparently was right in front of her.

But all she saw was how crazy she must appear in the eyes of the other three people sitting on blankets laid out on the floor.

"Who's Brian?" Danny asked.

"It's her brother," Ming whispered, but Anja still heard her, and the admission, even if made by someone else, made her hide her face.

Yuri had straightened up from his cuddling demonstration with Danny and was now approaching Anja. He didn't hold out a hand or try to coddle her. He just spoke to her.

"He doesn't look like you," he said. "I don't think he's American. I don't even think he speaks English. If he did, I think he'd be more interested in what we're saying, because we're talking about him. But he's not. He's just eyes closed, concentrating on you. He's a lot older. Wizened. If I had to guess ethnicity, I'd say, I don't know, indigenous South American? I don't know. Like I said, he doesn't really open his eyes."

"But you said he loves me," Anja said. "I don't know anybody like that, so how could he love me?"

"There's more than one kind of love," Yuri said softly. "There's more than romantic and familial love. But maybe what I should have said is not that he loves you, but that he is loving you. He's sending you love. He's protecting you from the energies of the other ghosts and the rift by his love, by sending you love. And he's doing it nonstop."

"Maybe he's a monk," Ming said.

Yuri nodded like that was a distinct possibility.

"Does he look like a monk? Monk robes and stuff?"

"Not really," Yuri said. "You remember how I said that Josh appearing in full body was a rarity for me."

They all nodded. Yuri helped Anja sit back down on her blanket, then sat in front of them again.

"I can't see all of this guy. I can see his head and his torso—he's wearing a short-sleeved shirt, kinda baggy—but the bottom of him is basically just light. Like the light in the clearing, actually. Don't laugh, but he's almost like a genie with no bottle, and he's not taking requests. He's just . . ."

"Loving me."

Yuri shrugged.

"You've thought this all along. That's why you didn't balk when I said I didn't need protecting."

"You didn't. He's got you covered."

Anja sat with that for a minute. She didn't know if she believed it, but she couldn't deny that she felt really good. A little distracted maybe, because for a second she'd thought he was her brother.

But then she remembered. How could she have forgotten, even for a second?

"What about last night?" She hoped the reference would be enough. She didn't want to have to describe and thus relive the attack by someone she couldn't see.

"She wasn't attacking you," Yuri said. "She was attacking him. You were just in the way."

"She would've killed me. Why didn't he stop her?"

"She had her cord wrapped around his neck. Your neck." He shrugged.

"I saw you," Anja said, "and I saw the boy. But not her."

"And that might be why he got caught off guard. He was helping you see what you can't normally see."

"How did you get her to go away?" Danny asked.

"I didn't really do anything. I just showed up, grabbed her foot. She was standing beside the bed, hunched over you, one knee on your stomach. I think she was just surprised to see me and vanished. Went back to wherever they came from. But that was the weird part. I've always felt invincible while out of body. Now I'm not so sure."

"What do you mean?" Danny asked.

"Her fear. The look on her face before she left. She seemed scared to see me, like I could hurt her, and she's obviously skilled, so . . . maybe I could've."

Anja sat there for a while, soaking up what Yuri had said. Ming patted her hand. Danny asked a few more questions, but then it was time to get to work.

They had a tear in the veil. Time to test that theory. Somehow.

But first:

"Just one more question, Yuri," Anja said. "If you get a tear in the veil? How do you close it?"

Yuri's shoulders slumped and he shrunk a few inches.

"I don't know," he said.

CHAPTER 40

They sat together on the hardwood floor for a while longer, just thinking, Anja squeezing and releasing fistfuls of blanket, Ming tapping her jar of holy water, Danny exhaling heavily, the monitor screens flickering softly to Anja's right, until Yuri said, "Are you guys as pooped as I am?"

Anja nodded. After so much conversation, she had much to think about. For starters, she needed to figure out how one might test the hypothesis that the rift is a crack in the veil. But her brain was down for the count.

Ming and Danny nodded, too, looking mentally drained, now that it had been mentioned.

"Good," Yuri said. "That's a good state to be in to learn how to OBE."

"I gotta pee first," Ming said.

"Get up. Go pee," Danny said. "Be back in five. Anyone else gotta go pee?"

Anja shook her head. Empty bladder or no, she didn't know how anyone could expect them to suddenly *go out of body*. Of all things.

Still, she lay back on her blanket, feet toward the door, and interlaced her fingers over her stomach. She stared at the ceiling. The welcoming center had single white pendant lights hung between exposed log trusses.

Danny lay down next to her, on her left side. He shifted a little, trying to get comfortable, then sat up and groped around for his pillow, which he stuffed under his head. Yuri told him it was better to lie flat, to elevate the feet if anything, but Danny said he'd fall asleep if his head wasn't elevated. Yuri adjusted the pillow under Danny's head.

"So what did I miss?" Ming said when she came back.

"Nothing," Yuri said. "Lie down."

"Feet to you or head to you?" Ming asked.

Yuri said it didn't matter. "This blanket setup isn't ideal," he said. "Just do your best. I want you to be completely still. If you move, it disrupts the process. Hands at your sides."

Anja unclasped her hands and placed them at her sides. But she wasn't comfortable. The welcoming center's old wood floor was harder and colder than she'd expected, even through her blanket. She adjusted her shoulder blades, bringing them closer together and down. It helped a little, but she wasn't sure how long she'd be able to stay like this.

To Anja's left, Ming said, "Shouldn't someone be watching the monitors?"

"I'll watch the monitors," Yuri said.

"But you're teaching," Ming said.

"I can do both. But you can't. You'll need to shut your eyes. Now, close your eyes."

Anja sighed heavily and closed her eyes.

To her left, Danny said, "Can we turn off the light?"

In answer, Yuri swiped at the wall, flipping the switch. It made a loud, frustrated click. But the resulting darkness only helped a little, thanks to the monitors shining out at her from the right. She thought turning her feet or head to the monitors might even things out, but she didn't say so.

At the rate they were going, they'd never learn a thing.

Yuri said, "Now imagine there's this pulse at the bottom of your feet. If you need to, pretend there's a fresh sore on the bottom of your foot, and it's pulsing with blood."

Anja frowned, remembering this one time as a kid when she was running after her brother. It was summer. Her dad had been cooking a hodgepodge of stuff out on the BBQ. There was only one hotdog, and Brian had taken it even though she'd already claimed dibs while it was cooking. She saw him sneak it off the grill while she was helping her mom set the outdoor table. She chased after him in her bare feet and tripped stepping up onto the sidewalk. She'd stubbed her big toe. The whole tip had flapped over. Boy, had that been an aching pulse.

She sat with the memory, feeling the ache, remembering it. Her brother said he'd get their mom, but their house seemed so far away. Anja had called for him to come back, and he helped her hop home. He'd eaten most of the hotdog by then, had stuffed it into his mouth, but he mock-offered her the last bite. She smiled now, remembering how she'd managed to take it.

"Got it?" Yuri said, his words like a distant voice-over in her memory movie. "Got the pulsing sensation?"

"Yeah," Danny said.

"Don't talk," Yuri said. "Don't move. Just relax. Relax, relax. Now move the pulse up to your ankle."

Anja focused on her big toe. She could fully feel the ache in her big toe. She tried to tug on it with her mind, as if the ache were attached to a string. But it didn't move.

"Allow it to move up your legs," Yuri said. "Just imagine the pulse moving."

Anja sighed. They were back to imagining again. Remembering, she could do. Imagining was a different thing altogether.

"It doesn't matter if you believe it," Yuri was saying now, as if he knew that Anja wasn't feeling the energy she was supposed to be sending up and down her body.

Psychic indeed.

Or maybe she was just frowning. She tried to make her face look more neutral.

"Just imagine it," he continued. "Just imagine a sensation, any kind of sensation, moving from your toes, through your ankles, up your legs. Up the body. Into the head. Feel it and push it back down again."

Well, no amount of imagining was going to make a *sensation* run itself up and down Anja's body.

And the not infrequent sound of Ming and Danny shifting around on their mats, on either side of her, said she wasn't the only one. When she was sure, from the slightly muffled sound of his voice, that Yuri was looking away from her, she peeked at Ming to see if she was having any luck.

Ah. Perhaps Ming had been the one with the frown. Her face was pinched in every way it could be pinched. Anja was ready to call it quits, but Yuri, seeming to read her thoughts again, said to keep with it, that they had to give it at least an hour.

But as Anja sighed, she heard Yuri moving to her left, near Danny.

"You got this," Yuri said. His voice was closer—he'd squatted down—and she could hear that he was smiling. "You got this. Just keep moving it up," he said. "Just stay with it." Then, "Now run the energy up and down your body."

What energy? Anja wanted to say. She couldn't understand what Yuri was talking about.

But it seemed Danny was having some success. Well, good for Danny.

And good for Jackson. Danny's who Jackson wanted to go into the rift, anyway. And Danny was a better choice than Anja.

When the hour was up, Anja told Yuri that she hadn't felt anything. No sensations moving up her body. Ming told him the same thing.

Yuri looked disappointed, but undeterred. He told them that moving energy was just one technique. There were many more. They each just needed to find a technique that worked for them.

"What do you mean work for us?" Danny asked.

Yuri reminded him not to talk, to just relax.

"The techniques loosen the body's hold on the . . . let's just go with *soul*. Or, more accurately, the techniques loosen the soul's hold on the body. But it feels like the body falling asleep and letting go while the mind stays awake. So the techniques relax you, raise your vibration, make you more energy than matter, until you—your soul—releases the body entirely, and rises."

"Cool," Danny whispered.

But Anja once again sighed, wishing Yuri would just stick to the techniques and quit mentioning the goal. She could follow instructions. Usually, anyway. But she knew she couldn't accomplish the goal. Not this goal. And thinking about it wasn't helping.

"You might pop out," Yuri said. "You might float out. Part of you might escape while part of you holds on. You might hear things as you get closer."

"What kinds of things?" Danny asked.

Yuri reminded him to stay quiet. "We'll get into specifics after a few more practices," he said. "I want you to be open to whatever you hear or feel or experience. As opposed to judging everything you hear and feel and experience, wondering if it's right or wrong, wondering whether it's an indicator of it working or of it not working. Judging is not a high-vibration activity. Relax. If you can imagine the energy moving through your body, relaxing every part, so much the better," he said. "But I'm not seeing a whole lot of resonance here, so let's try another technique. In fact . . . we don't have much time, do we? I'll describe a few techniques, and I want you to pick one, just one, the one that resonates with you the most, and then we'll stick with it for another hour."

Yuri ran them through two more techniques.

One was supposed to have Anja feeling like she was falling.

With the other, she was supposed to feel like a spinning top.

By the time they broke for lunch and a much-needed break, still no one had gotten out.

Anja had followed the falling instructions but hadn't felt or seen or done anything.

Ming said she'd felt like she was spinning like a teacup inside her body, but that was about it.

Danny said he thought he saw his leg come out.

Anja rolled her eyes. He saw his right leg come out? Please. What did that even mean?

But Yuri said, "You did. I saw it, too. The right leg, right?"

"Yeah," Danny said, in this calm, sort of reverent way.

Whatever. Anja was becoming more and more certain that this was probably all a waste of precious time.

But that would all change before dinner.

CHAPTER 41

After lunch, Anja grabbed a new journal from a supply box in the kitchenette cabinet under the sink and went for a walk.

It was actually closer to walk to Big Beauty than to drive, but the path from the campground to the tree was overgrown. Still, Anja wanted the solitude and the physical exertion after lying on the hardwood floor, sandwiched between Ming and Danny all morning.

The sun sat high in the sky and filtered through the trees, giving everything a reddish hue. No bird sounds, no insects. The only things Anja heard were her own footsteps and the Pacific Ocean miles to the west. The skunk smell hadn't been replenished in a while, and the fresh air was wonderful.

She wasn't the only one who'd had the idea to visit the big tree.

"Yuri?"

He was leaning against one of the split-rail fence posts, staring up at the tree.

"Oh, hi," he said. "Did you come here for privacy? I can go."

"No, it's fine. What are you looking at?"

Yuri shrugged. "I don't know. Josh told me about the rift and the coordinates, which were of the rift, but I haven't figured out why he mentioned this tree."

Anja nodded. She had no idea why he mentioned this tree either. "Maybe it was just a reference point to let you know you were near the right area."

Yuri didn't look convinced. "I had the GPS thing to tell me I was in exactly the right area. This tree's however far away." He gestured in the direction of the path that spanned the distance to the clearing.

Anja didn't say anything, just climbed over the fence, sat against the fence post nearest his, and opened her notebook.

She'd planned on jotting down her hypothesis and her plans for testing it, but she found herself watching Yuri.

"I'm sorry about your brother," she said. "I don't think I've said that yet. And I am. I'm sorry."

"Not your fault."

Anja winced, thinking about how her earlier tests may have caused Josh and the rest of the team to have seizures and nightmares. But if Yuri wasn't thinking about it, then she thought it best to not bring it up.

"What's your age difference?" she asked.

"Thirteen years."

"That's a lot. You were—what?—five when he left home?"

"Something like that."

"Were you close?"

Yuri shrugged. "When my mom died, when I was twelve, my dad kind of checked out. Josh didn't come home or anything, but he started checking in a lot more. Until my dad . . ."

"What?"

Yuri shrugged. "My dad blamed me."

"Blamed you?" Anja said, but more from recognition than surprise, and from the opposite side of the equation. In her family, she was the one who'd done all the blaming. In her mind, her parents should never have encouraged Brian, should never have praised his . . . whatever, his skill, his *talents*.

Until recently, she'd stood staunchly by that assessment. But now . . .

"Mom thought it was all fun, what I could do. I used to entertain her, exaggerate for her, tell her I saw famous dead people. And then one day she started saying she could see things too."

This was not the same thing that happened to Anja, not at all.

"What happened?" she asked.

"She got sick, and she didn't fight it. She wasn't afraid of dying. She said it would all work out okay. She'd be fine. We'd be fine. Everything would be fine."

"And your dad didn't agree?"

"He was determined to not be fine. And that was okay. I had Josh. And Mom wasn't gone yet. She didn't look great, but he could've enjoyed her anyway. But he didn't. He wanted everything to look fine. It never looks fine. But it always is."

"You mean Josh?"

"Sure, Josh. He looks bad right now, but I thought he'd died and was visiting me one last time before going wherever you go. But he's not dead. He's recoverable. My brother is recoverable, and we're going to recover him. You're going to save my brother."

Anja nodded, sniffed, because she didn't know what else to say, and because the talk of saving a brother reminded her about how she hadn't been able to save her own.

Yuri came closer and sat down beside her, rested his head on the bottom fence rail. "What did I say?"

"Nothing."

"You all of a sudden look like your hamster just died. I said something. What did I say?"

"You kind of remind me of someone. And then not. But then yeah." She laughed and sniffled. "I'm not making sense."

"No, I get you. I said something that reminded you of something. What?"

Anja looked up and stared at what she could see of the sunlit sky through the canopy.

"I had a brother."

"Had?"

Anja nodded. "Everyone thought we were twins. And we kind of were. Not twin-twins, but Irish twins. Born eleven months apart. He was older. Everyone says twins are these super connected, read each other's minds, always knows what the other's doing, super special relationship things, but Brian and I weren't that. We were opposites. Opposite interests, opposite worlds. You name it, we were opposites."

"I take it he wasn't a scientist?"

"Case in point," Anja said. "He was like you, actually. In fact, you probably aren't going to believe this, but when I first saw you in the clearing that night, for a second I thought you were him. I do that sometimes. Think I see him."

"Is he . . . missing?"

"No. I'm the one who found him. In the bathtub. He always said it helped him forget that he was quote-unquote *real*. And then one day it made him not real."

Yuri was sitting quietly, looking curious but unwilling to pry.

"He didn't hurt himself or OD or anything. He drowned. In the bathtub. They think he must've fallen asleep, which is the stupidest thing I've ever heard. I said so to the medical examiner. 'I'm just a wannabe med student, but I'm pretty sure you wake yourself up when you can't breathe. That's why all the people with sleep apnea never feel rested.' But I guess on the flip side they could've found some way to blame me, being the person who found him and all. And then I'd be in prison instead of having this conversation. So, what's that you were saying? Things never look fine, but they are? I don't know. I think I'd prefer they look fine, even if they're not."

"You and too many other people," Yuri said. Then, "Sorry about your brother."

Anja nodded.

"So, can I . . .?"

"Sure."

"When you say I remind you of him, do you mean in looks, or was he . . ."

"Gifted?"

"Yeah, did he have some kind of psychic or extrasensory or . . ."

"Both," Anja said. "At first anyway. You don't really look like him, now that I'm looking at you, but you did for a split second. And, yeah, he was . . . I don't know just how psychic or whatever he was, but maybe you could call him spiritual or enlightened. Is that the word?"

Yuri shrugged. "Maybe. Enlightened how?"

"He just seemed wise and above it all, and always wanting to escape, especially when he heard something evil or sad or whatever. He'd go do that bathtub stuff. Not always in the bathtub, but . . . anyway. Yeah. Wise and . . . enlightened. He'd say things, like he was a new-age Confucius."

"That's cool," Yuri said, and he said it in a way that Anja couldn't tell if he meant it sincerely or as a listening sound or as a blow-off or something else entirely. And then he said matter-of-factly, "But you don't—didn't—think it was cool?"

Anja hung her head and wished she could have been more open-minded back then, but she felt that she still wasn't that open-minded now. She shook her head. "Get real. Get a job. Quit being such a loser. It's so embarrassing that you look so much like me I can't deny your existence."

"You said that?"

"Probably. Thought it at any rate. Treated him that way. With major frustration. My parents thought he was special, too, you see. Like your mom thought about you. I was your dad. Except in my scenario, the parental units were on the same side and banded together against me. Fortunately, I was going to college that fall, and I dove in and never resurfaced. I found people who didn't believe in that crap any more than I did. And that just sucked me down further."

"And here?"

Anja laughed. "Not getting away with much here, am I? Definitely being poked and prodded by the things I'd rather not think about, here. But I think I'm okay with that. Every generation of scientists has thought they've gotten it all right, too focused and self-righteous to see anything else but the truth of their own theories, and every generation has been wrong about that. But I don't see that happening to me, not anymore. Assuming we get out of here, anyway."

Assuming they figured out the rift well enough to get permission to go home.

"You don't still have your GPS, do you?" she asked.

She'd meant it as a laugh; they could plot the coordinates for home and start walking, but when Yuri said no, it was suddenly less funny.

The only way out was through.

"We should probably get back to it," she said.

More OBE training. Yay.

But she could feel that her resistance to the unfathomable things had shifted just the tiniest bit. Maybe it was talking about her brother that did it. She had no doubt he could do it. And he would always be a part of her.

She pushed herself up to standing and pulled Yuri up too.

CHAPTER 42

"Like you're floating on water," Yuri said, his voice oddly distant, as he paced slowly, quietly, back and forth just beyond Anja's feet.

Anja lay motionless on the blanket-strewn hardwood floor of the welcoming center again. But in her mind, she floated on water. Bobbed up and down, up and down, as if a boat had just puttered by and she was riding out its wake.

Anja had forgotten how she used to do this with her brother, float in their grandmother's neighbor's pool in the summer. It was one of those above-ground deals, not too deep. They could each touch their toes to the bottom and stand with their noses more or less out of the water, their foreheads definitely. Seven or eight years old. Later, their grandpa died, and their grandmother sold the property soon after that. But for a while they'd spent every summer in that neighbor's pool, floating on the water with the jets turned on just enough to create some waves, not enough to have to paddle too hard.

While in the pool they were silent, an unspoken agreement between them.

Don't say a word. It will ruin the magic.

At least that's what Anja thought her brother was thinking.

Don't say a word. When I'm floating in the pool, I forget where I am, that we're at Grandma's, that Mom and Dad are fighting again. I forget that I have a body, that I even exist. Don't say a word. And whatever you do, don't touch me.

That last one wasn't so much unspoken as it was yelled, once, when one of the waves pushed Anja toward her brother and she bumped his shoulder with her foot.

"Don't touch me!" her brother said, capsizing at the waist and flailing his arms and legs to find his footing. "Don't touch me. I was out!" he said. "I was so out. I was nowhere near here. I was . . . never mind."

He reached for the edge of the pool and climbed out, jumped down onto the asphalt, and stomped away from her, water pouring off of his huge basketball shorts.

Anja had righted herself as well, but had otherwise stayed motionless in the water, staring after her brother with her mouth hanging open, taking in water. It was just a bump to the shoulder. Obviously accidental. She'd done way worse to him on purpose to far less outbursting results.

She wanted to know what was really the matter with her brother, but now was obviously not the time to ask him.

She got out, dried off, and played with the neighbor's orange tabby until dinnertime, when Grandma insisted they all eat together at the table.

Grandma never failed to ask them about their days, like they did important things in some office or laboratory or field somewhere.

Anja usually went first, eager to relay her exciting adventures of swimming and cat playing, but she remained silent, waiting for her brother to go first. To her surprise, he grinned from ear to ear.

"I went to the moon," he said.

"Did you?" Grandma said, showing no signs that she was indulging him.

"Only for a little bit." He glared at Anja. "I got pulled back right after I got there, but before that I was with Grandpa."

"Were you?" Grandma side-glanced her husband, who was sitting at the table in his wheelchair. He didn't respond or even appear to be listening. He still looked tired from his nap as he picked at a chunk of peanut butter and jelly sandwich Grandma had cut up for him. He would die a few months later.

"We went to the arcade," her brother said. "I didn't get to play. No money. But we watched a kid get through some game start to finish in under ten minutes."

"Uh-huh," Grandma said. Now she sounded indulgent. "And what did Grandpa think?"

"He said he once worked on the first home video game console."

At this Grandma frowned. "He said what?"

"That he worked on the Magnavox Odyssey, the thing . . . before Atari." Her brother was frowning now, too, picking up on Grandma's shifting energy. It was such a change even Anja could feel it.

"Did your dad tell you about that?" Grandma asked her brother.

Her brother looked at Grandpa—a goop of peanut butter and jelly on his chin and still not interested in the conversation, if he heard it at all—and back at Grandma. Brian shrunk a little in his chair and took a big bite of his sandwich.

Grandma squinted at Brian and then squinted even harder at Grandpa.

Her brother was telling the truth. Anja knew it, and she thought anyone who knew her brother would know it too. She was certain Grandma knew it was true. Her brother hadn't heard it from their father. He'd heard it from Grandpa. Grandpa had told him about his time creating the video game thing. And he'd told him today.

But how?

"I'm sorry I bumped you," Anja said.

Her brother looked up at her and nodded, mouth still full of PB and J. But then his eyes drifted to Grandma, still studying him. He shoved in the rest of his sandwich and took his plate to the sink.

"When'd you bump him?" Grandma asked.

"In the pool."

As was their routine, Anja and Brian went to the pool the next day. Her brother hopped in and began floating on his back, eyes closed, oblivious to everything around him. But Anja knew a second intrusion would be even worse for her than the first time. So Anja hooked a jump rope around her ankle so as to make sure she didn't float into her brother again.

And Grandma watched. At first she feigned visiting the neighbors, but she peeked out the window more often than she should have for that to be the real motivation behind her visit. Her brother didn't notice at first, but the next day Grandma brought over a lawn chair and joined them outside. She came after her brother had already gotten into floating position, eyes closed, but she was still there when he suddenly came to and found his footing.

They locked eyes and Grandma seemed to measure her words before settling on the ever lame "Enjoying the pool?"

Her brother nodded but then said he'd had enough and got out. On the third day, Grandma prepared to go to the pool again, but her brother said he didn't want to go. And he never went back.

But he suddenly showed much less resistance to taking his nightly bath.

It wouldn't be until after their parents came to take them home that he would tell Anja what he had done and how she could do it too.

"When I'm in the water, I'm just completely relaxed, and the world falls away, and I fall away, except I also rise, and sometimes I'm looking down at my body and sometimes I'm somewhere else entirely. Just relax, and float, and rise. At the same time."

It didn't come as easily for Anja as it did for her brother. But she did eventually do it.

And she decided she could do it again now.

"Like you're floating on water," Yuri said again. "Rising and falling with the waves."

When she was a kid, Anja, too, would practice in the bathtub. Once or twice, anyway. She'd let the water fill her ears and lift her hair, and she'd close her eyes and relax.

Relax and rise, she'd think to herself. *Relax and rise*.

But she didn't think she was doing either. Was there tension in her hips? Her shoulders? How could she think she was rising when her back was touching the tub?

But then one time she just let the whole intention go. She pitched a towel tent over the steaming water, anchored with her mom's candles and other bathroom junk, to keep the heat in, and she lay in the tub, letting the water fill her ears and lift her hair. She closed her eyes. And she left it at that, figuring she'd climb out an hour later with nothing to show for it other than being all pruny.

She dozed.

"*Come on,*" she heard her brother say. Like he was in her mind. But it was more than a dream. "*I got you. You can do this.*" She opened her eyes—or opened her consciousness—and she saw him standing next to her, holding out his hand like he would help her up.

Or out.

"*Yes,*" her brother said, excited but not too excited. A calm encouragement. "*Just relax,*" he said, taking her hand.

But not either of her real hands. Those were still in the water, under the towel.

"*Here we go,*" he said.

And Anja, too, had gone to the moon.

But they never talked about it. And he never helped her again. She never knew why. And after he died, she'd called it all a dream.

"Relax and rise," Yuri was saying. "Relax and rise. If you feel anything weird, it's normal. If you hear anything strange, it's normal. Just accept it as progress and keep relaxing. Relax and rise."

Anja didn't hear anything, not even Yuri's footsteps, and if she felt anything, it was an absence of feeling. An absence of the weight of her body holding her to the ground. As if she were in that pool again, floating with her brother, practicing without knowing that she was practicing the feeling. The weightless feeling. She almost thought her brother might show up standing next to her, to help her out once again.

But she knew that wouldn't happen. He was sixteen years dead. And he wasn't coming back. Not for this. Not for anything.

But she was hyperaware. And when her soul broke free, she got a visual of her surroundings:

She was standing over her body. The glowing monitors to her right.

Yuri had his back to her as he walked past her toward Danny, on her left side. He reached the end of his pacing route and turned around. His gaze tore away from the blanket-strewn floor, from his observation of the three people lying at his feet, and he locked eyes with Anja.

He made no sudden noises, no sudden movements. He continued his calm pace and his calming description of what he hoped his students would be feeling and accomplishing.

But his mouth quirked. A quick smile. And he nodded as if telling her to go, to take it for a test drive.

Show me the moon, she thought.

CHAPTER 43

N*ow take me to the rift.*

It felt like being whisked away, sucked into a vacuum with the air rushing past her. All Anja had to do was think the thought of where she wanted to go and her consciousness obeyed.

She was standing at the edge of the rift.

The rift wasn't doing much. She could tell that if she were in physical form—same as the perimeter watcher now circling the clearing—the rift would be dark, silent, inert. He couldn't see it, couldn't hear it, and if he was new, he was probably wondering why he was even out here at all, guarding this thing.

But the rift was still there. In whatever form she was currently in, sans body, she could see and hear and feel the rift.

It was a whitish-purple shape in the air, a triangular shape, rotating in a smooth motion yet morphing so that the triangle's apexes, its points, never pointed toward the ground.

And it hummed. It was neither soothing nor agitating, just there, like white noise—no-no—like the deep rumbling of brown noise and the swishing and hissing of blue. Like the slow rush of waves without the ebb and flow.

And she could feel its mood. Concerned. There was a palpable sense of concern in the clearing. And it was definitely coming from the rift, the rotating, triangular rift, because it was decidedly not coming from the humanoid shapes standing in front of it.

Anja could see and hear and sort of feel them, too, though not as clearly. And they could sense her, but they seemed to find her far less interesting in her current form than when she'd shined light and thrown a rock at them.

Less interested meant less threatening. Right?

She walked toward them.

Two of them noticed her approach.

A tall, slender woman with waist-long hair pulled over one shoulder and a smaller man with a dark bowl cut. They didn't prod any of the other forms around them to warn them that Anja was approaching, nor did they confer with each other. They just watched. Neither curious nor annoyed by her presence.

When she was close enough but still out of arm's reach, Anja smiled.

"*Hello*," she said.

They didn't say anything, but they moved as if shifting their weight, tilting their heads in new directions. Anja took that as acknowledgement. So where to begin? The five Ws?

Who are you? What are you doing here? What is this thing you're standing in front of? Are you guarding it or drawn to it? Are those two things mutually exclusive?

"*My name is Anja*," she said.

The tall woman smiled and nodded, and Anja heard a strange high-pitched sound. But if the ghost-woman shared her name, Anja didn't catch it. And she was pretty sure she just didn't catch it, because the smaller man looked up at the woman like he hadn't expected to hear whatever it was she had said.

The smaller man then said his name was Ralph. Anja heard it. She heard his voice, like white noise over the brown. But she also saw it, saw his lips move. His lips had parted like a small lion's roar, and his tongue tapped his top teeth before they dug into his lower lip. *Ra-l-ph*.

Anja was so excited—

She was suddenly back on the blanket-covered hardwood floor, staring up at the log-trussed ceiling. Yuri was still talking Ming and

Danny through the floating technique. Anja doubted she'd been out more than a few minutes. If she'd been out at all.

Yuri turned around, seeming to sense her return. Anja frowned at him, but Yuri grinned from ear to ear, and that made Anja grin too. And why not? She'd gotten out. And she knew she could do it again. She'd done it once or twice as a kid with her brother, until—

(Well, until he got obsessed with it. More interested in being asleep and out than awake and alive.)

—until her brother made it so it wasn't fun anymore. He always wanted to stay out longer and go farther. His silver cord got so thin . . .

But she realized now that she'd stopped doing it not because she grew out of the ability, but because she hadn't wanted to do it anymore. She didn't like what it was doing to her brother and what her brother was doing with it.

But she could do it. She'd just proven it to herself. And Yuri, silly psychic Yuri, was the proof. She'd gotten out, and she could get out again.

But could she stay out?

CHAPTER 44

At the end of the session, after Ming went outside to stretch her legs and Danny went to check on patrol, Anja told Yuri about going to the moon and the rift and talking to the ghosts.

"But right after they answered me, I was suddenly back in my body," she said.

"When the woman didn't quite answer, were you surprised when the man did?"

"Oh yeah," Anja said.

"Then it's probably because you got excited," Yuri said. "People are on this positivity kick, where negativity is this horrid thing and positivity is where it's at, and you should fake it until you make it, and milk all the positive moments you have with this uber excited energy . . . but uber positivity isn't the ideal either. And going out of body shows that. If you were scared, you'd pop back to body, but you'll also pop back to body if something wows you."

"So I have to be emotionless?" Anja asked.

Stay objective. Don't react. Keep it on the inside. Sounded good to her. She'd been practicing that technique for years.

"It's not the emotion," Yuri said. "It's the moodiness, the waffling. Things can make you mad, and you can throw a tantrum or take it in stride or anything in between. Same with the positive emotions. Things can make you happy, and you can spout off about how awesome it is or take it in stride or anything in between. But whether you're ranting in the positive or the negative, it's not sustainable—both because it's exhausting and because the thing outside of you giving rise to the rant will wear itself out on you eventually—and you'll eventually have to come back to neutral. But you never fall to just neutral. You always fall a little past neutral before you climb back up again. You're on a pendulum that just keeps swinging, when what's needed is plumb stability."

"So when something happens to me . . ."

"Take it in stride," Yuri said. "When you're OB, you're going to do what you usually do, whatever your habit is. Because most people aren't as clear-minded and aware when they're out as when they're awake. So if you want to become more emotionally stable when you're out, you need to practice becoming more emotionally stable when you're awake."

"How old are you again?"

Yuri snorted and smiled.

"So don't react," Anja said.

"Think of it more as judgment. Something awesome happened to you—that Ralph guy told you his name—and you judged that as this super great thing."

"It was," Anja said.

"It was. Yeah. I know it was," Yuri said. "And had you just rolled with it, without making a big deal about it, you might still be talking to him right now. I'm just saying."

"So don't react."

"Reserve judgment."

"Reserve judgment." Anja nodded. "I don't think I can do that."

Yuri smiled.

"I'm feeling judged," Anja said.

"Nope," Yuri said. "Just acknowledging that I see what the universe is doing."

"What's it doing?"

"What it does. Did you see the old wizened ghost?"

"The . . . no," she said, remembering what Yuri had said about the old ghost loving her, and shifting uncomfortably.

"He didn't go with you. He stayed with your body. Did you see your body?"

Anja thought about it. "No," she said. "I knew it was down there, but I saw you, and I thought you were telling me to take off."

"I was," he said with a smile. "Seeing your own body can be a mind trip. The first time, especially. You probably would've popped right back in. But you were out a while. Went a couple places, it sounds like. I think your guardian was helping you stay out."

CHAPTER 45

The next morning, Anja woke early, to the sounds of a vehicle driving fast into the campground. Headlights flashed through her window and onto the conex's walls. Outside, she saw Jackson's black truck pull to a stop in front of the welcoming center, the dust still settling. Anja dressed quickly in her rain gear and hurried across the dirt road.

The welcoming center smelled like they'd forgotten to wash the dishes after dinner last night. Ming and Danny were sitting at the monitors.

"Where's Jackson?" she asked.

Danny thumbed the room next door. "He's over with Doc. He said to give them a minute, that he'd be back over."

But Anja couldn't wait. She went back outside, ran around the side of the building, and barged into sick bay.

Jackson and Doc, with the baby strapped to her chest, were standing over Tyrese. Doc had her cart with her. A red backpack sat on the floor next to it. Jackson looked like he hadn't slept in a while, and his eyes were rimmed red. He was letting the baby grip his index finger.

"You're here," Anja said. "How's your wife and . . . and everything?"

He gave Anja a small smile. "I've been told to prepare for the worst."

"The baby?"

His face crumpled and he shook his head. "My wife."

"Oh, Darius." Anja wrapped her arms around his torso, trapping him in a hug. She hugged him until it became awkward, not knowing what else to do, what else to say.

Jackson said, "There might still be something I can do. That you can do."

"Anything," Anja said, releasing him. Though she had no idea what he might have in mind.

There was a knock on the door and Yuri entered.

"Hey, Yuri," Doc said, "Come on in."

"Thanks." He tiptoed past the guys at the front of the room, squeezing a shin or a bicep along the way, until he reached Josh. He looked down at Josh, then looked back at the men he'd passed, a frown on his face. Then he looked at Doc.

"Josh looks good," she said, but her tone sounded heavy.

Another knock on the door and Ming and Danny entered.

Danny said, "We watched people going in here, but no one was coming back out."

Anja wondered who was watching the monitors but figured, hey, even when people do make it on site, we don't catch them, so there was probably no harm, no foul.

Jackson must've agreed because he said, "It's fine. I was hoping to put this all together and then show you, but we might as well put it together, well, together."

He gestured them closer and waited for them to make their way past the seven men lying very still in the middle of the room. Yuri stood and joined them, too.

Jackson said, "My wife is having complications. Chest pains, mostly, although they can't explain why. They say it's not heartburn or anything. Anyway, I told her to keep track of her symptoms, and she"—he smiled and hung his head—"she took notes all right."

He opened the red backpack and pulled out a notebook, then another, and set them on Doc's cart, on top of her tools.

"Precise, to-the-detail notes," he said. "Thing is, I think at least some of her symptoms line up with the rift activity."

"You're kidding?" Anja said. "How could that be possible?"

Jackson glanced at Doc. "Same as how the boys reacted to the rift activity?"

Doc pulled the notebooks her way as Danny made a give-it-here gesture. Doc pushed one of the notebooks his way and opened the second one in front of herself.

Danny opened his and stepped away from the counter a bit so that Anja, Ming, and Yuri could peer at it too. But Anja couldn't concentrate on the bubbly blue handwriting. She was thinking about the news, about the reports of a rise in pregnancy loss. They'd started about a year ago. About the same time Darius's team had been tapped to guard the clearing.

But still, connecting them causally felt like a stretch.

"Waking nightmares?" Doc said, reading from one of Marisol's notebooks as she passed her fingertips under each blue-inked entry. "That's not a typical pregnancy complaint."

"Neither is temporary paralysis," said Ming.

"Wait," Danny said. "She's written the times here. Look at this one. November 2, 7:45 a.m., waking nightmares. What is today?"

"The fourth," Ming said.

"Two days ago," Danny said. "Yesterday we learned how to OBE. The day before that we tested the rift. Didn't the power-station boom happen about 7:45?"

"Almost exactly 7:45," Anja said. She remembered looking at her watch with Ming when Doc had said it took her an hour to arrive at the campground after the team's movements triggered her alarm.

"What about when Anja threw the rock?" Ming asked. Then, quietly, to Anja, "Sorry."

"Don't be," Anja said. "It's not the data I was thinking we'd get, but data is data. When did I throw the rock? It was right after sunset. What time was that?"

"I think about 6:10 or so—no, 5:10, daylight savings," Danny said. "Here it is. November 2, 5:20 p.m., sharp pain, temporary paralysis. You think it's connected?"

"I know it is," Jackson said.

"What about all her other entries?" Danny said. "We don't have anything matching those."

"We do, actually," Doc said, and she pulled a third notebook from the lower shelf on her cart. "I've been taking notes, too. The big things you've mentioned, but also other, more subtle things I've noticed. You can look at it, but I already recognize matching entries in Marisol's book."

"There've got to be other women in the hospital with your wife," said Anja, opening Doc's notebook. "What about them? Are they complaining?"

Jackson nodded. "Marisol heard some of the other women yelling and moaning at the same time she was having issues. She asked her nurse what was going on, but patient confidentiality, blah, blah, blah. So I can't be sure, but . . . yeah. I'm pretty damn sure."

Anja was still comparing entries between Marisol's and Doc's notebooks, running both index fingers down the pages, her gaze darting back and forth between Marisol's blue ink and Doc's black. She was finding quite a bit of overlap, and she felt herself nodding. Emphatically.

Yeah. She was pretty sure the pregnancy reports were connected to the rift, too.

Just like the team's.

Standing around Doc's cart, with the seven fallen team members lying quietly on their cots behind them and the baby gurgling, Ming, Doc, and Jackson, and Yuri and Danny in particular, seemed to suddenly radiate energy and purpose.

Anja felt it, too.

Jackson leveled his gaze on Yuri. "We gotta go into that rift," he said. "Now." He glanced at Danny, who was still studying Marisol's journal, then back at Yuri. "Can we go into the rift?"

Yuri was slow in answering.

Yuri could go into the rift. Everyone knew that Yuri could go into the rift. But Anja suspected that what Jackson was really asking was could *Danny* get into the rift.

And if Danny couldn't go, would Yuri go alone? Was it worth sending Yuri in alone?

This mission was on Danny.

And Danny seemed to know it.

"How much time do we have?" he said. "I did some more practicing on my own last night—"

"In the spare moments when you weren't watching the monitors or checking the skunk bombs or calling the perimeter guys for status checks?" Ming said, not unkindly. But Danny ignored her so effortlessly, Anja began doubting whether Ming had spoken at all.

"—and I think I've definitely got the sensation down, the energy . . . movement . . . whatever. The sensation." He looked to Yuri for confirmation.

"The pulse technique?" Yuri said.

"Yeah, yeah. The bouncing pulse. And I got my leg out." Danny pointed at Yuri, who nodded dutifully. "Just a little more time," Danny said, "a day, twenty-four hours. I can do this."

But Jackson had barely taken his eyes off Yuri. "Can he, Yuri?" he asked.

"Look," Danny said. "Whatever caused this—whoever caused this—they're hurting my friends, my family." He thumbed over his shoulder at the seven men lying on cots behind him. "These guys, and you, you're all I've got. I will do this. I will do this for them."

Jackson's expression remained unchanged.

"Let me do this," Danny said.

"I don't think we've got enough time." He looked at Doc. "Tell them."

Doc sighed.

"Tell us what?" asked Danny.

"Are they okay?" Yuri asked. "Is Josh okay?"

"Josh is okay," Doc said. "I should have listened to you, Yuri. The tranquilizer is proving too much, and even though I only gave them the one dose, it doesn't seem to be wearing off. Their blood pressures are . . . well, they were always dangerously low, but . . ." She gestured helplessly at Tyrese just behind her, and then to the others. "Only Josh's is showing up."

"Are they dead?"

"No . . . no, they're not dead. They're . . . I thought they were still alive in there—and I still do," she hastened to say. "But I think we need to get them to a hospital."

"They can't help," Jackson said. "You were right about that. Not to mention the hospitals are full of pregnant women who will take priority. No, you were right. They're better off here. You can prioritize them here."

"And I'm doing everything I can," Doc said, "but Death gets what Death wants, and these symptoms are the mark of Death. I don't mean to be callous. I just want to impress upon you how serious this is."

"And I believe you," Jackson said. "I'll see if I can find them a facility with more equipment."

Doc nodded, clearly appeased. More equipment would make everything better.

"In the meantime, I think the team's condition just adds to the reasons why we need to go into the rift now," Jackson said. "The team, Marisol and the other women, the"—he gently shook Gaia's little fist. He turned to Yuri again. "Even if it's just you, kid. Someone needs to go into the rift. And it needs to be now. Can we do it?"

Yuri nodded absently, and his chest rose and fell in deep coming-to-terms-with-it breaths. Jackson was saying *we*, but what he really meant was *you*. Could Yuri do it.

"I can go," Anja said.

"You got out?" Danny and Ming both said.

"I got out," Anja said.

"Beginner's luck?" Danny said in a joking tone.

But Yuri quirked his mouth into an expression of regret. “Unfortunately, that is a thing,” he said. “When people first start, they don’t really know what to expect, so they don’t really have any expectations, no resistance, and they just play with the techniques, and voila, they’re out. And then, once they know they can do it, they get too serious about it, too insistent, and they often do get out again, but not right away, sometimes not for a very long time. Not until it’s no big deal again.”

Jackson snorted. “Well, there’s no denying this is a very big deal.”

“Exactly,” Yuri said.

Anja considered telling them that she wasn’t quite a beginner, but ultimately decided to keep it to herself. “Okay, well, beginner’s luck or not, if Yuri’s going either way, then whoever gets out with him can go with him into the rift. Right?”

But Anja could see it on their faces. Jackson and Yuri had long ago made peace with the idea that possibly only Yuri would make the trek. But now Danny, Ming, and even Doc were seeing only Yuri, taller than all of them but still only fifteen, getting out of body and entering the rift alone.

“How many more days do the guys have?” Danny asked, but when Doc didn’t answer immediately, he amended his question into a word that rang like an answer. “Hours?”

Doc shrugged. “I just don’t know. People tend to hold on for longer than you expect, until they’re just gone faster than you could’ve imagined.”

“Can you give me a day?” Danny said. “Just a day. As soon as I’m out we can go. Right, Yuri?” But Danny didn’t wait for Yuri to answer. “I’m out and I’m in, so to speak.”

“If you can’t get in, you can’t get in,” Jackson said. “But I would prefer it if you got in.” Then, “Okay. Keep practicing. But go in as soon as you can.”

Yuri took it as orders, turning on his heel and heading out the door. Anja followed him, Ming and Danny right behind her, back to the other side of the building.

"Get your mat, if it's not already next door," Yuri said.

Anja's wasn't, so she ran to her conex, ripped the blanket and the thin mat off the bed, and hefted both at a run back to the welcoming center.

Jackson was there, too. He held the door open for her, then followed her inside.

Ming was sitting in the chair in front of the monitors, wearing a set of headphones Anja had never seen before. Ming noticed her staring. "Found 'em in my conex."

Danny was already lying on his blanket just behind Ming's rolly chair.

Yuri was sitting on the edge of the table, still pushed against the back wall, his feet on the hardwood floor, next to Danny.

"No mat?" Jackson asked him.

Yuri shook his head, seemingly distracted.

"I'll get out of your way," Jackson said, backing toward the door. "Do you need anything from me before I leave? Maybe I should stay."

Yuri shrugged helplessly, but Danny said, "Unless you're an OBE pro, there's nothing for you to do here. Doc's got the team under control as best as anyone can hope, and the perimeter guys are solid. Ming doesn't expect to get out, so she's volunteered to stay in and watch the monitors and hold down the fort. So go. Be with your wife. And your child."

"If she comes," Jackson said.

"She'll come," Danny said. "We're gonna make sure she comes, and that she comes healthy, happy, and smiling."

But Jackson still looked unsure.

Yuri said, "I'll get them out."

"And in," Jackson said.

"And in. I'll get them in. Me, anyway."

"And Danny," Jackson said.

Yuri nodded. "And Danny. I'll get Danny in."

"Okay, then," Jackson said. "Good luck."

CHAPTER 46

Anja spread her mat and blanket out on the hardwood floor, then put her hand over the light switch, to flip it off. "We ready?"

"No," Yuri and Danny both said.

Danny gestured for Yuri to go first.

"We've got some prep work to do," Yuri said, not uncalmly. But he was noticeably shaking, almost like a chihuahua dog. "We need some protection measures. Some defense measures."

"Ming's protecting us," Danny said, and Ming nodded confirmation, though Anja thought she looked a little distracted, a little in her head.

"She's protecting our bodies," Yuri said. "We need something that's going to protect our minds, our awareness."

"From what?" Danny said. "Negativity? Do we need to bring our positive attitudes?"

Anja guessed Danny was anxious too, what with the way he was rambling, but she chuckled along with him. Knowing the psychic, it probably was something woo-woo like that.

"That wouldn't hurt," Yuri said, "but I was thinking distractions. We need to protect our focus."

Anja couldn't argue with that. Focus was everything. She'd like to defend her energy, too, from stimuli that might cause her to get too excited, because God knew there would be plenty of awe and wow where she was going.

But she told herself not to worry about that. If she got out at all, then she could get out again. And again. As often as it took, she would get out.

And dare she think it, let alone say it out loud, she would do it for the experience.

The world needed saving, sure . . . but wow. What an experience. What an adventure, to experience pure awareness, pureness of thought, and to go where no one had gone before. They say space or the deep ocean is the final frontier, but not so. This—going into the rift, beyond the veil—this was the final frontier, the final journey. A metajourney.

And she guessed that made her a metanaut.

"What do you have in mind," she asked, "for maintaining focus?"

She expected an immediate idea, but Yuri didn't offer one.

"What about headphones?" Ming asked. "Anja listens to binary beats at work." She offered Anja an apologetic shrug, but Anja didn't mind the suggestion. She thought it was a good idea.

"Yeah," Yuri said. "Yeah, that'll work. Do you have any headphones? Where'd you get those?"

"I can round some up," Danny said. "While I'm at it, can you make me a recording? If you're lying down with us, I don't know who's going to talk me out. I tried to talk myself out last night, but it wasn't as good."

Yuri hesitated, and Anja could only guess he was thinking about time, but Ming said she and Yuri would see if they could find a suitable recording on the internet.

With the other three focused on their tasks, Anja tried to get calm. She turned off the lights, but the room stayed fairly lit, what with all the monitors flashing scenes of the woods and the campground. Their various computer fans droned on and on, under the desk. Anja sat down on her blanket, then stretched out on her back.

Relax.

"I've been thinking," Danny said when he returned with more headphones, presumably scrounged from the other conexes. He hooked them up to the computers under the desk. Yuri took one set and passed another set to Anja.

"You don't have the skill to carry something solid," Danny said to Yuri, "right?"

"No, and I pulled that shoe by accident. I don't know if I could do it again on purpose. Why?"

"I'm pretty sure I don't have the skill to carry something solid," Danny continued, "and Anja—can you pick up solids?"

Anja shrugged. She was feeling pretty confident, and she wanted to give them hope. "I can try."

"So, no," Danny said. "But that kid—"

"The kid who took the notebook?" Ming said.

"Exactly. I'm assuming he's not the bad guy in this scenario. But I bet he doesn't have that skill by chance, either. At least not as far as our bad guy is concerned. And I doubt he was recruited just so he could snatch your notebook; you weren't even in the picture until a couple days ago. So if our bad guy picked this kid for his rare skill, then he's probably trying to take something across the veil, into the rift. But if that's the case, how are we supposed to stop him?"

Nobody said anything. Anja wondered if that was because the stupid answer that had come to her mind had come to their minds as well.

But they didn't have time to judge their options. Someone needed to say it.

"Distraction?" she said. Nobody laughed. But she still felt the need to explain. "If we're protecting ourselves from distractions, they might be doing the same."

"He vanished as soon as he got the book, before the woman OBEr started attacking you," Yuri said. "I don't know if he left willingly or because he couldn't help it, but it may be our only shot. Course it's his shot, too. We've gotta be on guard for surprises like that."

"And probably other surprises," Ming said. "If he's far more skilled, he probably has far more tricks to play."

"I've seen some tricks," Yuri said, and even though he didn't elaborate, the energy in the room seemed to lighten. They could do this.

So long as Yuri could do this.

Soon, Danny, Yuri, and Anja were all wearing their headphones and lying together in a row, heads pointed at the table pushed against the back wall, feet toward the door. Ming was at the monitors to Anja's far right, on the other side of Danny.

Ming had offered to play Anja the recording she and Yuri had found, but Anja had opted for binaural beats. Two different tones entered her ears, creating a third. It helped that she used this same recording to help her focus at work in her lab.

Anja had succeeded in getting out using the floating-on-water technique, but she had started out remembering the pulsing pain in her stubbed toe. She moved it through her hips and into her lower back. But she feared that Danny or Ming or whoever had said it might be right. Her first time might've just been beginner's luck.

And they didn't have time for her to become a pro.

She pushed the pulsing pain into her shoulders and up into her head, then let it travel back down to her chest, where it diffused into floating on water.

She lay there, imagining the feel of floating up and down, up and down.

"*That's enough,*" a voice said over the binaural beats coming from Anja's headphones. Dammit. She'd forgotten all about the headphones. She'd entered a deeper, OBE-worthy state, and now she was in touch with the physical again.

But she drifted so easily back into the theta state, eyes fluttering, body vibrating, stubbed-toe pulse coursing through her body on its own, that she thought surely she must be . . .

"I'm going to help you out."

She heard it more clearly now. It was Yuri. And she had a clearer sense of what he was trying to do, too. And not just because he'd stated his intention.

Help Danny, she wanted to say, but she knew better. Like

excitement, movement, even moving her lips, would halt the process. And, anyway, she'd be able to convey her message telepathically once she got out.

And she was now absolutely certain that she'd be able to do so.

She could feel Yuri's hand, or something like it, taking hold of hers and pulling her up, as if out of a chair, as if asking her to dance. She rose slowly, as if she were stepping out of a pool while wearing a ball gown, and the waterlogged fabric was weighing her down.

Yuri looked just like himself, in his tie-dyed hoodie, only translucent. She could see the wall behind him.

"*Help Danny*," she said.

But he just frowned, like he'd already tried and failed.

"*Go outside*," he said. "*I'll meet you at the rift.*"

Take me to the rift—no, wait!

Anja's eyes fluttered lazily, sleepily.

Damn. She was back in her body.

After demanding she be taken to the rift, she'd imagined herself arriving in the center of all the other ghosts, got worried, and lost her out.

Fortunately, she hadn't been gone long, barely a second, probably. She didn't dare try to move. Didn't dare to even open her eyes wide. She was still hypnogogic, still in a theta state. She knew she was, because she could still see through the haze of her lashes what she normally couldn't see: an astral body.

Yuri's astral body stood, or hovered, to her right, leaning over Danny. Something told her she shouldn't strain too hard to see what he was doing. But she figured if Yuri was still here, then he wasn't having much luck pulling Danny into the ether. She closed her eyes.

"*I got excited again*," she said.

And the feeling happened again, that faint feeling of a hand on her hand, pulling her up, as if out of a chair, as if stepping, drenched, out of the water. And at the end of her hand was Yuri. Smiling, if also still looking a little disappointed.

"*I can't get him out*," he said. "*I think he's just too tired. And no wonder. He's been doing all this stuff with us and all the stuff with the perimeter guys, too."*

"Just you and me then," Anja said. "*We'll be okay.*"

It came out more question than statement, though she'd intended it otherwise.

"*We'll be okay,*" he said, still holding her hand. "*Let's go.*" And before Anja could demand a location or mess things up again, she and Yuri were standing at the edge of the rift.

CHAPTER 47

The morning sun was out, but the clearing was still pretty shady thanks to all the redwood trees. Ghostly human forms loitered in the clearing, in front of the rift, but they seemed agitated, twitchy, like junkies looking for a fix. Or maybe glitchy was the better word, as if their programming wasn't working properly. Their forms jerked, and some of them blinked in and out of sight.

The rift rotated behind them, churning faster, moving through a spectrum of colors, both on the color wheel and beyond.

"*Something's happening,*" Yuri said.

Well, duh, Anja thought, followed by *Whoops.*

She'd meant to say that comment only in her own mind, not to Yuri, but then she realized that her technique for speaking to herself was the same one she used to talk to Yuri. So had he heard that? Was he hearing this?

"*Stay calm,*" Yuri said, but it was hard for Anja to obey. She didn't know if he was saying that with his own agenda or saying it in response to the mini freak-out she was having because she didn't know just how much of her thoughts were being broadcasted.

"*Just observe,*" Yuri said, which made her feel better. Sort of. She still didn't know whether he heard everything or not, but at least he was ignoring what wasn't specifically intended for anyone's ears.

"*Just observe. Stay open-minded, like a beginner. A newbie. We're new here. We don't know what any of this means. Not really.*

We think it's caused by something we don't like, but we don't know that for sure. For all we know, what we're seeing could be the rift's own countermeasures to the bad thing. It could be the universe fighting back."

"It looks almost like a vent releasing steam," Anja said, *"like it's releasing pressure from whatever's causing all the problems."*

"Could be," Yuri said. *"Either way, we don't know. So we don't need to judge. Not yet. You're okay. I'd say take a deep breath, but . . . you know."* He gestured to their lungless astral bodies. *"I hope that wasn't so funny it breaks your focus."*

"*I'm good,*" Anja said with a smile. "*Thanks.*"

But despite her efforts not to judge, she was judging. She was scared. The rift was doing things. Things she didn't understand. Things the resident ghosts didn't seem to understand. And not only was her next task to get closer to the rift, but she was supposed to try to *get inside* it, to get past the ghosts and enter the rift.

Calm, she said to herself.

"*Calm*," Yuri repeated, and she thought she heard a smile in the thought. The butthead. He *could* hear all of her thoughts.

She felt a warmth near her hand, like he was intending to squeeze it, and he met her eyes. His were crinkling at the corners. "*Here we go.*"

Yuri stepped forward, like you would in a physical body.

"You're not just going to whisk us into there?" Anja asked.

"I don't know what 'into there' is. I can whisk myself to places I've been before or places I can imagine, but I have no idea what's in there. I have no idea how to whisk us into there."

"*You can't just say 'take us into the rift'?*"

Yuri took another step, pulling her along with him. "*Do you really want to try?*"

"I want to avoid having to pass through the ghosts," Anja said.

"We're ghosts too, remember? More or less, anyway. They won't care about us."

"You sure?"

"*I'm more concerned about not knowing what they do care about right now. Something's got them spooked.*"

A few more steps, and the ghosts still hadn't reacted to them. Yuri was right; they had other things to worry about. But what? Anja tried to put her scientific skills to work.

Knowledge, comprehension, application, analysis, synthesis, evaluation.

Nope, too complicated for right now.

She tried journalism: who, what, where, when, why, and how? Now *that* she could work with.

Where were they? In the clearing, headed toward the rift.

Was there anything different about the clearing? Was it hotter or colder than usual? Had the rift grown since they'd last been here? Was it growing now?

Anja tried to look in the direction of the trees, but her awareness wasn't as willful as it was when she was in her body. She twisted, but slowly and only slightly, as if moving through molasses. It wasn't worth the effort.

And they were coming up on the ghosts. The ghosts still weren't paying much attention to Anja and Yuri. In general, anyway. Ralph and the taller female ghost were floating toward them. Anja felt a rise of excitement at being recognized and remembered.

Calm, Anja said to herself.

"*What is it?*" Yuri asked.

"*The ghosts I talked to. The shorter one is Ralph.*"

Ralph had been the one to introduce himself, but the taller woman appeared the happier to see Anja again now. Ralph looked . . . skeptical? Hesitant? Worried that Anja had not only come back but had brought a friend?

Anja wasn't sure about ghost etiquette, so she stuck with what she knew.

"*Hi, Ralph. This is Yuri.*"

Ralph nodded and gestured to the woman. "*This is Janeane.*"

"*What's going on?*" Yuri asked. "*Why is everyone agitated?*"

Ralph looked like he didn't want to answer, but Janeane made the high-pitched noise, and Ralph started speaking over her, as if just to get her to stop.

"*We're not ghosts like you're thinking,*" he said. Anja heard him in her mind, but not like she heard Yuri and her own voice. And not like white noise over brown noise anymore, either. His voice was more like a lullaby underscoring her monkey mind. The melody was there, and she was translating it into lyrics. "*Not all of us, anyway. The twitchier, blinking ones are ghosts.*"

He smiled guiltily at Anja.

Great. Apparently he could hear her too, even from far away.

"*They're the kind of ghosts that were too addicted to stuff in the material world to bear leaving it behind,*" Ralph continued. "*They've come to the rift because of the energy it's producing. They'll have no need to glom onto humans for their fixes as long as it's here. The rest of us are guardian ghosts, helper spirits, ascended masters, like that man who's sticking close to you.*"

"*To me?*" Anja said.

"*Calm,*" Yuri said.

Janeane held out her hand. But she didn't grab hold of Anja's hand or even touch her arm. She grabbed at something Anja hadn't even noticed was there.

A cord.

A silver cord? It didn't look silver. But Anja had never seen the color before and couldn't describe it, so she figured silver was a good enough inadequate description as any.

The woman held it up, and Anja instantly felt calmer. Not only that, she felt aware. Focused. She felt as clear-minded as—no, make that the most clear-minded she'd ever felt in her life. She felt as if she could see the edges of the universe, the very fabric of the veil, the thoughts that wouldn't come into favor, let alone use, for hundreds of years. She saw genius. Genius in its every shade.

Janeane smiled and released the cord, releasing the spell.

"*Wow,*" Anja said, with all the awe imaginable and yet as calm as she would ever be in this lifetime. "*What was that?*"

"*And some of us are whatever is beyond ascended master,*" Ralph's melody said.

His face didn't really show emotion, not like Janeane's, but Anja thought she could feel his emotion anyway. He'd seemed negatively emotive in general about the situation and the exchange they were having—worried or annoyed or something—but also . . . irreverent. Like it was always fun to enlighten people about what more was out there.

Anja said, "*So the man sticking to me?*"

"*He doesn't want you to worry about him right now.*"

"*But I'm okay?*"

"*You could say he's the reason you're okay, that you're still here talking to us. Him and your buddy, Yuri, here, anyway.*"

"*But about the rift,*" Yuri said. "*What's going on? Why are you all here?*"

"*The veil has been breached—not here,*" Ralph hastened to add. "*You are right. This is more of a vent. But it's not the only one. There are six such vents all over the world. Seven, actually, when there isn't a breach. They're not normally this active, but they've opened up as a distress call, as a way for people like you to heal the breach. It's man-made, you see. Material. We can guide you, but you have free will here. And you have more power than you'll ever believe, enough power to impact even the beyond. Even us. For better or ill. But we can't take action to help you out of it. We can barely take action to help ourselves.*"

"*Then why are you here?*"

"*Because we can guide you, talk to you. And because certain of you can see us. And because certain of you can access us. And because people like you can set it right.*"

"*Okay,*" Yuri said, in a way that had Anja thinking maybe she should remind him to stay calm. "*So what counsel do you have for us?*"

"*Don't go into the rift.*"

—

"*What?*" Yuri said. "*If we're the only ones who can fix it, how are we supposed to do that if we can't go in?*"

"*Someone went in,*" Anja said. "*Or at least, someone came out. Didn't they? The kid who took my notebook. And the woman with the helmet hair. They made it in and out.*"

"*They're the ones who caused the problem,*" Ralph said. "*There should be nothing at all that can harm you beyond the veil. But the veil has been breached, and material intent exists there now. We don't know what dangers they've caused. They won't harm us, not yet anyway, not until they accomplish what we fear they're after. But we can't promise they won't harm you. And you're the only ones who have come this far to stop it. Of all six distress calls, you are the only ones who have answered us in nonphysical form.*"

"*And that's why you're here? Why she's here?*" Anja said, referring to the taller woman.

Janeane beamed at Anja.

"*You think I can go into the rift, don't you?*" Anja asked her.

Janeane's expression might have changed, but not enough to make her look anything less than the bright-eyed and energetic optimist she'd been before. Like even if she wanted to, which it didn't look like she did, she could neither confirm nor deny; she could only have faith.

"*So what are we supposed to do, then?*" Yuri said. "*Babies are dying.*"

"*They're not dying,*" Ralph said. "*They're just not being born. I know for your kind that can be a distinction without a difference. But love is necessary for life.*"

"*What do you suggest we do?*" Anja said.

"*We know you're going into the rift,*" Ralph said. "*You're human. Even if there were no threat to propel you any further on this journey, you'd go in out of pure curiosity, despite warnings, and be even more curious because of warnings. We're not trying to sway you. Too much. We just want you to know that you're making a choice.*"

If Janeane could look solemn, Anja thought she was doing it now.

"The ghosts aren't a problem," Ralph continued, *"so if you're going, now's the time. The people who caused this are making progress. They are moving on to the next phase of their plan. The rift will respond if they succeed, and not in any way you want to be present for."*

"We need to warn Danny," Yuri said.

"We'll take care of your team," Ralph said.

"I thought you couldn't help," Yuri said.

"We can't take physical action. But that leaves more options than you'd think. They'll be fine. Go. They're making progress now."

Ralph and Janeane stepped out of their way, leaving Anja and Yuri facing the still twitchy and uninterested ghosts. The rift loomed behind them. It turned faster and faster, spewing what looked like mist, and Anja could feel the pressure rising. From where, she couldn't tell.

"*Go*," Ralph said, and Janeane held a hand out toward the rift, swooshing all the twitchy ghosts aside, forming a clear passageway.

Still holding Yuri's hand, Anja stepped toward it and felt herself whisked inside.

CHAPTER 48

Or were they?

Huge trees with reddish bark trunks stood several yards in front of her, just beyond a dirt clearing.

She turned around—

"*Calm,*" Yuri said.

And it was a good thing he did so, because the rift rotated just inches from where she stood. Its triangular apex passed by her nose as it shifted flat to keep from pointing at the ground.

And just beyond it, the ghosts milled about, still agitated and needy.

Well, jeez. Everything around them looked the same as before.

"*Did it not work?*" Anja said. "*Why didn't it work?*"

"*It worked,*" Yuri said.

"*What?*"

"*It worked,*" Yuri said. "*We're in the rift. Or, we've leveled up or something.*"

"*What do you mean? That's the forest. Those are the ghosts. That's the rift, still rotating above us. If we're in the rift, how can we be looking at the rift?*"

"*It's not a building,*" Yuri said. "*We didn't enter any kind of structure. There is no structure. I'm not even sure there's trees and ghosts. We're just seeing them because we're the kind of beings who generally have to see something. Sense something. And it would be helpful if we agreed about what we were sensing, I'm guessing. So since we were already in the clearing and we stayed in the clearing even as we walked into the rift, continuing to see the clearing seems most logical? Least jarring? Most navigable? I don't know."*

"So then how do you know we're in it? How do you know we've leveled up?" It was even worse than superstitious talk; it was video game talk. *"What was the point of this if everything is still the same?"*

Yuri said, *"It's not the same. Look."*

Yuri pointed at the shape of the rift, the triangle, morphing as it rotated so as to keep its apex pointing toward the sky.

"It was doing that before," Anja said.

"Yeah, but look at the ghosts on either side of the triangle."

She looked, but there were no ghosts outside the triangle's bottom corners. Which was to say, Anja couldn't see the ghosts unless they were standing inside the triangle.

"So we are in a building?" she said, frustrated that Yuri had said they weren't.

He said, *"In that sense, I guess. In the sense that we can't see through walls, just through open doors and clear windows. But why?"* he said. *"Why can we see the clearing and the trees whether they're inside the triangle or not, but we can't see . . . oh, you know what I bet it is?"*

"What?"

"I bet we can't see the ghosts for the same reason they're stuck on the other side. They're too dense to come over here, too attached to the physical world. So they're not represented in the nonphysical world."

"But what about the trees? Nothing's more dense and attached to the physical world than trees."

"Yeah, physically, in physical terms, but not mentally, not spiritually, not emotionally. Trees, everything else besides humans really, are pure positive energy."

Yuri pointed through the rift, at something in the clearing. Danny had said there were no animals this close to the clearing, but Anja saw a mouse.

The mouse scurried among the ghosts crowded around the rift, but when it scurried beyond the rift's opening, Anja could still see it.

Just then, Janeane and Ralph floated out past the opening of the rift, too, and while the other ghosts standing around the edge were cut off, Anja could still see Ralph and Janeane.

"*So what you're saying,*" Anja said, "*is that if a human were walking around the rift, we wouldn't be able to see them unless they were standing at its opening, like the ghosts. And that's because both the human and the materialistic ghosts don't belong in here.*"

"*Not in their current state,*" Yuri said. "*We might be able to see someone like the Dalai Lama, someone like that.*"

So what did that say about their friends the OBEing book thief and his handler? His handler for sure had gotten in here, or at least had come out of here. You want to talk about baseness and attachment and what not, theft and causing whatever those two were doing to the universe sounded pretty base.

But they weren't entering one of the seven natural rifts, were they? Ralph had said they'd torn open their own entrance.

Anja sighed, and then noticed how that wasn't really true because she wasn't really breathing. She looked down at her free hand, her other hand still holding Yuri's. Like the rotating rift, the shape of her hand was there, but so was the dirt beneath it. She could see right through.

For a second she wondered how long it would take to get used to this, but then she realized she already was. She was already everything she needed to be. It was only habit that was making her question and put up roadblocks and problems and issues and whatever else where none need be.

But even after having that thought, it was replaced by more of those same doubts and roadblocks and problematic rehashings, more monkey mind.

Calm, she told herself. It was all she could do.

"*So what's next? What do we do now?*" she said, getting them back on track.

Something was causing this rift, and it was the same thing that was causing the birth problems, the team's problems, and this forest's problems. And probably problems in the other six rift locations as well.

At least two people who could get out of body were involved in the operation. And probably at least one other person who was putting the team together.

And somehow those people had torn open the veil.

Anja said, "*One of those seven rifts is their entry point, the tear, the first rift that caused the other six rifts to open. Isn't that what Ralph and Janeane said?*"

"*You think they're at that first rift?*"

"*Don't you?*"

"*Maybe,*" Yuri said, sounding doubtful, and Anja deflated a little, because it seemed so obvious to her. To make a hole, you'd have to be present . . . oh, but she was thinking in physical terms again.

"*How do you tear a hole in the veil?*" she asked.

Yuri didn't know.

Anja thought she should've asked Ralph and Janeane when she'd had the chance. Why hadn't she asked? She guessed she'd been too overwhelmed by it all to stay focused. But maybe she'd see them again and get another chance. She was getting better at this staying calm business.

"*Hey,*" she said. "*Is my ghost buddy, the guy who loves me—is he still here?*"

"*He must be.*"

"*What do you mean?*"

"*Well, I can't see him, but this is way too much activity, and you're nowhere near as calm as you'd need to be to stay out of your body on your own, given how little experience you have doing this kind of thing. So he must be. Janeane and Ralph said he was helping you, and you should know: he is really helping you. You're getting a pass.*"

Yuri looked down at their astral hands, still clasped together, and said, "*It's why I'm not letting go of you. I think he's helping me, too. I've never been this active and out this long before. Nowhere near this long.*"

Anja wondered if she should be focusing more on staying calm than on the mission—but no, clearly her focus was better placed on what they were encountering, and that's why the wizened ghost was helping her.

But why was he here? How did he even know she was here or needed her help? What was his involvement with this? Would he turn on her? What if he turned on her? If she couldn't see him, could she get him off her if he turned on her?

"*Are you sure he's good?*" she asked.

"*Pretty sure,*" Yuri said. "*It's not like I can see him to check.*"

Something about the ghost, about all of it, still left Anja uneasy. But she reminded herself what she was doing. She was out of body. Of course she was uneasy. She had to let the weirdness go. She had to focus on the mission.

They had to find the source, the cause of the tear. And why? Why had the veil been torn?

"*Where do we go from here?*" she said, and she gestured around them, at the clearing and the trees and the ghosts huddled up to the vent in the veil. "*This all makes sense now that I've seen it and you've explained it, but I was kind of expecting . . . I don't know.*"

"*Like, a corridor leading us toward a bright light and a prize?*"

"*Kinda. So what do we do?*" Anja said. When she'd gone to the moon, she just said *take me to the moon*, and she'd been whisked away. She'd never been to the moon before, but she saw it in the sky every night. She could imagine what it might look like.

But where was the tear in the veil? Where were the people who'd made it? What did their location look like?

Anja looked at the rift, at the ghosts huddling up next to it and disappearing beyond its edges. Did it look anything like this?

She looked at Yuri. He was looking back at her, and she could tell in her feeling, in the look on his face, that he knew that she had a plan, and that he trusted her. She closed her eyes and imagined the rotating rift behind her. But where might she find another one? Did she have to imagine where it might be, the rooftop or cornfield or lake it was in, or could she just say—

Take us to the First Rift.

CHAPTER 49

Just like when she'd asked to go to the moon, Anja felt whisked away, the world passing by her in a white blur. The sensation lasted for a couple seconds, tops, and then—

She and Yuri were standing at the threshold of another rift, its giant shape rotating around them. They were inside it. Anja knew, because ghosts stood visible through its center, but not to either side. And something felt off about it. She felt a jarring, low-thrum sensation, like an all-over electric body massage on a setting that was just a little too harsh. And it wasn't going away. It just sat there in the background, this harsh buzz.

"*Wow,*" Yuri said. "*Stay calm.*"

Anja got the feeling he was saying it for both their benefits, not just hers. Because the harsh buzz wasn't the only unsettling difference about this rift.

This rift stood on a wide sandy beach, in a huge circle of sand that stretched into the water. The sand in the circle was darker than the sand beyond it, like it had once been burnt. Anja saw no people or animals, not even seagulls flying over the waves or sandpipers running with the swash.

Whether the water lapping at the beach was ocean, or merely sea or sound, Anja couldn't tell. She stared out at the water, looking for land, but didn't see any in the distance.

The bright translucent lines of the rift's perimeter swept past her nose as it morphed in and out of shape.

It was a square, not a triangle, and it extended high into the sky, maybe even higher than the Redwood Rift.

Yuri raised his translucent hand and pointed at the sweeping, morphing outline of the rift's perimeter as it passed close enough to the ground to touch the sand. Ghosts hovered around it, just like ghosts hovered around the Redwood Rift. But as this rift's perimeter passed by them, Anja could still see the full shape of these ghosts, all the way to the sand.

The rift wasn't passing in front of them; it was passing behind them. These ghosts were in the rift. They were in the beyond, in here, with Yuri and Anja.

"*Calm,*" Anja said, not feeling calm at all. She sent a silent thank you to the old wizened guy helping her stay out. She couldn't deny he was earning his place, even if the thought of him hovering around her body, *loving* her, was still a little creepy.

"*We're all right,*" Yuri said, but Anja thought she could hear doubt in his message, a tremble of fear.

"*What now?*" Anja said.

Yuri shook his head. "*If they're on this side, then they were probably here before, right? Not stuck on Earth like the others? So that makes them safe, right? Kind?*"

"*You mean harmless?*"

"*You think?*"

Only one way to find out.

Anja didn't have a rock with her to throw, so she moved a little closer to the closest ghost-looking being. The being looked human-shaped, but neither male nor female. Anja took a second to take a closer look at some of the others to see if that was true of them all.

Not necessarily. Some were more distinctly female- or male-looking than others, but all were a little bit androgynous. None of them seemed to be doing anything, just standing around. Not in a junky kind of way, like the Redwood ghosts, but in a calm, mountain-post kind of way.

She continued with her plan with the original target ghost.

"*Excuse me,*" she said.

No response.

Pulling Yuri with her, Anja moved to stand directly in the ghost's line of sight—just in case that was still how this whole nonphysical vision thing worked.

But the ghost stared right through her. Better than those guards at Buckingham Palace.

"*Tap him,*" Yuri said.

"*Isn't that physical?*"

Yuri shrugged, and she didn't have a better idea.

"*Excuse me,*" Anja said as she lifted an astral hand to tap the ghost's shoulder.

Her hand slid right through.

Anja wasn't sure what to make of that. She and Yuri could touch; they were still holding hands, and Anja wasn't letting go for nothing.

So why couldn't she feel this guy?

She swiped a hand at the next closest ghost, and got the same result.

Was she the ghost in this scenario? Or were they? Were these beings considered even more nonphysical than Anja's current, decidedly nonphysical state?

As Anja pondered this, the ghost made no movement, and neither did the rest. If they could hear her, they weren't paying attention to her like Janeane and Ralph had done.

"*Nothing,*" she said to Yuri. "*It's like they're concentrating on something.*"

"*On the rift, probably,*" Yuri said. "*I don't get the sense that they're the cause of it, though. I think they're here like us, trying to help.*"

"*Help do what?*"

Yuri shrugged, or at least that's what Anja sensed.

"*It's huge,*" he said. "*Maybe they're keeping it from getting bigger. Or maybe they're making it harder for the OBErs to make it through. We don't know how long these guys have been here. Maybe they just arrived after the kid stole your journal. Taking something physical through the nonphysical and then back into the physical has got to be against the rules. Against the natural order of things.*"

"*If that's what he even did,*" Anja said. They didn't know for sure he'd gone through the rift. He might've just flashed out of sight, at her conex, and then appeared somewhere else.

"*So what now?*" Yuri said.

"*We exit the rift.*"

"*Go out onto the beach?*"

"*You got a better idea?*" Anja asked. "*We can at least look around for something that identifies this place, and then we can go back, tell Danny and Jackson, and they can get someone out here who knows what they're doing.*"

"*Yeah, okay,*" Yuri said. "*Landmarks. What beach this is. Got it. Let's go.*"

Anja thought she felt Yuri squeeze her hand, and she smiled to herself, thankful he had done so. This was scary and completely out of her comfort zone. She studied fluorescent worms, for goodness' sake. Usually in a lab. And definitely always while in her body.

Anja and Yuri weaved around the dozen or so higher-vibration ghosts, mindful of where they stood. Even though it seemed they could have just passed right through them, it didn't seem right to do so.

When they stepped across the threshold, Anja felt that harsh buzz spike just a bit, then dissipate into the general unease and malaise she normally felt as an inhabitant of Earth.

"*Oh, wow,*" Yuri said. "*Do you feel that?*"

"*I feel better,*" Anja said.

She stepped away from the rift, further and further up the beach, hoping to get a full view of the rift's shape. It was huge. Square, or maybe diamond. It seemed to want to be a square.

The Redwood Rift morphed as it rotated, seemingly so as to keep the triangle's flat base at the bottom, and it did this smoothly.

But this rift jerked as it morphed, as if it wanted to be a square, but something was keeping its apex pointing at the ground, despite the efforts of the ghosts inside.

"*Yeah, I got that relieved feeling too, like a pressure's been lifted,*" Yuri said. "*But that's not the feeling I'm talking about. I'm talking about the anxious, danger, do-not-enter feeling. Do you feel it?*" he said. "*It's coming from over there.*"

Yuri pointed to the strip of beach that stretched to the right of the rift, which looked just the same as the strip that stretched to the left. Anja tried to feel the fear that Yuri described, but she didn't feel anything.

Then again, she didn't want to go right. Going left seemed better. Felt better. Was that the feeling he meant?

"*Well,*" Anja said, "*I'd like to go left, and it sounds like you'd prefer to go left. But I'm thinking if going right feels bad to you, then that's probably where the bad guys are, and where our answers are.*"

"*But we're not looking for the—*"

"*Aren't we?*"

"*No,*" Yuri said. "*We're looking for landmarks, remember? Non-confrontational things. Safe things.*"

"*I don't see any landmarks anywhere,*" Anja said. "*And this looks to me like it could be a private island. And why not? Because really, if you're going to tear a hole in the fabric of the universe, you probably want some privacy while you're at that. And if you've got rare Chinese kids and OBEr bodyguards, you've probably got the money for your own private island. Which means we probably won't find anything identifiable about this place unless we find the bad guys' lair.*"

Yuri didn't say anything.

"*And just to be clear,*" Anja said, "*we are not splitting up.*"

"*Agreed,*" Yuri said eagerly.

"*Good,*" Anja said, "*then let's go.*"

"*We're walking?*"

Their apparent change of roles wasn't lost on Anja, but she didn't know whether to find that comforting or troubling.

She said, *"Do you want to whisk yourself there and get caught off guard like we did here with these ghosts? We got lucky this time. These ghosts are docile. But the OBEr bodyguard and the notebook thief and whoever else our Big Bad has on staff . . . I'd rather see them before they see us."*

Yuri said, *"They might already know we're here."*

A rush of anxiety and fear spiked through Anja's body. *Calm,* she said to herself before asking her next question.

"*What makes you say that? Are you getting a feeling?*"

"*No,*" Yuri said, and he sounded defeated. "*I can see them coming. They're already here.*"

"*What do we do?*" Anja said, mentally squeezing Yuri's hand. "*Do we go back into the rift? No, they can follow us there, obviously. And they know where we came from, so they can follow us back there, too. So what do we do? Do we go to the moon?*"

"Calm," Yuri said. *"We're out of body. We're safe. No harm can come to us when we're out of body. At least, I hope. So let's just be calm. We'll have a conversation. Ask them what's going on. Maybe they didn't mean to do this. Maybe they're looking for a way to fix it. Maybe they're hoping we can help."*

Anja stared at Yuri with her nonphysical jaw dragging on the sand. This was the most naive kid she'd ever encountered. He had to be kidding. People with the arrogance to do this kind of thing in the first place don't all of a sudden mea culpa and ask for help.

And what about Anja's thoughts? Yuri could hear her thoughts. She couldn't hear his, not unless he projected them at her. But she was pretty sure he could hear hers. Would *they* be able to hear her thoughts?

Given the skill of the bodyguard and the little notebook thief, Anja had to assume they probably could. She had to guard her mind.

How does one guard one's mind?

"Calm," Yuri said.

Calm, Anja thought. On repeat.

And she reminded herself quickly that she had a failsafe. If something happened, if she had to do something, she could whisk them away to the moon.

CHAPTER 50

"That's her," Yuri said.

A tall woman in translucent out-of-body form had appeared in the distance and was moving toward them. She could have come up quickly or even whisked herself right here, instantaneously, but she moved slowly as if not wanting to startle them.

"That's the woman I saw at the Halloween night market," Yuri said. *"Before I saw Josh. She was out of body then, too, with a businessman. That's her."*

Anja and Yuri had both clearly seen her; Anja knew the woman could sense that. And yet she seemed to slow down, seemed to hesitate about coming any closer.

Anja couldn't read the woman's expression. It wasn't happy, and it didn't look angry, but it also didn't look like she was entirely comfortable with the forthcoming situation, either.

Behind her, the little kid who'd entered Anja's conex and taken her notebook appeared like a blink of light, as if he were running late.

Or as if he hadn't been invited.

The woman turned to look back at the little book thief. But if she and the kid shared any kind of communication in that look, it was quick. She turned around once more and picked up her pace until she stood on the beach before them, about eight or ten feet away.

She was the same apparition who'd given chase after Anja had thrown the rock at the redwood ghosts.

She had small eyes and a larger nose with deep nasolabial lines, even out of body. But Anja thought she was probably younger than she looked, like a Russian Baba Yaga.

The kid trotted up behind the woman, coming to a stop at her side. He wrapped an arm around one leg and clung to her thigh like a much younger child. For a moment, nobody said anything.

Anja shifted a little closer to Yuri. More out of habits of physicality than because the movement was useful now. Did being out of body make her safer right now or even more on her own?

Beside her, Yuri was pulsing. She hadn't noticed before, hadn't really paid much attention, she guessed. She'd been much more interested in the rifts and the ghosts and the sensations of whisking from here to there in a moment. But she saw him now, and he was pulsing. As if his whole out-of-body body was breathing, pulsing with . . . what? Some kind of energy?

As she focused on him, she started to hear him.

Calm. Calm. Calm. He kept repeating the word *calm*, stretching it into four beats, with a two-beat pause between repeats.

And it seemed to Anja like it might be working. He appeared calm. And when he pulsed, he appeared bigger. Anja had read once that hackles—humans' tiny hairs rising on end—were a vestigial reflex left over from when we had to stand and face wild animals, like wolves or tigers and bears, and we needed all the intimidating size we could get.

Anja felt like that now, like she and Yuri were facing a fierce mama bear protecting her cub.

The kid looked up at the woman, at Anja and Yuri, and then back again. Anja couldn't tell if he was worried or excited. Was he about to do something? Was Baba Yaga?

"*Where are we?*" Yuri said, and his tone was that of a lost tourist. Lost, but not scared yet. Like he was still enjoying the adventure. "*This is really cool,*" he said, pointing at the rift. "*What is it?*"

"*Nice try,*" said Baba Yaga. Her voice felt different from Yuri's and different from the voices of the higher ghosts. It felt almost physical, as if coming into Anja's ears in surround sound rather than being in her mind. Like she was actually hearing it. How was that possible?

"*Where's the man you were with,*" Yuri said, "*the one you flanked at the Halloween market in Seattle, the business guy?*"

Baba Yaga quarter-smiled, a rise at the corner of her thin lips.

The little book thief looked at her, then looked at Anja and Yuri. He looked confused. Maybe he only spoke another language and couldn't understand them. Anja couldn't decide if he was scared or twitchy. Whether he was eager to leave or waiting for a signal to act.

"*Why were you there?*" Yuri tried.

"*To make look at you, yes,*" the woman said.

Anja felt a jolt of uncalm excitement at the small victory of getting the woman to speak.

Beside her, Yuri must've been slowing his mantra into an even longer word, because he was pulsing larger and for longer moments at a time.

Baba Yaga snorted as if she'd heard Anja and found her amusing.

Calm, Anja told herself.

"*Why did you come see me?*" Yuri said.

"*To make see if you are fraud.*"

"*And?*" Yuri said.

Her head tilted to one side, and then she shrugged, noncommittally, like she couldn't decide and it didn't matter either way. She didn't seem totally aligned with whatever the game plan was, despite the fact that she seemed to be its most active player.

So then why was she doing this?

Anja pointed at the rift circling behind them in a jerky rotation. "*Why did you tear a hole in the veil?*"

"*Is not tear. Is rift. Natural. Come. He will show you tear. He wants to show you.*"

"*Who wants to show me?*"

"*Your businessman,*" Baba Yaga said, with a glance at Yuri.

The woman then looked at Anja, and her mouth quirked. And

for the first time, Anja thought she could read the woman's expression.

Pity.

But why?

"It's what we came here for," Yuri said.

Anja looked at him, but he was looking straight ahead, at Baba Yaga, who was warily eyeing them in return, like she knew they were communicating but didn't know what they were saying.

Yuri was outdoing himself somehow. Somehow he was keeping their conversation private.

The little notebook thief sat in a flat-footed squat, poking his disembodied finger at something in the sand. And making divots.

"We're here to find out how to close the rift," Yuri said. *"Learning how they opened it might tell us how to close it. And learning* why *they opened it . . ."*

Might reveal to Anja whose side they were really on.

Baba Yaga smiled and stepped toward them, lifting her hands toward Anja and Yuri. Yuri might've been shielding his own thoughts and feelings, but Anja's, apparently, were still in full broadcast. The woman had sensed Anja's willingness to see the tear.

"We'll go with you," Anja said, more to maintain her feeling of control than because it was necessary—because it wasn't. It was already happening. The woman opened her arms wide and wrapped them both in what would have been a hug, except that Anja felt the whisking sensation.

CHAPTER 51

The whisking sensation stopped, and Anja's vision cleared. She and Yuri were in some kind of room with silvery walls and a high ceiling. Windows looked down on them from high up on the wall to her right. The space felt sterile and reminded Anja of a surgical theater. Except instead of an operating table, there was a box in the center of the room. The box was about the size of a steamer trunk, and it was made of wood with a rich, heavy grain of golden, medium, and dark brown waves.

Anja didn't see anything in the room that looked like a tear in the veil. Where had Baba Yaga brought them?

The woman smirked. *"My name Marfa,"* she said. *"Baba Yaga . . . she nothing."*

Fair enough.

Anja squeezed Yuri's hand and pulled him away from her.

And her back hit a wall.

The silvery walls looked solid, but they felt more like a fine mesh net. It pulled and stretched with her as she struggled against it.

"What's going on?" Yuri asked Marfa as he struggled with the mesh. *"What is this?"*

The woman said nothing. She and the little book thief remained standing in the center of the room, the box just behind them. The kid clung to her leg, and she kept one hand resting on his shoulder. She offered Anja and Yuri a sad smile.

In the upstairs viewing room, Anja saw a shadow.

Around them, the silvery room reverberated with a voice.

"Amazing, isn't it?"

The little book thief looked over his shoulder at the upper floor's viewing room, then switched sides, moving to Marfa's other leg and away from the incoming visitor.

Anja understood the instinct. She wanted to get away, too.

The shadow moved closer to the window. He wasn't out of body. He was completely solid.

Physical.

And Anja knew who he was.

"Jim?"

"Anja." He sounded pleased to see her. And nowhere near surprised. Anja felt her spiking emotions threaten to send her back to her body.

"*Calm,*" Yuri said.

Calm, Anja thought, feeling the steadiness of her protector and trying to match it. Somehow, the wizened ghost protecting her body had dampened the spike. But she didn't want to rely on him. She had to help. *Calm*, she repeated.

Jim wore his trademark black raincoat, heavy-rimmed black glasses that looked ridiculous, and a big grin on his face. It was a grin she'd seen only a few but memorable times before, when he'd been on the verge of a breakthrough.

It was no wonder to her why he wore that grin now.

"Where are we?" she asked.

"In my centralized bunker," Jim said.

Anja hadn't known Jim Lugner to be psychic, not like Yuri, able to see nonphysical things while still in his physical body. In fact, she'd known Jim Lugner to eschew such superstitious things. To mock and deride them. It had formed the foundation of their mentor-mentee bond. And yet he was answering her like they were just two physical people sitting across from each other at a table.

"I knew you'd help us," he was saying, "but I had no idea you'd help us like this."

He gestured down at her out-of-body state. In his hand, he carried something black the size of a brick. It was wired to his glasses as well as to an earpiece. Some kind of signal translator?

So he wasn't seeing or hearing her after all, not on his own.

"What's in the box?" she asked, pointing to the one in the center of the room.

"Nothing yet," Jim said. "But we're on the verge of something big here, Anja. Really big. And I'm so glad you're here. We need your help. We need the information you've been keeping out of the article you've been submitting about your studies."

Something not unlike a shiver ran through Anja's astral body.

Maybe Jim Lugner was psychic after all.

"*Calm,*" Yuri said.

And Marfa smiled at her, mischieviously. But then her eyes shifted to the air around Anja, and her expression changed.

Anja had seen that look before, on Yuri. Did that mean Marfa was seeing the old wizened ghost? Yuri had said he'd stayed with Anja's body, and she could feel her emotions bucking against her protector's calm. It bridled her excitement, helping her maintain her out-of-body state and her lucidity, her awareness.

But now that she was focused on it, she could feel that his help was growing brittle.

Calm, she thought to herself. Then, for the others to hear: *"That article has been rejected from every publication I've sent it to. How do you know about it?"*

"Ah," Jim said, and her mentor, the businessman, the scientist on review boards, the budding politician with fingers in all the pies, suddenly looked sheepish, guilty, and Anja knew the answer to both questions.

"*You're on the boards. Or your friends are. You shot it down.*" She thought about it some more. "*You knew it was big. You knew I was onto something. And you didn't want anyone else to know. You wanted to keep it to yourself,* for *yourself. Probably like that headgear you got there. To do . . . what? What is all this? How did you tear the veil?*"

Her tone was rising far beyond calm, but she felt the calming pressure of Yuri's pulsing hand squeezing her own.

"You want to know what I've been up to?" her mentor said. "Come. I'll show you."

Anja heard a clanking thud, followed by a whoosh. A section of the wall below the window her mentor was standing in was sliding open.

But why? They'd gotten in here without using a door. So why the pretense?

Anja looked up at her old professor. He'd been her admired, trusted mentor. But that was a long time ago, before his son's murder, before his sabbatical. Clearly he had changed since then. She couldn't trust him now. Not fully.

But on the whole, he did seem happy to see her and not like he'd just been caught doing something he shouldn't be doing. He seemed proud of his accomplishments. Eager to show her, to brag about it.

Maybe it wasn't all bad. Maybe this rift problem really was temporary. You have to break eggs and all that. Science made a lot of omelets breaking dozens of millions of eggs.

The people who first studied bioluminescence decimated the population of glowing jellyfish that used to thrive in the Puget Sound. A tragedy, sure. One that haunted Anja. But that once-living light was now used in cancer research.

From destruction, rebirth.

Jim was still smiling like he'd made the breakthrough of a lifetime. And maybe he had. Because, holy cow, there were rifts in the veil. And she could see them. She could travel through them.

"It's what we came here for," Yuri said. But he gave off an energy like he really didn't want to go through the door or see whatever was on the other side.

Anja didn't either. But Yuri was right. It's what they had come for.

Still holding Yuri's hand, Anja stepped toward the door. Marfa stepped aside to let them pass, then followed close behind them.

CHAPTER 52

The door opened onto a corridor that passed beneath the upstairs viewing room.

At the other end was an enclosed, open-air courtyard, maybe fifty yards square. The ground was covered in paving stones. The walls were several stories high and composed of that same silvery-white metal. Only one wall had windows—it was the back side of Jim's viewing room—but all four walls had doors, and a gallery walkway connecting those doors, on the second level.

Wherever you were in the building, you could easily take a break, apparently, and come take in the view.

The courtyard's paving stones had spots of exposed dirt. Anja presumed that trees once grew from them.

Well, not anymore.

Purplish-white energy strained against the courtyard like a caged monstrosity.

"*What is that?*" Anja said.

"Isn't it amazing?" Jim Lugner said. He was descending a set of exterior stairs one triumphant step at a time. Anja could feel his pride, his ownership. "It's a rift in the veil."

"A rift," she said, *"not a tear?"*

"Semantics."

This from the man who'd drilled her in precision.

A *rift*, a *tear*. Neither word did it justice. It was a gouge in the fabric of the universe. It pulsed with pain and warning like a head wound.

Whereas the Redwood Rift and the First Rift had been openings through a distinct shape, the tear looked like a puncture in a balloon, a ragged hole in a shirt. The purplish-white-neon edges flapped, as if waving at each other, trying to come back together.

But the hole was only getting bigger.

Metal mesh netting rose from the floor to high above the courtyard's walls. Somehow it was keeping the tear from spreading horizontally into the building.

But the sky offered no such limit.

The tear was ripping, mushrooming out of the top of the courtyard.

"*It's tearing families apart,*" Anja said. "*This, or whatever you did to make it happen, to cause it, is also causing all those pregnancy issues.*"

"It's temporary," Jim said with false regret. "But it's a benefit too, don't you think? So much overpopulation. Disasters thin the herd, spread out the resources, make everyone else just a little bit kinder, a little more altruistic. More loving," he said. "At least for a time."

"*But why?*" she said.

"I just told you."

"*To thin the herd?*"

He pressed his lips together and sighed. His look of disappointment. She'd focused in on the mission's lesser benefit, and on the cost. Her old mentor had expected her to be smarter than that, to understand the work's deeper purpose.

As usual.

"*Why would you even want to tear the veil?*" she asked. "*You're not even out of body. You can't interact with me without that headgear.*" She pointed into the tear. "*Can you even see the beings on the other side?*"

So many beings, there was no space between them. They stood crammed inside the tear, confined by the shape of the courtyard.

Whereas Janeane and Ralph were lighthearted and friendly, and the beings at the First Rift were focused and indistractible, the ones inside the tear were straining. Like if any more energy tried to pass by them, they would burn out.

"They don't want your rift," Anja said.

"They don't have a choice," Jim said, refusing to look at them. Anja was almost certain that was because he couldn't see them, not even with his headgear. "We might be like them, but they're not like us. They don't have the will we have. They can't do the things we do. They can only act at the request of one of us. But us? We can do anything."

"And what are you trying to do?" Anja said.

"Can't you tell? It's your design."

"What's he mean?" Yuri asked her.

Anja could feel indignation rising within her being, but also a sense of wonder. She should have told herself to stay calm, but she didn't have the mind to do so. She couldn't help surrendering all the responsibility for maintaining her lucidity to her invisible, wizened protector.

This, this tear in the veil, this was not her design.

But as she ran through the setbacks and accomplishments of her years of study, both as a student and as a postdoc, she could see how someone might use her work to do something like this.

The astral body was energy. And what she'd done, what no board or publication seemed to care about, was that she'd discovered a new way to manipulate subtle energy, the energy of light.

The most fundamental energy of the universe.

"Not most fundamental," said Baba Yaga. *"Light useful, but life finds way without it."*

"There is one thing we can't live without, though," her mentor said. "The pregnancy losses are proving that. They're not willing to come into a world that lacks it. We've been attacking each other and been out for ourselves for so long. We live in a world that shuns love, that favors violence and ridicule and hoarding . . . but I'm going to fix that," he said. "I am fixing that."

Mankind had been stinking up the air and polluting the water and poisoning the food, and shutting down research that could cure cancer with the energy of sound and create cars that could run on the sun, all for a few financial interests to continue peddling lucrative but harmful wares.

Were babies, new souls, unwilling to come to a place that was being exploited, neglected? Sure, we were here to learn. But under what conditions?

"Those things you list still only physical things," said Marfa, listening to Anja's mind. Then, to Anja's mentor, *"You tell."*

Jim said, "There's an energy far more fundamental, and it's all around us. Or, at least, it should be. We act like there's a shortage, but there's plenty to go around. It's just not being wielded in the most productive manner. And so it feels as though there's a lack. But I'm going to fix even the illusion of lack."

Beside her, Yuri pulsed in time with his mantra. *Calm. Calm. Calm.*

"Calm," he projected, for Anja's benefit.

But she was not calm. Nor could she instantly become so. Calm was for yogis and people who sat on mountaintops humming *Aum*. Calm was for people who had plenty of money for their work and everything taken care of for them. Calm was for trust fund babies and for people with loving, friendly families. Calm was for others. It wasn't for Anja. Anja was a doer. Anja saw what she wanted and made it happen. Forced it to happen. Like Jim. He saw an opportunity and he took it. Using her research. No matter the collateral damage. She wasn't calm, and she wasn't becoming any calmer now.

She felt a pull on her energy, like her awareness of this place, of this moment, was being drained from the sink. And the plug that was her wizened protector couldn't stop the leak.

"You left information out of your publication submissions," Jim was saying. "I tried your experiments, and replicated them beautifully—you really do stunning work—except for one aspect."

"The part where the same energy can cause the color to change," Anja said.

Jim Lugner smiled at her. "Did you leave it out on purpose? Did you hope we'd all overlook that part? You never complained to me about not getting your paper published. So I figured that's what you'd done. But then you submitted again and again, and you still didn't put it in . . . because you didn't actually have it, did you? And why would you?" he added, sounding like he was speaking more to himself than to Anja. "You never did believe in any of this. You thought it was all bogus. You led the way in making fun of that wise man we visited in Brazil. And you did it with such conviction. The rest of the students followed you whether they agreed with you or not."

"I may not have had the solution then," Anja said. *"But I have it now."*

"Does she?" Jim said. And for a second Anja didn't understand. But then Marfa, who had been hovering just inside the corridor with the kid clinging to her side, glided closer, and Anja received the distinct insight that Marfa was trying to get in better range of Anja's brainwaves.

"Calm," Yuri said, and Anja took up the practice herself, repeating calm, calm, calm.

"She does," Marfa said with a smile, *"but she not giving it up."*

"Can you get it from her?"

"Da. Give time. Just need get beyond their mantra."

"What are they saying?" Jim asked.

"Calm," said Marfa.

Whatever she was doing, the woman's astral body didn't touch Anja's at all. She merely studied Anja, giving off an energy of intention and determination.

Still, Anja gripped Yuri's hand tighter and backed further away from Marfa, putting the courtyard stairs between them. She repeated their mantra, trying to steel her mind.

"Calm?" Jim Lugner laughed. "Was that Yuri's idea? I'm sure it was. He's a fraud, you know."

Anja flinched, and for a second her mind wasn't just wide open, she was back in her body. She glimpsed the log beams in the welcoming center's ceiling, saw the light from the campground's monitors shining to her right.

But then just as suddenly she was back in the courtyard with Jim and Marfa and the tear. She credited her wizened protector. It had to have been him, because her mind was reeling. Jim had called Yuri a fraud.

"Got it," Marfa said.

"Calm," Yuri said, and Anja renewed her effort to repeat the word, as if doing so could claw back the information Marfa had taken. Anja felt her energy pulse in time with Yuri's light-flickering body.

But she couldn't help noticing that her grip on his hand had loosened. She was no longer squeezing his as strongly as he was squeezing hers.

"He's a table kicker," Jim continued, no longer saying things just to shock her so that Marfa could invade her brain. "A Sherlock Holmes-caliber observer maybe, but he's no psychic. I can show you a good psychic. But of course, you know that. You've seen what my team can do. What real psychics can do."

Marfa put her arm around the little book thief's shoulders. *"Time to go,"* she told him.

Anja tried to tell herself that it was just the kid's nap time, that Marfa wasn't dismissing him because it was about to become unsafe for the kid to be here anymore.

"Calm," Yuri said, but he didn't sound calm. He sounded like he, too, knew that if it wasn't safe for the kid, then it definitely wouldn't be safe for them either.

The kid pouted, wanting to stay.

"You still have work to do, yes?" said Marfa.

The kid eyed Yuri and Anja and then looked down. He nodded.

"Go, then," said Marfa, and the kid disappeared.

Jim Lugner was still talking.

"But what have you done with *your* psychic, hmm?" he said to Anja. "What have you seen? Did you see a few quote-unquote ghosts? Did you see our tears in the veil? Do you really think you're doing anything more right now than just dreaming?"

Jim pointed at Yuri. "He told you some nonsense story about someone latching onto you, didn't he? Some kind of old man who *loves* you. *Is* loving you."

"How do you—"

"I know real psychics," Jim said, gesturing to the tall, out-of-body woman. "And yours is a fraud. You're dreaming. And despite the major emotions you're feeling in this dream, you're still dreaming. And why? Because you're sleeping heavily. Ever hear of a roofie? Mix it with some melatonin and you've got yourself a dream-filled cocktail."

"But then how are any of you in my dream? How are we here having this conversation?" She'd never felt more lucid.

"Because of *my* psychics," Jim said. "You want to see your old wise man? He's not really there, but I can show him to you anyway."

Jim Lugner made a gesture, a double twitch of his index and middle fingers, indicating some kind of order to Marfa. Anja knew, because Marfa smiled sadly at her and then stepped closer.

The only time Anja had seen her own silver cord was when Janeane had pointed it out, but now she saw it again. Marfa found it and lifted it. Connected to it.

Anja felt none of it.

But then she saw him. Her wizened protector. He appeared just where Yuri had said he was, at her side, on the floor of the monitoring room. He had an arm around her shoulders, his ghostly elbow deep in the floor. His head tilted to touch hers.

He looked very old, with broad cheeks and deep lines that started at the corners of his eyes and spread all over his face.

And she recognized him.

He was the elder she'd met in Brazil, on a hopscotching field trip down through South America to see the southern lights in Chile with Jim Lugner. The old man had taught them calmly and quietly about energy and about love.

And her class had made fun of him afterwards.

He didn't say anything to her now. He didn't even look at her. And Anja thought of some experiences she'd read about, where people saw projections while in the hypnogogic state, between sleeping and awake. He was like a vision.

A hallucination.

And so she was dreaming. Her mind had gathered from her past experiences the one old man she knew of who would fit this strange scenario and cast him to play the most important role in this, her dream.

Beside her, Yuri vanished.

"Yuri?"

She looked around her, behind her, across the courtyard. She looked at Marfa, but all she saw, all she felt, was the woman's sad smile.

Yuri was gone.

"He's not necessary anymore," Jim Lugner said. "And he's also not cueing his presence anymore in the room where your physical body is sleeping. He has left that room. Left the site entirely, really. And so he's no longer making the noise that was causing you to dream about him in the first place. You'll see, when you get back."

Anja shook her head. Yuri had saved her from an attack. He had. He had saved her from an attack by Jim Lugner's so-called super psychics. If they were super, then Yuri was just as talented because he had saved her, saved her when not even Danny could help her. Yuri had saved her, and he had comforted her, and they had shared with each other stories from their pasts that Anja, at least, had never shared with anyone. Stories about her brother and about what she had done, both with Brian and after he'd died. She'd OBEd with her brother. And she'd done that before she'd ever met Yuri.

"No, you didn't." Jim Lugner said. "Those were dreams too. Yuri's mention of the phenomena now merely brought them back as memories. But where you went back then, what you witnessed—the moon—it was nothing verifiable. Just something to make you think you were as talented as your brother. But you weren't. Neither was he. It was all just dreams."

Anja shook her head. *Not calm, not calm*, she told herself. *I am not calm. Take me back. I want to go back to base. Take me home. I want to go home.*

"Go ahead. Wake up," Jim was saying, but Anja barely heard him, barely noticed him turn away from her and start to climb the stairs. "I have an email to respond to. Your email. Though I'll be forwarding it. Time to dismantle your mission."

"*Take me home!*" Anja said, but she felt a resistance coming from somewhere, like the whisking motion wanted to happen but couldn't gather any momentum. She felt stalled.

But then it was like a flick of a switch. *Whoosh.*

CHAPTER 53

Anja was lying on the hardwood floor, staring up at the welcoming center's log-style beams. The lights from the campground monitors shined down at her from the right.

She heard someone speaking. Faint. Distant. Danny was kneeling beside her, but the voice wasn't his. His lips were pressed hard into a concerned line.

"You okay?" he asked.

The glow of the surveillance monitors behind him felt really bright. But Anja could barely squint her eyes against the glare.

She couldn't move at all.

A jolt of fear shot through her.

But she'd experienced this before. She knew what to do.

She focused on her toes, on trying to wiggle them, trying to feel them touch the toe box of her shoes. The paralyzed sensation slowly subsided. She rose up on her elbows.

"Where's Yuri?" she said.

"I don't know," Danny said. "I went to check something I saw on the video feed. I came back, and everyone was gone."

Everyone?

"Ming?" Anja said, struggling to sit all the way up and look around. But Ming didn't answer. And Anja didn't see her. "Where's Ming?"

"I don't know," Danny said. He unhooked the walkie-talkie from his belt and pressed the big red button. "All call. Have you seen Yuri in the past half hour? Over."

"Negative."

"Negative."

"Negative."

Anja rubbed her face and ran her hands through her hair. Her fingers bumped into something that felt like a headband.

Headphones. Right. She was wearing headphones over her ears. Ming had found her some focus music to listen to, to help her relax. Some binaural beats.

But that's not what the headphones were playing.

Anja put her hands over the earcups and pressed the speakers to her ears.

The faint, distant voice she'd been hearing was still faint, but now not so distant. It was speaking short, soothing sentences over calming music.

"*You don't trust him. . . . You want to be away from here. . . . You sense that he is bad. . . .*"

She pulled off the headset and showed it to Danny. "What is this?"

"What do you mean? You put it on earlier. We all did. To keep us focused. Or unfocused. However it works."

"Not this," she said, shaking the headset.

The cord tugged in a way that felt loose and yet still connected to something. Anja grabbed the cord and followed its ten feet of length through the table legs and toward the computer tower set up beneath the monitoring desk.

But that wasn't what it was plugged into now.

Anja picked up the little digital audio player she found next to the tower.

"That wasn't there earlier," Danny said.

No kidding. Anja rewound the recording.

Danny still had the headphones, and he put them on. But the player had its own tiny speaker. Anja unplugged the headphones.

"*You're on a beach,*" said the hypnotic voice, almost robotic through the player's tiny speaker. "*Behind you the rift is circling. . . . You're whisked away to a building. . . . The room is sterile, but you're not alone. . . . The woman and the child are here with you. . . . In the windows above, you see a man. . . . You don't trust him. . . . You want to be away from here. . . . You sense that he is bad. . . . He's the one causing this. . . . He wants to manipulate you. . . . He wants to exploit your skills. . . . You can't get away. . . . You should be able to go through the walls, but you can't. . . .*"

"Where's your headphones?" Anja asked.

Danny picked a set up off the monitoring desk.

"Okay, then, where are Yuri's headphones? And where's Ming?"

"I don't know," Danny said, looking around the monitoring desk for the missing set.

Anja studied the player, but there was only one jack and no adapter that would accommodate a second plug. So this player was meant just for her.

She got up to help look around the desk while Danny reviewed the feeds.

"Anything?" she asked.

"No, you?"

"Nope."

So Yuri probably still had his headphones. Wherever he was.

Had he left on his own?

Anja hefted the player in her hand. It was light, but she figured it was heavy enough. And the computer tower was even heavier. And the way their cords had been weaved under the table, around the legs. "All our headphones were plugged into the tower, weren't they?" she asked.

"No," Danny said. "Yuri and I were listening to ocean waves."

Danny pointed at a much smaller tower, about the size of a kid's shoebox. It had been set on the floor near the door, presumably in a place where Yuri's and Danny's headphones could both reach it.

An adapter that could accommodate two plugs was sticking out of the jack.

If Yuri had been forcibly removed from his place on the floor beside Anja, then his headphones likely would have pulled loose—but not without some resistance. The tower would have moved. It would have skidded a bit toward the pull.

“Is it just me?” Anja asked. “Or is that tower sitting flush against the wall?”

Danny sighed heavily and nodded. “Right where I left it.”

CHAPTER 54

In the opposite back corner of the room, the toilet flushed.

Anja looked at Danny. How did they miss that someone was in the bathroom?

"Ming or Yuri?" she asked.

He shrugged.

The sink turned on and off, and then the door opened.

Ming came out wiping her hands on her pants. "Hey, you're back," she said. "Did you find . . . er . . . what's wrong?"

"Have you seen Yuri?" Danny asked.

"No," Ming said. "I mean, he was doing his thing on the floor with Anja when I went in."

"How long ago was that?" Danny asked.

Ming nodded from side to side. "A while. Blame all the oatmeal. He wasn't there when you got up?"

Anja shook her head. And held up the audio player. "So you don't know where this came from?"

"No. What is it?"

"Audio player," Anja said. "Playing me a creepy meditation."

"No," Ming said. "I had you plugged into the computer."

"I know," Anja said.

"So where did that come from?" Ming asked.

Anja shrugged.

Danny said, "We need to find Yuri."

CHAPTER 55

"Did you check the sick bay?" Ming said.

Anja felt her face release its tension. "Yes. Good call," she said. "I bet he's in sick bay."

Danny didn't look so sure, but he led the way at a fast clip out of the building and around the corner. But then he veered across the dirt road.

"Where are you going?" Anja asked.

"Just checking something," Danny said. He ran up to the window of Yuri's conex, peeked inside, then ran back across the road, shaking his head.

Doc's Honda was parked behind the log building.

They burst into sick bay without knocking on the door.

Doc barely noticed, struggling as she was with Kumar, trying to keep him from rolling off his cot. Danny stepped in to assist.

"Thanks," Doc said, stepping back with a sigh and wiping her brow.

Despite the activity, all seven men seemed as comatose as ever.

Yuri's brother was the only one not moving. But he'd pressed himself against the wall at an angle that looked really uncomfortable. Anja tucked a pillow between his head and the wall and tried to straighten him out.

"If Yuri had been here, he would've done this himself," she said. "He wouldn't just leave Josh like this."

"Yeah, I didn't think he'd be here." Danny said. "The cameras would have picked up anyone entering, and no one's entered in the last hour, so . . ."

"So where is he?" Anja said.

Ming shook her head.

"Yuri?" Doc said. "I thought he was with you."

"He was. But now he's gone."

"Gone? Did you check his room?"

"Did on my way over here," Danny said. "And he's not on the feeds."

Doc shook her head. "I don't see him leaving. Not without telling you. Not without Josh."

"Yeah," Danny said. "It doesn't make sense."

"Is there anywhere else to look?" Ming asked.

Danny shrugged. "The woods? I could take another look at the feed. We could check the clearing."

As Anja, Danny, and Ming headed outside again, Anja found herself fidgeting with the little audio player. "And you guys swear you didn't plug my headphones into this thing?" she asked.

Ming and Danny both shook their heads.

"And the perimeter guys didn't show up on the feeds as coming near this building, either," Danny added.

"So that only leaves Yuri to plug me into this thing," Anja said. "Why would Yuri play me this message? And where would he get it?"

But then Anja remembered her mentor appearing in her out-of-body dream, standing in the second-floor viewing room, calling her out on her hypocrisy, and showing her the original tear.

CHAPTER 56

Anja's mentor had said Yuri was a fraud. She'd thought she'd been out of body, holding it for a miraculously long time. But her mentor had said that she was just dreaming, that Yuri was a fraud.

Anja looked at the little audio player in her hand. The recording had described what she'd seen while out of body: the rift on a beach and the sterile silvery room and not being able to leave.

It described what she'd *thought* she'd seen.

Had it all been a dream?

A fraud?

But why? Why would Yuri come here and—

His brother.

But Josh was still in sick bay, still as comatose as ever. So what else had Yuri come here for?

"Jackson says this place is secret, right?" Anja said. "You took my phone, wouldn't let me call out. I barely got to email my mentor." She snorted to herself—*that* was probably why he'd appeared in her dream as the prompted bad guy. "We need to check the rift. If Yuri blames what happened on the rift—"

"And he should," Danny said. "I do. The rift attacked my team."

"If there even is a rift," Anja said.

"What do you mean?" Danny said. "We saw it. We saw it when you shined lights on it and threw that rock."

"Maybe we saw it. But Yuri was there. And he was so eager to rehash with us what we'd seen. Remember? So maybe he used one of those . . . I don't know what you call it."

"No, I know what you mean," Ming said. "Like a more sophisticated version of one of those Christmas light things that project red and green dots all over the house. Only his thing projected the image of the rift."

"And the ghosts?" Danny said. "Did he create them, too? Make them seem like they were running after us, after you? When he was already at the car?"

"Why not?" Anja said. "It makes more sense than the idea of a rift in the veil of the universe. Doesn't it? It makes more sense for all this to be a trick, a fraud, than to say there are harmful things we can't see in the clearing, ghosts and a tear in the veil and whatnot."

"But something really did harm them," Danny said, pointing toward sick bay, and Anja pictured the seven men lying on cots. Juan and Tyrese twitching. Darryl, Nick, and Steve grimacing like they were having nightmares. Kumar trembling like he was silently crying. "Something did this to them," Danny said.

"I know," Anja said, trying to soften her voice. "But for all we know, someone flew by and dropped a chemical on them, soldier-dusting same as crop-dusting. Did you hear anything that night?"

Danny shrugged. "I was in here."

"Which would explain why you're still fine," Ming said.

Danny didn't look convinced, but he also looked doubtful all around. About his team, about the rift, about life.

"Look," Anja said, "I don't know what happened. I just know that what's happening right now—Yuri missing—doesn't jive with what we thought was happening. It doesn't jive with where we thought we were going. I thought I was going out of body."

"Didn't you?"

Anja closed her eyes and felt herself rising out of her body, jumping to the rifts, meeting Marfa and the little book thief and her mentor. It was all so vivid. So real.

Too real.

"I don't know anymore. But even if I did. Our mission was to find out what's causing the rift so that we could stop it. So that we could save your team, save Yuri's brother. There's no one but us here, right?"

"Right," Ming said.

"I mean, the team's here, and the new guys are nearby, keeping a lookout," Danny said, "but if you mean we're the only ones here clued into the rift and capable of doing anything about it, then, yeah. It's just us."

"So if you didn't take him," Anja said to Danny.

Danny shook his head.

"And you didn't take him," Anja said to Ming.

"I was watching the feeds until nature called. And he was lying on the floor next to you," she said.

"And I didn't take him, being asleep and all," Anja said. "Then who took him? Pretty sure it wasn't the perimeter guys. They're all accounted for, right? They all confirmed they hadn't seen him. Do you believe them?"

"Yeah," Danny said, but then his expression changed to one decidedly less sure.

"What?" Anja said.

"These radios have a huge range," Danny said. "You could radio in from Sacramento." Then, "Let me recheck the feeds."

Danny led Anja and Ming back to the front of the building and into the welcoming center. He and Ming took seats at the monitoring station, and Anja stood behind them while Danny rotated the monitors through all the camera feeds.

They found three guys in fatigues on three different feeds. They were lurking among the trees, checking deterrence devices, taking notes. Before Anja could ask about the guys who were off duty, Danny shifted to three other feeds, each showing a guy snoring in accommodations that were still rustic, but looked better than hers.

"They're all doing what they're supposed to be doing," Danny said. "And I'm not seeing any signs of stress or anomalous activity or feed tampering."

"Could they fake that everything's okay?" Anja said. "Do a quick job with Yuri and then pretend it's business as usual?"

"Sure," Danny said. "But why? Why would they take Yuri? There's just no reason to. They just met him yesterday, and they're used to acting on orders without full information of what's going on."

"Maybe he paid them," Ming said.

"With what?" Danny said. "We searched him. He had a couple bucks and a debit card."

"I think you should question them," Anja said.

Danny shook his head. "No. I trust them. They know they're replacements. They came in to do the job knowing something bad had already happened. They're risking their lives to guard a clearing that's already taken out another team. And the clearing itself is spooky, but they thought Yuri stumbling into it without tripping any of the sensors was even spookier. I just don't buy it. And they're there, on the feed. I'll go through the last hour again and see if I missed any of them moving, but I just don't think it was one of them that took Yuri. They're good guys."

Anja nodded.

"Wait," Ming said, "Why were you checking cameras?"

"Why?" Danny asked. "Yuri was still here when I left."

"Sure, but I faced Montezuma's Revenge in that bathroom," Ming said, pointing at the back right corner. "Maybe you slipped something into my tea."

"Are you serious?" Danny said.

Ming shrugged, not backing down.

"Fine," he said. "Let's check the feeds for me, too."

"Why were you checking the cameras?" Anja said.

"Because one of the alarms went off, but there was nothing on the camera, so I went to look."

"And?"

"I didn't see anything."

"Then, what was it?"

"I don't know."

"Bird? Animal?"

He shrugged. "It's possible, but that's one of the things about the rift. Birds and animals go around it. Remember? You're the one who commented on how silent it was when you first got here. No bird song, no animals breaking twigs."

"So what tripped the alarm?"

"For all I know it was a branch falling," Danny said.

Anja deflated a little. That explanation seemed quite logical, especially given that it was fall, and windy. Even if the wind veered around the rift, it was still pretty windy elsewhere. They were quite close to the ocean.

She didn't know what to make of this. Yuri had reawakened her ability to go out of body. Hadn't he? This most recent time was probably a dream, but what about the time before?

Or had that been a dream too?

Probably.

Yuri was gone now. And she'd been left with evidence suggesting this might have all been a ruse. Not an out-of-body experience at all, but just a dream. Just a dream, guided into a particular scenario by the recording someone had switched out for her meditation music.

It all sounded like a hoax. And definitely felt like a waste of time.

CHAPTER 57

Outside the welcoming center, Anja heard a vehicle coming in fast down the driveway.

"Are we expecting someone?" she asked.

"No." Danny returned the monitors to the current recording time and started flipping through different feeds of the surrounding area until he found one showing an unfamiliar SUV kicking up dirt as it slammed to a stop just outside the welcoming center door. Rock grit and debris pelted against the log building. The SUV had a rental sticker on the windshield.

"Jackson?" Danny said.

Sure enough. On the black-and-white screen, Jackson opened the driver's door and stepped out of the vehicle. He said something Anja couldn't hear and pointed over the roof of the vehicle as three of the perimeter guys climbed out of the SUV's other seats. They nodded and went around the back of the log building.

The welcoming center's door cracked open.

Jackson quietly snuck his head in.

"Oh, you're up," he said. He opened the door wider and stepped inside. "Does that mean you've gone and come back or that you weren't able to get out?"

"I didn't," Danny said, "but Anja did."

Anja grimaced and shook her head in rebuttal. "I don't know about that. My mentor was there. The more I think about it, the more I think it was just a dream."

Jackson nodded as if the distinction didn't matter. "The client called," he said. "The job's off. I sent the new guys over to help Doc pack up the team. You're the punch list," he said to Danny. "Let's grab the equipment we can carry and head out of here."

"What about the rift?" Danny said.

Jackson shrugged. "No action since the attack on the team. But either way, not our focus anymore. We've already been given a new assignment."

"Since when?" Anja said.

"But what about the team?" Danny said.

Jackson said, "Since about an hour or so ago. I choppered in. I'll take the team out that way. We've been given access to a medical facility of some kind as a parting gift. I'll need you to prep the conexes for transport and then drive out. You'll meet us in Sacramento. Let's go."

"What about Marisol?" Anja said. "What about the baby?"

Jackson looked pained by the question, but he put on a brave face. "Her mom's with her now. I'll join them again once I get the new assignment set up."

Anja noticed that he didn't mention the baby, but she didn't say anything. It seemed that whether or not what caused the rift was also causing large-scale pregnancy issues, Jackson no longer had the resources to care. It was too late for any more mavericking on his part. He'd done all he could to save everyone's families. Now he just wanted to be there for his own. He was a man of orders again.

"What about us?" Ming said.

"You're free to go."

CHAPTER 58

"So that's it?" Anja said.

"Hurry up and wait," Jackson said, like it was the story of the contractor's life. "You can fly out to Sacramento with me if that helps you get home."

"Can we make calls now?" Ming said.

"Sure," Jackson said.

Ming made a give-it-here gesture, and Danny hopped to, saying he'd left their phones in his conex. He bolted out the door to go get them. Anja had half-expected him to just dig their phones out of his pocket. She was pretty sure he'd been wearing the same pair of dirty cargo pants this whole time, since he'd first picked them up. And he probably had been. Anja didn't think he'd had any time to do anything but eat and keep an eye on them.

And now it was all just . . . over.

"So that's it," she said again.

Jackson put an arm around her shoulders and squeezed. "Thank you for coming. Thank you for working so hard. Both of you. And thank you for keeping this secret. If I could give you a better farewell, a better thank-you, I would, but . . ."

But this was it.

Anja snorted and shook her head. "Okay," she said, wriggling out of his grasp. The job was over, and that was fine. She was over it, too. She wanted to get back to what she knew, back to her science and her research.

But whether or not she'd actually been talking to her mentor when she'd been dreaming out of body, she felt like she understood her mind's underlying message. Her subconscious had been telling her that publication and success in her current position was probably never going to happen.

Fine. She was over that, too.

Might as well just leave it all behind.

Danny came back into the welcoming center, peeling off the tape he'd used to secure the batteries to the phones and popping the batteries back into place. He handed Anja's phone back to her looking sheepish about having taken it in the first place.

Jackson had offered them a lift, but she didn't want it. She powered her phone back on and called a cab to the airport.

Ming took her phone back. She looked at it, hefting it in her hand, and then looked at Anja. "Do you mind if I go see my son?" she said. "All this has got me kind of—"

Anja wrapped her friend in a hug, cutting her off, and pressed her temple to Ming's. "Of course," she said. "Go."

CHAPTER 59

Anja wondered if the tourists knew her smile was fake. She flashed it whenever one of them looked at her on their way up the ramp into the Gasquet visitor center. Danny had dropped her off at the Smith River National Recreation Area Headquarters so that the cab wouldn't have to drive to or learn about the rift site.

Anja's cheeks burned with the tension that only a fake smile could cause. She wore it over this strange feeling she had but couldn't place.

She still wasn't sure whether what she'd seen—her mentor in his viewing room, showing off the tear he'd made in the veil—was a dream or not.

He'd said it was a dream. But it had seemed so real. More real than real. More real than the moon.

Anja's cab was a traditional yellow cab driven by a guy who smelled like incense. A silver guardian angel hung from his rearview mirror. He had the radio on low volume. Classic rock. She tuned it out.

She'd asked him to drop her off at the nearest airport with a direct flight back to Portland. He'd said it was in Medford, Oregon. The Gasquet visitor center fronted US-199, and the cabbie took a left, heading north. Eventually the classic rock station started to crackle with static, and the cabbie started scanning.

Classical . . .

'80s . . .

Rap . . .

"*They're dying, Steve,*"

"Leave it on," Anja said to the cabbie, before the scanner could change channels.

The radio hosts and a couple of guests were debating about a proposed drug that could help pregnant women carry to term "in the face of today's new challenges."

It was a drug they'd have to take for the full nine months.

And the side effects?

Well, certainly there would be some. You don't pinch something off here and not expect a mess to come squirting out over there.

And that was just thinking of the mothers. What about the babies? What would they have to endure for the rest of their lives as the price of being born?

Anja figured it would be the same thing they would have received had their mothers *not* taken the drug.

Soullessness.

Literally or metaphorically.

Yuri was a fraud.

They told Jackson about him disappearing while Danny was checking the feeds, Ming was in the bathroom, and Anja was still confused and out of it.

"Well," Jackson said, "officially, he's not supposed to be here. And if he hiked in, he can hike out. And he hiked in. Past all your security measures without a peep, if I recall."

"But he didn't take his stuff," Danny said. "And I don't think he'd leave Josh."

Jackson said, "Unless you've got proof he was taken, a lead we can follow, I've gotta pretend he was never here. He was never supposed to be here. And unless he turns up, we don't have time or resources to look for him."

But Anja didn't think he'd turn up.

He'd come like a flash in the night, like sleight of hand. And Anja was sure he'd left the same way, taking whatever he'd come for with him. Like a fraud.

She was an idiot for letting him get into her head.

But she couldn't just forget what she'd learned from him over the past few days. Trying to do so would leave the rest of her life feeling empty. Meaningless.

She'd had a glimpse of that emptiness before. The so-called robotic meatbag. She'd clung to it like a life preserver. The irony. But she knew better now.

Yuri was a fraud. But she felt the futility of insisting that Yuri had somehow faked what she herself had made visible using her own equipment.

Something had attacked her. That was real.

They had all seen the mirage of ghosts at the rift. That was real.

She had caused the rift to reveal itself, not Yuri. Yuri, in fact, had told her not to do it.

His sensitivity to things, to energy—her sensitivity. That was all real.

She felt the truth of these things. And she couldn't let it go. She didn't want to let it go.

Scary and unknown and unexplainable. So be it. It was also exciting and real and worthy.

And true.

And it had given her hope.

She couldn't go back to not believing in more.

And she didn't want to.

There was light in believing in more. Hope, light, and love.

"Really?" one of the radio people said, sing-songing the melody of bank notes and getting Anja's attention. They were talking about the drug's economic opportunities now. Parents would do anything for their kids, after all. They'd try any drug that might save their kids.

They took a commercial break.

"Sad," said the cabbie.

"What's that?"

"Babies are dying."

Anja winced. Both because that was putting it far cruder than any ticker at the bottom of most news programs would put it, and because it was probably far more accurate.

"Animals are dying too," said the cabbie. "Did you hear that?"

"Animals?"

"Pets, mostly. Companion animals. Some small-farm livestock. Some people are saying—Hey!" The cabbie honked his horn, telling an SUV that had gotten bogged down in the fast lane that now was not the time to swerve around the holdup.

Anja waited for him to relax and resettle, and then asked him to repeat what he'd been about to say about *some people*. *Some people* usually meant the industry people who had attended the same schools and learned the same rules and guidelines as the mainstreamers but now claimed outlandish hypotheses and otherwise failed to conform to the materialism message.

People not unlike Yuri.

Anja felt a pang in her chest about Yuri. He had abandoned them, and yet every time she reminded herself of that, she felt guilty.

"They're saying the animal thing is the same thing causing the rise in stillbirths, and now the rise in SIDS."

"SIDS?" Anja froze, as if her brain needed all available energy to let the gears of her mind work. "What about older people?"

The cabbie shook his head. "I haven't heard anything about older people."

Anja scooted into the center of the bench seat and leaned closer to the driver. The air up there smelled faintly of fries. Anja blamed the crumpled fast-food bag in the front passenger footwell.

"This thing with the animals and the kids," she said. "Have you heard whether it's been a gradual thing?"

She'd only been away from the real world for a few days, but it seemed like everything had had plenty of time to change.

Anja couldn't see the cabbie's face, so she watched him through the rearview mirror. He was frowning, seemingly entirely focused on the traffic.

Anja nodded and sat back in her seat, resigned to let it go.

But then the traffic spread out a little. The cabbie relaxed and said, "It started a few days ago. They say they can pinpoint it to within ten minutes. *Ten minutes.*"

"And have they?"

"Yeah, Halloween, between 5:40 and 5:50 pm."

Anja felt shivers ripple down her arms. But it was hard to keep her face schooled into the same somber expression the cabbie wore. Anja was begging to show her dread.

Halloween. When the team was attacked.

The news program then brought on experts to offer their best guesses as to what was causing this rise in issues, their suggestions for how to resolve it, and their predictions for the future. But they couldn't come to a consensus, and they were all wrong anyway.

Anja thought that she should be on the program, but then again, who would believe her? But she knew. She'd felt it when she was in the dreamworld, and her mentor had told her the cause. She'd heard him then but had focused on something else.

"What?" said the cabbie. His gaze was darting back and forth between the rearview mirror and the road. "You got an insight into all this?"

Anja leaned forward in her seat again. No more wearing that fake smile. Her mentor may have just been a placeholder in a dream, but what her mind had been telling her was real. Anja could feel the truth of it.

But the proof was in the victims.

Pets and small children were unconditional love. And they needed it in return. Everyone did. Because the most fundamental energy in the universe was love. That's what her mentor was saying.

And now love was being threatened. And unless it was saved, all of these new problems in the world were just going to keep getting worse.

And Anja was the only person left who could do anything about it.

"Weird request," she said, "but can you take me to the nearest police station?"

The driver must've sensed the urgency—or known personally someone who could benefit from a solution to USBS—because he merged into the fast lane, whipped across the median, and screeched a U-turn onto the freeway going the other way.

CHAPTER 60

The cab driver said, "I don't know where the nearest police station is off the top of my head, but I saw a speed trap back near Selma. Will that work?"

Anja didn't like the idea of talking to a cop who might put her in a cop car, but she reminded herself that she would be approaching the officer rather than the other way around. "That'll work."

She worried the officer might've found a speeder and fled away, but when the roadside pull-off came into view, the roof of the cruiser was still peeking over the concrete guardrail, the car tucked mostly but not quite out of sight. No red-and-blue lights on top, but no one was fooled. Everyone was slowing down.

The driver eased the cab into the breakdown lane just past the cop car.

"I'll wait here," he said.

Anja got out.

The cop had a radar gun propped up on the concrete barrier, like a sniper perch, and was ducked down low, watching the numbers. When Anja shut the door, the cop looked over at her, whipping a ponytail out of the back of her uniform. She stood and rounded the side of the cruiser. Her cheeks were windblown. Her brass name tag said *Williams*. She was probably a few years younger than Anja. "Can I help you?"

"Yeah." Anja had been running what to say through her mind as they'd driven down the highway, but there was no good way to put it. "You've heard about the stillbirths?"

The cop frowned, and Anja couldn't blame her. Stillbirths were a medical thing, not a cop thing. Officer Williams turned her head to the side, as if positioning her ear to hear better, and waited for Anja to say more.

"I know what's causing it," Anja said, "and who's causing it."

Officer Williams's brows rose. She settled her weight on one leg and rested her hands at her waist, thumbs hooked on her gun belt. "Okay. I'm listening."

But would she keep listening once Anja started talking?

"Someone tore a hole in the veil between the physical and nonphysical worlds. I don't know why. I don't know how. But it's threatening love, the most fundamental energy in the universe that everyone needs to survive."

The cop stared at her. "I'm sorry, say that again."

"I know it sounds ridiculous—"

"No," the cop said, "just say it again. Slower."

Anja couldn't believe she wasn't being immediately shut down. "Really?"

"Yeah. Tell me again."

Anja took a deep breath. "Okay. I know it sounds crazy. But someone tore a hole in the veil between the physical and nonphysical worlds, and—"

Officer Williams was laughing. "Okay, honey," she said, holding up a hand that said she'd heard enough. "Is that your cab?"

Anja stood in silence, head hanging, as Officer Williams told her in jovial, disbelieving tones that Anja could get in her cab and have it take her to a station in Grants Pass, Oregon, where an officer there could help her fill out a police report.

"Ask for Officer Bruce," said Officer Williams with a barely suppressed giggle. "Kenny J. Bruce."

Anja had a feeling that poor Officer Bruce was a friend or maybe a frenemy that Officer Williams was hoping to harass with Anja's crazy talk.

Officer Williams took Anja by the elbow and walked her back to the cab and got her seated in the back. Then she asked the cabbie if he was okay taking Anja to the station—or just home, if Anja preferred. The cabbie said yes, ma'am, yes, ma'am, and Anja couldn't fault him for it. Of course he didn't want to spend any more time with the cop than he had to.

And of course the cop didn't believe her. Anja knew her colleagues at the station wouldn't either. Why would they? Anja hadn't believed it herself. Hadn't wanted to believe until she'd been forced to face it.

When the cab pulled back into the traffic lane, the cabbie asked Anja where she wanted to go: airport, police station, home?

But Anja said none of the above. She had a different destination in mind.

CHAPTER 61

Anja had the taxi drop her off at the old campsite's camouflaged gate.

"Do you want me to wait?" the driver said.

Anja looked at her phone. She had a full battery, a decent signal, and the Gasquet visitor center was only a couple miles back down the hill. She shook her head.

"You sure?" he said with a sudden shudder, like he was cold even though he had the heater blasting.

"You feel it, don't you?" Anja said.

She sure felt it. Like something breathing up and down her spine. A mere distraction as it bore down from above. It had grown worse, more prominent, harder to ignore the higher they'd driven up the hill. The closer they'd gotten to the rift.

She had no proof, no evidence that the sensation was caused by the rift, and what was strange was she didn't care. She'd never been more sure in her life, not even when so-called proof was staring her in the face. And not just because today's proof was so often refuted by something else that came along later. This, this feeling, this sensation, this subjective sensation in her body—it was irrefutable.

For the first time ever, she put her whole trust in her intuition. And it told her that she and Yuri and Danny and the team at the rift had been onto something.

The rift was real, and what had caused it—and was still causing it—was real, too. It was all real, and it was all still happening.

And getting worse.

And there was no one looking to help, not directly.

Indirectly, sure, there were plenty of people exploiting the problem and calling it help, offering skewed and therefore patentable bandaids, frankensteined protocols to help carry babies to term. She knew. She'd worked on such projects. But no one was looking for the cause, not anymore.

No one but her.

"You do, don't you?" she said. "You feel it in the air."

The driver gave her a look that said *So what if I do?* as he suppressed another shudder.

Anja felt a ripple of tingles slice through her own strange feeling and shiver across her shoulders. Objective proof was one thing, but there was no greater proof than shared subjective experience. No known tool would measure it, could measure it, but she felt it, and now she knew this guy felt it too.

And the closer she got to the rift, she knew, the stronger the feeling would become.

"Get away from here," she said as she opened her car door and stepped out, confirming her theory. "Drive until you can't feel it anymore."

If there was such a place.

She'd expected him to scowl at her, say *Sure, lady*, but he only nodded, like he felt relieved.

"Do you want me to contact someone?" he asked.

Anja thought about it for a second, but everyone she thought might help already knew and had left the area. The cop she'd tried to tell had laughed at her, and Anja couldn't say she blamed the woman. The materialism bias was strong, Anja knew; she'd helped perpetuate it. There was no point in telling anyone else.

"No," she said. "But thank you."

Anja waited for the cab to leave and then tried to open the gate. It was locked. She clambered through the brush growing up around it and headed for the welcoming center. She expected that everyone was gone, but she wanted to go to the last place she knew they'd been and feel their strength.

She was going to need it.

The old campsite was deserted. The welcoming center was quiet, and the monitors were gone. The food was gone. The cots in sick bay were gone. Anja's steps echoed on the hardwood floor. It felt like no one had been to this campground in years rather than just four or five hours ago.

Anja went from conex to conex, and every one of them had been stripped of all personal items. Nothing remained but empty furniture bolted to the floor.

In her old conex, she found a note from Danny.

I knew you'd be back, it began, and she snorted a wistful little laugh.

> We found Josh's journal during cleanup. He must've stashed it near Big Beauty right before the attack. His dates and times align with those listed in Doc's notes. Marisol's, too. Just thought you'd like to know.
>
> Yuri didn't turn up. But this did. If you find him, tell him I believe him. You should, too.

Under the note was Yuri's blue-and-purple fluorite crystal. His protective talisman.

The chain was broken.

He'd worn it under his shirt. It shouldn't have caught on anything.

And yet the clasp was broken in half.

Like someone had ripped it from his body when they couldn't get it over his sleeping head.

Yuri wasn't just gone.

He was taken.

Where to?

But Anja could only think of one group who would want him, one place he could be.

She'd been planning on going to that place anyway, but now she was gripping the stone and dashing out of the conex at a run, unable to get there fast enough.

And alone. How was she going to get there all alone?

She raced through the campsite, past the welcoming center, and into the woods. Instead of skunk, the woods smelled like damp earth and fresh green air, and the redwood canopy hid the sun and cast shadows on her path. The direct path she was taking to the clearing wasn't as well-trodden as the path that led from Big Beauty, and she tripped on more than one tree root, more than one fern.

She didn't know what time it was, except that it was getting close to evening. The sun would be setting soon.

Not that the time mattered. She was going to do what she had to do regardless, and she had to do it now. It had to be now. Today. November 4. Her memories of the past couple days were racing as fast as she was, and she remembered something Yuri and Ming had said about the middle of Scorpio being the time when the veil was thinnest. They'd said it would get thinner and thinner until November 6.

But her mentor wouldn't wait until then.

She couldn't deny how lucid she'd been, how real he'd seemed, when he'd shown her the tear he'd made in the veil, when he'd said love was the most fundamental energy. She hadn't seen him in years, except on TV, and they never depicted him the way she remembered him. He'd shown up in her out-of-body experience in a manner she just didn't believe she could both recreate in a dream and now remember in such vivid detail.

That, and the pieces fit together. He'd mentioned their stop in Brazil. He was never the same after Brazil, even before his son had died.

And he'd gone back to Brazil soon after.

To see the old wise man, she had no doubt.

The man who'd said such crazy, relevant things about energy and about love.

The apparition who now hovered over her shoulder, protecting her with love.

Her mentor, Jim Lugner, was the man behind the tear in the veil and the attack on Danny's team. Anja didn't want him to be, but she was absolutely certain he was.

And she knew what he was after.

It was so obvious to her now.

And he wouldn't wait until the last minute to pull off his heist, even if November 6 was the veil's thinnest day.

His son had been murdered on November 4. And if Jim Lugner was stealing love, Anja had no doubt he was doing it for love.

He would do it today.

CHAPTER 62

Anja ran to the rift. Eventually, the redwoods parted. She reached the edge of the clearing just as sweat broke out on her forehead.

Beams of sunlight were angling through the canopy and hitting the old scorched earth. She stepped closer to the clearing's demarcation line, gauging any rise in sensations in her body like it was some kind of compass. Like it was playing a game with her, telling her when she was getting warmer, when she was getting colder. She stepped closer, closer to where the rift had been, where it had appeared to her during her light experiment and while she was out of body. She willed her body to tell her that she was hot, hot, hot.

But it didn't.

She felt something else. An absence. A quiet.

It felt like the rift was gone.

Anja collapsed to her knees in the center of the clearing, the sun spilling around her.

Now what?

If she was right about the thing that babies and animals have and need that was making them more vulnerable than others now, then someone had to do something.

If it wasn't already too late.

It felt like the rift was gone. Did that mean Jim Lugner and Marfa and the little book thief had already gotten what they needed?

She didn't know. But just in case they hadn't, just in case there was still a chance, she had to do something to stop it. It was getting worse. And if they weren't done, it was only going to get worse still.

Because if she was right about what children had, it wasn't that they had it and others didn't. It was that they had more of it. Everyone had at least a little. Even Anja herself. Which meant this wouldn't stop with young ones and pets. It would extend to older children. Adults. Until no one was left to help.

Saving children was enough reason to do what she had to do, but it wasn't just them. It was everyone. Everything. Even these trees rising high into the sky, towering over her. These beautiful, majestic trees. Even them. And the birds. And the plants. And the bunnies. Everything. Everyone was vulnerable.

They just didn't know it yet.

But even if there wasn't a whole world to save, whoever had caused the rift—Jim Lugner—he'd taken Yuri. She knew he had. Not Jim, himself. No. He couldn't. But his team could.

Yuri had held her hand. He had calmed her. He'd had no intention of leaving her, not in the rift, not at the base. Not ever. And he never would've left his brother.

Anja gripped Yuri's fluorite crystal. The broken chain dangled from the jump ring.

He wore it under his shirt, for protection. For protection from unseen things.

But seen things? They could touch it. They could pry it out of his shirt while he lay on the floor in a trance. So that the unseen could take him.

Just like a book.

Anja's whole body trembled with the truth of that thought.

Yuri had been taken.

And she would get him back.

CHAPTER 63

She looked around, compelled to stall, but she already had everything she needed. Or at least she hoped she did. Yuri would have told her she did. If he were here.

That pang in her chest came again. She'd be on her own this time.

But there was no time to wallow or mourn. She hadn't expected anyone to help her anyway. It was time to get to it.

But she wasn't alone in the forest.

"Anja?"

Anja looked around. "Danny? What are you doing here?"

He stood at the six-o'clock point of the clearing, on the path that led back to Big Beauty.

"Last man out," he said. "Just making sure we leave no trace." He had a trash bag and a metal detector with him. "What are you doing here?"

"It's getting worse."

"The rift?" he said. "USBS?"

Anja nodded, and appreciation swelled inside her. What a feeling to not have to explain herself. To be eminently understood. "And SIDS is rising. There's talk of pets dying, too. In greater numbers, actually, but—"

"People care less about that."

She nodded. "But I think that's the key. To what's going on.

Usually when kids are vulnerable, so are older people. But there's no upsurge in geriatric vulnerability."

"Huh," Danny said. "So what do kids have that pets have that older people don't have?"

Anja thought she knew. There was a pulse, a pitter-patter of two words in her heart, in her mind.

But she didn't say it.

"Any ideas?" she asked.

"I've got some things pets and kids don't have that elderly people do have," he said.

"If you say wrinkles."

"Gray hair. Stiff bodies. Jaded attitudes."

"Yeah," Anja said, swelling again at the last idea he'd mentioned. But she still couldn't say what she suspected. *Just say it, Anja.*

"We gotta go back in there," she said instead, and then she remembered that Danny hadn't gone in with them the first time. "Someone's gotta go back in there."

A radio on Danny's pants squawked and asked for Danny's ETA. Anja recognized Jackson's voice.

Danny shared a long look with Anja, both of them saying nothing. Though she felt her gaze begging him to stay, to stay with her at the clearing.

He clicked the red button. "I need more time," he said. "I'd like to follow a lead with . . . with Anja. Over."

"Granted," came the immediate reply. And Anja thought she heard just as much hope and gratitude in Jackson's voice as she was feeling herself. Not to mention relief. He then told them good luck and for Danny to get in touch when he was done.

A lump formed in Anja's throat. She no longer had to do this alone.

Danny set his stuff down and walked into the clearing. "The rift is gone."

"What do you mean gone?" she said. "I thought so, too—you can feel it. But how do you know for sure?"

"I checked it one last time with all the equipment before the perimeter guys packed it all up. Used your little lights and rocks trick, too." He smiled a little. "It's gone."

"But things are worse now," Anja said. "How can it just be gone?"

"Maybe whoever caused it in the first place didn't need it anymore. And didn't like you coming through it. Did you get my note?"

Anja held up Yuri's crystal, the broken chain still wrapped around her wrist.

"I think the book thief took him," she said.

Danny nodded. "Yeah. That's my conclusion, too. And . . ." He squinted at her and sighed. He had more to say, but he wasn't saying it.

"What?" she asked.

"Nothing."

Anja scoffed.

"Nothing important right now," he amended. "We're getting him back, right? And saving the world?" He grinned, trying to make light of their impossible situation. And Anja tried to smile back, if only in appreciation for his effort. His presence. For keeping her from having to do this alone.

"So?" he said, opening his arms as if to say *I'm at your service.* "What's the plan?"

CHAPTER 64

Anja lay on her back in the center of the clearing. The ground was softer and damper than she'd expected. Above her, the canopy of redwoods encircled a clear space of blue sky. The sun had fallen far below the treeline and its rays had stopped shining through the canopy.

The atmosphere around her felt warmer, fuller than the crisp autumn air she was used to. She wondered if that was the ghosts.

Except, weren't ghosts supposed to make things colder?

Wow, did she really just think that?

Focus, Anja.

"If any of you can help us get out of body," she said to any ghosts that might be in the clearing, "I'd appreciate it."

She waited for some kind of response, but she felt nothing. Like she was talking to no one. Or, worse, just talking to herself. Like a crazy person. Like a crazy person who might one day haunt a place like this.

"What about your ghost guardian?" Danny said.

"I don't think he's here anymore," she said.

"Why not?" Danny asked. "Why wouldn't he be?"

"I don't know. But you know how you all felt weird after the power-station incident?"

"Yeah."

"Do you still feel that way?" Anja asked.

"Yeah. It just feels heavy. It was less so when I drove you down to Gasquet. Even less in Crescent City."

"Yeah, well, Yuri thought he was keeping me from feeling that heaviness. And I feel it now."

"Oh," Danny said. "Okay."

She shook the worry about her old protector away, telling herself he was already a ghost. What more could be done to him?

"Do you remember Yuri's instructions?" she asked Danny. "Or do you need me to say them?"

She'd meant to truly offer help, but her tone made it clear what the correct answer was, and Danny said he was good on his own.

Anja closed her eyes. She tried to feel like she was floating on water, but the damp ground undermined her efforts.

Not a good start.

She focused on her big toe, remembering the sensation of stubbing it. The surprise, followed by the pain, followed by the ache. She waited for it to swell into a sensation that she could move up and down her body, but the stubbed toe remained nothing but a memory.

She bent her knees and put her foot flat on the ground, then used the other foot to stomp her toe. She grunted. And closed her eyes. Her toe throbbed, but so did the ones next to it. And it was more than a memory now. It was present. It was pain.

It was distracting. That feeling of frustration and anxiety rose in her chest until tears threatened to fall. She whacked her elbows against the ground to release some of the feeling, some of the energy. Bits of flung dirt landed on her face.

What made her think she could do this? Not only was it all nonsense to begin with, but what had ever made her think she could do it even if it weren't? It was easier when Yuri was guiding her, doing all the talking and the orchestrating for her. Doing it herself left her brain too active, too focused on the physical sensation in her body. And she didn't want to be in her body. She wanted to be out.

She wanted to be out!

She took a deep breath and huffed it out, shaking her arms and legs out at her sides. She closed her eyes.

Yuri. She pulled his crystal from her pocket, curled the chain around her wrist, and let the charm rest in her hand. She'd seen him less than eight hours ago. But it seemed so much longer. And he'd been holding her hand, whispering *calm*. She squeezed the crystal as if doing so would somehow let Yuri know she was coming.

Trying to, anyway.

Calm. She closed her eyes. He'd helped her and been patient with her and kept her calm when she couldn't have done it herself. And the moment someone pitched shade on him, she'd shunned him. She'd let them just have him.

I'm sorry, Yuri.

And she let go. She gave in to the earth beneath her and the fire in her heart and the tears in her eyes. She buried and burned and drowned. And when it was over, she was still and completely in her own little world. Floating on an unnamed sea. The cosmic ocean. The primordial waters.

And she was out of her body.

CHAPTER 65

Sitting at his office desk, in his underground Kansas bunker, smack-dab in the center of the lower forty-eight of the United States, Jim Lugner received a text message. He already knew who it was from and what the message would say, but he checked it anyway.

> *Scientist at redwood rift and out of body.*
> *Now let him come get me.*

The first part meant his protégé would be here with him at any moment.

The second part was more aggressive than he thought the situation warranted, given what a favor he'd done for the woman, what moment in history he was letting her be a part of.

But she'd be out of his life soon enough. They both would be.

He's busy, he texted back.

And then he stood and hustled up the stairs to the compound's viewing room, with a smile on his face.

CHAPTER 66

Anja was out of body. She could tell because her body still lay at her feet.

But she was having a hard time seeing it. It was blurry. She could barely make out that she was wearing her white blouse and designer jeans, her once-cream ballet flats, now covered in mud. Everything in the clearing, whether it was physical ground and trees or nonphysical rift and ghosts, looked blurry, like it was all muted and blending together. Nothing was as crisp as it had been when she'd traveled with Yuri.

And her movements felt slow. It took effort to look around or to step closer to Danny, who was another blur on the ground a few feet away.

It all meant that she had a tenuous hold on her lucidity, that she could slide back into her body at any moment.

Calm, she told herself. *Clear. Lucid. Calm.*

The statements helped, but she still didn't feel as clear and focused as she'd felt when she'd been out of body with Yuri.

Ah, but Yuri had said, then, that she'd been aided by her old wizened protector.

"Are you here now?" she asked. She looked around, but everything was a blur.

She imagined the old man in her memories, from her university trip to Brazil with Jim Lugner. She couldn't remember the man's name. But she recalled his lined face, his kind smile, his knowing eyes. She imagined him in her mind, hoping it would help her see him now, if he were still here.

"Are you?" she asked again. *"Are you here? Can you help me?"*

He appeared before her.

Just the top half of him, like Yuri had described.

But only his face was clear. His torso was blurred out, and faded to nothing at the waist. He hovered before her.

Anja felt a spike of emotion, of joy and relief. It threatened to pull her back to her body.

Calm, she told herself. Then, *"Can you help me?"* she said to him. *"Help me get more clear?"*

He nodded.

Anja thought he'd kneel down and touch his head to hers, like Yuri had described. But instead, one of his arms became more clear and he touched her astral forehead.

She didn't feel a thing.

But the circle and the redwoods became more clear.

He dropped his hand and his arm blurred into his torso again.

"Thank you," she said. *"Thank you. What about Danny?"* She pointed, slowly, her movements still labored, at Danny lying on the ground. *"Can you help me get him out?"*

The wizened half-bodied ghost nodded and turned toward Danny with fluid motion. Anja followed, but nowhere near as fast. She felt like she was walking into a wind tunnel, except there was no roar in her ears. There was only silence, punctuated by her own thoughts.

But after a few steps the feeling of drag went away and her pace sped up.

The half-bodied ghost lowered to the ground next to Danny, like he was kneeling, and his left arm became crisp again. He touched Danny's forehead.

Danny's eyes opened.

But after a moment, Anja realized that it wasn't Danny's physical eyes that were open. It was his astral eyes. The ghost's touch had made Danny's astral body pop out, and it was visible now as it lay over the top of his physical body.

Danny's astral eyes darted around, stopping when they alighted on Anja's. His astral hand rose up and out of his body.

Anja looked to the old wizened ghost to do something else, the next step in helping Danny out, but he didn't. He nodded at Anja.

"Me?" she said.

He nodded again.

"But how do I . . . ?"

But she didn't finish the question. She could feel herself getting anxious. *Calm*, she told herself. *Stay calm*.

And with a little moment of calm, the *how* became obvious.

She grabbed Danny's astral hand and helped him rise up, pulling him out of his body.

"Holy shit, this is crazy," she heard Danny say. Or think. She figured he was probably thinking it, because she'd never heard him talk like that in word or tone before. And the thought that maybe he'd cleaned up his vocabulary for her caused another spike of emotion.

Calm, she told herself, the tone of her statements to herself becoming more terse. At this rate, they'd have no chance of even getting back to the tear, let alone doing anything to stop Jim Lugner's plan.

"Am I out?" Danny was think-saying as he looked down at his astral self and then at his body. *"I think I'm out. Holy shit, I'm out. This is amazing."*

"Try to stay calm," Anja told him.

Danny startled, glancing her way for just an instant before disappearing with a silent whoosh back into his body.

Calm, Anja told herself. *Calm. You must remain calm. You must not let this frustrate you. No matter what, Anja, you must stay calm.*

Then, to the old wizened ghost: *"Can you help me get him out again?"*

The ghost nodded and touched Danny's forehead.

Danny's astral eyes opened and he raised his hand. Anja helped him out again.

"Hey," she said, still holding his hand and looking him in the astral eye. *"Whatever you do, you need to stay calm, okay? Strong emotion, good or bad, will send you back to your body. And we only have one chance to surprise them."*

"Yeah," Danny said. *"Okay. Calm. I can do that. Calm."*

"Calm," Anja said, saying it with more calm than Danny had. *"It helps to feel it when you say it."*

"Calm," Danny said, with more ease.

"Calm," Anja said. Then, to the old wizened ghost, *"Can you help us stay out again, the way you helped me last time?"*

The ghost shook his head.

"No?" Anja said, followed immediately by *"Calm."*

The ghost shook his head again.

"Why not?" Anja asked.

Both of the ghost's arms became crisp, and he touched her and Danny's foreheads.

Anja saw her mentor standing in his viewing room, the tear in the veil reflecting in the window's glass.

"Wait," Danny said. *"Isn't that Jim Lugner, the guy running for senate? The guy whose kid was murdered?"*

"Yeah," Anja said.

"Isn't he your mentor?"

"Yeah."

And the image in her mind changed. She was suddenly back in Brazil in the wise man's dirt-floor hut.

The wise man had been a tourist attraction on their trip, not part of their curriculum. He'd rambled on about something Anja had found too woo-woo to listen to. At the time, she'd let the other students clamber for spots on the worn furniture or the area rug, and she'd taken up post against the wall, staying as far away from the woo-woo as she could.

But now it meant she could see everything.

And everyone.

The wise man had props that went along with his tales. One was a book. And when he put it down in exchange for something else, Anja's mentor had picked it up and thumbed through it. When the old wise man finally realized it, he asked Jim for the book back and then hid it in a drawer.

"What is this?" Danny asked.

"Shh," Anja said. She watched Jim Lugner's face, his reaction to the book being taken. He'd tugged on it, not wanting to let it go.

He'd been different from that moment forward on their trip. Distracted. Lost in his own thoughts.

The image in her mind changed again.

But this time it wasn't a memory.

She saw *herself*, on that trip, standing against the wall, next to the front door, with her arms crossed and a scowl on her face.

She was seeing how she had looked, then, to the wise old man.

Sorry, she thought. *I didn't know. I didn't realize.*

The image changed again. She was still looking at the wall next to the front door, but no one else was in the hut. The old wise man was alone.

Until the front door opened.

Jim Lugner stepped inside.

The image changed again, but not entirely. It fast-forwarded in time, the action speeding up enough to cause squiggles across her mind's screen, like an old VHS tape.

And Anja didn't like what she was seeing through those hastened blurs.

Calm, she told herself, not feeling it at all. It was probably helping that the old ghost was still touching her astral forehead. *Calm*.

But even with the statements and the old ghost's help, it was hard to remain calm as the fast-forward continued to play. If Jim Lugner had done what she thought she was seeing—

The image resumed real-time speed.

Anja saw the old wise man lying face down on the ground. A big bleeding gash on the back of his head.

And Jim Lugner walked out the front door with the old wise man's book.

Anja remembered how eager Jim had been to get them all to the airport.

Calm, Anja told herself.

"Your mentor killed a guy?" Danny said, his tone impressively calm. Calmer than Anja felt, for sure. *"For a book?"*

Anja couldn't remember the stories the old wise man had told them when he'd been holding the book, but she had enough context from the memories and the past couple days to put together what was going on.

"The book was Jim's inspiration," she said. *"His starting place. For doing what he's doing now. For why he recruited the psychics. For why he tore a hole in the veil."*

"Isn't he the guy you wanted to email?"

"Yeah," Anja said, trying to say it like she was saying *calm*, hoping it would do double duty. *"And I did email him."*

And she remembered how Jim Lugner had told her out-of-body self that he'd gotten her message, that he was going to respond with an email of his own. Anja was sure that he had—but he didn't send it to her.

"I think he's the one who hired your team. I think he's why your assignment was shut down as soon as I got back in body."

"Then he's why my team was attacked," Danny said, with a scary amount of calm. *"Let's go get him."*

CHAPTER 67

Danny, still managing to stay in his astral body, looked around the clearing, probably wondering how to proceed, but then he stopped, motionless, and he stared at something behind her.

"Wow," she heard him think as he backed away from her, to the edge of the clearing.

"Calm," Anja reminded him. She turned around to look for what he might be seeing and then backed away herself.

The trees bordering the clearing were crisper now.

And so was the rift.

It wasn't gone. But it was rotating so slowly that for periods of time it looked like it was standing still. When it did move, it was jerky. It reminded Anja of the First Rift, the one she'd stepped out of with Yuri, on the beach.

And like the First Rift, there weren't many ghosts lurking around their rift anymore. What ghosts Anja could see were standing inside it, clearly concentrating.

"Do we go through there?" Danny asked, sounding like he was ready to do it if he had to but would rather not.

"I don't think so," Anja said. *"I don't think we want to be inside the tear, on the other side of the veil. Mankind ruined the veil on this side. My guess is we fix it from this side. It looks like the ghosts are doing what they can on that side, anyway,"* she said. *"Take my hand."*

Danny grabbed her hand and squeezed. She looked at him, grateful that he was here with her, and squeezed back.

"There's one other thing," Anja said as she held on tight to Danny's hand. *"About Yuri. The book thief might've taken him. But I think Jim Lugner has him. And I can't imagine Jim wanting him for no reason."*

Danny looked down. She couldn't hear him, but she saw his astral body pulsing, almost like a heartbeat slowing down to calm.

"You good?" Anja asked.

Danny nodded. *"We gotta help Yuri."*

Anja squeezed his hand, thinking the same thing.

Still standing by their bodies, the wizened old ghost nodded once at them and then vanished.

Godspeed, Anja thought after him. Then, to herself, to the universe, to the magic that made it happen, she said, "*Take us to Yuri.*"

CHAPTER 68

Darkness surrounded them. And Anja didn't know where she was.

She'd felt herself being whisked away immediately. But that was several moments ago, and they still weren't in a new place. And if she wasn't mistaken, she still felt a phantom of the whisking sensation. Like it had slowed down, because it didn't know where to take them. Or how to get there. Like they'd only made it halfway and were now stopped in a dark void.

No light.

No joy.

"Yuri?"

No answer.

No materialization in the void.

Where was Yuri? There was nowhere to look because there was nothing to see. No depth, no dimension. What had Jim Lugner done to him?

Calm, Anja told herself. And then she said it again. Over and over. She couldn't let herself think right now about what might've happened to Yuri, of what Jim Lugner might've done to him. She had to believe that Yuri was okay, that he would be okay.

Anja squeezed Danny's hand and then had to remind herself to stay calm again when he squeezed back. She tried to look left, tried to see Danny, but there was nothing but black. Anja didn't know if her astral head was even moving, if she even had her astral body anymore.

If Yuri was here, in this void . . . and why wouldn't he be, since that's where she'd asked to be taken? She'd asked to be taken to Yuri. She'd demanded it. If he was here . . .

Then Jim Lugner had put him here.

She had to get Yuri back.

And she would all but destroy her mentor.

"Take us to Ji—"

"Wait," Danny said.

CHAPTER 69

"*What?*" Anja asked, squeezing Danny's hand just to reassure herself that he was beside her in the darkness, that he was the one who'd told her to stop. *"What are we waiting for?"*

"You said 'take us to Yuri' and we ended up here. Where are you taking us now?"

"To Jim Lugner."

"We're just going to pop up in front of him?"

"Uh . . . yes?"

"And do what?" Danny asked.

"I don't know. We need to close the tear. I don't know how to do that. But he does."

"I think we should sneak up on him," Danny said. *"Do some reconnaissance."*

"How? I don't know where he is."

"What do you mean? I thought you saw him when you were out with Yuri."

"I did, but Marfa—"

"Who?" Danny asked.

"The OBE woman who attacked me. Tall? Curly hair?"

"Got it."

"She whisked Yuri and me into some weird room with an observation deck on the floor above. The tear was outside, in the building's courtyard. It wasn't raining, but other than that I have no idea where we were."

"Where do you think he'll be?"

"Jim? I don't know. Not in the courtyard; the tear takes up all the space. The viewing room, probably. That's where he was before. But the building looked pretty massive. Like a mansion. He could be anywhere. He might not even be there at all." Anja thought about it and reconsidered. "No, he'll be there. They're doing it now. It's the anniversary of his son's death. He'll be in the viewing room." Her astral body rippled with the truth of that guess. *"So what do you want to do?"*

Danny squeezed her hand. *"You didn't see any other spaces?"*

"There were doors on the second-floor balcony in the courtyard. But I don't want to show up there. The tear's not like the rift."

"What about the room Marfa took you to?"

Anja recalled backing away from Marfa and hitting some kind of mesh wall, a barrier her astral body couldn't pass through. She described the experience to Danny. *"It was like some kind of Faraday cage."*

"Like Ghost Busters*?"*

"Doubt it. That was decades ago. This is something more advanced."

"So how did you get out?"

Anja told him about getting into the courtyard through a tunnel under the viewing room. *"Then, once Yuri was taken, I just thought about going home, about how I wanted to go home."*

"So if it's a Faraday cage, they turned it off."

"Must've. I wasn't immediately whisked away. I could feel it trying, but then, whoosh, like the flick of a switch, I was back. What do you think?" she added when Danny didn't say anything.

"I think if you don't know where you were, don't want to go to the courtyard, and I don't want to pop up in front of Jim without knowing something about my surroundings, then we'll have to take our chances with the Faraday cage. If it could keep you in, then it would have to be turned off for us to get in in the first place, right? You think that's why we're in the void now? Because Yuri's in the Faraday cage?"

"Maybe," Anja said, but she doubted it. She thought the magic whisking sensation would've gotten them as close to Yuri as they could get. Outside the cage, if he was in one. She thought she'd at least be able to see him.

No. She had a dark suspicion Yuri was somewhere in this void.

She just hoped he wasn't the void itself.

CHAPTER 70

Still holding Danny's astral hand, Anja brought to mind the high ceiling and silvery-white metal-looking walls of the Faraday room, with the viewing room windows looking down from above.

"Take us there," she said.

The magic whisked them out of the void, and in an instant, Anja was back in the silvery-white room.

Standing beside her, Danny let go of her hand.

"No, no, no," she said, her lucidity flickering. Then, to herself, *Calm. Calm.*

"What?" Danny said.

Anja fumbled for his astral hand. *"Yuri let go of my hand and—"*

"Got it," Danny said, giving her hand a double squeeze. *"But we might have to be strategic about it."*

"Understood," she said. But she had no intention of letting go of his hand. Logically, she knew it probably didn't make a difference. It wasn't his physical hand; it was an astral hand. No substance. Nothing to really hold onto if something wanted to suck him away—or if he wanted to leave. But she wasn't operating on logic much at the moment. Gut feelings and instinct were guiding the way.

Something passed by her. It wasn't anything she could see, but she felt it brush past her ever so lightly, like arm hairs tickling arm hairs.

"Did you feel that?" she asked Danny.

"Feel what?"

Anja looked around the silvery room, seeing nothing, then studied the windows high up on the wall in front of her. For a second, she thought she saw movement, a shadow. But it was gone so fast, she doubted she'd seen it at all, and her mentor never appeared. She didn't see any other astral beings, either.

Guess Jim Lugner and his psychic team were otherwise occupied. She and Danny were alone.

"Never mind. See that left window?" she said. *"There's a door in the wall panel below it that opens onto a tunnel. It leads to the courtyard. That's where the tear is."*

"Okay," Danny said. "What about the box? Anything in there?"

Anja looked at the wooden box still sitting in the center of the room. *"Jim said no. Or, he said 'nothing yet,' anyway. So I don't know. Probably nothing. You want to check?"*

"Yeah." Danny bent down and stuck his astral head through the box. *"Too dark,"* he said, and he waved his hand through it. *"Nothing in it as far as I can tell. Anything else I should know?"*

"Probably, but I don't know it either."

"So we've seen what's to see in this room. Right?"

"Yeah."

"Then now it's my turn." He squeezed her hand and said, *"Take us to the back door of this place."*

One whisking moment later, and they were standing on the back stoop of what appeared to be an old American farmhouse. The door had a window with peeling crosshatching across the glass. The interior was dark.

It was night wherever they were, but the moon was full, and in the distance, Anja saw nothing but grass and fields, privacy hedges, and the occasional copse of trees. She heard a pair of owls hooting back and forth, and the wind tickling a wind chime.

"Uh," Danny said, *"Did I not do it right?"*

He stepped off the stoop, pulling her with him.

Around the side of the house was an old two-story red barn with white trim and what used to be a gambrel roof with five flat edges forming an upside-down U. But now the roof was gone, and the barn had greenish-yellow light shooting out of the top.

Like a fire hose spewing the Northern Lights.

"No, it worked." Anja said, pointing at it. *"That's the tear. The room we were in must be underground. The barn's covering the courtyard."* But it couldn't contain the tear, clearly.

"Makes sense," Danny said. *"Normal people put their evil plans in the basement. And they probably don't expect us to come in through the barn."* He tugged on her hand, pulling her toward it.

"I don't expect us to go through the barn," she said. *"The tear's no joke. The only reason it's not spreading toward the house is because it's contained by a net. Another Faraday cage, probably. If it can't get out, we can't get in."*

"We don't need to get into the tear. We just need—"

"Privyet, comrade."

Anja startled and whipped around to see Marfa standing behind them on the back stoop.

Calm, Anja told herself, trying to hold on to her lucidity as she fumbled to back further away and untangle her arms from Danny while maintaining a grip on his hand. With less than stellar lucidity, her surroundings looked like a black-and-white movie with the sound turned off. *Calm,* she repeated, trying to draw out the word.

Standing next to her, Danny seemed to be doing better at staying calm. But he was probably trained for this. For being in action, in places unknown to him with foes trying to sneak up behind him at every turn. For Danny, this probably *was* his calm place.

"You're the one who tried to attack Anja," Danny was saying.

"Orders," Marfa said. *"Sometimes I obey. Sometimes . . ."*

She shrugged.

"What are your orders now?" Danny asked.

"Turn on cage. Catch you when you come into viewing room."

"You let us go," Anja said.

Another shrug.

"Why?"

"I warn him. I will hurt bad persons. Fine. Good person?" She shook her head.

"Yuri?" Anja asked.

"Him, too."

"What did Jim do?" Anja said, *"What happened to Yuri? We need to help him."*

"Yes," Marfa said. *"You help. You come."*

Marfa said it as if they had a choice, but she stepped toward them and gripped them each by the shoulder, whisking them away without another word.

CHAPTER 71

Anja was back in the silvery room with the viewing windows high on one wall. She didn't see anyone standing in the viewing room.

Marfa let go of her shoulder. *"Stay here,"* she said. *"I open door for you."*

And she vanished.

Calm, Anja told herself as she squeezed Danny's hand.

He squeezed back. *"Do we trust her?"*

"No. But she's clearly got a moral compass, skewed though it is, and apparently this whole situation has it pointing south."

"My take, too," Danny said. *"We might have aligned interests. For now. Let's go stand by the wall, out of view of the windows. Just in case."*

"Okay," Anja said.

She probably could've whisked them to the spot, but the physical mindset is hard to shed. Her astral body trudged toward the wall, the difficulty of the movement, like stirring peanut butter, confirming just how tenuous her lucidity was. *Calm,* she said with every step, trying to make her muted surroundings appear more luminous in color. *Calm*.

But they didn't make it more than a couple steps. She felt a sensation of stirred-up energy. Sparks flashed and dropped from the ceiling.

A cage came down.

The flimsy wires and the metal base of the cage clanged to the ground around them and vibrated against each other. The ground at their feet crackled like novelty sparkler fireworks, throwing up flashes of light and the smell of ozone.

Calm! Anja ordered herself to remain calm, but it was doing no good. She could feel her anxiety rising.

Danny stepped closer to the cage wall, pulling on her hand. It was a decent-sized cage, eight-foot by eight-foot, maybe. His astral head tilted up. She looked up, too, at the viewing room windows.

"Take us there," Danny said.

But they didn't move. Anja didn't feel the blowing-wind sensation whisking her off to her chosen destination. She felt nothing.

She put her hand out and stepped toward the walls of the cage. She couldn't touch the wires. They put out some kind of field that gummed up her hand. It felt like pressing on thick memory foam. And if she pushed it too much, it repelled her, like she was the wrong end of a magnet.

Calm, Anja thought. But she didn't need to think it. She was stuck in here. She was stuck in this cage, she and Danny, whether they liked it or not.

And she didn't like it.

"Guess that answers the question of whether we can trust our comrade," Anja said.

"I don't think she's the one who did it," Danny said. *"Look."*

CHAPTER 72

Jim Lugner was standing in the upstairs viewing room, staring down at them from the middle window. He wore his translator headset, the ultraviolet glasses, and the earpiece. The black brick-shaped thing Anja figured was probably a battery pack was gripped tightly in his hand.

But he wasn't alone.

Anja didn't see Marfa, but she saw ghosts. At least half a dozen. The less focused, more dazed and wandering hobo kind.

"And here I thought you ultimately wouldn't believe," Jim said. "That you'd take my dream explanation and make it your excuse for rationality and doubt, and bail yourself out of this mess. But look at you. I still haven't mastered the art of leaving the body, and here you are, twice in one day. And you brought a frie—"

Jim held up a finger, cutting himself off, and he touched his earpiece.

"He's almost got it?" he said, and he rushed to the other side of the viewing room to look out the opposite windows, the ones that looked out over the courtyard. Anja didn't know who he was speaking to, whether it was someone in another room or one of the ghosts or someone Anja wasn't seeing.

"He's almost got it," Jim repeated, this time with a giddy certainty.

"Who's 'he'?" Anja said. *"What's he got?"*

"Can't you feel it?" her mentor said, returning to the window. "They can feel it."

He closed his eyes, opening his arms wide and tilting his head back. He sucked in a breath and seemed to glow with the effort.

Anja didn't feel a thing. Except maybe some kind of vibration, like a tiny earthquake. She wasn't sure she would've noticed it at all if Jim hadn't mentioned anything, and she figured she might only be imagining it now because he'd suggested it.

She looked at Danny to see if he felt it.

He looked back at her and shook his head, then squeezed her hand.

Calm, she told herself. She didn't want to be out of the habit of staying calm once they got out of this cage. Because they would get out of this cage. Somehow. They had to.

"'They' who?" Anja asked, because there was no one else in the viewing room with Jim. No embodied human anyway. Just the ghosts.

But then she realized that was probably who Jim meant. They were glowing too. Looked better, too. As if uplifted by something stronger than any downer known to man.

"What's he got?" Anja asked again, still not knowing who *he* was.

"The love," said her mentor. "He has the love at the core of the universe."

The light in the upstairs viewing room dimmed to almost nothing. No light at all. And then all of a sudden it was the brightest light Anja had ever seen, the brightness of the sun or of the angels, the brightness you shouldn't look at directly because although it gave life at most spots on the spectrum, the tip end of it would harm you.

That was this light.

And it was coming from the tear.

"Want to see?" Jim Lugner said.

The panel door opened, revealing the tunnel to the courtyard. Beyond it, Anja could see that it wasn't the tear that was bright. The tear had dimmed. What had looked like the Northern Lights now looked like a Bunsen burner.

The new bright light was on the other side, coming through the tear.

Someone was bringing it forward, stepping up to the edge, where the veil separated worlds.

The book thief.

He held the source of the light in his hands.

CHAPTER 73

"Ha!" Jim Lugner cried, and he raced out the door at the back of the viewing room. "Help him," Anja heard him yell over the metal sound of him running down the stairs. "Help him. There's nothing left for you now, so help him."

Anja didn't know who he was yelling at, but there seemed no cause for it. The building was silent. As far as Anja could see, her mentor was the only being around who was capable of making physical noise. The book thief was out of body, and she hadn't seen Marfa since the shielding cage came down.

But being physical, maybe Jim Lugner was experiencing the light in the kid's hands in a different way. Maybe it was blinding and deafening, warming and flowering. Maybe he could taste it. Anja thought of love and thought of hearts and thought of her grandma's fresh-baked cookies and chocolates on Valentine's Day. She smiled—and then felt ashamed.

Was that the best she could do?

The kid stepped out of the tear, and the tear dulled. Whether it disappeared entirely or was still there without its vibrance, Anja couldn't say.

But she suddenly felt a low-grade hum.

The kid staggered into the tunnel with the brightly shining love gripped to his chest. And the ghosts followed him. They followed the love. They followed as close as they could, as close as they dared. But they kept their astral eyes averted.

Anja was shielding her eyes, too, but this was different. The ghosts weren't looking away as if the light was too bright. They looked away as if they were ashamed to be seeing it: the love at the core of the universe.

The kid was struggling. His head was down, and his once quick and limber astral body was trudging like the oldest and weakest of physical man.

Jim Lugner appeared at the back of the tunnel, with the dim rift and the courtyard behind him. He cupped the rims of his glasses to block out the light.

"He's not done yet," Jim said. "He needs more energy. Go and check the Fraud."

"Yuri?" Anja said. *"He's gotta be talking about Yuri."*

"That's my guess," Danny said.

Anja didn't know who Jim was talking to, but she doubted it was one of the ghosts. The only being she could think of was Marfa.

But then Anja saw something ghostlike appear next to the book thief, like it had been surrounding him but was now standing up.

Whether the being was a higher-vibration ghost or another out-of-body person, Anja couldn't tell. The light was too bright.

The apparition appeared to stoop down again and hug the book thief—but then it vanished. Without its help, the kid could barely stand, let alone keep moving forward.

Then movement in the upstairs viewing room caught Anja's attention.

Marfa was rising, standing up with effort as if she'd been lying on the floor. She looked out the window and locked eyes with Anja.

"Hit the button," Anja said. *"Get us out of here."*

Danny yelled at her, too. But Marfa was in physical form. She probably couldn't hear them.

Marfa's eyes slowly closed. She slumped down and then perked back up again.

"Something's wrong," Anja said.

"She's bleeding," Danny said. *"Look at her hair."*

Marfa turned her back to the window, and Anja saw. Marfa's curly hair was flat and matted with blood. She staggered to the back of the room and pushed open the door, banging it against the wall and letting it slam shut. Anja heard her stomping heavily down the stairs.

She had to be checking on Yuri. In physical form. That had to be a good sign, right? He had to be alive. He had to be okay.

But Marfa slunk around the corner at the back of the tunnel.

The book thief was still struggling with the love. Jim Lugner and the ghosts were all following behind him.

Did Jim not hear the door slam? Did he not hear Marfa stomping down the stairs? He was hovering behind the love thief like he wanted to push the kid along. Like it was his only concern in the world.

Marfa snuck up behind him.

She snatched his translator off his head.

"No!" Jim cried, grabbing for the headset. He tried to use the tethered brick battery to yank it away from her.

But Marfa threw the headset against the wall behind him, breaking it into pieces.

Then she slumped to the ground.

"Damn you," Jim said, then, to the ghosts, "Get it to the ark. Help him get it into the ark."

Anja squeezed Danny's hand. *"He can't see us anymore, can't hear us. His translator's busted. We gotta get out of here. The love at the core of the universe? You* know *that's not meant to be here, on the physical plane."*

"In the hands of someone like Jim Lugner," Danny added.

"Exactly. We've gotta stop whatever he's doing, and we've gotta find Yuri," Anja said. *"We've gotta find a way out of here."*

CHAPTER 74

Jim Lugner couldn't hear her anymore, but Anja thought maybe the ghosts could.

"*Hey!*" Anja yelled. "*Hey! There's got to be a button to get this thing off us. Or to turn it off. Something. Someone hit the button. Anyone!*"

Anja looked around herself for a solution, for a way out of this cage. She was definitely not calm. She was anything but. She was anxious and afraid and riled up with energy. She felt like even she could pick up a notebook if she had to, like she could pick it up and throw it.

But there was nothing around her. The floor was pristine and white and clean, and there was nothing there.

Nothing but her own two feet. That, and her high emotional energy, her anxious, negative emotional energy, that had her feet, her body, looking more solid than they should be.

Could she?

Maybe. The book thief had stolen a book. Yuri had taken a shoe. Many strange things had happened in the past couple of days.

But more than that, she had nothing to lose. She mimed the action of toeing off one of her ballet flats.

"What are you doing?" Danny asked.

"I don't know yet. Maybe nothing."

But the shoe came off.

It landed with a thud on the ground.

She picked it up.

The wires? Could she get the shoe through the wires? She hit the shoe against the wires. They felt fragile. She hit the shoe again, slowly but deliberately, through the feel of molasses and memory foam. And the more she hit at the cage, the weaker the molasses felt.

"Give me the other one," Danny said.

Anja toed off her other shoe and handed it to Danny. She worried it might fall through his hand, but he kept hold.

"Too bad you weren't wearing heels," Danny asked. *"Got anything sharper?"*

Anja shook her head, but then—

"Yuri's crystal!"

It was still hanging off her wrist. She took it in hand, willing it solid, and went to work on the wires, twisting the wires around the edges of the crystal until the tension forced them to snap.

Danny pulled out his St. Christopher medallion and started doing the same thing.

"Why didn't we think of this before?" she said. *"We could've been doing this the whole time."*

Back in the tunnel, the kid was still inching deathly slow toward his destination. But Anja could tell from her mentor's face that the kid was making progress. He would get there soon.

And her and Danny's task was taking too long. They weren't going to make it. They'd made a small hole. It was barely big enough for her to stick her arm through.

"What are you thinking?" Danny asked.

"I don't know yet. Keep working on the wires."

Anja looked up at the viewing room windows. They needed someone to push the button and raise the cage. There used to be ghosts up there, but now they were all in the tunnel.

Anja said, *"How's your aim?"*

Danny said, *"Where am I throwing?"*

"Into the tunnel."

"I take it I'm throwing the shoe?"

"It's all we've got," Anja said.

Danny stuck the shoe through the hole they'd made in the cage and lobbed it into the tunnel.

"Is that you, Anja?" Jim said.

But he wasn't the only one who noticed. The shoe got the attention of the ghosts. And they all looked at the cage.

"Help us," Anja said, waving her hands. *"Get us out of here."*

Most of the ghosts found them uninteresting and turned their attention back to the love, following it as closely as they dared.

But one ghost did not. He looked at them longer than the others, kept looking at them, and as he looked, Anja thought she recognized him.

Danny said, *"Isn't that—"*

"My wise protector."

He was keeping tabs on the kid and the love, and almost looked as dazed and out of it as the others. But then he slipped into a moment of lucidity, and understanding dawned on his face.

The ghost vanished into the side of the tunnel and reappeared in the viewing room. Anja felt some of her anxiety transform into hope.

But then the ghost vanished from view again and was back in the tunnel following the love.

Anja cried out in defeat. She shook the wires of the cage and hung her head.

And the cage began to move.

"It's rising!" Danny said with a laugh. *"It's rising!"*

"Calm," Anja said, reminding them both. She could feel that it mattered again.

"Go to Yuri," she said.

"Does that mean you're calling for the strategic release of hands?" Danny said.

Anja looked down at their hands, still clasped together after all this time.

"You're not wrong," he added.

"I think we should," she said. *"Go find Yuri. I'll take care of the tunnel."*

"You got it," Danny said, and then she heard him say, *"Take me to Yuri's body."*

Jim Lugner was still in the tunnel. It was maybe thirty feet in length, and they'd barely traveled halfway. Her astral body could walk to him. But that wasn't who she was today.

"Take me to Jim Lugner," she said.

CHAPTER 75

Bad idea.

Anja whooshed away and was suddenly standing behind Jim Lugner in the tunnel, her vision murky and blurred.

She was surrounded by ghosts. They paid her no mind, and neither did Jim. He didn't seem to notice her presence or that she was out of the cage. Or if he did, he didn't care. His eyes were on his prize.

And that was a very good thing, because Anja wasn't ready. She felt the astral equivalent of lightheaded.

She should've had the upper hand. But she no longer had the assistance of the shielding cage keeping her out of her body. Her anxiety no longer made her physical. It just made her less lucid. More likely to spontaneously return to her body, back in the redwoods.

She wouldn't be able to do anything until she got her full lucidity back.

Calm.

Calm. Calm. Calm, she chanted. But the effort was making her anything but calm. She couldn't force herself calm.

The kid exited the tunnel and trudged to the center of the silvery-white room.

Like Jim and the ghosts, Anja followed. She just wanted to be near the kid, near the thing he held in his hands. She just wanted to be in its presence.

When the kid—the love—was almost to the wooden box, Jim Lugner ran ahead of him and opened the lid.

He looked like he'd just won the Nobel Prize, the Lifetime Achievement Award.

The kid dropped the love into the box.

And the low-grade hum became a vibration, a tremor. Maybe even an earthquake.

But Jim Lugner didn't seem to notice.

"Thank you," he said as he closed the box's lid. "Now go back to your mother."

The kid vanished.

Jim bent down and reached for the handles at both ends of the box, trying to pick it up.

And he picked it up with ease.

"No," Anja said. She had to stop him, but it seemed it was already done.

"We have to stop him," she said, but the ghosts weren't listening.

They were gathering around Jim Lugner. Following him, same as they'd followed the kid. They followed the box. They just wanted to be near it, to feel it, and Anja could feel why. Jim turned in a circle, showing off his prize. And as the box passed in front of her, she felt the warmth of the love radiating right at her, surrounding her, making her feel, making her know, that everything was ultimately okay. That nothing could harm her. Nothing bad or even interpretively unpreferred could happen—as long as the love was near.

But as soon as it passed her by, she noticed she no longer felt love in herself. There was no more faith in her heart, in her soul, in her astral body. There was only this physical love here, this artifact in this box. Love was only in the box now, only there. And if she wanted to feel it, that's where she needed to be.

But the box was in Jim Lugner's hands, and he was pulling it away. And Anja felt like the ghosts, felt herself acting like the ghosts.

She had to follow the box for fear that love might get away, might leave her without. Jim and the love were turning away.

She had to stop him.

She couldn't stop him.

It was already done.

CHAPTER 76

Finishing his victory twirl, Jim stooped to set the box back down on the ground. But he stumbled. He dropped the box, and the box fell open.

Anja wasn't sure what had happened, but she was electrified as the ghosts surged through her toward the box, toward the naked light of love.

"No-no-no! Kid!" Jim yelled. "Bring the kid!"

For a moment, Anja had all the lucidity in the universe, borrowed from the mob of ghosts. She saw the love for what it was and for what it would be if it remained here.

And she saw one ghost who remained upright.

Her protector.

"Put it back," he said.

Jim Lugner was up and scrambling for the box, yelling for the kid. The box's lid had fallen open, and the love had rolled out onto the floor. The light was shining again, but it wasn't nearly as blinding as before. Not so blinding at all. It was like looking at a sixty-watt lightbulb.

Anja waded into the ghosts and tried to pick up the light. But her hands went right through it.

Jim, for all his wailing for the kid to help him, picked it up no problem.

"How do we stop him?" Anja asked.

"We will stop him," said her protector. *"You will put it back."*

"How?" she asked. How would her protector stop him? How was she supposed to put it back? She needed a Faraday cage. She needed something to help her get solid, solid enough to pick up the love.

"*Calm*," she heard.

"Yuri?" She looked around for him. *"Danny?"* But they were nowhere. Where were they? Were they together?

Behind her, she heard a crash. Jim Lugner had stumbled again, and the love flew out of his hands.

Marfa's ghost had her arms wrapped around Jim Lugner's head. Anja knew it was her ghost, and not her astral body, because she could only see the woman's top half.

Jim swooned, like he was drunk and disoriented. He put his hands to his head, like he had a headache, like he didn't feel well.

Anja's protector ghost touched Jim's forehead. "*You will be respectful from this day forward,"* he said and the timbre of his voice reverberated.

Jim Lugner's head twitched like a dog who had heard something high-pitched.

"Who is that?" Jim Lugner said. "Anja? *Marfa?* Who is that?"

"Go," said the protector ghost to Anja. *"Take it back."*

But Anja still hadn't figured out how.

"It is not physical," said the ghost. "*At least, it is not meant to be. You must believe that you can pick it up. Just believe."*

Anja looked at the love's dimming light and judged it a lightbulb. Just a lightbulb. *It's just a lightbulb*. She picked it up.

She thought it would be a slogging trudge back through the tunnel to the tear in the veil. But the love knew where it wanted to go, and it was eager to get there. And Anja suddenly realized why the kid had had such a hard time walking it forty feet.

The love was like a magnet to the dim tear, to its home. It tugged her back to the rift, back to its purpose.

She moved as if on rollerblades, being pulled by a small dog, and as the love heaved itself into the rift, she pitched forward and let it go.

It was done.

But Anja couldn't allow herself more than one calm's worth of relief.

She had to find Yuri.

Danny hadn't come back, so she had to assume that he'd found Yuri, that his words had worked.

"Take me to Yuri's body," she said.

CHAPTER 77

Anja was whisked away to another silvery room, another cell, this one smaller with a lower ceiling and no viewing windows.

Yuri was lying on the floor. Or his body was, anyway. His physical body.

His nonphysical body was crouched next to it. He had a gaping wound not unlike the tear in the veil, in his astral chest. And he was holding the trailing length of his own silver cord.

Danny, kneeling next to him, held the cord's severed end.

"Yuri?" Anja said, *"Omigod. What happened? Have you been out of body this whole time?"*

"The little kid took my body," Yuri said. *"Jim, your mentor, he said it was just a precaution. He said I'd . . . he'd said I'd get to go home soon, but then . . ."*

"Whatever the kid was doing, he didn't have enough juice, enough energy," Danny said, taking up the story when Yuri couldn't finish. *"Marfa wanted Jim to stop the mission, but he wouldn't. Just kept saying they were so close, they just needed more power. So Marfa left—and found us outside—and Jim Lugner cut Yuri's cord and wrapped it around the kid's physical body. The kid's body was still in here then. And the trick must've worked, because Jim left—we saw him upstairs in the viewing room, remember?—and the kid came back with the love or whatever, right?"*

"Yeah," Anja said. She'd tell them about how she'd returned the love after they fixed up Yuri.

"So I'm guessing mission accomplished," Danny was saying, *"because a few minutes ago, the kid came back into his body and ran out of here like he'll be having nightmares for the rest of his life. Poor kid. But now . . ."*

Danny held up the end of Yuri's severed cord.

"I don't know what to do," he said. *"And now, seeing you in here . . ."*

He glanced pointedly at Yuri.

And Anja understood. And she knew Yuri did, too.

Yuri's astral body wasn't as visible to her as Danny's was.

Yuri was starting to fade. And she didn't want to think about what would happen in the next few minutes as he continued to do so.

Anja looked around for her own cord, for Danny's. But if either of them had one, she didn't see it.

"Do you see mine?" she asked.

"It's just thin," Yuri said, pointing at her chest.

A tiny, silkworm-like thread flowed from her chest. Danny tugged on it. She didn't feel anything.

"How do we put it back?" she asked, having never wanted to accomplish anything in her whole life as much as she wanted to accomplish this. *"How do we reattach it?"*

"I don't know," Yuri said. *"I don't think we can."*

"We have to be able to. You're still here. There's no point in you still being here if there's nothing we can do."

Calm, she told herself. *Calm. Calm. Calm.* But there was nothing calm about her. She knew her words were a lie. She knew of far too many people who'd lingered only to succumb.

Calm, she told herself. *Believe,* she told herself. But she was having trouble doing either.

And yet she was holding on. Maybe the moment of lucidity granted to her when the ghosts had all passed through her was helping her stay out of body now. Because there was no way she could be doing it all herself.

And something *was* helping her, but it wasn't the effects of the ghosts.

"We got this," Anja said, and she took Yuri's cord from Danny.

"You're gonna be fine," she told Yuri. *"You. Are going. To be fine."*

And she jammed the cord into the tear in his chest, penetrating Yuri's astral frame.

Yuri's mouth and his eyes opened wide. But he didn't make a sound.

And nothing happened.

At least, nothing happened to Yuri.

CHAPTER 78

Around them, the low-grade hum, the vibrational tremor sensation, was strengthening, becoming a shaking, a rumble. And even though it hadn't quite felt like an earthquake before, it started to feel like one now. Like a physical earthquake, but also like a haphazard thrum jarring the air.

Like the veil around them was quaking.

And breaking apart.

The veil around her started to crack.

"Stay with him," she said to Danny.

And then she stood and turned away from them and imagined what it might be like to be omniscient.

"Show me," she said. *"Take me up."*

Anja swooshed, and she was suddenly above the farmhouse and its red and white barn, above the flatland state of Kansas. She just knew.

Take me above Portland.

Anja swooshed, and she was suddenly above downtown Portland. It was late evening, and people were outside beneath the streetlights. They'd been going to dinner or meeting with friends. They'd been going about their lives.

But now they were no longer living.

Bodies lay on the ground.

And around those bodies stood the disembodied forms of all mankind.

But they didn't look riveted by it. They didn't look in awe of the universe, didn't look as excited as Anja had been to suddenly find themselves out of body.

They looked like Yuri.

They looked scared and crumbled and despaired about how this could be happening to them.

It has to go back.

Anja wasn't sure if she'd thought the words herself or had heard them, or if they had come from the light of love itself, talking not about itself but about the form someone had forced it to become.

"*Take me to the love,*" she said.

And Anja was back in the tunnel with the ghosts, mere feet from the edge of the tear.

Most of the ghosts were butting their heads against the tear's edge.

The love's lightbulb's worth of light was flickering on the other side.

Marfa had her arms and legs wrapped around a still struggling Jim Lugner.

And Anja's protector ghost stood next to her. Patient and wise.

"*It has to go back,*" he said. "*All the way back.*"

"*Where is that?*"

"*It knows the way,*" he said. "*But physicality brought it here, and it needs physicality to take it back.*"

"*But I'm not physical.*"

"*You are. You are human. You are the only one here now who is and the only one here now who can help it get home. You must return it to the center of the universe.*"

"*Will I make it back?*"

The ghost looked sad for her.

Calm, she told herself, but she was anything but. "*I'm not going to survive, am I?*"

"*If you do not hurry, none of you will survive.*"

Anja nodded. She wanted to take one last look around . . . but one last look at what? This underground bunker full of wayward ghosts and hateful traps?

This loveless world full of empty bodies and frightened astrals?

Calm, Anja told herself.

But she didn't feel it. And she now knew what was helping her.

It was time for her to help it.

She stepped inside the tear.

She picked up the love.

And it pulled her toward oblivion.

ALL SAINTS DAY

Danny Diega had never worn a suit before, unless you counted his military uniform from back in the day.

The suit he wore now was black, all-purpose, and recommended by the shop assistant for weddings, interviews, and funerals.

He still couldn't believe he was alive and walking around in this body, feeling the warmth in his heart—the love—whenever he chose to focus on it. Sometimes he'd stop wherever he was and put his hand over his chest and feel the feeling and close his eyes and say thank you. *Thank you.*

He would never take that feeling for granted again.

The rest of his team had made it through the Rift Attack, too, as they'd taken to calling it. So did the dog. He turned out to be a great dog and pretty smart, too, so they'd made him part of the team. It took some recovery time to get up and running again. More for the other guys than for Josh and Rifter, the dog. But the guys weren't too much worse for wear, considering all the horror stories they'd told him about the four-day nightmare they'd lived through following the attack.

Four days. Danny still couldn't believe all that had happened and how much his life had changed in only four days.

As soon as Anja . . .

Well, as soon she'd saved the world, Danny could tell.

The earth stopped shaking.

The cracks in the veil disappeared.

The ghosts stopped bumping into the tear in the veil, like brain-dead automatons.

Marfa's body wouldn't be rising again, but her ghost seemed satisfied to be suffocating Jim Lugner from the other side, like that ghost that's hanging all over Joshua Jackson at the end of the movie Shutter.

It would have to be consequence enough for Jim Lugner, because aside from her murder, the state of Kansas said he hadn't broken any laws.

Anja's protector ghost crossed the veil to join the other high-functioning, high-vibe entities Yuri and Anja had mentioned. But before he did, he'd given Danny the saddest of smiles.

Some things should never happen. And some people don't come back after setting them right.

All dressed in his suit, Danny took a taxi to the airport, where he met up with Josh. Man, it was good to have that guy back. Danny didn't think he'd ever make fun of his journaling again.

Well, maybe a little.

The two of them flew into Sea-Tac, and then he and Josh met up with Yuri and took a train down to Portland.

Yuri, man. That kid was impressive.

After Anja had gored his astral body with his own silver cord, Yuri had somehow gotten it to reattach with nothing but the power of his mind. Incredible.

He'd then returned to his body, popped up standing, and ran to call for help. He'd handled everything at the Kansas farmhouse—the ghosts, the cops, the logistics—until Danny was able to get back to his own body in California, confirm that the Redwood Rift was closed, take care of Anja's body, contact Jackson, and get a team back out to Kansas.

Specifically, to Lebanon, the center of the lower forty-eight. Jim Lugner had intended to hoard the love at the core of the universe, but not only for himself, it seemed. He'd wanted it for the whole of America. To bring peace to the US. The rest of the world didn't matter, apparently. But still, not entirely selfish. Noble even, however misguided. But as they say, the road to hell and all that.

Anyway, Yuri did it all like a champ, like he was Mr. Can-Do, like he hadn't just been stuck in limbo, scared out of his wits that he might never again be able to return to his body.

And he'd been doing it all ever since. Going public with his skills. Teaching people to OBE. He'd even had a guest appearance on one of those debunker television shows, and he'd schooled 'em. Ha!

Danny loved knowing that he was the kid's first student.

Well, one of them anyway.

"Should we go in?" he asked.

The MAX train had dropped them off ten minutes ago, but he, Josh, and Yuri were still standing outside the building.

It was a beautiful day. Blue skies and fall leaves. Danny told himself that's why they were still standing out here.

Josh opened the door.

Their group was meeting in the Oregon Convention Center's big room. Yuri had been there before for some event, and so Danny and Josh followed after him.

Danny saw the rest of his team saving seats in the back row. Looking out at the rest of the room, it felt like thousands of other people were sitting in front of them.

Good. Anja deserved that.

Danny shook hands and exchanged jabs with every one of his teammates. Never mind that they'd just finished a mission together and would be starting another on Friday.

Tyrese. He'd been in the worst shape after The Rift. But for Tyrese, that just meant he'd come back strongest.

Darryl. His compass-rose doormat and rudimentary thermometer had come in so handy that Danny had requisitioned him an upgraded set. Darryl carried it in his go bag. You really never know when you might need that stuff.

Nick. The team's self-proclaimed chef. After eating nothing but oatmeal and spaghetti by himself during his team's recovery, Danny would never again complain when Nick wanted to "cook up something new."

Steve. He'd been all-in and full of ideas when Danny had suggested they update their equipment sensors. Next time someone asked him if their stuff could see ultraviolet as well as infrared, Danny would say *that, and so much more.*

Kumar. The team's token monk. He'd been one of Yuri's first OBE clients and was now using the skills on missions. Remote viewing, astral travel. Not even the sky was the limit.

Juan. The team's leader. The one who used to interface with Jackson when need be. He'd decided to retire after the Rift Attack and had passed the role of team leader to Danny. Before the attack, that might've caused a stir. But the rest of the team approved unanimously.

And Doc. She'd come today sans grandkid swaddled to her chest. Not an official team member, but so, so valued all the same. Instead of saying hi, Danny said to her what he'd probably be saying to her for the rest of their days: "Thanks, again, for bringing them back."

"You bet," she said, like she always did, "but you know it wasn't me."

"I know."

"You made it," Jackson said when he saw Danny, Josh, and Yuri, but he was mostly just talking to Yuri. He wrapped the kid up in a one-armed hug. "I was hoping you would. I wanted to introduce you to Marisol."

Marisol was wearing a dark dress with a high waist that was forgiving over her stomach. She had long, wavy hair and pretty dark eyes, and on one hip, she carried her and Jackson's daughter.

"Yuri," Jackson said, "this is Marisol, and this"—he let his two-year-old daughter grip his index finger—"is Anja."

"Guess what the bun's name is," Josh said.

"I don't know," said Yuri.

Marisol said, "We'd like to call him Yuri."

Yuri nodded. A lot. "He'll probably get teased," he said, "so pick a good middle name, too. But, yeah, I like it."

Josh laughed and hugged his brother with both arms before giving him a noogie. "Love you, kid."

"Love you, too," Yuri said into his chest.

Up front, someone was testing out the microphone.

"Should we sit?" Jackson said.

Danny sat, on the aisle where he could be the first person on the scene, should a scene erupt. Not that he was expecting one, but, habits.

"Thank you all for coming," said a male voice over a sound system.

A loud *shhhh* rang out through the room.

"Anja Aura Copenhagen was a lab leader who was studying bioluminescence when she was called to investigate an electromagnetic anomaly in the redwoods of California. Four days later, the unthinkable, the unbelievable, happened.

"Many of you probably still don't believe it. I'm not sure I do either. That moment still feels like a dream, doesn't it?"

Murmurs from the crowd.

"But she saved you," the man said. "She saved me. She saved us all."

The man nodded to someone off to the side, and behind him a screen lit up with images of Anja working on stuff.

Glowing worms. Glowing mushrooms. Glowing rocks.

But then the Northern Lights. The fluorescence of galaxies. The electromagnetic spectrum.

The man continued:

"After that moment that rocked the world, she shifted focus to electromagnetism and vibration, and went to work on what some of us have long been calling the big TOE. A true theory of everything. A merging of sci and psy.

"And she succeeded. You may have heard about it on the news?"

Laughter from the crowd.

"Some of you might've even read the article posted online on her own website—back when no one would publish her work."

More laughter.

"Now, as I'm sure you all know, that article and many more have been picked up by every major peer-reviewed journal and news outlet in the country, and throughout the world."

Cheers.

"And now," said the man, "I'd like to welcome to the stage the woman of the century. Here to tell you all about it herself.

"Ladies and Gentlemen: Anja Aura Copenhagen."

Calm, Anja told herself as she took the stage to huge applause.

But she'd come a long way from the woman squeezing Yuri's hand, frantically telling herself to stay calm. Now when she said it, she could feel the love at the core of the universe giving her an extra boost. And it was infinite.

She still didn't know where the love had taken her, because she could feel that it resided everywhere.

She hadn't let go of it so much as she'd felt the love radiate away from her hands, becoming nothing. The nothing it was supposed to be. The nothing that is everything.

But even though she'd returned it, the light remained dim.

The warmth was not returning.

She'd been tugged backward then. She'd never forget it. It was as crystal clear in her mind right now as it had been when she'd first experienced it. She'd been tugged backward, to another realm. The realm of the undecided, of limbo, between life and life again.

"I knew you had it in you."

Anja knew the voice. She knew it, and she hadn't heard it in sixteen years. Hearing it now shocked her to her core. If she hadn't been here, in this liminal realm, she would definitely have returned to her body. But she was here. And no matter what level of joy she exuberated, she wasn't going anywhere, it seemed.

"Brian?"

She felt him more than she saw him. He was here, but then he was there, because he was everywhere. He was like love. He was love.

"Did it work?" she asked. *"Is it returned?"*

Brian didn't answer.

But the love, radiating from its home at the core of the universe, at the core of herself, had wrapped around her and had once again shown her the world.

All of the people of the world were still standing less than naked, bare and astral, beside their bodies.

"Help me," she said to them. *"We have to all want to put it back."*

Anja palmed her chest now, as she stood on the stage, remembering the feeling of all the people of the world hearing her, of all of them helping her return love to the core of the universe.

"Thank you," she said to the applauding crowd, "but I had lots of help. Lots of it."

She visored her eyes as she scanned the back of the room. "Stand up, guys," she said with a smile. "I couldn't have done it without you, either."

She spotted the whole team in the back, where Jackson had told her they'd be sitting despite her wanting them up in the front row, next to her mom. Anja could thank them for her reconciliation with her, too.

Way in the back of the auditorium, Danny and Yuri were sinking down low in their chairs.

"There you are. Stand up," she said.

They looked at each other and stood up, waved quickly, and immediately sat back down again.

"Thank you," she told them. "For your thoughts, challenges, and deeds. Thank you for everything you did to inspire and to provoke me. To suggest things I wasn't ready to consider and to help me advance my thinking. I am here because—"

Behind them, to the left of Danny, the auditorium doors opened, and Anja saw something that made her speech hitch, but she managed to finish.

"—because of you."

Two figures slipped through the open door at the back of the room.

The first was Ming.

And next to her, hugged to her side, was a human being Anja had seen several times—but never in physical form.

A kid.

A book thief.

A little boy she'd never seen smile.

A gifted child who had been caught up in someone else's schemes.

Well, he was smiling now. And when Anja made eye contact and smiled back, he smiled bigger. Though sheepishly.

His mother brought a hand to her heart and mouthed with exaggerated movement, *I'm sorry. I'm so sorry.*

Anja nodded. She understood. She'd already suspected. And she'd had the last two years to piece together what had happened.

Ming's son had been trapped in China, an asset of the state. And once Jim Lugner had set eyes on her son's abilities, getting a job with Anja and spying on her for him had become the way for Ming to get her son back.

Anja understood.

Anja had forgiven.

And one day, Anja hoped to feel ready to contact her old friend.

Ming slipped out the door again as Anja launched into her speech.

She was here for an award, believe it or not.

Anja sure couldn't believe it. After all those years of rejections . . . and now those same gatekeepers were showering her with awards.

Life, right?

The audience was wonderful. Attentive. Engaged.

At the end of her talk, Anja asked for questions.

An eager young teenager was sitting in the front row, and he'd been raising his hand like crazy. Anja had seen him right away—he kind of reminded her of Yuri—but something about him had told her to call on him last.

"Yes," she said, pointing to him now.

The kid stood up and said, "Is human bioluminescence actually the soul?"

The people behind him started to snicker and jeer.

But Anja smiled. She'd known his question wouldn't disappoint.

She held up a hand to quiet the crowd. Even after the strides she'd helped mankind make in the field, its practitioners still, as a group, couldn't imagine anything further.

But after her four days with Yuri and the rift, after being returned to her body safe and sound and alive by *the love at the core of the universe,* Anja had vowed to never again automatically dismiss someone's crazy ideas.

"That's very intriguing," she told the young questioner. "I've never really thought about it before. Please, tell me more."

AUTHOR'S NOTE

Thank you for reading!

I am thrilled that you picked up this book, and I hope that you enjoyed it. If you want to see more books like it from me, **make sure to leave a review!** Reviews help me in many ways, but especially when I'm wondering what to write next.

Also...

I have a newsletter! I send out updates, exclusive content, and other goodies to subscribers about once a month. The monthly newsletter is free, and you can sign up using the QR code at the bottom of the page, or at meganbledsoe.substack.com.

Make sure to read the newsletter's welcome email. You'll find your first subscriber goodies in that email, including a **deleted scene from *The Metanaut*.**

Talk to you soon!
Megan

MORE BOOKS BY MEGAN BLEDSOE

Glitching the Matrix: *a novel . . .*
The Metanaut: *a supernatural thriller*
Girl, Incorrupted: *a love-horror story*

The *Corbin Kohl In Hell* Series
fun low-fantasy mysteries
Corbin Kohl Adrift in Hell
Corbin Kohl Baited in Hell
Corbin Kohl Cornered in Hell

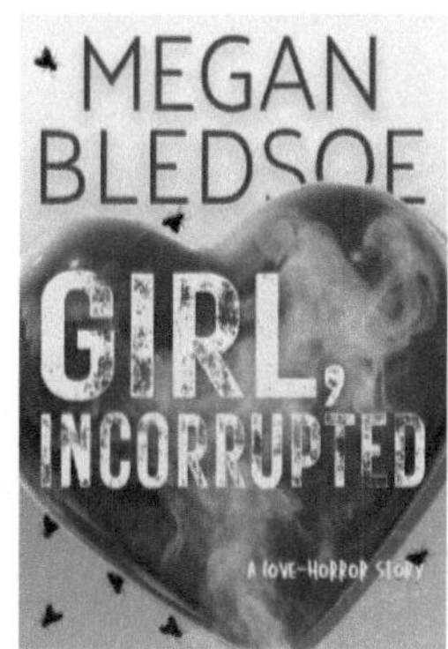

ABOUT THE AUTHOR

Megan Bledsoe takes inspiration from the world's unexplained but still undeniable phenomena. She used to be an attorney but now writes in the Pacific Northwest, where she lives with her family. She is the author of *Glitching the Matrix*, *Girl, Incorrupted*, *The Metanaut*, and the *Corbin Kohl In Hell* series. Find her online and join her newsletter at meganbledsoe.com.

www.ingramcontent.com/pod-product-compliance
Lightning Source LLC
Chambersburg PA
CBHW020504310726
48979CB00016B/2777/J

* 9 7 8 1 9 6 9 2 6 5 0 6 8 *